RAVE REVIEWS FOR J. F. GONZALEZ AND *SURVIVOR!*

"It pushes your eyes off the page and then pulls them back, forcing the kind of visceral relationship between writer and reader that the best horror writing can produce."
—*The New York Times Book Review*

"Fans of Jack Ketchum are definitely going to enjoy *Survivor.* You need to buy this book."
—*Cemetery Dance*

"Quite possibly the most disturbing book I've ever read in my life."
—Brian Keene, Author of *The Conqueror Worms*

"J. F. Gonzalez is a writer to watch."
—Bentley Little, Author of *The Policy*

"There's something very unsettling in the way *Survivor* seems to prod at the slippery slope of violent entertainment; how the book...places a great deal of personal responsibility onto the reader.... It's not enough simply to ask why anyone would commit such horrors; we also have to wonder why we're so fascinated by the details."
—*Fangoria*

SOMETHING NOT HUMAN

"Hello, Cindy."

Cindy whirled around, her heart in her throat. Her finger squeezed the trigger and there was a deafening boom and her right arm was thrown back by the force of the Colt going off. She didn't even hear the bullet strike the wall; she was too busy trying to keep her balance and her eyes on the figure in front of her, keep her mind fixed on the single purpose she had come here for.

Diana stood at the threshold of the hallway that led to the master bedroom. She was naked. Cindy's mind was still frozen in shock from the surprise and the unexpected realization that Diana had tricked her, and the underlying compulsion that had screamed at her to break into the house and kill her now pulsed through her brain. *Do it now! Shoot her! Shoot her!*

Cindy raised the Colt and aimed.

Diana smiled, and then her face melted.

Cindy's reflexes froze. She watched with eye-widening, mind-numbing horror, her finger frozen on the Colt's trigger. Time seemed to slow down incredibly. Diana's flesh seemed to slough and drip off the bones of her skull....

Other *Leisure* books by J. F. Gonzalez:

SURVIVOR

J. F. GONZALEZ

BELOVED THE

LEISURE BOOKS NEW YORK CITY

. A LEISURE BOOK®

December 2006

Published by

Dorchester Publishing Co., Inc.
200 Madison Avenue
New York, NY 10016

ISBN 0-8439-5694-1

Printed in the United States of America.

Visit us on the web at www.dorchesterpub.com.

To
Bob Strauss
and Garrett Peck,
who never stopped believing.

And for
Zack Venable,
who still believes.

ACKNOWLEDGMENTS

I'd like to acknowledge the following people for their assistance and the support they provided during the writing of this novel:

Jesus and Glenda Gonzalez, for obvious reasons.

The Becker family, for reasons they can't imagine.

Gil Schloss, for continuing to show faith in such a tough marketplace.

Brian and Cassie Keene, Garrett Peck, Zack Venable, David Nordhaus, Pam Chillimi-Yeager, Geoff Cooper, Gord Rollo, Brian A. Hopkins, Bob Strauss, Judi Rohrig and Hellnotes, Del and Sue Howison, Jeff Gelb, John Pelan, Richard Chizmar, Paul Melniczek, Jane Letty, Gary Zimmerman, Bonesaw, Shane Ryan Staley, Matt Schwartz, and Gene O'Neill for various reasons, among them their friendship, support, and online camaraderie.

Cathy Gonzalez, for somehow putting up with me, and coming up with the perfect title for this novel when I couldn't.

And to Hannah Gonzalez, who I will always be there for.

PROLOGUE

The escape route was planned perfectly.

The first thing he would do was walk through the court-yard to the apartment where his wife's new lover lived and knock on the door.

He knew the man was home. He'd seen him pull in to the gated complex in his Lexus. Don Grant had been sitting in his car across the street, watching through a pair of binoculars.

Lisa's lover wouldn't recognize him; of that, he was certain. Don had made the necessary preparations today. He was normally bespectacled, thinning blond hair neatly trimmed and clean shaven. He'd worn contact lenses today instead of his glasses, and he hadn't shaved. His bags were packed, and his bank account had been emptied yesterday. He had a Mexican passport, and if he could get over the border this afternoon he could make it down to San Paulo by Saturday. He could lay low for a while, head to Mexico City, where a new identity and passport could be bought. Then he could wait until his appearance had changed drastically enough for him to drift north again.

He didn't want to get caught.

What the hell am I doing? Don thought as he walked through the apartment complex's courtyard, hands in the pockets of the light blue windbreaker he was wearing. In the right front pocket of the windbreaker was a cheap .22 pistol he'd bought at a gun store. He'd never fired a gun in his life, and when he'd decided to kill his wife's lover, he'd simply gone into a gun store in Pasadena and picked out the first thing he saw. After the mandatory waiting period and filling out the appropriate paperwork, he'd picked the weapon up along with a box of shells. He wasn't worried about the weapon being traced back to him. He'd never broken the law before, so his fingerprints weren't on any government computer database. They'd be on the gun, of course, but they'd never find that. If he made it down to the southern tip of Baja he'd throw it in the Pacific.

What scared him most was the incredible sense of hatred and rage he felt toward Lisa's lover. And the fact that he was so *driven* to kill the man.

Don's hand trembled in his jacket pocket as he meandered slowly through the courtyard of the apartment complex. It was a Thursday afternoon, and the complex was empty. He'd planned well. There'd be no witnesses, and he'd be in and out of the complex in less than five minutes.

But he was still scared to death.

I've never committed a violent act before in my life, Don thought as he scanned apartment numbers on his walk to the rear of the complex. *I am a peaceful, God-loving man. I love my wife, I love my country, I love God. I am a man of faith. I believe in the Ten Commandments, especially the one that says Thou Shall Not Kill. And I can't help wanting to kill the motherfucker who's been fucking my wife!*

Yet at the same time he was experiencing these twin feelings of murderous rage and hate, he felt perfectly sane.

Don had tried offering up a small prayer, trying to hear the still, small voice of God, trying to ask Him for guidance, to protect him from the strong temptation he was feeling. But he'd felt and heard nothing from God.

All Don felt was the calm, warm feeling that accompanied the visions of watching himself walk into the man's apartment, seeing his wife there, then opening fire on him, ending his life in a hail of bullets. Whenever he replayed the image, he heard a voice—the same one that gave him such a strong feeling of peace and contentment when he prayed—say to him, *You'll feel better if you kill him, Don. He's the cause of all your problems. He seduced your wife, and now she doesn't want to have anything to do with you. She loves him now. Kill him and maybe—just maybe—you'll win her back. You need to prove your strength and show you can't be taken advantage of. A strong man always takes care of himself. So do it. Kill him.*

Two weeks ago he'd followed Lisa when she left for work. He'd called in sick to his own job at Kaiser Permanente, where he worked as a systems analyst. He'd followed Lisa discreetly as she drove to Hawthorne, then watched as she'd gone into the apartment complex. He'd gotten out and followed her, staying far enough behind that she never detected him, but also close enough that he got a general sense of which apartment she entered.

He stood before that apartment now.

Apartment Twenty-five.

He stood before the door to apartment Twenty-five trying to calm the anger and rage that pulsed through him. He'd checked out the man who lived there, found out his name was Bruce Miller, that he drove a black Lexus and had the looks of a typical upper-middle-class yuppie fuck. Don had gotten his name from the bank of mailboxes at the front of the apartment, and he'd confirmed his wife was screwing Bruce when he scrolled through the phone list on her cellular one evening while she was in the shower and came across his name. He'd almost gone into the bathroom then to confront her but something had made him stop. *She won't listen,* he'd told himself. *If I confront her she'll just deny it. Accuse me of snooping in her personal life and besides, what proof do I really have that she's fucking around?*

The late night calls to her cell phone, which she took with a feigned air of casualness, always stealing away into the kitchen or upstairs to take it in hushed whispers; her answers that it was only "her friend Ann or Marge" who had called; the mornings he called her office when he knew she should be there and her secretary informed him that Lisa had an appointment; the evenings she came home late from work, proclaiming that meetings were keeping her in the office till six, seven, sometimes eight or nine o'clock in the evening; the harried expressions, the flush in her cheeks, the slight rumple of her clothes when she came home from such meetings. Oh, she was fucking Bruce Miller all right. The signs were there. And he knew that she'd deny it even if he pointed out all the circumstantial evidence against her.

Therefore, he had to kill Bruce.

He'd been agonizing over the decision for weeks. He'd been distraught when his instinct told him Lisa was having an affair. He'd cried, bawled his heart out, actually. His sadness weighed heavily on him the week he'd put everything together. He would have thought Lisa would have sensed his mood—she used to sense the change of his moods so often, and would always inquire if he was okay or if anything was bothering him, but this time she didn't seem to notice. That made the sadness weigh in more heavily, and it was then the whispering suggestions of murder began. They had quickly grown into a persistent roar.

And now he was here to follow up on it.

God help me, Don thought as he wiped a tear from his face. *God help me because I can't help it and I just need to kill this sonofabitch.*

He knocked on the door.

For a moment there was nothing, but then he heard footsteps approach. The door flew open.

A good-looking, tanned and youthful man stood at the door to apartment Twenty-five. He grinned. "Yes?"

"Bruce Miller?"

"Yeah?"

Don heard a voice in the background. He instantly recognized it as Lisa's.

He barreled past Bruce into the sparsely furnished living room, shoving the other man roughly against the door. He pulled the .22 out of his jacket pocket and pointed it at Lisa as she emerged from the back bedroom, gasping in surprise. She was dressed in the skirt she had worn this morning when she'd left for work, a red satin bra, and her black pumps. Now her black hair hung in her face in disarray and Don noticed with rising anger that Don's shirt was unbuttoned, showing off a tanned, washboard chest. The zipper of his slacks was down, too. "I knew it," Don muttered, pointing the gun at Lisa, fighting back the tears. "I fucking *knew it!*"

"Don, please put the gun down!" Lisa said, and there was something in her tone of voice that got to him. He gasped, steeling himself from the image of what he wanted to do: plug holes into both of their adulterous faces, but especially hers. The urge to empty the chamber of his newly purchased .22 was so strong it washed over him, seeming to whisper, *Do it now, do it now now nownownownownow!*

"Don't do anything foolish, Don," Bruce said, seeming to take the confrontation in stride. He made no effort to close the door or take a defensive stance.

Don couldn't think straight. He glared at both of them, alternating the aim of the .22 from one to the other, as if unsure which one to shoot. Lisa looked frantic, scared, but not guilty. No, not guilty at all.

"Why?" he asked her, gun aimed at her lover.

Tears streamed down Lisa's face. "Please don't shoot him, Don. Please!"

"What if I do?"

"Please don't," Lisa begged, and there was something in her voice, something that seemed so desperate, so *hungry,* that it spoke to him. "Please don't kill him. I don't think that . . ."

Don't think that what, Lisa? Don thought, suddenly find-ing the power he held over Lisa's emotions now . . . well, kind of exciting. He hadn't been able to arouse any kind of emotion in her lately, and here he was inspiring fear. It gave him a feeling of confidence. He kept the gun trained on Bruce, who stood at the open doorway calmly, as if he were used to the spectacle of jealous husbands.

"Please!" Lisa sank to the floor on her knees and sobbed. *"Please, you can't kill him . . . he's . . . he's all I've got!"*

And hearing her sob like that, recognizing the tone of her sadness for what it was, brought the anger and hate rushing back to Don Grant once again. Lisa was deeply in love with Bruce Miller; he could tell by the gut-wrenching sobs, so heavy with emotion. This wasn't just an affair of the flesh, something that could be forgiven and worked through with marriage counseling and a lot of love. This was a betrayal of the deepest sort. She had given not only her body, but her heart and soul to an-other man.

And she had ripped his out in the process.

And that hurt more than anything.

But it also made him angry and hate-filled until it burst out of him in a sudden fury.

Don squeezed the trigger, emptying all six shells into Bruce Miller, who staggered and fell back against the open door, the jamb stopping him from tumbling to the Pergo en-tranceway. Lisa let out a long wail. *"Noooo!"*

Don turned back to Lisa one last time; he wanted the im-age of her crying visage to be burned into his mind forever. He wanted to savor the moment of when he had killed her lover.

He turned and stepped toward the doorway to make his retreat when he stopped suddenly, amazement and con-fused fear vying for equal attention in his already jumbled emotions.

Bruce Miller was getting to his feet, grinning. Don saw the six wounds the .22 shells had rent into his body where he'd shot him, the bullets easing out of his body as the wounds closed. The sound of the spent lead hitting the floor made the reality of it more final, and as Don stood there rooted to the spot, staring at Bruce with a sense of numb awe, he noticed Bruce wasn't finished.

He was still changing.

Don heard a dull *thump* as the gun fell from his limp hand.

Bruce Miller laughed; his mouth became a twisted thing, filled with rows of rotten, jagged teeth. His eyes were burning orbs set in a skull that was bony. As he laughed, Don smelled the sourness of his breath. He watched in growing horror and cold, blind fear as Bruce's body morphed and contorted into a shapeless thing, and then a grinning leering wraith of indeterminate sex.

He heard Lisa give a gasp—not of fright, but of surprised joy. *"Bruce!"* She ran past Don and embraced the still-morphing thing, hugging it, laughing with joy. *"Bruce! Bruce!"*

Bruce looked at Don over Lisa's shoulder as he hugged her. His hair had grown and thickened, becoming tangled dreadlocks. His skin had become bruised-colored, almost a sickly green. He licked his lips with a tongue that looked diseased.

Lisa grasped the Bruce-thing's face between her hands and kissed him deeply. Don's stomach plunged down an elevator shaft as he watched the Bruce-thing's tongue undulating in Lisa's mouth.

The sound of his screams snapped him out of his frozen shock, and he bolted out of the apartment.

He didn't know how he made it past them without flinching in revulsion and dread, but he managed. Instinct will do that; kind of like the way an arachnophobe will stand frozen in fear when a spider scuttles down its web ten feet away from him, but in a life-or-death situation, he'll blunder through the web without a second thought of the spider becoming entangled in his hair or clothes. That was how Don made it past the Bruce-thing and his wife—he just bolted past them, screaming at the top of his lungs, and ran through the courtyard, his sense of self-preservation compelling him to flee.

He took the stairs leading down to the sidewalk at the front of the complex three at a time, ran across the street without checking for traffic, almost got hit by a Federal Express van that honked at him and fumbled for the driver's-side door of his car. He opened it and dove in, started the engine and peeled away from the curb, his terror racing through his heart. It wasn't until he was a mile away that he realized he was doing sixty in a thirty-five-mile-an-hour zone and slowed down.

Back at the apartment complex, Lisa Grant stepped out of the apartment with a very normal-looking Bruce Miller. The two lovers had put their clothes on and their features showed concern as they looked toward the front of the complex where Don had fled. An older man stepped out of his apartment across the courtyard and looked around. "What was that man yelling about?" the old man asked.

"He was upset," Lisa said, not wanting to get into it further. "He'll be fine."

A woman from two doors down also stepped out. "Everything okay?" she asked. "I thought I heard gunshots."

Bruce nodded and smiled. He'd buttoned his shirt and zipped up his slacks. "Everything's fine."

"Was somebody shooting a gun?"

"No," Bruce said, turning to her, shrugging. "I don't know what that was."

"Hmmm." The woman nodded, lips pursed. She appeared to dismiss the sound of the gunshots. "That man sounded like he was mad."

"He is," Lisa said, frowning. "It's really very sad. He's been this way for a while."

"Oh," the woman said, looking embarrassed. She looked too old to be playing hooky from school and too young to be retired. "I'm sorry to hear that."

"He really should get some help," Bruce said, mostly to

Lisa. The woman two doors down went back into her apartment. "It's getting worse. He could have killed us."

"That doesn't matter now," Lisa said, her face flush. She was practically swooning. "What matters is us." She took his hand, pulling him back into the apartment. "Come on and finish what you started."

Bruce grinned. "As you wish."

They went back into the apartment and closed the door behind them.

PART I

BEGINNINGS

CHAPTER ONE

"What do you think of this?" Laura Baker had her finger set in the open page of a cookbook she was reading, and she looked over the kitchen counter at her daughter. "The recipe calls for fresh basil and oregano, but I'm not sure if—"

"Let me see." Elizabeth set down the latest issue of *People* magazine, which she'd been perusing casually, and walked over to where her mother was standing in the kitchen. They'd been talking about preparing some baked ziti, and while Elizabeth had a recipe at home, her mother had found this particular recipe in a new cookbook she'd picked up at the fire hall fund-raiser last month. She looked down at the cookbook and nodded. "Yep, that's identical to my recipe. We can do that easily."

"Okay, fine," Laura said, flipping the page. "That's what we'll do then."

Elizabeth smiled. The subject was closed as far as her mother was concerned. When Mom got it in her head to make a certain dish for whatever event she was planning, she usually didn't budge.

Elizabeth had left school right at the three o'clock bell

and headed straight home. She worked as a high school English teacher by day and as a writer of paperback novels by evening. She lived with her husband, Gregg, and nine-year-old son, Eric, in a modest two-story home in Lititz, about five miles away from her mother. Once at home, she'd responded to some e-mails, did some research on the publisher who asked if she had anything he could publish and decided she would allow him to have limited-edition hardcover rights to her next novel—whenever her agent got around to selling paperback rights for it. Then she'd headed to her mother's to pick up Eric. Her mom picked Eric up from school on Fridays and sat for him until five or so, giving Elizabeth an hour or two to get some business taken care of and some housecleaning done before Gregg came home. Eric was outside playing with the Sullivan twins, and Elizabeth had told him they'd be leaving shortly. Elizabeth and her mom had been chatting about what had been going on in their lives the past week—the usual stuff—and then Mom mentioned that Ronnie's new girlfriend, Diana Marshfield, was finally moving out from Ohio.

"Oh, it's this weekend?" Elizabeth asked.

"Yes," Laura answered, starting the dishes in the sink. "Ronnie left this morning for Ohio to help her pack the truck, and they're supposed to leave tomorrow morning and get back by the afternoon. That's why I thought I'd make something for them here."

Elizabeth nodded, knowing exactly what her mother was talking about. She'd want her son and his new girlfriend to have a nice home-cooked meal when they arrived, and she also wanted to make Diana's arrival a welcome one. After all, the woman was uprooting from her life in Columbus, Ohio, where she'd been born and raised, and was starting a new life in Lancaster County, Pennsylvania. Gregg had received the same welcome when they'd first started dating twelve years ago. "So he's really going through with it," she said.

"Yep, he sure is," Laura said. Elizabeth knew from the tone of her mother's voice what she meant by *that.*

Elizabeth's father, Jerry, had already expressed his disapproval of the developments in Ronnie's life months before. These pronouncements were always made when Ronnie was at work and when Mary, Ronnie's daughter, was outside playing, or with her mother, and Elizabeth always happened to be around when her father made them. Elizabeth agreed with his opinion on the situation; she, too, felt her brother was rushing into the relationship too quickly.

Ronald Baker was thirty-seven years old, three years younger than Elizabeth, and, until this weekend, he and Mary had been living with her parents. Three years before, Ronnie had moved out of the small two-bedroom duplex he had been living in since his wife, Cindy, left him for another man. He and Mary had moved into Laura and Jerry's house so Ronnie could pay down some bills. Elizabeth had predicted that the "few months" Ronnie proposed would turn into "a few years" and she was right. Ronnie and Mary lived with Laura and Jerry for three years rent free. Then Ronnie met Diana through some Internet dating service and things changed drastically.

It had started innocently enough. Ronnie never talked about his girlfriends, so it was months before anybody knew he was seeing Diana. One morning he'd asked Laura if she could watch Mary for the weekend; he was going to Ohio. When Laura asked why he was going to Ohio he'd answered, "I'm meeting somebody there." When pressed on the issue, Ronnie had grudgingly admitted he was going to Ohio to see a woman. He later admitted he'd met her on the Internet.

At first Elizabeth had been amused by the incident. She'd never known her brother to troll for women on the Internet. He'd always met his girlfriends at the local bars or at parties. He'd met Cindy at the Cocalico Tavern, and the few girlfriends he'd had after the breakup and divorce were women he'd met at other bars. But with the acquisition of a new computer a year before, Ronnie spent the time he wasn't working and playing with Mary in their parents' basement on the Internet. And what kind of websites does a thirty-something recovering alcoholic/drug addict who has just been through a divorce usually find most attractive?

Elizabeth approved of Ronnie having a long-distance affair; what she didn't approve of was her brother's sudden plans to have a house built and move Diana and her two children in with him, settling into a sense of domestic bliss. She and Mom had talked about this constantly in the months during the building of the house. "I think he's making a mistake," Elizabeth had said one day during an afternoon visit when the two women were alone together. "Going from a divorce right into another relationship. Hell, he didn't even play the field that much when he was living with you guys. He should have done that for a little bit, but he didn't. And Diana . . . I mean, yeah, I think it's fine to have a long-distance affair, but they're rushing into it. At least they're not getting married."

And that's when her mother had told her what she'd found one afternoon when she had cleaned Ronnie's room: unpaid credit card bills and letters demanding payment; credit card receipts from Ohio for dinners at expensive restaurants; and a credit card slip for Gordon's Jewelers for two thousand dollars. The last was for a diamond engagement ring. Elizabeth had been flabbergasted not only at the price, but the willingness with which Ronnie had bought the ring. When he and Cindy had gotten married they'd been poor—Cindy's wedding ring had cost Ronnie two hundred dollars, and it had been a beautiful wedding band cut with small diamonds. Cindy hadn't been the type of woman to have pestered Ronnie for something gaudy anyway, and Ronnie was notoriously cheap when it came to spending money on family. The only person Ronnie wasn't cheap with was Mary; he showered his daughter with gifts at every available opportunity.

Mom hadn't said anything to Ronnie about what she'd

found. This had been during a period when relations between son and parents were beginning to become strained. Ronnie had already announced his plans to move Diana and her kids out to Pennsylvania and get a place together, and the rent they had suddenly imposed on him two months earlier ceased. His excuse for not paying the two hundred a month to his parents for room and board was he didn't have the money. Which translated to, "I have the money, but it's already earmarked for anything Diana wants, so don't ask me for any."

They'd met Diana three times. She'd called the house once and announced she was driving out to pay Ronnie a surprise visit and wanted directions. She'd been seeing Ronnie steadily since June and had made the surprise visit in December, shortly before Christmas. Ronnie had been surprised, and he'd hustled her into the room he normally shared with Mary and didn't come out until the next morning. Mary had slept on the sofa in the living room that night, and Elizabeth had been furious when she'd found out. She'd been a trifle miffed her parents hadn't been more firm, but as Mom had explained to her a week later, "What could we have done? He wouldn't have listened to a word we said."

"But it's your house, Mom!" Elizabeth had said. She had been over with Gregg and Eric that afternoon, and Gregg had nodded in silent agreement. Eric had been downstairs playing with Mary. "I mean, he's living under your roof and not paying rent. You call the shots. Hell, you're practically raising Mary anyway! Just tell him if Diana comes to visit next time, you prefer he get a motel room for her. It's not fair his daughter has to sleep on the sofa while her father is screwing his girlfriend!"

Only that hadn't worked. The next time Diana visited a few months later, her mom had politely asked Ronnie if he could get a motel room in the area for her to stay in and he'd exploded. Mother and son had wound up having a huge fight, and Mom had backed down. Diana had slept with Ronnie in his room, and Mom wound up buying an air mattress to set up in the study at the end of the hall for Mary to sleep on. Jerry had fumed silently but said nothing.

The third time Diana visited she'd brought her children. Rick was a silent, brooding twelve-year-old who was almost as tall as Elizabeth. Lily was also silent, dark-haired, with a perpetual frown. Elizabeth had been at the house with Eric, and she'd tried to get her son to play with Rick and Lily, but Eric shied away. Elizabeth didn't pursue it—it wasn't in her or Gregg's nature to force their son to play with certain children, and they certainly weren't going to start now to make nice with her brother's girlfriend.

The plans were for Ronnie and Mary to move out of the house and into the new place with Diana and her two children, forming a Brady Bunch of sorts. Mary was looking forward to gaining step-siblings, even if they weren't close to her age; Mary was seven, two years younger than Eric, and was more of a sister to Eric than a first cousin. Elizabeth thought her niece was looking forward to having a mother figure again, too; Cindy hadn't really been much of one lately. She was more interested in sex, drugs, and rock and roll than her daughter.

"So are they still bringing that dog with them?" Elizabeth asked. Diana owned a rottweiler and was adamant about bringing him along.

"Apparently," Mom said, rustling in the kitchen. "I'm not too happy about that but we'll see what happens."

Elizabeth was about to ask her mother about Diana's ex-husband, then decided to drop the subject. The few times she'd met the woman, Diana hadn't mentioned him. What they'd learned about the situation had come from Ronnie, who said Diana's ex had suddenly walked out on her and the kids, leaving them destitute. Diana and her kids had been living with her mother in Ohio when she'd met Ronnie, and Elizabeth silently wondered if perhaps Diana was using Ronnie as a meal ticket and a way out of her situation. Despite his tightwad way with money, Ronnie made plenty as a welder at a sheet metal factory.

"Well, if you want some company, give us a call," Elizabeth said. She rose to her feet, moving toward the front door to call Eric in. "We'll be around all weekend."

"Okay, honey," Mom said. "I'll probably be calling you."

Yes, you probably will, Elizabeth thought. Then she called Eric to come in, and a few minutes later the two of them were pulling out of the driveway of her parents' house, heading home.

CHAPTER TWO

The weekend was uneventful. For the first time in weeks, Elizabeth and Gregg watched a movie together while Eric played in the basement with Stephen Peck, the kid next door. The following morning they ran some errands, and Gregg went to get the cars washed while Eric played outside. Elizabeth did some laundry and got some writing done. Ronnie and Diana were due to arrive at their new home that afternoon, and with the friends he had coming over to help, along with two of Mom's brothers who had promised to lend a hand, they'd probably get the truck unloaded that evening. Ronnie and Diana would spend the rest of Sunday unpacking and arranging furniture, and because he wasn't due to report back to work till two P.M. on Monday, he'd have part of that morning to get stuff done, too. Mom had said if all went well she'd have everybody over for a brief dinner Sunday afternoon at her and Dad's place, so Elizabeth made sure to tell Gregg the possible plans Saturday afternoon.

Sunday morning they did some work in the yard, and Gregg headed off to play a round of golf with some of his friends from the office. Elizabeth ate lunch in the dining room—a BLT sandwich and an apple—and Eric rode his bike to the McDonald's on Route 501 with Stephen. She told him to be back by three o'clock, and she spent the rest of the day reading the new Norman Partridge collection.

Mom called at two-thirty. "Ronnie and Diana are coming over around four for supper. You guys want to come?" Elizabeth said they did. Twenty minutes later Gregg and Eric came home, and after Eric washed his hands, they headed to her parents.

Ronnie and Diana were reclining on lawn chairs in the backyard, sipping cans of Budweiser when they arrived. Diana's son, Rick, was playing with a football in the backyard and Lily was sitting by her mother, her expression forlorn and silent. Elizabeth gave the little girl a smile and tried to meet her gaze, but she looked away. *She's shy. I was shy when I was her age. And she's been through so much.*

"So where were you guys yesterday when we were unloading the truck?" Ronnie asked, and the tone of voice he used seemed to say, *So why the hell didn't you come over to help us?* He was wearing sunglasses, his puffy tanned face tipped up at the afternoon sky, and Elizabeth could sense fatigue in his demeanor. He was wearing a tank top, which showed off his tattooed biceps, and a pair of shorts and sandals. One arm was draped casually around the chair next to him where Diana sat.

Diana smiled—smirked more like it—at Elizabeth and chuckled. "Yeah, we missed you, Elizabeth. I could've used the help."

"Nobody called me," Elizabeth said. She gave her mother a hug and the look Mom gave her told her something was up, but she didn't pursue it; she'd find out sooner or later. "Besides," she said, turning to Gregg. "We had ourselves a relaxing weekend. First one in a long time."

"Oh, a relaxing weekend, huh?" Ronnie said, taking a sip of beer. He nodded at Gregg, his long brown hair blowing in the summer breeze. He looked like the type of guy who would rent you a Jet Ski at Lake Havasu. "What'd you guys do?"

They hung out for a while, making small talk; Elizabeth filled Ronnie and Diana in on what they did yesterday and today. Eric sat on a small bench on the porch with Elizabeth, and she could tell he was reluctant to join the older boy. The sliding-glass door that led to the daylight basement slid open and Mary stepped out. "Hey, Eric!" she said. Eric turned, his face brightened and Elizabeth smiled. Mary smiled and ran to join her cousin. She had her mother's face and dark hair, but she had Ronnie's personality—gregarious, outgoing and active. She was wearing a pair of shorts, a T-shirt and white tennis shoes, her hair pulled back in a ponytail. She joined Eric on the bench and began telling him about the drive to and from Ohio.

Jerry was standing by the grill, where hamburgers were sizzling; apparently Mom had decided against the baked ziti. "Want a beer, Elizabeth?"

"Sure."

"I'll get it." Gregg went into the house after Jerry for the beer, and Elizabeth settled herself into trying to be sociable with Ronnie and his new girlfriend.

It was almost a perfect early summer late afternoon. The day had been warm, and a light breeze cooled things down as the afternoon died. Rick invited Eric and Mary to a game of catch, and before Elizabeth knew it, the kids were enjoying themselves. Even Lily was in the yard playing. Ronnie had retrieved more beers for himself and Diana, and between talking with them and Mom, Elizabeth began to feel a little more relaxed. Diana related how the move was going. "The place is full of boxes, and we've got the bed set up in the master bedroom. The kids slept in sleeping bags last night, and we should have them in their beds this evening. Tomorrow we might have most of the house set up."

"So quickly?" Mom asked, reclining in her favorite rocker with a glass of lemonade.

"Most of it," Diana said, nodding. Despite being skinny as a rail, she wasn't bad looking, but Ronnie had been with more attractive women in the past. Elizabeth tried not to focus too much on Diana's hair, which looked slightly unwashed and frizzy, or her complexion, which looked like it had just gotten over a bad case of acne. "Of course I've got my curtains I want to put up, and Ronnie has his things he wants to set up. We still have to set up the computer—"

"And we're setting up *my* computer," Ronnie said, in that subtle *we're-doing-things-my-way* tone.

"What's wrong with my computer?" Diana said, turning to Ronnie. Her hazel eyes dared him to continue.

"It's a piece of shit," Ronnie said, matter-of-factly, sipping his beer. Elizabeth recognized that tone all right. It was his holier-than-thou voice; since getting his computer, Ronnie had become a PC specialist in his own mind. This happened with everything Ronnie got into. When they were kids and Ronnie wanted a guitar, their father had bought him a Gibson Les Paul. Ronnie had taken lessons, never practiced and never become very good on the instrument, but he proclaimed himself the next Eddie Van Halen anyway. He did the same thing with cars, motorcycles and the other toys with which he'd held brief infatuations. Now it was computers. She remembered him telling her that he had spent three grand on his computer when he bought it. Three grand for a guy who only used it to e-mail his girlfriend and download porn off the Internet. But that was Ronnie.

They ate supper on the back deck. Laura put a nice spread of condiments for the burgers on the table, and Elizabeth brought a salad and they all dug in. Diana told them Himmler, the rottweiler, was being acclimated to the house; she'd put a pen in the basement where the dog was staying while they were gone. "Don't know what to do with him without a fenced-in yard," she said. Elizabeth agreed, but silently wondered why she brought the dog with her if she knew the house didn't have a fence around the yard. Couldn't she have tried to find a home for it?

For the most part it was a casual dinner, but Elizabeth could sense a slight tension in the air from her brother. It was a sense she got from him the moment he introduced them to Diana three months ago, as if he were forcing her on them. As if he were saying, *This is my new girlfriend and you're all going to like her, okay?* She was getting this feeling from him again, and as the afternoon changed to evening and she helped Mom clear the table when supper was finished, she dismissed the notion. *He's just nervous,* she thought. *He just wants everything to be okay. He wants her to be accepted by his family. She seems okay enough.* She paused at that thought, watching Diana out of the corner of her eye. Like Ronnie's ex-wife, Cindy, and the few girlfriends he had deemed worthy enough to bring home to meet the family, Diana had a slim, somewhat skinny figure with shoulder-length black hair and dark eyes. If her face hadn't been so badly scarred and she had more meat on her bones, she'd be very attractive. She seemed nice enough on the surface, but . . . come to think of it, Diana hadn't really been that friendly with her when they'd walked in this afternoon. She'd acknowledged her, yeah, but she seemed to carry this condescending aura, a feeling that said, *You are so beneath me that you don't merit my time.* Elizabeth shook her head. *I'm letting my imagination get the best of me. Give her a chance. You're not going to like her immediately; you've got to get a chance to know her, and she has to warm up to you. She's probably nervous.*

One thing she did notice, however, was that she did not like Diana's kids.

She disliked them the minute she met them.

The revelation hit her suddenly, and as conversation went on and she engaged in it, the thought remained at the back of her mind for her to dwell on. She'd never felt such a dislike for children before. She'd known people who had kids who were brats, but she never felt the kind of dislike she felt for them as she did with Rick and Lily. She wondered where the feeling came from, since it came so suddenly and seemed to spring from no particular event or series of events for her to form an opinion on. It seemed to have just sprung out of her instinctually, the way one felt a dislike for spiders or snakes.

And as the afternoon bled into evening and she found herself supervising the kids, babysitting her niece as well as Diana's two kids, she thought about it more. She began to think of Diana in a different light. Maybe that's why she felt such an intense dislike for the woman's children—it was really Diana she didn't like, and the feeling was beginning to be projected onto her kids. Whatever the reason, the rational part of herself knew it wasn't fair to Diana or her kids—or Ronnie for that matter—to begin formulating opinions on them based on being around them for only a few hours. Relationships took time to develop. She'd get to know them better, and in doing so would slowly begin to like and accept them. She was sure of it.

They left her parents' house around eight P.M. and got home twenty minutes later.

That evening as they were getting ready for bed, Gregg said something that surprised her. "There's something about Diana that doesn't seem right."

Elizabeth turned to him. "What do you mean?"

Gregg shook his head as he slipped into a T-shirt. He'd put on some pounds over the last few years. His once flat stomach was now beginning to balloon considerably, and his hair was graying rapidly. His face hadn't changed, though; he still had delicate features, high cheekbones and an aquiline nose; an actor's face. When they'd met over a decade ago, Michelle was a struggling writer, selling stories to small-press magazines and the occasional paperback anthology, and Gregg was a struggling actor. He'd done mostly plays and a few independent films with one, *Voyeur,* actually receiving good reviews. He'd dropped out of acting entirely when Michelle became pregnant with Eric, and she always got the impression that he resented the fact that he'd had to give up his dream while she'd continued to pursue hers during her rare moments alone.

"I don't know," he said. He went to the master bathroom.

She followed him and waited for him to continue as he brushed his teeth. She could tell he was thinking about what he wanted to say, that he probably didn't want to offend her, so she said, "To tell you the truth, I'm not sure if I like her, either."

"Really?" He paused in mid-brush, mouth full of toothpaste.

"Yeah. I don't know what it is, but . . ."

"You don't like her?"

Elizabeth shrugged, not sure how to answer. "I don't know. I mean . . . I *want* to, but . . ."

Gregg finished brushing his teeth, his eyes not leaving hers as he watched her in the mirror. "There's just . . . something about her," he said.

"Yeah." She nodded. She rubbed her arms. "It's just a feeling, I guess. Kind of silly, isn't it?"

"Not at all," Gregg said. He finished brushing his teeth, put his toothbrush away, turned off the light and joined her in the bedroom. "We've probably developed this subconsciously over the past few months since hearing she was going to move out here and finally meeting her. I mean, look at the situation. They met on some Internet dating website. He drove out to spend a weekend with her and got hooked. All we heard was that her husband suddenly left her and she made her living as a debt collector for a credit card company. Then we met her and the kids when they came out that one time. Remember that? Rick was downright sullen, didn't say much. I thought he was spooky, myself. And Lily? She had this air of . . . oh, I don't know . . ."

"She almost looked cowed," Elizabeth said. "Like she was afraid to do anything. Like she was afraid her mother would yell at her if she did the slightest thing to provoke her."

"Yeah."

"And Diana just reeks of . . ." The phrase was on the tip of her tongue and she hesitated before saying it. "White trash."

"Yeah," Gregg said, settling back into the pillows. "White trash. That's just the phrase I was looking for."

"The minute I saw her that first time she reminded me of Cindy. It's like Ronnie has this certain type of woman in his mind he keeps hooking up with. Remember Linda, that woman he was seeing for a while after Cindy left?"

"Yeah, I remember. She did kind of look like Cindy."

"Exactly. Put all three of them together and they'd look alike." Cindy was a petite, lithe brunette; Linda, whom Ronnie had dated for a year after Cindy left him, was a petite, lithe brunette. Diana could have been a carbon copy of both women. All three favored tight-fitting blue jeans and blouses, black leather jackets; they smoked and drank, hung out at the same kind of bars bikers tended to congregate at and sported the same style of makeup; cheeks rouged, eyelids blue, lips glossy red or pink. And their hair always looked like it had been microwaved into a frizzy 'do.

"You're right. They do look alike."

They lay in bed, silent for a while. Then: "Gregg?"

"Yeah?"

"You don't think it's silly of me to not like Diana right away?"

"Not at all."

"I know it's wrong. And I'll try to get to know her. I really will. It's just . . ."

"Trust your instinct, Elizabeth. Get to know her at your own pace, on your own terms. If your instincts about her are true, then there's no law that says you have to get along with her just because she's your brother's girlfriend. But if you give her a chance and she turns out to be okay, so much the better."

"Yeah." Elizabeth sighed. "You're right." She turned to her left side, snuggling up to Gregg. "'Night, honey."

"'Night, babe." Gregg turned to her, and they kissed.

Then Gregg rolled over back to his side and was snoring within five minutes.

Leaving Elizabeth awake and wondering about Ronnie and Diana and her own relationship with Gregg, telling herself she shouldn't even worry about liking Diana right now. She had her own marriage to worry about.

Cindy Baker was well into her sixth or seven beer at the Cocalico Tavern when the trouble started.

She'd spent most of the evening venting to Ray Clark, her drinking buddy at the tavern. She'd had a lot to bitch about. "First my fucking ex starts fucking this new bitch from Oh-fucking-Hi-Oh, then he moves her skanky ass back here and buys her a fucking house, moves her fucking kids and my daughter in with them. Can you believe that? He's got *my* daughter living with that bitch and her fucking kids. And then Gary got a bug up his ass about something and filed for custody of Jason. Can you believe that shit?"

Ray Clark shook his head, his weasely features stubbled, his eyes red. He was wearing a dirty baseball cap over his brittle collar-length blond hair, a black T-shirt, biker boots and ratty denim jeans over his too skinny frame. He clutched a bottle of Budweiser in his fist. "That's fucked up."

"Goddamn right that's fucked up!" Cindy proclaimed, voice raised. She pounded down a hearty slug, thunked her bottle on the bar top. "First he moves out of the house and takes Jason. Okay, I don't mind him taking Jason because I didn't really have a place for him to stay after we lost our apartment, you know? But then he had to turn around and file for *full* custody? Of *my* son?"

"That's fucked up," Ray said again, confirming to Cindy that things were fucked up indeed.

Cindy took a drag from her cigarette. Her voice was rough from cigarettes and hard booze. Cindy and Ray both looked like they came with the bar when it was built. "The hearing for custody is Thursday and no way in hell I can be there. I've got a job interview that afternoon, and I *need* this job because if I don't get it, I won't have a chance at being a part of Jason's life, you know? At least if I can get a job and work for a while I can come back later when they have that family mediation thing and they'll see I'm working. Know what I mean?"

"You see a lawyer?" Ray asked, taking another swig of beer. Ray looked forty-four shades of fucked up. He'd already been drinking at the bar when Cindy showed up two hours ago.

Cindy took a drag on her cigarette and gave Ray a look. Damn, but he was a dumb fucker. Hadn't he been listening? "Not yet," she said, biting her tongue. She wanted to tell him he was dumber than dog shit, but she didn't want to drive him away. She needed a place to stay tonight, and she was hoping she could crash with him. She couldn't piss him off now.

Cindy Baker was thirty-three years old and had been officially homeless now for almost a month. Fortunately she didn't live out of her car; she'd spent the first two weeks after she and Gary lost the apartment staying at her mom's. Then when her mom had got on her shit for drinking, she'd left and stayed with Carl Eastman, a fuck-buddy she'd been banging on the side while Jason was at Gary's parents' and Gary was at work. She'd been in the process of dumping Carl since he was never around anyway—he was usually hanging out with friends of his who were members of Satan's Slaves, a local motorcycle club. Shortly after Gary filed for full custody of Jason, she'd lost it, spending a few days in the psych ward at the local hospital. She'd spent another week with her mother but finally left. Two weeks were spent bopping around various friends' apartments, sleeping on their sofas. This week she'd spent a night at her brother's house, and she'd bitten the bullet and stayed one night at her mom's. Then she thought of Ray, so she had come to the Cocalico because she knew that tonight was his Saturday night—Ray worked a graveyard shift at the Acme warehouse in Reamstown. She'd had a hundred bucks on her that she'd gotten from her last paycheck at her last job, which she'd quit a few days ago because her boss was a chainsaw Nazi-bitch, so she had enough to get by for another night or two. If this new job came through she'd be fine. But then she'd have to deal with this other shit.

Namely Ronnie and his new girlfriend.

She hadn't liked the situation the minute Laura told her about it a few months ago when she was over at her former in-laws' house to see Mary. She'd called Ronnie that night when Gary was at work and yelled at him, in the end breaking down in tears. "Why?" she'd sobbed. "Why do you have to bring her out here, Ronnie? I love you, and I want to be with you. Please don't do this!"

But Ronnie had told her to fuck off. They were divorced—remember? She'd left him for Gary, whom she'd been sleeping with while they were married, he sarcastically reminded her. Cindy had cried harder, shaking her head as Ronnie ground the salt into the wound. "I gave you two years to come to your senses and come back. Did I file for divorce immediately? No. I didn't. I tried to get us into marriage counseling, and you refused. I held out all hope, but you never came back, so what was I supposed to do? Besides, by then you were already pregnant with Jason, and you and Gary had already been living together for almost two years, so as far as I was concerned we were through. It's over, Cindy. It's been over since you walked out on Mary and me four years ago."

Cindy had screamed and slammed the phone down, hanging up on him. Then she'd grabbed her leather jacket and headed to the Cocalico where she'd gotten shit-faced and fought with some skanky bitch.

Knowing that Ronnie was fucking another woman made her angry. Couldn't he see that she wanted him just as badly, if not more, than any other woman? Yeah, so she'd fucked up—but she'd been scared. She was a new mother, and she didn't know what the hell she was doing, and the work she was getting just wasn't challenging and she was bored and then she'd met Gary and it had just happened. They'd started messing around. He was giving her what Ronnie couldn't give her, which were his time and a nice stiff one. If Ronnie wasn't working, he was being dad to Mary or spending time with his parents or his friends. Being husband came last.

Shit, but she needed something stronger to drink. She signaled for the bartender, an older guy named Bill, who worked days at the Acme warehouse. "Shot of Jack," she said, fishing in her purse for her wallet. She turned to Ray. "Want one?"

"Yeah," Ray said, his eyes getting a little more animated at the news Cindy was buying him a shot of Jack Daniels. "Damn straight!"

Bill set down shot glasses and served them up. Cindy picked up her shot glass and held it up to Ray's. "To us," she said, clinking her glass against his. "Because you're the best drinking buddy I've ever had in this whole damn county!"

"Damn straight!" Ray said, and they tipped their shots back and drank up.

The whiskey went down smooth, and Cindy chased it with a hearty gulp of beer. She was halfway to being high now. If she only had some blow on her, this could be a good night.

It would help her forget.

Cindy motioned for another shot, and Bill poured it. She drank it down, her memory simmering. First Ronnie takes Mary from her; then Gary takes their son Jason. And he had the *nerve* to file for full custody! And to petition the court that she wasn't allowed to take Jason or see him without supervision! What kind of shit was that? Hadn't she raised Jason since he was fucking born? Like it was really her fault the last time she and Gary fought the ashtray she'd thrown at his head missed because he'd ducked—and had hit Jason instead. Like Gary was the perfect parent; he'd done his share of blow with her; had two DUI convictions on his record, had been convicted of attempted murder stemming from a bar fight ten years before and served three months in prison for it. And he had the nerve to say his shit didn't stink?

Fuck him!

And then there was Ronnie, her ex-husband. Moving his new whore in and buying her a house, moving her and her stupid kids in. No fucking way was Mary going to be raised by this woman. Besides, if Ronnie had only taken Cindy back the way he should have, things would have been fine with them. The house Ronnie and Mary were moving into would be *hers* as well! That cunt from Oh-fucking-Hi-Oh wouldn't even be in the picture.

The thought of going over to the house to pick up Mary for visits made her blood boil.

She signaled the bartender for another shot.

"Damn," Ray said, an almost empty bottle of beer raised to his lips. He looked at her with drunken amazement. "You're doing some heavy drinking there, girl."

"Fuckin' A," Cindy said, knocking back her third shot. She wiped her mouth with the back of her hand and was just about to reach for her beer when she felt a presence behind her.

"Well, well, well, if it isn't Miss Psycho-bitch who just can't get enough cock up her stinking pussy."

Cindy whirled around and came face to face with Karen Murphy.

Karen's blue eyes were smoldering pits of anger. She was nearly a head taller than Cindy, but was just as skinny. She was wearing blue jeans, a Harley Davidson T-shirt and Tony Llama boots. Her cheeks were scarred with acne, and they now blazed a bright red. Her frizzy blond hair hung in her face, her mouth set in an angry scowl. "Yeah, I'm talking to you," Karen said. "What, you deaf?"

"What are you getting in my face for, bitch!" Cindy yelled, and now the adrenaline was pumping through her. Before she knew it, she shot off the barstool and was standing, trying to pump her height up. Ray scampered back, his weasely features bearing a *what the fuck?* look.

"You already on to the next one or something?" Karen sneered. "Forget you were fucking my boyfriend last week, bitch?"

Then Karen pushed her.

Cindy exploded. She swung a wild haymaker that landed on the side of Karen's face and as Karen fell back, Cindy jumped on her and they were at it. Karen reached out and grabbed a fistful of Cindy's hair as she crashed to the ground, and Cindy swung her fist down on Karen's face. She felt Karen's nails rake her cheek, coming dangerously close to her left eye, and she was screaming at the bitch. "Take it back! You fucking bitch, take it back!" And she was hitting Karen, and Karen was pulling her hair with one hand and slapping her face and scratching her with the other, and then strong hands were grabbing Cindy, pulling her off the other woman. The bar, which seemed to have been practically empty before the fight, was suddenly filled with people as they crowded in to watch, and several men stepped into the fray to break it up.

CHAPTER THREE

Elizabeth was stacking dishes in the dishwasher that evening, Friday night, when Eric told her about what he and Mary saw while they were riding bikes in Mary's new neighborhood.

They'd just had dinner and Eric was helping her with the dishes. He was clearing the table, telling her about his day at Mary's when he paused. "Mom, can I ask you a question?"

"Sure, honey. What is it?"

Eric looked troubled. He set the dish he was drying on the center island and glanced into the living room, as if he were afraid of being overheard. When he turned back to her he looked nervous. "You know Himmler? Diana's rottweiler?"

Elizabeth frowned. In the month and a half since Diana and her kids had moved in with Ronnie, Elizabeth had voiced her concerns to Mom about that dog. She felt Himmler was aggressive, and she didn't like for Eric to be at the house because of it. Diana and Ronnie had convinced Mom that Himmler was actually a good dog once he got acquainted with you, so she'd backed down a little. She'd insisted on being at the house the few times Eric went over to play with Mary, and the dog was actually pretty good with her niece; she'd been afraid the animal wouldn't take to Mary, but he did. Mom had been a little apprehensive at first, but now seemed to be won over. It was the general consensus of the family that influenced Elizabeth to let her guard down and consent to Eric going over without her supervision, something she still struggled with, and now that Eric mentioned Himmler, bearing that funny look on his face, her original feelings came back. "What's the matter?" she asked.

"Well . . ." Eric looked nervous. He squirmed uncomfortably.

"What happened?"

Eric looked ashamed, as if he were going to be punished for doing something. "He almost attacked another kid. A kid named Andy who lives four doors down."

Hearing this confirmed all the feelings she'd had for the dog. She felt a strange relief that she had been proven right and that somebody would finally listen to her. She also felt a sudden dread at the implications of what had happened. "Is he okay?"

"Yeah, Andy's fine," Eric said. "It's just . . . it was weird. I was in the backyard with Mary and Lily, and Himmler was with us. Lily had Himmler on his leash, and he was being real good. And then Andy came by, and when he stepped into their yard, Himmler got this funny look. He just . . . well, he growled at Andy and Andy froze. Mary and I were playing catch with the baseball, and she stopped and turned around and said, 'Hey boy, what's wrong? It's just Andy.' And then Himmler lunged at him. And I mean, he took off. He dragged Lily to the ground, and she started screaming. Andy ran and Himmler would have chased after him and got him, but then Rick was suddenly there and he grabbed the leash from Lily and pulled, and it took all his strength to pull that dog back. I . . . I almost wanted to go over and help him because I could see he was struggling to hold the dog back, but I was scared. Mary and I, we were both scared, and we ran a little ways into the neighbor's backyard and just stood there and watched. Andy . . . he'd already run home, and Rick got Himmler under control and herded him into the garage and into the house, and Mary and I were too scared to go back for a long time."

Elizabeth was livid. "What happened next?"

"You're not mad at me, are you?" Eric burst into sudden tears.

"Honey, I'm not mad at you." Elizabeth pulled her son to her, hugging him. She smoothed his hair back, kissed him. He cried briefly, and she could tell his tears were from the pent-up fear he experienced back at Ronnie's. "I'm not mad at you. If anything, I'm mad at Diana. All she did the first two weeks she moved in was brag about how vicious that damn dog was, like it was something to be proud of, and look what happened. Andy could have been killed."

"I know," Eric said, his sobs easing. He wiped his face with his hands. "He's okay, though. Mary and I, we went over to see if he was okay. His mom was mad, though. She called over at Ronnie and Diana's and chewed Diana out over the phone."

"Good."

"She didn't even look at us. She told Andy he wasn't allowed to play with us until Diana got rid of that dog, so we left. Mary said Himmler was probably in the basement, so we went in the house." Diana had taken to locking Himmler in a large cage in the unfinished basement during the day; might as well put the dog in a kennel. "Diana and Lily and Rick were acting like nothing happened. Himmler was in the basement like Mary said, but they weren't . . . they weren't even bothered by what happened."

"What were they doing?"

"Rick was playing some kind of computer game, and Diana was on the phone," Eric said. He looked up at Elizabeth and she nodded, understanding what he was getting at. Every time she and Eric went over, Diana was either on the phone, or she was sitting in front of the computer surfing the Internet. She chain smoked Marlboros and drank Diet Coke constantly. Lily had to practically beg to be fed, and when Diana did feed her it was usually something out of a can, unheated. She'd never seen Diana prepare anything for her son, or for Ronnie, for that matter. Ronnie was never around since he was always working at the plant. The plan was for Diana to stay home during the summer and look for a job once the kids were in school, giving Ronnie relief on the overtime. Elizabeth had a feeling Diana had found her meal ticket in Ronnie, however, and wasn't going to do anything except sit on her skinny ass.

"What happened then?" Elizabeth asked.

"Nothing. I came home."

Elizabeth rubbed Eric's shoulders, then turned back to stacking the dishwasher.

"Mom?"

"Yes, honey."

"Can Mary start coming over here instead?"

"Of course. In fact, I insist on it." It would mean having to drive over to Reinholds to pick the girl up and drive her back because she knew damn well Diana probably wouldn't do it, but she felt better about having Mary and Eric play at her house.

"Mom?"

"Yeah."

"What are we going to do?"

Elizabeth closed the door to the dishwasher, threw back the lock, pressed the button to start it. It began to hum, the sound of rushing water filling up as it began its first cycle. "I don't know," she said. "I really don't know."

Ronnie Baker lay on his back in the king-sized waterbed, naked as Diana showered after their bout of lovemaking.

Ronnie lit a cigarette, drew the smoke deep into his lungs. It was late—just after two A.M., and he'd gotten home early from work. His normal shift was three-thirty to midnight, but he always put in at least two hours of overtime. Tonight he'd skipped out of the overtime and come home. He'd worked overtime for the past month. Time for a little R&R.

The light in the bedroom was low, and the rest of the house was silent. Rick had been watching *The Blair Witch Project* on the TV in the living room when Ronnie came home and Lily had been up with him, staring at the TV with a kind of hollow-eyed vacant look, her face puffy with fatigue. Diana had been sitting at the computer desk browsing through some Web page and he'd shut the front door, making sure the lock engaged, then crossed the living room to Diana. He'd kissed her, ruffling her hair. "How's it going, hon?"

"Okay," Diana had said, eyes riveted to the screen. "How was your day?"

"Fine." Ronnie had looked around the house, at the living room, dining room, the kitchen. "Where's Mary?"

"She went to bed a couple hours ago," Diana had said.

Ronnie had nodded, then headed back to their bedroom to shower.

Diana had joined him thirty minutes later, and he figured she'd sent her kids to bed because she'd fucked him with a sense of ferocity he'd never seen in her, even in the nine months or so they'd been together. She'd rode him hard, driving him into her, her hands tugging at his hair as she bounced on him and she'd kept him hard and inside her for what seemed like hours. When she'd finally rolled off him and headed to the shower, Ronnie stole a glance at the clock on the nightstand on his side of the bed and saw that only an hour had passed. *Damn, but she was hot tonight! What got into her?*

Ronnie smoked, feeling that relaxed sense of pleasure he always felt after sex. This was why he had gone through all this hell—the arguing with his parents about moving Diana and her kids out, getting a new house built, moving in, the overtime—it was all so he could have some sense of normalcy. So he could provide a sense of comfort and a home to Diana and her kids and Mary. He wanted a family, wanted Mary to grow up knowing what it was like to have a mom and a dad around. She didn't know what that was like; Cindy had left when she was only three, and while Mary saw her mother regularly and had spent evenings over at her and Gary's apartment until just recently, it was hardly a traditional family situation. Ronnie felt bad that Mary had to be shuttled back and forth like that. She was seven now and it was all she knew. What kind of life was that? That wasn't what he remembered growing up; he wanted Mary to live in a stable environment, with a mother and a father in the home. He didn't want to raise his daughter alone.

That was something his father didn't understand. His mother was a little more accommodating and open-minded. But Dad . . . he was ramrod straight conservative, and he didn't like Diana one bit. Ronnie could tell. When his parents came over they looked normal enough, but Ronnie could detect his dad wasn't too happy. In fact, he appeared downright disgusted. Ronnie didn't give a shit. Far as he was concerned, his dad could fuck off. What mattered was Ronnie had found a woman who loved him and whom he loved, and she had moved three hundred miles just to be with him. Now *that* was love!

Meeting Diana had really proved to be a turning point for him. A year ago he'd been living at Mom and Dad's, drifting aimlessly in his personal life and trying his best to raise Mary on his own and share custody with Cindy. He'd waited two years for Cindy to come back, and when she showed no signs of making any efforts at rekindling the relationship, he'd quietly filed for divorce. He'd messed around with other women between Cindy and Diana—but not like he'd used to when he was single and fifty pounds lighter. Ronnie rubbed the spare tire that had grown around his mid-section. He used to be in great shape; tight muscles, well-defined abs. He used to work out. Not any more. No time for working out now. The only workout he ever got these days was in bed with Diana.

Ronnie grinned. He'd never thought he'd meet somebody over the Internet. He'd met Diana on an adult matchmaker website. He'd bought the computer—a Pentium III with 1.5 GHZ of speed and a 40 Gig hard drive—a few months before and become obsessed with learning everything he could about it. He'd discovered the Internet, and the first thing he had typed in a search engine was "sex." He'd spent weeks perusing various sites, spending about a third of that on the various adult and pornography sites. And through his Web wanderings he'd come across various match-making sites. Most of them were fee based, which he steered clear of. All of them, however, contained tantalizing personal ads. *Hi, my name's Tina! I'm thirty-two, single, and looking for a casual sex partner. You must be clean, professional, HIV negative and be prepared to prove it with a certified test result, and in good physical shape.* The accompanying photo would show a woman, sometimes nude or semi-nude, and most of the time the women were average looking. Some of them were real hotties, though, and he wondered why they felt the need to advertise for a bed mate on an Internet site.

Of all the sites he went to, he was drawn to one in particular—Friend Finders for Adults. It was free to peruse ads; all one had to do to view bios and photographs was sign up for the age-verification service by punching in a credit card number. The only time your credit card was charged was if you answered an ad or placed one. And it was only $19.95 a week to place an ad! Because he felt it wouldn't hurt to at least look, Ronnie spent most of his time perusing the ads and photos on Friend Finders for Adults, spending more time on the ads from women who were only interested in sex (and some of those photos were quite explicit—one, from a young Chinese-American college student, showed a close-up of her smiling face as she clutched an erect penis, and Ronnie had almost been tempted to respond to her).

One evening, bored after a night of work, he'd been perusing the Friend Finders for Adults classifieds when Diana's ad popped up out of nowhere.

It hadn't been there before, and he didn't know how he'd missed it because he was pretty sure he'd cruised through all of them at least once that evening. But there it was, and it showed Diana in all her naked glory, smiling at the camera, legs spread. Her ad was simple: *I know I can excite you. I will be the best fuck you've ever had. I love anal sex, S&M, giving blowjobs, and I swallow. Write to me and I'll be your whore. Will travel anywhere.* Ronnie had clicked immediately on the Contact This Person link, filled in the appropriate fields and hit the Send button. He didn't know what it was about her that had compelled him to act so compulsively, but there was just something about her. She represented everything he fantasized about in a woman, creamy complexion, dark hair, curvy figure, full breasts, flat stomach, long shapely legs. She was perfect.

Diana had responded immediately, asking for a picture. Ronnie had an electronic file of one he had scanned a few days before from a family picnic, and he'd sent it to her. She'd responded immediately again, and that started a two-week correspondence where they simply traded information: past lives, their jobs, marital status. Diana told him her husband had left her suddenly, that she lived in Columbus with her two kids, that she was devoted to raising her kids but she just needed to let loose every once in a while and that's what had led her to place such a daring ad. What Ronnie found in the two weeks he spent corresponding with her was a woman with a tender soul, a traditionalist at heart who had gone temporarily wild when she'd placed that ad.

He had to meet her.

She'd invited him out to Ohio, set him up in a hotel near her home. He'd driven out one weekend and called her when he arrived. They'd met at a bar down the street from the hotel, and seeing her in the flesh swept him away. She was more beautiful in person than she was in the photo, and as they sat in the smoky booth at the bar talking, feeling awkward, Ronnie knew he was falling for her. He could sense she was falling for him as well, and it was inevitable they ended up back at his hotel room in bed.

And the sex . . . God, the sex!

Ronnie finished his cigarette, stubbed out the butt in the ashtray. The sex with Diana was incredible. He'd never been with a woman who could keep him hard all night the way Diana did. She seemed to draw something out of him, something that kept his appetite for sex with her insatiable. When they were together it seemed that all he wanted to do was make love to her, and Diana was always willing to comply. Her appetite for sex equaled, if not out-rivaled, his own. She was a dream come true.

He'd spent that entire weekend in bed with Diana, and the following week he'd been ragged and tired and sore. She'd further tantalized him with provocative e-mails, complete with jpeg attachments of herself nude. That kept the fires stoked, and he quickly arranged to see her two weeks later. That's when Mom had found out—no big deal there. But when he wanted to go out to see her again the following weekend Mom said, "What about Mary, Ronnie? You've already gone out to Ohio last week to see Diana. Can't you spend the weekend with Mary instead?"

He'd grown a little annoyed at this, but quickly agreed. He called Diana to apologize for not coming out and she understood. "I like a man who understands the importance of his children," she said in that seductive purr. "That's just *so* sexy."

The following week she drove out from Ohio to visit him. Ronnie had been surprised at the visit, and immediately ushered Diana into the room he shared with Mary, where they spent the rest of the night making love. It was only when she left Sunday morning he realized he had neglected Mary all weekend—she'd even slept on the sofa in the living room. He apologized to her profusely, but then had to dash off to work. He spent the next few days feeling guilty about throwing Mary out of their room like that, and went out to Toys R Us one afternoon to buy her a doll to cheer her up. That had seemed to do the trick, and she forgot about the incident. Unfortunately, Mom and Dad hadn't.

He could tell Mom was pissed off, but she didn't say anything about it. His dad was furious as well, and it was a good thing their paths never crossed during the day; otherwise there would have been heated words over it. Ronnie kept his head down and blazed through the rest of the week, continued his relationship with Diana long distance, and after a few more months and some more trips and visits, they'd decided to move in together.

It was a natural decision. He felt close to Diana whenever he was with her. She understood him; she loved him, and she was great in bed, simply the best lover he'd ever had. She never complained about anything, and she didn't tell him what to do. When he talked to her about raising Mary, she listened, offering advice at just the right time. ("A young girl needs a mother figure, Ronnie, and Cindy surely isn't providing that for her. I hope she'll soon think of me as her mother.") She sympathized with his situation. ("I know what it's like to live with your parents. That's why when you come out to see me I have you stay in a hotel, and I sleep with you there. You don't want to see my parents' place or meet them. Trust me. Your situation is paradise compared to mine.")

He understood *her* as well; they shared the same interests in NASCAR and rock and roll, and the same tastes in beer and cigarettes. Diana had a similar philosophy as Ronnie when it came to raising their kids. ("I let them pretty much do what they want to do as long as they don't hurt themselves. This lets them learn on their own terms, teaches them lessons.") It was slightly different from Ronnie's own approach to raising Mary, which was to basically be there to guide her, but he understood where Diana was coming from. Soon they were talking about moving in together with both sets of kids. The more they talked about it, the more Ronnie began to be sold on the idea, and then right after Christmas, when they'd been seeing each other for six months, he felt compelled to go out and buy her the ring.

Mom had been pissed; he could tell, but she'd never voiced her feelings. And Ronnie went out and had a house built from scratch instead of renting a place. "We need a place that is totally our own," Diana had said during one of the many marathon phone sessions they had in the months leading up to her quitting her job and moving out. "We need to be in a new development, in a new house. We're both starting over, Ronnie. Building this house will be a representation of that."

And now she was here.

The shower had stopped a few minutes ago, and he could hear her drying off in the bathroom. When she entered the bedroom she was a smoky silhouette, a large towel wrapped around her body, another towel wrapped in her hair. She sat on her edge of the bed and began drying her hair. Ronnie reached out and touched her. "I love you," he said. The impulse to tell her he loved her came suddenly; this happened a lot now. He'd never had such intense feelings for somebody before, and he was always expressing his love for her through touching her, telling her he loved her, doing everything he could to help her and her kids. Sometimes he felt that wasn't enough, though, so he told her.

She smiled, drying her hair. "I love you too, babe."

Ronnie settled back in the pillows feeling contented, at peace, yet tired. Diana slipped the towel off her body and joined him in bed, snuggling next to him. And as he drifted to sleep, Diana pressed up against him, he thought about how much better things were going to be. Sure, a few wrenches had been thrown in the motor this summer, but that was inevitable. Himmler, for instance, had become an unexpected burden, but Diana insisted on keeping him.

Her kids seemed a little lazier than most kids, but hell, it was summer. His ex-wife, Cindy, was becoming an increasingly annoying presence despite his winning temporary full custody of Mary. She refused to stop at the house to visit Mary, and she refused to have Diana drop Mary off and supervise the visit. She insisted either he or his mother be present and since he was always working, his mother handled the burden. And the twelve-hour-plus shifts were beginning to wear on him, but it was only for another few weeks until Diana got a job.

Just a few more weeks.

It wouldn't be that bad.

Diana loved him.

CHAPTER FOUR

Motherfucker.

Cindy Baker sat in her car, an old Ford, smoking a cigarette. She had parked five houses down from Ronnie's new home, and had watched the comings and goings of the house for the past thirty minutes. She smoked cigarettes as she watched, the ignition powering the electrical system of the vehicle so she could listen to the radio. System of a Down wanted to blare from the speakers, but she had the volume turned down low. It wouldn't be good to attract attention to herself.

She hadn't shown up at the custody hearing a few days ago. Ronnie had told her it was happening, but she told him she wasn't showing up. When he'd asked why, she said, "Why the fuck should I? Why should I have to ask a judge to see my own daughter?" Ronnie had started spouting a bunch of bullshit, something about doing right by Mary and about Cindy getting help and counseling and bullshit bullshit bullshit. She didn't need any fucking help, and she didn't need counseling. What she needed was Ronnie, and she needed him to be away from that cunt from Oh-fucking-Hi-Oh and her two kids.

From this vantage point she could see Mary playing with another little girl who looked to be about five—a neighbor's kid, maybe? Diana's daughter, Lily, was sitting sullenly on the porch as the other two girls played. Cindy was surprised she could remember the names of Diana's kids. The older boy, Rick, was in the front yard somewhere tooling around on a skateboard. She hadn't seen Diana since she pulled in, and she didn't want to see her now. She had to psych herself up for it.

At first she had refused to see Mary at Ronnie's house for visits. Especially since the custody bullshit started. No fucking way was she going to have Diana supervise her while she visited her own daughter. So she'd refused to come to Ronnie's house and insisted that he bring Mary to his mother's. He'd complied for a while, but lately he hadn't been able to do it. Something about all the hours he was putting in at work, so Diana was bringing Mary instead. That didn't sit well with Cindy either, having that bitch drive her daughter to visit her. Cindy had dealt with the humiliation and pain of this the only way she knew how: She'd drowned it in alcohol and cocaine. And look where that had gotten her.

She rubbed the side of her head. The bruising from her fight with Karen was gone now but was replaced by a new one from a few nights ago. The fight she'd gotten into at the Cocalico Tavern a few weeks ago was still fresh in her mind, but it was now a distant memory to the bar's patrons. She'd been banned from the club for a week, and she hadn't been back since. There was no need to run into that Karen bitch again; Cindy would just kick her ass again if she saw her and she didn't want to waste the effort. She wanted to save the energy for Diana.

Cindy stubbed out her cigarette and lit another one. She wished she had a drink. There was nothing but a can of

Coke in the car, and it had grown lukewarm. There'd been no booze in the apartment; Ray was supposed to have gotten some at the state store, but he was a lazy-ass bastard, even if he had been kind enough to let her move in with him. Her visit with Mary wasn't until tomorrow, but she had wanted to drive out to Ronnie's house and park up the street just so she could watch her daughter play without being under the gaze and the thumb of Ronnie or Diana.

Cindy smoked, watching Mary and the other little girl playing, wondering about Diana. Why would Ronnie take up with her? She was a skinny little bitch. She walked like she had a stick up her ass, she was skanky, and she had two ugly kids. The thought of that woman living under the same roof as Mary made her skin crawl. Knowing she was a horrible person made her blood boil. She knew what kind of person Diana was the minute she'd laid eyes on her. And those suspicions had borne fruit within the past few days.

It was no secret Cindy and Diana hated each other. Cindy could tell from the moment she met the woman two months ago that Diana couldn't stand her. No telling what Ronnie had told her. Cindy had tried to make the best of the situation and had been friendly to the woman, but she'd been snubbed. Diana's voice was always snotty when she spoke to Cindy, and it seemed she was always looking down her nose at her. When Cindy asked Mary how she liked her father's new girlfriend, her daughter had shrugged and said, "She's okay, I guess. Daddy likes her." That just made Cindy angry, and as the weeks passed and Ronnie pulled the custody thing on her, her problem had only gotten worse. Cindy had blown up at Ronnie over the custody issue and refused to go to the house to see Mary, insisting that Mary be brought to her ex-mother-in-law's. That worked fine until Diana started bringing the girl over. Then Laura announced she was just too busy on the days Cindy wanted to see Mary, and it would serve everybody's interest if Cindy would just visit with Mary at Ronnie's.

Cindy hadn't liked the idea, but she wanted to see her daughter, so she'd bit the bullet and done it.

The first few weeks had gone fine. She sat with Mary in the living room, playing games with her, while Diana surfed the Internet and smoked. Diana practically ignored her, and her kids walked around as if Cindy wasn't even there. There was a brief moment when Cindy thought that maybe Diana wasn't so bad after all; she'd even tried making light conversation with her. But all she'd gotten back was attitude and short, clipped responses, suggesting Diana didn't want to deal with her. Cindy had stopped trying to be friendly and made a passing remark to Laura one day when she was leaving Ronnie's after a visit that Diana was "Queen Cunt."

Then the shit hit the fan.

So far it was just phone calls. They started three days ago, at Ray's apartment. Ray picked up the phone one night and handed it over to Cindy. When Cindy said, "Hello," a female voice said, "You're a pathetic wench, you know that? Just pathetic."

"Who's this?"

"Lost your husband, lost your home, lost your boyfriend and your other child," the woman said. "Then you lose job after job, bounce from apartment to apartment, and now you're in the process of losing your daughter. What kind of a mother are you?"

"You fucking bitch!" Cindy had screamed.

Diana hung up.

Cindy had been boiling mad; first thing she'd wanted to do was drive over to Ronnie's and rip the woman's head off and piss down her neck. Ray had talked her out of it, and Cindy opted for calling Ronnie's house instead. When Diana answered Cindy screamed at her, "Don't you ever fucking call me again, do you hear me you bitch!"

"Cindy?" Diana had asked, her voice taking on that, *Whatever are you talking about, dear?* tone.

Fifteen minutes later she'd gotten another call. "Think you can threaten me, huh? You're dumber than I thought you were."

"I *said* I don't want you to call me again, you cunt! I'll kick your *fucking* ass—"

"Oh, threats now, huh? So we've decided to escalate things? How exciting. A word of advice, Cindy. Take a number and wait in line."

"I'll cut to the front of the line, bitch! I'll—"

Diana hung up.

She'd gotten into a fight with Ray that night about going over. Ray ended up forcing her to the bed and tying her up with duct tape to keep her at the apartment. Cindy had almost lost it—it felt like the afternoon she'd lost it at Gary's day job when he'd filed for full custody of their son. She still only remembered patches of that day: how she'd driven to the warehouse where he worked, how she'd screamed at the receptionist to see him, how she'd struggled with the security guard; how she'd fought with the police officers who came to take her away; how she'd screamed at Gary that he was killing her, that by taking her son away he was killing her slowly. The next thing she remembered was waking up at the hospital in the psych ward, her arms strapped into a strait jacket. That had been three months ago, and the experience seemed to lessen the shock two months later when Ronnie pulled the same stunt. There had been no reason to go berserk again; she'd already done it.

But the night Diana called to rub salt in the wounds had almost tipped her over the edge again, and luckily Ray was there to calm her down and . . . well, tie her up. That had done the trick, because once Cindy calmed down she could think straight. And when she could think straight, she was more reasonable. She'd suggested they call the police that night, and they did.

The officer who showed up took a statement and said he would talk to Diana. A few hours later, another officer came to the house. "She said you're the one making the harassing calls, miss."

Cindy had taken a deep breath to calm the rage that wanted to explode out of her and explained everything. Yes, she'd lost her mind and done a stupid thing by calling Diana back and yelling at her. She shouldn't have done it. But *Diana* had started it, not Cindy. In fact, Cindy had explicitly told Diana not to call her apartment again, and she'd called anyway with more harassment. Ray backed her up on this, and the cop had listened sympathetically. "Aside from going to the phone company to check your phone records, it's a case of 'he said, she said.' If she does it again, hang up on her. If she keeps it up, call the phone company to have your number changed, and then call us. Whatever you do, don't engage in the behavior with her and don't call her back. That just makes it worse."

Cindy had agreed and promised not to escalate the situation further should it occur again. The officer thanked them and left.

The phone calls started again the following night. Both times Cindy hung up on her. Ray answered the phone a few more times that night, expecting to get Diana, and reported only a dry clicking noise on the line. Cindy felt proud that night; she was proud she hadn't let her emotions get the best of her and was able to react to the situation like an adult. After all, *she* was the better person. Diana was just a cheap whore.

Two nights later, however, Diana crossed the line.

"You hang up on me again," Diana said the minute Cindy answered the phone, "I'll whip Mary with the riding crop I have."

At the mention of physical threat to her daughter, Cindy froze. "What did you say?" Her mouth had suddenly gone dry, and she felt a sudden sense of dread in the pit of her belly.

"You heard me and you heard correctly, so I'm not going

to repeat it," Diana said. Her voice dripped with venom, with an edge of superiority.

"Then I'm hanging up," Cindy said, starting to replace the receiver in the cradle.

"I'll be sure to make a tape recording of your daughter screaming in pain," Diana said sharply, and Cindy brought the receiver back to her ear to make sure she was really hearing this. "In fact, I'll not only send you a copy, I'll be sure to get some money out of it. I hear there's a market for audio tapes of children being whipped by their parents in the pedophile underground. Should we split any profits from such a sale?"

Cindy saw red. Her body was tense. When she spoke, her voice cracked with the intensity of her fear and blinding anger. "If you lay one finger on my daughter I will fucking kill you."

"Threats again? I thought we agreed not to cast such idle threats. In fact—"

"You're dead." Cindy hung up the phone and before she knew it she was in the bedroom she shared with Ray, rummaging through his closet searching for his nine millimeter. She had just found it and was checking the clip when he came home.

"What the fuck are you doing?" Ray had asked, eyes widening in surprise. His long blond hair hung in his stubbled face.

"I'm going to kill that bitch," Cindy had said, and it was the last thing she remembered saying with any sense of clarity. Ray told her later that when she walked by him he had taken a swing at her, his fist slamming into the side of her head. She'd fallen against the wall of the living room, and the gun clattered out of her hand. He'd retrieved it and hidden it in a more secure location by the time she regained consciousness. When she woke up, she'd cried as she told him how Diana had threatened to hurt Mary.

She had been pouring this story out to him, crying uncontrollably, when there was a knock at their door.

It was the police. They were investigating a claim from Ronnie Baker that Cindy had threatened his girlfriend and was making harassing telephone calls. Cindy had screamed at them from where she was sitting on the sofa, a wet washrag pressed against her temple to quell the rising lump from Ray's blow. "That fucking bitch threatened to whip my daughter and tape it to sell to perverts! Why aren't you pounding at *their* fucking door!"

She didn't know how Ray managed to keep the cops from hauling both their asses to jail that night, but he had. Between her screaming and crying, and Ray trying to get her to shut up, and the cops wanting to poke their nosy asses in their business, it was a wonder she was sitting in her car right now. The cops had insisted on taking a look around the apartment, and as they conducted a search Ray sat on the sofa next to her. "Just be cool," he'd whispered. "Let me get rid of them." She'd shut up, pure emotion over the vile ugliness of what happened getting to her. While one cop searched the apartment, the other questioned them, asking how Cindy had hit her head. It took them five attempts to convince him she'd fallen in the kitchen, and when his partner came back the officers told them that, a) they didn't believe Cindy had fallen down and hit her head and, b) if they got a call like this again, they'd both be residents of Lancaster County Jail for the evening. Ray had thanked the officers and seen them out the door. It wasn't until an hour after they'd left when she realized how much Ray had really saved her. If he hadn't hit her as she'd been trying to leave with his gun, she would have walked right into the cops on her way out and she'd *really* be in trouble. Diana had set it all up.

And for that she was going to pay.

It had been three days since the cops had come to her apartment, and Diana hadn't called since then. Cindy hadn't spoken to her, and as far as she knew the woman was aware of her scheduled visit with Mary tomorrow. No way was she going to call to remind her, though. And forget talking to Ronnie. That asshole was never around anyway. What the fuck was wrong with *him* lately?

Thinking about Ronnie led her to consider how she should approach telling him about how Diana had threatened their daughter. In the days following Diana's phone call, Cindy had called Laura three times a day, asking if Mary was okay. Laura had been puzzled. "Mary is fine, Cindy. What's gotten into you?"

"She's really doing okay over there?" Cindy had asked at one point, stifling back tears. She could tell Laura knew she was crying, but she didn't care. "Ronnie's taking real good care of her, and Diana isn't . . . you know . . ."

"Mary is fine," Laura had said. "Ronnie is taking good care of her, and Diana has been wonderful with her. There's nothing to worry about."

Cindy hung up before she could blurt out what had happened between her and Diana, and now as she sat in her car watching her daughter play, she felt better about Mary's well-being . . . at least for now. The girl didn't look abused or neglected in the least. She watched as Mary laughed, jumping up and down, her auburn hair flying as her playmate said something. Then the two of them ran into the backyard, laughing. Lily trailed along after them, but Cindy ignored her. She smiled. It felt good to see her little girl laughing and playing like that. It felt good to see her child playing and happy, without a care in the world, the way it should be when you were a child. And as she watched Mary play, a sudden pang came to Cindy and she stubbed her cigarette out in the ashtray and leaned back in the front seat, looking out at Ronnie Baker's new home, her eyes pooling with tears.

That could've been me in there, she thought, her chest growing heavy with the sudden hurt. *If I hadn't been such an idiot; if I hadn't been so stupid and gone fucking around with Gary and left Ronnie, we would still be together. I'd be living there with him and Mary. It would be me in that kitchen watching my daughter play in my own backyard. Oh*

God, I just want it all back. I want my family back, I want Ronnie back and I want my little girl back. I just want every-thing back the way it was. I wish I had never gone and fucked things up the way I did.

And thinking about everything brought all the anger and despair and rage back, and she felt her head clouding up with pain again. The itch to quell it was strong, and she extracted another cigarette from the breast pocket of her denim shirt and lit it with the dashboard lighter, taking the smoke deep into her lungs. It calmed her down, but it wasn't enough. Her cheeks were damp with tears, and her chest hurt from holding her sadness in. She was angry and she was sad and she didn't know what to do. Part of her just wanted to break down and cry, while another part wanted to rush over to the house and hug Mary and beg her to come live with her. Yet another part of her wanted to kick the living shit out of Diana and burn down the fucking house Ronnie had built for her. Cindy's emotions swarmed like a cyclone, creating a vertigo of pain, and when she could stand it no longer, she started the car, put it in gear and headed down the street and out of the subdivision, tears stinging her eyes as she drove.

CHAPTER FIVE

Elizabeth Weaver was at her mother's house picking up Eric and perusing a Lane Bryant catalog when she heard her mother say "trouble." She looked up. "What trouble?"

"Oh, Ronnie and Diana are having trouble with Rick," Laura said. She opened the refrigerator and began taking out condiments for the hamburgers—ketchup and mustard bottles, lettuce and onions. "Apparently Ronnie's having trouble with Rick; the boy is challenging him, you know, being rebellious. He's not listening to his mother, and he's being truant in school, staying out at all hours, that sort of thing. And Ronnie's temper hasn't been the best lately, what with those double shifts he's pulling down at the plant."

"He's still working double shifts?" Ronnie had been working double shifts for the past three weeks, including weekends.

"He has to if he wants to make that mortgage payment," Laura said. She stood at the stove, checking the progress of the sizzling burgers, and then began transferring them to a plate. "I don't think Mary's seen him in three weeks. And it's proven to be very tiring, especially when you bring Cindy's visitations into the mix."

"Oh yes, there is that," Elizabeth said. God, her brother was such a loser. He goes from one nutcase to this latest prize, whom Elizabeth was beginning to dislike the more she heard about her. Granted, Elizabeth hadn't had a very good feeling about her when she first met the woman, but in the last few months Diana had proven to be rather . . . well, lazy.

She's a lazy bitch, she thought. *Admit it. She saw a meal ticket in Ronnie and jumped at the chance. She hooked him with whatever bullshit she told him, and he's so gullible he fell for whatever sob story she told him and now he thinks he's happy to be in a relationship, any relationship. He should have just stayed divorced for a while and spent time with Mary and gotten to know himself better as a person before deciding to go jumping back into another relationship.* But nooo . . . that wasn't how Ronnie Baker did things. He had to be in a relationship. He had to have the perfect nuclear family, or as near to one as he envisioned it. And now look where it was getting him.

She decided to throw out a line to her mother. "So Diana hasn't gotten a job yet?"

"Hell no! She actually refuses to work."

"Refuses?"

"Yes, refuses." The burgers were now on a plate and Elizabeth stood up. Her father was getting to his feet, and she knew the conversation would have to be cut short soon. The kids would be coming in for supper, and she knew it wouldn't be good for Mary to hear what Laura was saying. "Diana is the laziest woman I've ever met. She won't get a job, and the only thing she does is spend money."

"She's damn worthless," Jerry said. He began to help himself to hamburgers and the baked beans that had been simmering on the stove. He was a big man with a crew cut; he was an ex-Marine and he still kept in shape. "Diana doesn't do a goddamn thing but sit on her ass and play on that computer and smoke cigarettes. And she does that all day. She doesn't even clean up the house."

"Enough of that," Laura said, heading to the sliding-glass door that opened up on the back porch. "We'll talk about this later." She slid the door open and called out, "Supper's ready!"

"I better get going," Elizabeth said, picking up her purse. As much as she wanted to talk more about this latest travesty in her brother's life, she knew it wasn't the time or place to do so, not with Mary here. Her heart went out to her niece, who was a sweet kid. Mary had been through so much—a turbulent early childhood courtesy of Cindy's mood swings, both parents' heavy drinking, and finally Cindy leaving her brother. Her parents had been the only constant adult figures in the little girl's life and now she was out of that secure environment, once again thrust into a volatile home. The few times she had been at her brother's new house, she had the faint impression that Diana treated Mary differently from her own kids. Not bad, mind you, just . . . different. As if she resented that she had to share Ronnie with the girl. Elizabeth had the impression that in Mary's worldview, living with Diana and her kids was like being Cinderella, living under the thumb of a wicked stepmother.

"I'm getting damn tired of it," Jerry said, still rattling on. He spread mayonnaise and mustard on potato rolls and extracted a pickle from a jar. "Ronnie's working double shifts to pay for not only himself and his daughter, but Diana and her kids. He's paying for everything—food, clothing, shelter, all the bills, everything. And she doesn't appreciate any of it."

The clatter of running footsteps thundered up the back steps and the sliding-glass door slid open. Mary and Eric ran into the house, followed by Lily, her dark eyes reflecting a sense of anger that seemed to be etched in her facial features as well. *That kid always has a damn smirk on her face,* Elizabeth thought as she watched the little girl trail after the two older kids. Laura turned into an instant grandma the moment the kids came in, and Elizabeth caught Eric's attention, motioning him over. Lily watched as Eric went to his mother, and for a moment Elizabeth's eyes met Lily's and those eyes were—

So cold.

Elizabeth feigned a nonchalant attitude, putting her hand on Eric's shoulder. "Why don't we get going, sport?"

"Okay." Eric grabbed his windbreaker and, after saying goodbye to her parents, Elizabeth and her son left.

CHAPTER SIX

Something was happening, and Mary Baker was scared.

She huddled under the covers of her bed, terrified. She knew if she told her daddy, he wouldn't believe her. He'd say she was lying, or that it was just her imagination. But she'd *seen* it—or at least she *thought* she'd seen it—and it had terrified her, and she didn't know what to do.

She risked a quick peek at the bed on the other side of the room where Lily slept. Lily wasn't in bed, and when Mary had gone into their bedroom she thought she had heard the little girl in the kitchen while her mother sat at the computer, surfing the Internet. Lily's brother, Rick, had been playing with a Game Boy in the living room, silently immersed.

Something wasn't right. And Mary knew it. She couldn't describe it, didn't know how to put what she felt into words, but something was very wrong here.

Diana and her kids weren't . . . *right*.

Mary turned toward the wall, bunching herself up under the covers. She told herself not to cry. She'd been living here for four months now, and if Lily were going to do something to her, she would have done so by now. But just the thought of sharing a bedroom with that . . . that . . .

Monster? Was that the word she wanted to use?

Maybe I was just imagining it, she thought. *Maybe it was a bad dream. Maybe it was because they were watching those scary movies the other night and I stayed up to watch with them when I should have been doing my homework. Maybe I should have called my grandma and had her come get me, but Rick and Lily were watching the movies and Diana was gone. I don't know where she went, and Daddy was working, and there was nothing else on TV. They wouldn't let me turn the channel so I could watch Sponge-Bob, and I watched it too and it was some movie about a Blair Witch, and then something about demons or aliens and then Lily's face . . . her face . . .*

Mary shivered, tears streaming down her face. She'd begged them to change the channel; she didn't want to watch this scary movie, but Rick had told her to be quiet and they'd sat there in the darkened living room as the horror movie blared from the TV, Rick leaning back watching with a smug grin, Lily staring transfixed at it with that vacant look she had, and Mary cringing and trying to look away, not wanting to even be there.

Then somehow Diana was back and the TV was off, and the house was lit up and Mary must have fallen asleep because that was the last thing she remembered—them watching the scary movie and then it suddenly being turned off and Diana was back in the room. Mary had jumped up and headed straight to her room and dove into bed. Lily hadn't come with her; she'd remained in the kitchen, where she was now.

Maybe it was just the movie, she thought. *Maybe I was having a bad dream because of that movie we were watching. Maybe my imagination got to me. My grandma always said that watching scary movies will mess with your imagination, make you see things that aren't really there.*

That made her feel a little better, but not much.

Because she could've sworn she saw it. Even though it was brief.

She could have sworn she'd seen Lily's face changing into something else.

She'd caught a quick glimpse as she was heading to the bedroom she shared with her stepsister (that's what Tina, her friend at school, called Lily; her stepsister, and it was confusing to Mary because Grandma and her daddy and Diana were saying that Lily was her *sister*, but she didn't feel like a sister, not really). She had just woken up and seen that Diana was back in the living room in front of the computer and that horror movie was turned off. She realized then she must have dozed off, so she'd gotten up and headed to the bedroom, catching a glimpse of Lily playing on the kitchen floor out of the corner of her eye.

Only it wasn't Lily. Well . . . it had Lily's body. And it kind of had Lily's face. But Lily's face had been . . . shifting . . .

It was so sudden that Mary didn't know if she had really seen it or not. Lily had looked up as Mary rounded the corner on her way to their bedroom and the movement in her face was shimmering, as if the skin of her face was elastic and there was something beneath it moving around; her eyes had become black pits, her mouth turning upward into a grin for the first time since Mary had known her.

And then just as quickly it was gone. Lily's normal vacant stare was back.

Mary hadn't stopped. She'd dived into the bedroom and into bed, not even bothering to put on her pajamas.

Where she'd been ever since, trying to tell herself that what she saw was just her imagination.

I just want my daddy, she thought. The more she thought of Lily, the more she tried to remember if what she had seen happened, the more confused she got. And the more confused she got, the more scared she became. She started to cry silently. *I want my daddy!*

She hated living here. Daddy was never around; he was always working, and whenever he was home he was either grumpy or too tired to play with her or listen to her. He was always asleep when she woke up to go to school, and he didn't even take her to school anymore—Rick did now, walking her to the school bus every morning. At least Grandma picked her up in the afternoon, but on those days when she couldn't, Diana was there to pick her up. Once home, it was just her and Lily and Diana, and Diana didn't like her anyway. She never even made supper. Mary usually wound up calling Grandma, asking for Pop-Pop to pick her up, which he did. Those were the only good times of the day—being at school and being with her grandparents. Sometimes her cousin, Eric, was there and she always had a good time with him. But then Diana would either come to pick her up or, most likely, Pop-Pop would drive her back to her house and she'd have to face the long evening with Diana and her two kids *(they're not my brother and sister, they're not, they're not, they're not!)*. The few times she had tried talking to her new step-mother (that's what Tina said Diana was; her step-mother; she wasn't her mom; *Cindy* was her mom and Mary knew there was something wrong with her mother but even if there was, she much preferred her real mother's company to her step-mother's; at least her real mother loved her and paid attention to her, even if she was drunk a lot of the time), Diana had acted as if she was annoyed as all hell. That's the phrase her grandmother sometimes used when she overheard conversations Grandma had with Aunt Elizabeth. "Whenever Diana is forced to do something with Mary or her own children, she always gets that annoyed-as-all-hell expression." Diana got that expression a lot, and Mary understood clearly the woman wasn't the least bit interested in looking over her homework or looking at her drawings or playing a game with her. Mary had the feeling Diana didn't want to have anything to do with her. For the first few months she wondered if she was going to be like the evil step-mother in *Cinderella*, but Diana seemed to treat her own children the same way. She ignored them, too.

Mary had tried playing with Lily, and while that went well most of the time, she got the impression the younger girl was going through the motions and wasn't really serious about it. And in the past few weeks she'd gotten an even stronger impression that Lily was somehow different.

She'd started noticing Lily's blank stare, her eyes. At first she merely attributed it to the girl's behavior, but as she observed her more, she realized there was something creepy about it. Sometimes Lily could go for hours without speaking. She'd sit on the sofa in the living room staring blindly at the TV, like she was a robot or something. And Rick, while he was no better, would usually flip the channels disinterestedly. He mostly ignored Mary. But then he ignored Lily, too. And his mother.

In fact, they often ignored each other.

The more Mary thought about it, the more frightened she became. The only time she ever really saw them interact with each other was when her daddy was home or when Grandma or Aunt Elizabeth or Eric were around. When it was just the three of them, they didn't talk to each other at all.

That wasn't right. Even though Mary was only seven, she knew brothers and sisters talked to each other and their mother at some point. Mary had never even seen Diana yell at her kids. She yelled at Mary all the time, but—

Gooseflesh erupted on Mary's skin, and she shivered under the blankets as she heard the door creak open. A shaft of light spilled into the room and she held her breath, telling herself not to cry. *Don't cry, don't cry, don't cry, don't cry, don't—*

Soft, silent footsteps padded into the room.

The creak of bedsprings from Lily's bed.

The rustle of blankets.

Lily had gone to bed.

Mary listened for other sounds, but there was none. She could imagine Lily on the other side of the room, lying in her bed, her flat gaze staring up at the ceiling with those dark, soulless eyes.

I hate living here, and I wish Daddy had never met this woman. I don't like Lily and Rick and Diana, and I just want to go back and live with my grandma. I just want my daddy and my real mommy!

Thinking about her real mother brought a burst of sadness, and now she couldn't help crying. Silent tears rolled down her cheeks. She felt a sense of shame that her family was not normal. Her friends all had normal parents; Eric's mommy and daddy were normal. She felt like an oddball because her mommy and daddy didn't live together, weren't married, and now everybody was trying to make Diana her real mommy when she *wasn't.* Mary *had* a real mommy and she just wanted to live with her and daddy in their own house, away from Diana and her kids.

I just want my daddy. I just want my daddy.

She cried silently, thinking these thoughts, as she finally fell asleep.

While in the next bed Lily lay on her back staring at the ceiling, her eyes open and vacant, her face expressionless.

The closer Ronnie Baker got to his home, the more the feelings of dread solidified.

Maybe it wasn't exactly dread. It was more like a feeling of apprehension.

And he was horny, too.

It was a weird thing to harbor feelings that were polar opposites of each other. He and Diana made love every night, even when it was her time of the month. He'd always avoided sex during a woman's period before, but not with Diana. He thought he would be repulsed by it, but he'd actually grown to like it!

So he was looking forward to tonight's romp. But he was also apprehensive about coming home.

Ronnie yawned as he made a left on Fir Road, which led

down to his development. The roads were relatively deserted at this hour of the night, and Ronnie liked driving home with nobody around. He liked having the road to himself. But lately the drive was beginning to wear him out. It wasn't so bad when he drove to work, but lately after a twelve-hour-plus shift, he was starting to feel tired. He couldn't really afford to work fewer hours. Diana wouldn't work, and in a way he liked having her home during the day to be with the kids, but it was beginning to take its toll on his well-being. He never had time for anything except work and driving home to fuck Diana, eat, sleep, wake up, scarf a quick breakfast and drive back to work to do it all over again.

And for the past month, the work schedule had been seven days a week.

It was starting to really get to him. Ronnie felt irritable and tired. He didn't know how much longer he could work this brutal schedule, but he didn't know what else to do. He had the mortgage, the utilities, his car payment, Diana's car payment, insurance for both vehicles, his credit card, her credit card, food and clothing for the kids, and the usual miscellaneous expenses that went with running a house. Diana was expensive, too. He'd bought her diamond rings, bracelets and necklaces, all from the best jewelry stores in town. Her engagement ring alone cost more than two grand. And even though he made over fifty thousand dollars a year, that barely covered things. Actually, he made less than that—it was only through working the overtime and on weekends and holidays that he was able to pull in double-time, which boosted his salary to a mid-five-figure level.

He had to work these grueling shifts. If he didn't, he'd fall behind on a payment. And if he fell behind on a payment, started slipping financially, he might lose what he had.

He didn't want to lose Diana.

But she was beginning to piss him off.

Ronnie thought about this as he cruised home, the radio

playing Bad Company as he drove slowly through the back roads of Reinholds, the town he had moved to. As great as Diana was in the sack, she wasn't very supportive when it came to paying her share of the bills or giving him some support. You'd think if she were home all day she'd clean the house and do the laundry and have dinner ready for him when he got home, but the house was becoming a pigsty. She didn't clean, she didn't dust, and she didn't cook. There was never any food in the house, and the few times he'd seen Mary this week she'd complained they'd been out of cereal and milk and eggs for almost a week.

Thinking about his daughter brought a frown to his face. He hated being apart from her so much, but he didn't know what else to do. He loved Diana, and he wanted her in his life. If he could only convince her to do something like get a job, maybe he could scale back on his own hours and spend some more time with Mary. Actually, he could spend more time with Diana and her kids as well. They could be a real family, do things together. He could take them on trips; they could do normal family things together. He could be happy.

He made a right down Elm and yawned. As much as he loved Diana, he hated arguing with her about this. He'd tried bringing it up to her, tried to convince her he just couldn't take working like this anymore, but she wouldn't hear it. She told him if he really loved her he would just shut up and go to work like a real man and provide for his family. She had uprooted her life in Ohio to be with him; she'd made plenty of sacrifices already, especially with her children. Couldn't he sacrifice a few extra hours for them? When she put it to him that way it made sense, and Ronnie would back down. But lately he'd been mulling it over and the more he thought about it, the more fucked up it was sounding. It wasn't until he was bitching about Diana at work while on the assembly line when his co-worker Mark Shank overheard him and said, "Well shit, man, maybe she's just stringing ya along. You know, digging for gold and all that."

Ronnie's first impulse had been to punch Mark, but he'd resisted. In a way, what Mark said made sense.

He was thinking about this now as he turned down his street and pulled up in the driveway and killed the engine. Diana's car was safely inside the closed garage and as Ronnie got out of the car feeling tired and achy, he saw movement out of the corner of his eye.

He almost jumped back but relaxed when the form solidified into a recognizable face. It was Cindy, his ex-wife.

And just as quickly as he recognized her, so did his anger rise. "What the fuck are you doing here?" he asked, making no effort to lower his voice.

Cindy stepped forward. She looked like shit. Her hair was a stringy mess, and it looked like it hadn't been combed or washed in days. She had gotten super skinny. Her tattered jeans barely clung to her bony hips, and she was wearing a long-sleeved black T-shirt with some kind of white tribal design that snaked up the arms. Her eyes were large, the pupils wide, and Ronnie could see that her face had broken out with some bad acne. Evidence that she was on something. "I had to see you," Cindy said, rushing up to him, clutching his arm. Ronnie pulled away from her, and she clutched at him again. "Please, Ronnie, you've got to listen to me!"

"Do you know what time it is? It's three in the fucking morning!"

"I know what time it is, but you've got to listen to me," Cindy said, lowering her voice a little. "This was the only way I could think of getting in touch with you. I'm sorry if—"

"Go home, Cindy." Ronnie felt wide awake now. Confrontations with Cindy always did that to him, and he brushed past her and started walking toward his front door.

"Ronnie!" Cindy ran after him and grabbed his arm, pulling him back. "Listen to me!"

Ronnie yanked his arm out of her grasp. Now his anger flared. He resisted the urge to yell at her, especially this late at night, and it was a good thing he was now more awake to keep his anger in check. If he'd still been dead tired he *would* have yelled at her. "Get the fuck off my property."

"Diana is harassing me, and she's threatening our daughter," Cindy said. "I'm scared for Mary and—"

"You're fucking crazy!"

"*Listen* to me!" Cindy pleaded, and for a moment there was something in her voice that got to him, something that got through the hard exterior of his stubbornness and suggested there was a hint of truth in what Cindy was trying to tell him. But then it was quickly gone as he took in her physical appearance. "I know it was stupid of me to call her back and fight with her, but I've been trying to stay away from her and she keeps calling me and saying the most awful things about me and Mary and—"

Ronnie snapped. He leaned forward, jabbing his index finger at Cindy. "You think I'm going to believe the ravings of a lunatic like you? You're a drunk, drug-addict psycho bitch, Cindy! You make shit up all the time, you always fuck things up, and you go looking for trouble. I know you, okay? I know from experience so please spare me your bullshit, okay?"

"*Please,* just listen to me for *once* in your life!" Cindy was actually crying. He could see the tears streaming down her face. "I know I've fucked things up between us and there's no chance for us getting back together, but this isn't about that. This is about *Mary* and—"

"You still think we can get back together? You're out of your fucking mind."

"—it's about her welfare. You're never home, and I'm sure Diana paints a totally different picture of what happens during the day and she'd probably deny everything anyway and—"

"Goddamn right she would, because she doesn't have the time to mess with you," Ronnie said. He was quickly growing bored with this charade.

"Did you know Diana's threatened our daughter? Do you know she's called me and threatened to have Mary whipped to within an inch of her life and to sell a tape of her screaming to child molesters?"

"You're sick!"

"She's done more than that. Look at this." Cindy pulled a photograph out of her pocket and held it up. Ronnie squinted at it. It was Cindy's first-grade school photo, and somebody, most likely Cindy, had taken a red pen and drawn a butcher knife across Mary's throat, complete with blood spilling down her shirt. Ronnie drew in a breath of surprise. "Jesus, Cindy, what the hell is wrong with you?"

"Aren't you *listening?* Diana *sent this* to me! It had a Reinholds postage stamp on it and—"

Ronnie grabbed for the photo, but Cindy was too fast for him. She pulled back and they grappled for it. Ronnie's right hand encircled Cindy's wrist, squeezing. "Give me that picture, you fucking bitch!"

"No!" Cindy struggled, her body thrumming with what felt like live wires. She doubled over, the hand gripping the photo drawn up against her chest. "Ronnie let me go!"

Ronnie reached down with his left hand to try to pry Cindy's arm back. He was getting that picture. If he could get that picture, he was calling in sick tomorrow and going to the lawyer with it to try to convince him to end the supervised visitations. If Cindy were drawing pictures of knives stabbing his daughter, he didn't want her around Mary at all. "Give me that picture, you bitch!"

The front door of the house opened, but Ronnie didn't notice. "Give me that fucking picture!"

Cindy lashed out a kick that connected with Ronnie's left shin, and he automatically loosened his grip on her wrist, enabling her to jerk away. She scampered back to the sidewalk. Ronnie was just about to chase after her when he noticed Diana standing in the doorway to the house. He hesitated, torn between wanting to chase Cindy and going into the house. The brief hesitation was enough time for Cindy to run crying to her car, which was parked two houses down.

Ronnie stood on the driveway and watched while Cindy hobbled to her car. He could sense Diana behind him. They watched as Cindy got into her car and then drove jerkily down the street, turning down Fir Road and heading out of the development.

When Cindy was gone, Ronnie turned to Diana, who stood waiting for him, still in the doorway. He walked up to his front porch. Diana was watching the taillights of Cindy's car recede in the distance. "What did she say to you?"

"The same crazy shit," Ronnie said, dismissing Cindy with a wave of his hand. He motioned Diana inside the house, shut and locked the door behind him. "I don't really give a shit about her. All I'm really interested in now is one thing."

Diana turned to him and smiled. She was wearing a red satin bathrobe, and the front was loose enough to show the tops of her breasts. "And what's that?"

"What do you think?" Ronnie said, taking Diana's hand and leading her to the bedroom. He didn't even bother to turn off the lights in the living room. Diana was ready for him; the bedspread was down, and the candles she had placed on saucers and candelabras around the room were already lit. Once in the bedroom he disrobed and joined Diana in bed. He fucked her twice and passed out three hours later, sleeping until one P.M. the following afternoon. He didn't even think about Cindy or what she'd told him. He didn't even ask about Mary. And when he woke up and got ready for work the only thing he could think of was that he couldn't wait till his shift was over so he could get home and fuck Diana again.

CHAPTER SEVEN

It was Saturday morning, and it was already promising to be a beautiful fall day.

Elizabeth loved October. It was her favorite month. It reminded her of childhood, of running through fallen leaves, the crisp chill promising winter and Halloween. Most of her association with autumn was because of Halloween, which was her favorite time of year. The daytime temperatures had been in the low sixties during the week and the nights in the mid-forties. Occasionally thunderstorms rolled in, bringing rain and wind and thunder and lightning, but they were quickly gone within an hour. And sometimes at night when the wind kicked up and blew around the eaves, Elizabeth would snuggle in bed and think about her childhood, of reading the dark fantasy of Ray Bradbury (she still owned her tattered paperback copy of *The October Country*, which she'd discovered when she was ten), playing with her friends in the neighborhood, making jack-o'-lanterns, creating elaborate Halloween costumes. And even when Halloween was over, its magic touch remained with her for the rest of autumn as it slowly gave way to winter.

Elizabeth stood at the kitchen sink emptying the dishwasher. Eric was upstairs in his room playing with a game he had gotten for his last birthday, and Gregg was in the basement working out. Elizabeth had spent most of the morning drinking coffee and watching the news, with occasional forays into reading the latest Stephen King novel. Gregg had started making inquiries at the Fulton Opera House, a local theater group, for next year's season, and she was pleasantly surprised and pleased by this. He'd been invited to send a resume, which he had done a few days ago, and she was certain he would be called for an audition. She felt good that he was seriously thinking of taking up acting again. Today they had talked about going into Lancaster and running around—visiting the mall, maybe taking in a movie and dinner. She had mentioned this to her mother earlier in the week, and Mom had offered to take Eric for the evening to give her and Gregg the night to themselves, and Elizabeth thought she was going to take her up on it. In fact, she was going to give Mom a call right now and—

The phone rang and she closed the dishwasher and answered, thinking to herself, *You beat me to it,* as she saw her mother's name and phone number flash across the LED readout of the caller ID system. "Yello!"

"Hello, Elizabeth," Mom said. "How are you doing?"

"I'm doing okay. What's up?" Mom sounded tired, like she'd been up most of the evening.

"Okay, I guess. Didn't get much sleep last night. Mary spent the night and is probably going to spend the weekend over here."

"Oh?" Elizabeth frowned. Ever since Diana moved herself and her brood into Ronnie and Mary's house (because it *was* her brother's house after all; he paid the mortgage, and she was pretty certain his name was the only one on the deed), they seemed to think Mom and Dad ran a free babysitting service. Lily and Mary were dumped off at their home every other day. They were there every weekend, it seemed, as well. Elizabeth objected to Ronnie taking advantage of their parents that way, but had remained silent. It was Mom's issue, not hers, and Laura had simply smiled and accepted the kids readily, but lately Elizabeth could tell her mother was not happy at being taken advantage of. Diana would drop the kids off while Ronnie was at work, claiming she had to go grocery shopping or run errands, and she'd be gone for six hours or more at a time. They didn't mind sitting for Mary, but Diana seemed to expect Mom and Dad to watch Lily all the time. Her father wasn't happy with that, and had remarked to Elizabeth a few weeks before he felt they were being forced to accept Lily as one of their grandkids. Dad was getting ready to burst at the seams, but Mom was holding it in, trying to be diplomatic about it. Elizabeth knew her mother was trying to make the best of a bad situation, but in her opinion she was doing anything to be accommodating. Whenever Mary stayed over, Lily always wound up at the house, too. "So you had the kids last night then?"

"Just Mary," Mom said.

"Oh, so Diana let you get away with just having Mary, huh? How hard was it to get her to keep her own kid at home for a change?"

"I'll have to tell you all about it. Think we can come over for a little bit?"

There was something in the tone of Mom's voice that told Elizabeth there was more to what happened last night than Mary simply spending the evening with her grandparents. Something had happened, and Mom didn't want to talk about it over the phone. "Sure. Come on over."

"Good, because I have quite a story for you. Think Gregg can take the kids somewhere for an hour or so while we talk?"

"Yeah, I think I can arrange that," Elizabeth said, now brimming with curiosity. "Come on by."

"Okay. I can be there in half an hour."

When Elizabeth hung up the phone she replayed the conversation back to herself. No, she hadn't been imagining things. Her mom really wanted to talk to her in private. Something serious must have happened last night. Maybe Diana and Ronnie were breaking up!

Brimming with anticipation at hearing her brother's new romantic relationship was falling apart, she headed downstairs to talk to Gregg about the latest development in the day's plans.

By one thirty P.M. the house was clean, and Gregg had taken Eric and Mary to Chuck E. Cheese for an afternoon of pizza, soda and video games. Mom had arrived with Mary thirty minutes after they'd gotten off the phone as she'd promised, and Elizabeth smiled at Mary as she came in the house. "Hey Mary, how's it going?" Mary had smiled and gone over to hug her aunt, but Elizabeth could tell something was different about the girl. Both Mary and Laura appeared tired, but it also looked as if a tremendous weight had been lifted from their shoulders. Laura's hair was down, and she wearing a gray sweater. Mary was dressed in blue jeans, a white blouse, and a blue jacket, clothes Mom kept on hand at the house for her. Elizabeth had told Gregg something was going on with Mary and asked if he could take the kids somewhere for an hour or so while she talked to Mom. Gregg had readily agreed. Eric had come downstairs when Mom and Mary arrived, and fifteen minutes later he was out the door with his father and cousin. Elizabeth had still been fiddling with house cleaning and her mother joined in, making idle chatter as they finished. When Elizabeth suggested brewing a pot of decaffeinated coffee, Mom sat down at the kitchen table and looked out the sliding glass doors that led out to the porch. "Coffee sounds fine, honey. I probably need it. Make it the real stuff, too. I didn't get much sleep last night."

"So what happened?" Elizabeth got coffee out of the refrigerator and poured the fresh beans into the grinder.

"Well, Mary called last night around eight o'clock crying. She wanted Jerry to go out there and pick her up."

Elizabeth nodded as she ground the beans, then emptied the coffee into a fresh filter-lined percolator. She poured a full pot of water into the coffeemaker, musing over this. Mom had related a week earlier that Mary had taken to calling her grandparents, often in tears, begging to come over and spend the night. Jerry would go over to Ronnie's house to get her, and Diana would talk him into taking Lily with him, which only made Mary change her mind about wanting to come over, causing Diana to banish them to Jerry and Laura's anyway. Elizabeth thought it was pathetic Diana was forcing her own child on her parents when their own granddaughter clearly wanted to spend time with her grandparents alone. Mom had told her last Friday that Mary wasn't happy whenever she came over with Lily. "Diana pushes Lily on us whenever Mary wants to come over and it almost feels like we have no choice but to take her. And I don't want to take her every time. Every once in a while is okay, but not all the time. She isn't our grandchild, but . . ."

I don't want to offend anybody, Elizabeth had thought, finishing her mother's sentence. That was the trouble with Mom. She didn't like to rock the boat. She didn't like to offend people. She'd let people walk all over her before she would lift a finger to stand up for herself, and she and Dad were paying for it now. Elizabeth remained silent through Mom's recitation of those events last week, and now as her mother sat in her kitchen waiting for the coffee to brew, she suspected the subject of Lily always being pushed on them whenever Mary wanted to come visit her grandparents by herself had finally come to a head.

"Well, you know Jerry and I haven't exactly liked the idea of Lily always coming over whenever Mary wanted to come spend time with us," Laura said. She was sitting at the table gazing out at the backyard. "I could tell Mary didn't like having her around because she became more clinging toward us. She actually started carrying her blanket around and sucking her thumb again last week."

"Really?" Elizabeth frowned again. Mary had a security blanket from the time she was a year old until just last year, when she turned six. She had also sucked her thumb well into her sixth year.

"Yes," Laura said. "So last night when Mary called I'd just about had it. I mean, I was really at the end of my rope. And I know it isn't fair to be angry at Mary because it's really Diana I should be angry at. She doesn't show those kids any attention whatsoever, and she's always dumping them on us whenever she damn well feels like it. Well, when Mary called last night she started crying right away, and I cut right though and said, 'Now Mary, stop it! You have to stop this crying right now and just calm down. You're fine, I know you don't like it over there but it's just something you're going to have to get used to.' And Mary wouldn't stop crying. She insisted on coming over, practically *begged* to come over, and there was something in her voice that got to me, so I told her I'd have her grandfather go over and get her. And when I got off the phone with her, I told Jerry to bring Mary home and to not bring Lily over no matter how much she cries and begs to come over and no matter what Diana says. And Jerry's just about had it with the situation too and he said, 'Don't worry about that. I really don't give a good goddamn if I make Diana mad or not.' And he went to pick Mary up."

Laura paused, and the only sound in the kitchen was the coffee brewing. Elizabeth gathered the spoons and a bowl of sugar and set them out on the table as her mother continued. "There was something different in Mary's voice this time when she called. She actually sounded frantic, like she was scared to death of staying over there. She sounded like . . . well, she had that tone of voice you only hear when women scream in horror movies. There was this underlying tone of genuine terror in her voice. That's the only way I can describe it. I've never heard a child sound like that before, and when I heard it in Mary's voice it scared me to death. I actually started thinking that maybe Cindy was right in what she was saying."

Elizabeth immediately thought of Cindy's accusations against her brother's new girlfriend. Laura had related last week that on a supervised visit with Mary, Cindy had told her (while Mary had been playing with Eric in the basement out of earshot) about the harassing phone calls and the threats Diana made against Mary. Laura hadn't believed her and told Cindy she found it hard to accept such a story. Cindy had been insistent though, and Laura had even talked to Ronnie about it, warning him that Cindy might try to use the story as ammunition in a custody battle. Elizabeth didn't know what to make of the story either way; she didn't like Diana, and her respect for Cindy had been on a steady decline since her former sister-in-law left her brother and began sliding into her present drug and alcohol state. Cindy's behavior of late, as indicated by a DUI she had acquired over the summer, her constant changing of addresses and boyfriends, living with drug dealers, and the numerous fights she'd gotten into at area bars clearly indicated she was unstable, and Elizabeth wouldn't put it past her to resort to lies and false accusations against her brother in a custody battle. Mary was at the right age to be easily manipulated, and an allegation of abuse was just the sort of leverage Cindy would need to throw a wrench into Ronnie's case, even if she couldn't prove it.

"So Jerry went to the house," Laura continued, looking out the sliding-glass doors to the backyard. "When he pulled up Mary ran out and opened the driver's-side door, crying that she wanted to go. Jerry tried to calm her down, and by then Diana had come out. She was apparently shocked Mary had run out of the house like that, and Jerry said later she looked surprised he was there, as if Mary had placed the call to us secretly."

Elizabeth nodded. Her niece probably had made an effort to catch Diana off guard.

"Jerry told Diana that we were going to have Mary over for the evening," Laura continued. "He made up a story, said I had arranged this with Mary a few days before. By then Lily was standing at the door looking outside, and Diana told Jerry she was going to go inside real quick and get Lily and Mary's things. Jerry stopped her and said, 'That won't be necessary. Mary has plenty of clothes at the house.' Diana said something about going inside to pack a bag for Lily and Jerry said, 'Lily isn't coming over. She's staying with you.' He said Diana got this look on her face, as if she were about to say, *Well, Lily* is *coming over whether you like it or not,* and Jerry held his ground. Diana tried to pull her sweetie-pie thing on him. You know, 'Oh come on, Jerry. I could really use the night off. Ronnie and I will be more than happy to come over and mow the lawn or run errands for you sometime' or some other bullshit, and Jerry told her no, we *weren't* keeping Lily tonight and if she didn't like it that was just too bad. While all this was going on, Mary was in the car crying. Jerry got mad and I'm afraid he told Diana off and she stomped back in the house and said 'Fine! We'll see how your son likes it,' and she pushed Lily into the house in front of her and slammed the door. Mary was crying hysterically and as much as Jerry wanted to calm her down before he started driving, he felt this urge to pull out of the driveway and head home, so he did.

"Mary cried all the way home. Jerry asked her if Diana had hit her or hurt her in any way and she just shook her head, not speaking, just crying. When they got to the house, she had calmed down a bit, and when she came inside, she came to me and started crying again. I held her and let her cry. Jerry caught my gaze, and he looked troubled. We both sat down with Mary in the living room and tried to calm her down. By then I was all up in arms with worry that Diana had done something to Mary, that she'd beat her or done something worse, but the more we asked if Diana had hurt her, the more she shook her head. Finally when she had calmed down, she said she never wanted to go back to that house, and then she started crying again, asking if she could live with us instead of with her father and Diana and her kids.

"Jerry was pacing the kitchen and the living room, and I could tell he was both angry and scared, and you know how he gets when he's like that. He becomes agitated. I had to calm him down before I could get any useful information out of Mary, so I got his pills and a glass of water and made him take some. Then I made some hot chocolate for Mary, and Jerry actually went downstairs to the bar and brought up a bottle of 151 and made us some rum and Cokes. Of course, he put more rum than Coke in it, but it did the trick with him. It calmed him right down."

Elizabeth was about to ask the inevitable question about mixing alcohol with her father's prescription nerve medication, then decided against it. Her father rarely drank, but he had an unusually high tolerance for alcohol.

"Finally," Laura said, her gray eyes reflecting fatigue, "when we all had our drinks and Mary had calmed down sufficiently, we sat down at the kitchen table, and Mary started talking. She started by talking about Diana and her kids, telling us that they don't interact with each other, that they hardly talk to each other. At first I didn't think much of it, but Mary said, 'Grandma, they never talk to each other. The only time they do is when you're around, or when Daddy is around and sometimes when I'm around. But most of the time when it's just us they don't do *anything!* It's like they don't even know the other one is there!'

"You know Jerry and I think Diana is lazy and that she doesn't do anything—"

"And that she doesn't pay attention to her own kids, much less Mary," Elizabeth said. The coffee had finished brewing, and she brought down two big mugs and poured it. She returned to the table with the steaming mugs and the two women prepared their coffee silently.

Laura stirred hers, now a rich golden color, and took a sip. "Thanks. I needed that."

Elizabeth nodded, sipping.

Laura continued the narrative. "At first when Mary related that Diana and the kids don't interact with each other, I didn't know how to react. I still believed Mary was throwing a tantrum and resented having to share her father with them and was using this as a way of venting the last few months of whatever pent-up emotions she'd been holding in. I asked her if anything had happened that day that would lead her to call us in the state she did, and at first she wouldn't answer. Then she started repeating what she'd said earlier, that Diana and her kids don't talk to each other, and then she started focusing more on Lily, saying that Lily was a monster and a freak, and again I chalked it up to feelings of alienation and her situation. Jerry tried to talk some sense into her, but Mary shook her head and said quite calmly, 'No Pop-Pop, I know what I saw, and Lily isn't what you think she is. They *all* aren't what you think they are!' She started to cry again, then took great effort in stemming the tears, then took a sip of hot chocolate and told us what had happened that afternoon.

"Yesterday afternoon Mary went down the street to a friend's house. I think this is Leslie Allman, who lives three doors down. Leslie is in Mary's class. She told me that usually when she goes over she tells Diana, who makes Lily go with her, which Mary hates. This time, though, she didn't tell Diana where she was going. Rick never tells his mother where he goes, and Diana never seems to notice where Lily is or what she's doing anyway, so Mary figured Diana wouldn't care if she didn't tell her she was going to Leslie's. She slipped out of the house and ran down the street, and once at Leslie's, the girls played for a while. Then Leslie had to have dinner with her parents so Mary went home.

"It must've been around six o'clock, maybe a little later," Laura said. She sipped coffee as she related Mary's narrative. "The first thing she noticed was that her father's car was in the driveway. She was surprised he was home, and she thought maybe he had come home sick. It was starting to get dark, and she felt better that her dad was home because she knew otherwise she would have to find something to eat in the house since Diana rarely made the kids supper. She got to the house and let herself inside through the front door, and at first she thought the house was empty. There was nobody in the living room or the kitchen and for a moment she stood there quietly, trying to listen to where everybody was. Her first thought was that Lily and Rick had gone somewhere and that Ronnie was in the bedroom with Diana. So she tiptoed to the master bedroom door and paused outside, listening.

"It was right at that moment Mary said that she knew Diana and the kids weren't in the house, but she sensed there was something wrong. She could tell her father was home, that he was in the bedroom, but she was afraid to go in there. She didn't know exactly how to explain it to us, and it took Jerry and me a good thirty minutes of questioning to get it out of her, but what we both got out of it was this: Her instinct told her Diana and the kids weren't in the house, but theoretically she knew they *should* be in the house.

"She wanted to see her father so badly she pushed the door open gently in case he was asleep. Keep in mind I still don't know what to make of this next part of Mary's story. Jerry and I were up most of the night talking about it and doing so worried Jerry more than ever. We're both of a mind to have Mary looked at by a child psychologist."

Elizabeth felt her stomach turn into shaved ice as she clutched her coffee cup. "What happened?"

Laura took a sip of coffee. She was looking down at the table as she spoke, as if she were still trying to make some kind of sense of what she had heard Mary tell her last night. "Mary said that the first thing she noticed was that somebody had lit all those scented candles Diana keeps in the bedroom. They were the only source of light. She took a step into the bedroom and saw something move on the bed. At first . . . when she got to this part I honestly thought she had been traumatized by the sight of her father and Diana having sexual intercourse. But . . . it wasn't that at all."

Elizabeth listened with growing dread, her hands gripping the coffee cup.

"She saw her father on the bed. He was lying on his back and he looked like he was asleep. She also saw what she first thought to be Diana lying next to him, but as she got closer to the bed she saw that it wasn't Diana. It was . . . well, the best way I can describe it is that it was this . . . this large mass."

"Large mass?"

"She said her first impression of what she saw was that there were several . . . people . . . crowding up against each other on the bed," Laura said, speaking slowly and methodically. "She could make out a large shape mashed up against her father. She said there were also other shapes, and they were moving, making a rustling sound. Mind you, I still thought Mary had walked in on her father and Diana having sex, especially when she mentioned the smell that came up, but . . . well, I still want to believe what she saw was probably a combination of her imagination or . . ." Laura shook her head, her features troubled. "I just don't know."

"Mom, what did she see?"

Laura looked up at her, her eyes wide, scared, troubled. "She said it was like one big mass all bunched into different lumps. One of those lumps was attached to Ronnie."

"*Attached?*"

Laura nodded. For the first time since she began spinning Mary's narrative, she looked disturbed. "Mary said that was the only word she could think of to describe it. It was like this mass melded seamlessly with Ronnie, and he was asleep and the rest of the . . . mass, or whatever you want to call it, was lying there like some gigantic tumor. It had skin, she said that much; it was like Ronnie's skin had morphed with whatever this thing was and that . . ." Laura took a sip of coffee, seeming to struggle with what to say next. ". . . well, part of it, the part farthest away from Ronnie, was moving."

Elizabeth let that sink in, not knowing what to say. Laura continued and Elizabeth was momentarily grateful for this, as it kept the silence from becoming too great. "The part that was moving . . . she said it was like there were lots of other things underneath it moving around. That they would strain against the surface of the skin, like somebody being underneath a blanket . . . and that she could see shapes moving around in there."

"Shapes?" Elizabeth couldn't believe what she was hearing.

"Sounds crazy, doesn't it?" Laura took a hearty sip of coffee. "I don't know how long Mary actually stood there watching it. She was frozen for a moment, trying to make sense of what she was seeing. And what she was seeing— what she *insisted* she saw—was this huge mass that became formless with lots of eyes and mouths and claws that rippled and disappeared, then reappeared over and over again. She said it shifted and changed and in some cases she saw faces erupt to the surface, faces that seemed to scream. And as the shapes began to coalesce into one huge mass, the faces became more distinct and she made out three different figures—Diana and her kids. That's when she bolted out of the house."

They were silent for a moment, and Elizabeth didn't know what to say. *How do you respond to a story like that? Especially from a seven-year-old?* She sipped her coffee and looked at her mother, who met her gaze with that same worried expression.

"Mary ran back to Leslie's house," Laura continued, hands still clutching her coffee cup. "She ran back and sat on the front porch for a while, trying to convince herself what she saw was a nightmare. When she began to sense from the movements inside the house that supper was over at Leslie's, she rang the doorbell and Leslie's mother answered the door. Mary asked if Leslie could play, and Mary was allowed to go inside and play with Leslie for about an hour. She said she didn't know what else to do; she didn't really want to play with her friend, but she couldn't go back to her own house. She asked Leslie if they could watch cartoons, so the girls went in the family room and watched TV for a while, but Mary said she didn't really watch the TV. She mostly thought about what she'd seen. And the more she thought, the more scared she became. When Leslie's mother told Mary it was time for her to go home, Mary asked if she could use their phone to call her house real quick. She was allowed to use the phone in Leslie's brother's room and that's when she called us."

"So she didn't even go home?"

"Oh, she went home," Laura said. "After she called Jerry, she ran home and waited on the porch. The lights were on in the living room and she heard the TV. Ronnie's truck was still in the driveway—Jerry confirmed the truck was there when we talked about it later. She was too afraid to go inside. She peeked in the window and saw Diana sitting in front of the computer and Rick sitting on the sofa watching TV. She couldn't see Lily, and she didn't want to go inside, so she huddled on the front porch. When Jerry pulled into the driveway she ran out to meet him. He didn't even know she'd been waiting for him on the porch."

Laura sipped her coffee and sighed. "It's when things like this happen I sometimes wish I still smoked. I could use a cigarette now."

"Sorry I never started," Elizabeth said. Laura looked at her, and the two women burst out laughing.

"That's basically it," Laura said, wiping her hands on a napkin. "That's what Mary told us happened, and she insists she won't go back to that house. Jerry didn't realize she'd been sitting on the porch waiting for him when he pulled up, and it was that little part that really got to him. I mean, the fact that the child was too afraid to go inside her own house and get out of the cold. It made him furious, and it scared him. We were up all night talking about it."

"Did Mary get any sleep last night?" Elizabeth asked.

"She finally got to bed a little after midnight," Laura said. "I gave her something to help her sleep, and Jerry and I stayed up till two o'clock talking. Twice Jerry got up to call Diana to yell at her, and both times I took the phone out of his hands. Then he ranted and raved about Ronnie all night, talking about how inconsiderate he was and how he was being stupid in letting this woman and her children move in with him, and how he was paying more attention to them than the welfare of his own child and it just went on and on. I didn't want to defend Ronnie, but he *is* an adult now and we don't want to make his decisions for him. You know what I mean?"

Elizabeth nodded. "Yes, I know what you mean." She sipped her coffee.

"Why does Ronnie pick those kinds of women?" Laura asked.

Elizabeth glanced at her. "You think I know what turns him on?"

Laura shrugged. "Well, look at his past history. All his girlfriends are dark-haired, skinny, and they all drink. They're party girls. Look at Cindy. She was a wild one, if I ever saw one. And what about the girl he was seeing for a while after Cindy left him? What was her name?"

"Linda."

"Right. Look at her. Just like Cindy. And Diana is just like Cindy as well, only she doesn't drink all day and run around the way Cindy does."

"Give her time."

"I don't want to give her time," Laura said. "I just want him to grow up and find somebody who is mature. All he goes after is party girls."

"Well, Mom, Ronnie always did let his little head do all his thinking."

"You got that right."

The two women sat at the kitchen table sipping coffee and thinking. Elizabeth finished her cup and rose to get a refill.

"The more I thought about what Mary told me, the more I realized she seems to be right."

Elizabeth turned to her mother, a fresh cup of coffee in hand. She frowned. "What do you mean?"

"Diana doesn't talk with her kids," Laura said. "She *yells* at them and she talks to them sometimes, but she doesn't engage them in conversation. She doesn't pay attention to them. She spends all her time sitting in front of that goddamn computer, and the kids don't talk to each other much."

Elizabeth still had that frown on her face. She thought about what her mother just said as she sat back down at the table with a fresh cup. "I don't think I can comment on that. I've never been over enough to notice."

"Jerry and I talked about that all night," Laura said. "About how Diana treats the kids. There's never food in the house, and it's always a mess. She's home all day long and won't get a job, so you'd think she'd clean the house and cook, but she doesn't."

"That's one thing that's always bothered me," Elizabeth said. "Diana refusing to get a job."

"It makes Jerry angry. Ronnie is working himself ragged in order to pay for a roof over their heads and put food on the table and clothes on their backs, and she won't do anything to help. You'd think she'd pitch in and do her part by keeping the house clean, making sure there's food in the house, cooking, tending to the welfare of the kids, but she doesn't. She sits on her ass all day and runs up the phone bill. Jerry wants Mary to move in with us, and I agree with him."

Elizabeth was surprised at this. "You serious?"

"Serious enough to discuss it at length last night." Laura finished her coffee. "Jerry is afraid for Mary's safety over there. Ronnie isn't seeing what's going on. I don't think it's so much that he doesn't *want* to see it, but he's not around enough to experience how things really are."

"He doesn't notice his house is a mess and there's no

food in it?" Elizabeth found it hard to believe that her brother, even as much of a loser as he was, would not notice his house was messy.

"He works all the time," Laura said. "How could he notice? He comes home, drinks a beer or two, goes to bed, gets up and does the whole thing over again. He spends more time at work than he does at home, and you know it. I'm sure Diana is being as sweet to him as she can to keep him on her good side. Probably why he doesn't notice anything is wrong."

"That little head in control again."

Laura laughed. "Well, Ronnie never was the sharpest knife in the drawer when it came to women. I must sound like a horrible mother to be talking like that about my own son, but it's true. He was always more into taking the easy way out than working hard to achieve something. He flunked out of college and when he was working for your father, Jerry fired him at least half a dozen times. He's always been what you kids would call a fuckup."

You missed several things, Mom, Elizabeth thought. *The time he was busted for smoking pot when he was fourteen. All the fights he used to get into at school. The DUI he got when he was twenty-one. Being charged with vehicular manslaughter stemming from an accident he got in one night when he was twenty-three and making a beer run with his buddies. And then what about the times you and Dad were visited by his drug dealer, who demanded payment for Ronnie's coke habit? I think that happened twice, and I believe the demand was something along the lines of, "Pay up or something bad will happen, maybe to Ronnie, but maybe to you or somebody else in his family." You and Dad shelled out nearly ten grand to pay off his drug debts. Oh, he's been more than inconsiderate over the years, I'd say. Putting his family in danger due to his selfish actions is just one of them. The only reason he entered rehab was because of his last arrest for driving under the influence, and he did that to avoid prison. Thank God for that, because he would have gotten himself killed if he'd kept it up. Although I must say, even though he stopped attending NA meetings and continued drinking, he appears to have learned from the errors of his ways and hasn't abused drugs and alcohol to the extent he did ten years ago. Although that very well could change with the pressure he's under now. Yeah, I'd say he's a fuckup all right. And that's putting it mildly.*

"The closest he's come to anything in which I felt I could be truly proud of him was when Mary was born," Laura said. "He really seemed to settle down and get his act together. He and Cindy moved in together and got married. He was doing good at the shop with your father. He and Cindy moved to that little condo in Ephrata. They were doing really well there. He really cut down on the partying, and he was a good father to Mary."

"And until Diana came along, he continued to be a good father to Mary," Elizabeth said. She had to admit, despite his history of being the consummate fuckup, having Mary helped Ronnie maintain the straight and narrow road. Elizabeth had to admit that in the five years or so he was married to Cindy he had straightened out so much, had redeemed himself from his past sins so greatly, that he had truly become a different person. He had actually been fun to be around. That had changed when Diana arrived.

Laura nodded. She took a hearty gulp of coffee. "You're right."

"So what happened?"

"Diana."

Elizabeth thought about that for a moment while she drank her coffee. Granted, she didn't like Diana either, but she still felt it was Ronnie's responsibility to make sure Mary was taken care of. She tried putting herself in Ronnie's shoes; if it had been she raising Eric as a single mother, she wouldn't have been so quick to jump into a new relationship. She would have given herself time to grow into being a single parent. And even if she had met somebody and decided to shack up with him, she wouldn't have allowed herself to be the sole breadwinner; she'd have insisted her new mate bring in an income too, and if he didn't his ass would be out the door.

But then she didn't think with her little head. That was her brother's territory. She had to remember that.

"Do you think Diana's abusing Mary?" Elizabeth asked.

"Physically, no. Psychologically and emotionally?" Laura thought about it. She shook her head. "It's hard to say. I don't think there's any abuse going on in that house. But it's obvious something's happening."

"You mentioned before that you thought Mary was going through these crying tantrums as a way of protesting the situation. Never able to see her father, being thrown into an environment she's uncomfortable in . . ."

"I believe that's where most of this stems from," Laura said. "I think it's led to stress, and the buildup reached its peak last night."

"You think Mary hallucinated what she saw?"

"What else could it be? What she described sounds like something out of one of your books."

"That's what I was thinking," Elizabeth said. She took a sip of her coffee. "It's too unreal."

"Jerry and I discussed getting Mary to see a child psychologist," Laura said. "We went around with what we've been discussing, all the changes Mary's been through, being in a new house, not liking Diana and her kids, never seeing her father, being affected by the incompetence of her mother. And he agrees Mary probably needs to see a professional."

"So you and Dad decided on this last night?" Elizabeth asked, sipping her coffee.

"Yes," Laura said. "We decided to keep Mary for the weekend to give her some fun, take her mind off things at home. Before we came over I called Dr. Wagner and arranged to have her seen by him Tuesday afternoon. Jerry called Ronnie's to tell him we had Mary, but he was asleep.

I decided to come over here with Mary while Jerry deals with Ronnie."

Elizabeth snorted laughter. "Oh I can see *that* going well."

"Jerry assured me he would be level-headed."

"Dad, level-headed?"

Laura grinned. "Well, at least he won't let Ronnie walk all over him, which is what he would have done with me. I'm usually more liable to let Ronnie have the upper hand, but your father isn't. Your father can reason with Ronnie. And Jerry's calmed down sufficiently from last night. He's going to tell Ronnie we're keeping Mary for the weekend and he'll bring her back Sunday evening, and I'm taking her for a checkup Tuesday."

Elizabeth nodded, digesting this latest bit of information. She knew something would blow up at her brother's house eventually. She just didn't think it would involve Mary.

"Does Mary know about the accusations Cindy is making against Diana?"

"No, and she doesn't need to."

"And you don't believe them?"

Laura shook her head. "At this point I don't know what to believe."

Elizabeth didn't know what to believe either. What she did know, however, was everything that represented trouble in Ronnie's house centered on one person.

Diana Marshfield.

The friction between Cindy and Diana was understandable, and if everything else was fine in Ronnie's life that tension could be chalked up to jealousy on Cindy's part. But when you added the other elements in: Ronnie working twelve, sometimes fourteen hours a day, six and seven days a week because Diana wouldn't work and they needed the money from the overtime to meet basic living expenses; Diana not pitching in at the house to help out with things; Diana's treatment of her own children; the effect it was all having on Mary—no wonder it was taking a toll on the girl.

One thing Elizabeth couldn't get over, though, was the supposed accusations Cindy was making against Diana.

Diana threatening to hurt Mary.

Elizabeth didn't know Diana very well, but she knew Cindy. And as much of a fuckup as Cindy had become of late, Elizabeth didn't think her former sister-in-law had the capacity to make up an accusation as ugly as that. Especially against her own daughter.

She had a feeling Cindy's accusations might be correct. She didn't know why she felt this way—it certainly wasn't because of her own dislike of Diana—but she felt it nonetheless.

It was a gut feeling.

"How long have they been gone now?" Laura asked.

Elizabeth glanced at the clock. It was after two. "About an hour and a half maybe."

"Why don't you call Gregg and see if they want to meet us at Park City?" Laura suggested. "We can do some shopping."

Elizabeth smiled. "Sounds great.

They spent the rest of the afternoon shopping at the mall and, as discussed with Gregg when she called him from the house, they met at five o'clock at an Applebee's for supper. They drove back to the house, where Elizabeth suggested her mother and Mary spend the evening with them. They could sit up and watch movies all night and eat popcorn. Mom thought that was a wonderful idea, and they swung by Jerry and Laura's home to make a pit stop for clothes. On the way back, Laura told Elizabeth that Jerry had talked to Ronnie and said everything was fine over there, then dropped the subject. Elizabeth nodded, trading a glance with Gregg, who had been brought up to date in bits and pieces over the course of the afternoon while the children were out of earshot. Gregg nodded, put on a smile and said, "Why don't we watch something funny tonight? How 'bout *Shrek*?"

To which the kids gave a resounding, enthusiastic "Yes!" in reply.

CHAPTER EIGHT

Cindy Baker sat in her new boyfriend's car watching Ronnie's house.

It was one-thirty A.M. on Sunday. The October evening was chilly, and Cindy was wearing a long-sleeve T-shirt and a black leather jacket. She smoked a cigarette, watching the house for any sign of movement and thought about what she had come to do.

The Colt .45 lay on the front seat beside her, fully loaded. The gun was Scott's, and he had stolen it a few years ago in Kansas, where he had been living. She had just moved in with Scott two weeks ago after having left Ray's apartment due to a sudden argument. Ray wanted her to start paying rent, but Cindy had a mountain of debts over her and couldn't afford it, and besides, her new job didn't pay for shit. Ronnie's latest bitch was still calling the apartment, too, and Ray had gotten tired of calling the police. The last time he'd called the cops they didn't even bother to show up, and Ray was still smarting over the incident from last month when Cindy had been determined to go over there with his gun and blow the cunt to hell. So she'd packed the few belongings she had into a duffel bag and headed over to the Cocalico Tavern where she's spent the evening drinking, and then crashed at her friend Jacob's house.

The following day, though, Jacob told her she couldn't stay. His wife wouldn't like it, so she'd had him take her back to the Cocalico Tavern where she'd met Scott Anderson.

Scott had just gotten off work. He was a construction worker with a local contracting firm, and his weathered face looked ten years older than his thirty-five years. He'd just served six months in Lancaster County Jail for possession of heroin, and he claimed that he'd been sober now for over a year. Well, okay, truth be told he was off smack, but what was wrong with beer? Cindy agreed wholeheartedly, and they drank up. She ended up at Scott's place a few hours later, in his bed, where they'd had sex and passed out.

And since she didn't really have a place to live she'd stayed with him ever since.

She was still working the day shift for Kelly Services as a "cleaning specialist." Scott had gone to Hershey last night with some friends to see a Rush concert and crashed at a friend's house. He'd called her this afternoon and told her he was going out with the guys again, this time to Philly to hang out with other friends. Cindy didn't mind; they needed to resume their relationships with their friends, and she felt that's what made romantic relationships work—giving your mate his space. Besides, it would give her time to do what she knew she had to do.

Cindy picked up the Colt in one leather-gloved hand. It was heavy. She'd been careful to wipe it down with a cloth while wearing the gloves before she left the house so there wouldn't be any prints on it, and she'd also been careful to make sure that it wouldn't be traced back to Scott. He'd told her a few days after they met that he had spent a year in Kansas working construction, and he had been using heavily then. To support his habit, he'd broken in to a few houses and lifted whatever he could find. He'd come across the Colt during a break-in and taken it. If the gun was registered, it was likely reported as stolen, and since Scott had never been implicated in the B&E's in Kansas, or even questioned, it wouldn't be traced back to him. Besides, she hoped it wouldn't be found when she was finished. The Cocalico Creek was on her way home from Ronnie's and would provide the perfect resting spot.

The thought of committing murder didn't bother her in the least.

I'm not committing murder, she thought, her emotions warring within. *I'm protecting my daughter because nobody else will!*

The sudden revelation that she had to take such drastic measures to save Mary had come to her throughout the day. She'd called Ronnie's house to arrange a visit with Mary, since Scott wasn't expected back until this afternoon, and Diana had told her in that indifferent tone that Mary had spent the evening at Jerry and Laura's. When she asked to speak to Ronnie, Diana had told her he was still asleep. *He's always asleep,* Cindy had thought as she hung up. *He doesn't know what the fuck is going on anymore.* Cindy had called her ex in-laws and Jerry had answered, telling her that Laura had taken Mary over to Elizabeth and Gregg's for the day. Cindy had felt a little disappointed at that; she'd really wanted to see Mary today and she voiced this to Jerry. "I'm sorry, Cindy," Jerry had said. "I can have Laura call you. Maybe we can arrange to have you see Mary tomorrow."

Cindy thought Jerry sounded tired. "Yeah, that sounds good. I haven't seen her in two weeks, and it's just been so hectic here."

"I'll do that, Cindy," Jerry had said.

"How's Mary doing?" Cindy had asked; the question seemed to come to her suddenly, and she had the burning need to know.

Jerry hesitated. Cindy's senses weren't altered yet this morning from drinking, and she could tell there was something on his mind. She'd felt the curious need to not have to wake up this morning with a glass of beer or a shot of whiskey and she'd actually had a few cups of coffee while reading the paper. She'd felt relaxed, at peace with herself, and she found herself thinking, *This is sobriety? My God, this is what I've been missing? I feel great!*

"Well, Mary wanted to come over last night," Jerry said. "So I went over and got her. In fact, she'll be spending the weekend with us, so you can call here anytime this weekend and she should be here."

"I'm glad she's with you instead of with Ronnie and Diana," Cindy said. "No offense against Ronnie, but I don't like her being with Diana."

"I don't either, Cindy." There was that hesitation in Jerry's voice again. Then: "Cindy, can I ask you something? Just between us?"

"Sure, Jerry."

"Laura told me you'd mentioned Diana had threatened Mary. That Diana called your house harassing you, saying she would harm Mary. Is that true?"

Cindy felt a great relief wash over her. Somebody wanted to *believe* her! "Yes," she'd said, closing her eyes. "She said the most horrible things."

"What did she say?"

"You don't want to know."

"I do."

So Cindy had told him. And as Cindy related the numerous threats Diana had made, how she'd threatened to whip Mary and record her screams and sell them to pedophiles, how she'd threatened to torture her daughter and whip her with a riding crop, she heard Jerry gasp. Then she told Jerry that she'd had to move out of the apartment she'd been living in because Diana had kept calling there and whenever her boyfriend—well, ex-boyfriend now—tried to call the cops, they didn't believe her. She related the numerous incidents when the police were called. Jerry listened in stunned silence. When she was finished, Cindy said, "I told Laura, but I don't think she believes me."

"I believe you. Don't worry about that. I don't like Diana and I know Laura doesn't, but you have to look at this from her side too. She's caught in the middle. Diana is with Ronnie now and she feels this . . . I don't know . . . this need to be civil with her because of the situation. Do you understand?"

Cindy nodded, then realizing Jerry couldn't see her, she said, "Yes."

"Just be patient," Jerry said. "We're working on the situation from our end."

"What are you going to do?"

"I don't know yet. I want to talk to Ronnie, but—"

"He won't listen. I've already tried to talk to him."

"Well, if I talk to him—"

"Do you think he'll listen to you? No offense, Jerry, but Ronnie's as hard-headed as you can be. When he gets a notion to do something, he does it, and damn the consequences. Diana's got him wrapped around her finger, and everything she tells him is the gospel truth in his eyes. And he doesn't see Mary enough to know what's going on."

"What *is* going on, Cindy?" Jerry asked, that tone of desperation in his voice. Cindy's heart went out to him. He was confused and scared; of what, Cindy didn't know, but she had an idea.

"I don't know what's going on," Cindy said, trying to keep her voice calm. "All I know is that Diana is an evil woman, and she's been threatening Mary for over a month. She's been increasingly disgusting with the level of threats, too, and I've had it."

"Do you think Diana is abusing Mary?"

The thought had occurred to Cindy, and in the past few weeks when she'd seen Mary she'd tried to search for the tell-tale signs of physical abuse but had seen none. It was hard to talk to the girl about it since the visits were always supervised. She couldn't very well ask Mary if her father's new girlfriend was abusing her when the woman was in the same room with them, and the few times Cindy had tried tiptoeing around the issue when Laura was present, her former mother-in-law told her to stop it. Mary had looked at her mother with something like fear in her eyes, and Cindy could tell that the girl wanted to tell her something, that she was hiding some dark secret but was either afraid to tell her or felt awkward in opening up when there were other people around. The few times she'd talked to Mary on the phone when she knew it was safe, she'd asked Mary if everything was okay at her father's house. "Everything's fine," Mary had said. Cindy had pressed her on the issue, but Mary insisted everything was okay. One time Cindy had asked her if she liked Diana. Mary had hesitated briefly, then said, "I guess." It wasn't a very convincing answer.

"I don't know," Cindy had said. "I don't know, but we have to do something."

"If she's abusing Mary, Ronnie won't stand for it," Jerry said. "I know that."

"You're right," Cindy said. Ronnie wouldn't stand for anybody laying a hand on his little girl. Cindy doubted Ronnie was aware of anything malicious happening in his own home, and with his new sex slave to suck his dick every night, he wasn't going to pay attention.

Cindy's conversation with Jerry had left her confused, frightened, angry and desperate. She'd spent the afternoon replaying the last two months' events and trying to connect the scenarios together. It was possible Diana's phone calls were just that: harassing phone calls. It was possible she was making shit up about hurting Mary just to yank her chain. Ray had thought that was the case as the phone calls continued, and Cindy had been too blind with anger to listen to reason then. For a while she was seriously considering that fact.

Now she wasn't so sure.

Mary's behavior hadn't been the same in the last two months. The little girl had become withdrawn, forlorn and shy. When Cindy had her visits with her, Mary acted like she was afraid of her—her own mother! For a while Cindy thought that Mary was ashamed of her; she'd just gotten fired from her last job and had gotten into that fight with Karen Murphy at the Cocalico, and she knew Laura and Jerry were clucking in disapproval at her lifestyle, and there was no doubt that news had floated back to Ronnie and Diana and, finally, to Mary. That bitch Diana had probably chortled about it at the house in Mary's presence, said disparaging things about her. It probably embarrassed Mary, made her feel ashamed of her own mother. Maybe that was why she'd been acting that way lately.

But then why did Cindy have this feeling that Diana really *was* trying to hurt Mary?

Call it a mother's intuition, but she really felt her daughter's life was in grave danger.

She knew she couldn't go to the police. They wouldn't believe her, especially with all that had gone on before. And she really had no solid proof that Mary was being abused at all.

She just had a hunch it was happening.

And she felt powerless to do anything about it.

She couldn't go to the police. Jerry and Laura would drag their feet before anything was done. Ronnie had them wrapped around his finger, too. He didn't know what the hell was going on in his own house, of that she was certain. He didn't believe her when she told him Diana was threatening Mary, and he wouldn't listen to her if she told him that Mary had sprouted a second head, a third arm, and a pair of gills. So she couldn't talk to her ex-husband rationally about the welfare of their daughter.

But she had to do something.

Toward the end of the afternoon she thought about kidnapping Mary and driving off with her somewhere, but she knew she'd be tracked down and caught immediately, and Mary would be placed right back into that abusive house.

It was then that the phone had rung.

Cindy sat in the car, replaying that phone call in her mind. She could hear the timbre of Diana's voice in her ear as clearly as if she were sitting next to her. Cindy had answered the phone and the first thing Diana had said was, "The little bitch is with her grandmother and aunt now, but when she comes home I've got a surprise for her."

Cindy had felt her knees go wobbly. She'd been drinking coffee all day and hadn't had the slightest urge to have a drink, but at that moment the need pulsed through her. "Please leave me alone," she'd said.

"Himmler's horny," Diana had said, her voice menacing, throaty. "When he gets in this mood he'll fuck everything. The sofa, your leg, whatever's handy. You've seen Himmler, so you know a dog his size is pretty well hung, and Himmler's got a big cock. Shit, he's bigger than most guys. When Mary gets home from her lovely weekend with Grandma Twat-face and her book-loving cunt of an aunt, I'm going to strip Mary naked and hog-tie her in the basement and let Himmler have a go at her. A slut like you will agree that Mary's the right age, don't you think? I mean, you started whoring around when you were seven, right?"

Cindy had fought hard to control her voice. "If you hurt her—"

"Who said anything about hurting her? All I said was that I was going to let my dog fuck her."

"You are a sick woman," Cindy had said.

"I'll let you come over and watch."

And with that Cindy had picked up the phone and thrown it against the wall, where it crashed against a shelf that held Scott's beer mugs. They crashed and splintered, spilling thick glass shards all over the floor. Cindy had stomped her booted foot into the phone repeatedly, screaming, "You fucking bitch, I'll kill you, I'll fucking kill you!"

The next thing she remembered she was rummaging in the bedroom she shared with Scott. She had slipped on the gloves, which she'd gotten from her leather jacket, and she'd found the Colt in an old shoebox at the bottom of the closet. It had been unloaded, but she found shells for it in one of Scott's drawers and loaded it easily. She'd been trembling with fear and rage, and as she worked at formulating her hastily made plan, she told herself, *I didn't imagine that, the bitch fucking threatened to have her dog rape my daughter and if I report that to the police, those fuckers won't believe me, nobody will believe me, Jerry and Laura won't believe me, and Ronnie won't believe me and doesn't he care that his daughter is being cared for by that psycho bitch?*

Now she was sitting in Scott's car while he was in Philadelphia with his friends, not knowing his new girlfriend was about to commit a felony.

It was the only way she could protect her daughter. She might be a fuckup, she knew that's what her old friends and her family thought of her lately, but one thing she'd always maintained was a strong love for her children. She'd do anything for Mary, and right now she felt a strong instinct to protect her from Diana. She'd already explored all legal avenues; if the police had taken her seriously two months ago, the calls would have stopped. Maybe Ronnie would have seen Diana for what she really was and left her, but that hadn't happened. She'd tried reasoning with Diana, tried talking to her in-laws about it. Nobody believed her. Thus, she was left to do the only thing she could think of.

She'd been sitting in Scott's car for two hours now. She'd driven out earlier and watched the house from a distance, noting movement within. Then she'd pulled away from the curb and gone back to Scott's apartment, trying to talk herself out of it, trying to come up with reasons why she shouldn't do what she was going to do.

She couldn't think of any, so she'd come back.

She had watched the house for the past two hours and noted when the lights were finally extinguished: one-thirty A.M. The porch light was on. There wasn't even faint light emanating from behind the curtains from a television set, at least none she could detect.

When the dashboard clock read two-twenty she picked up the Colt, put it in her jacket pocket, and smoothed the knit cap she was wearing over her head, drew the ski mask over her face and opened the car door. She got out, quietly closing the door. She paused at the curb. The neighborhood was silent. The houses within the immediate vicinity of Ronnie's were dark.

The plan was simple. She had seven rounds, with one already chambered. It might take two or three rounds to take the dog down, and she was positive they let that fucking mutt loose all over the house. She didn't think a dog like that was trained to attack stealthily—it would probably bark the minute it sensed her outside. If it didn't, if she were able to gain access to the house, it would still give away its location with its growling. Hopefully she'd have time to shoot the fucker before it sprang on her. Besides, she'd been in the house a few times and knew the dog was more clumsy than anything. She also knew that Diana constantly stepped out on the back porch to smoke and always left the sliding-glass door unlocked. And if Diana was as stupid as Cindy thought she was, she probably forgot to lock that door all the time. If the door was locked, one round would shatter the glass to pieces and it might scare the dog off, too. Then she could slip inside quickly and flip on a light. If she hadn't shot the dog by then she'd do so at that time. Then she'd head to the bedroom and shoot Diana. There was no need to make any dramatic entrance or utter some witty proclamations. People only did that in movies. She'd go in quickly, blow away Diana and the dog, and then get the hell out. She didn't want to hurt the kids, but if they got in the way, or if the dark-haired brat tried to stop her, she'd blow him away, too. She didn't think anybody would see her, and she didn't think the kids would recognize her with the ski mask on. And as for an alibi, well . . .

She'd worry about that later.

Taking a deep breath, she stepped onto the sidewalk and headed toward Ronnie's.

The closer she got, the heavier her heart felt. The air was cold, damp with a rain storm that had blown in earlier in the day and was still lingering. The feeling of dread solidified in her belly. The Colt felt like it weighed a ton.

She crossed the lawn and began heading along the side of Ronnie's house.

She listened for any sounds from within.

There was nothing.

She paused in the backyard, letting her eyes grow accustomed to the dark. She couldn't make out movement at all. If that dog was there, it was probably hiding in the dining room, watching her. She'd just have to take her chances. She moved slowly toward the porch, and when there was no barrage of furious barking from within the house, she placed one gloved hand against the glass of the sliding door and peered inside.

She saw the dining room table and chairs directly in front of her. To her right was a kitchen, arranged in a horseshoe pattern. Beyond the kitchen and dining room was a large living room with a sofa, easy chair and an entertainment unit flanking the right-side wall. Just past the kitchen was a computer desk with a computer on it. Down the hall beyond the computer desk was the master bedroom, where Diana was probably sleeping. Toward the left was a hallway that led to the two bedrooms where the kids slept.

The dog was nowhere to be seen.

When her eyes were fully adjusted to the darkness of the house, she peered under the table. The dog wasn't hiding under there, either. She tried peering around the kitchen to see if there were any blind spots. The dog could be hiding anywhere if it had sensed her, but the only place she could think it could hide was either around the corner, close to where the master bedroom was, or in one of the kids' rooms, or the hallway that led to them. Of course, it could be in the basement or the garage as well.

Cindy's heart was pounding. She felt hot and sweaty beneath her leather jacket and the ski mask. Realizing it was now or never, she reached out and tugged at the handle to the sliding-glass door. It slid noiselessly in its track as it opened.

She almost lost her nerve then. For a brief moment she thought, *What am I doing?*

Then Diana's voice, menacing and hateful, came back to her. *Who said anything about hurting her? All I said was that I was going to let my dog fuck her.*

Over my dead body, bitch, Cindy thought as she stepped into the house.

Once inside, she reached toward where she thought the light switch was and couldn't find it. Cursing under her breath, she glanced around the dining room. Seeing the light switch on the other side of the room, she drew the Colt out of her jacket pocket and headed over to it and, with one fluid motion, flipped it on. The dining room was bathed in light and with the Colt gripped firmly in her gloved hand, she headed down the hall toward the master bedroom, her body primed and tense, her adrenaline flowing.

She was wound up so tightly that if anything came at her now she'd shoot first and ask questions later.

The door to the master bedroom was closed. She pushed the door open and raised the barrel of the gun, pointing it at the bed as she burst into the room, her adrenaline compelling her to *get it over with, shoot the bitch, shoot her and the dog, then get the hell out of here now!*

The master bedroom was empty.

"Hello, Cindy."

Cindy whirled around, her heart in her throat. Her finger squeezed the trigger and there was a deafening *boom* and her right arm was thrown back by the force of the Colt going off. She didn't even hear the bullet strike the wall; she was too busy trying to keep her balance and her eyes on the figure in front of her, keep her mind fixed on the single purpose she had come here for.

Diana stood at the threshold of the hallway that led to the master bedroom. She was naked. Cindy's mind was still frozen in shock from the surprise and the unexpected realization that Diana had tricked her, and the underlying compulsion that had screamed at her to break into the house and kill her now pulsed through her brain. *Do it now! Shoot her! Shoot her!*

Cindy raised the Colt and aimed.

Diana smiled, and then her face melted.

The moment Diana's face melted, Cindy's reflexes froze. She watched with eye-widening, mind numbing horror, her finger frozen on the Colt's trigger. Time seemed to slow down incredibly. Diana's flesh seemed to slough and drip off the bones of her skull; from the neck down, her skin had taken on a muddy appearance and a thick scent wafted up, overwhelming her. It smelled like meat left in the refrigerator for too long, which caused another block to her senses. *What the fuck?* she thought, confused now as to what to do. *What the fuck is happening?*

Who cares what's happening, just shoot her! Shoot her!

Oh my God, she's not normal, she's not—

She felt light-headed and fuzzy, and her body felt warm. She felt like she was floating, like she was caught in some bad acid trip. Diana stepped forward and smiled. When she spoke, her voice sounded like it was being processed through one of those special-effects systems that make your voice sound demonic. "Put the gun down, Cindy."

Cindy raised the weapon again. "Don't come near me!" she screamed.

"You really don't want to do this," the Diana-thing said, its voice chortling. Now Diana's face was morphing into something else. Her eye sockets had sunk deep into her skull, and her eyes became black pits. Her mouth widened, becoming a shapeless maw of ragged teeth.

"Don't come any closer, you bitch!" Cindy screamed. Her

blood pounded; she could feel her nerves tingling. She had never been so scared in her life.

"What do you think you will gain out of this?" the Diana-thing said, cocking its head to one side. "Just put the gun down."

Cindy squeezed her eyes shut. *Oh why did I do this, why oh why, what the fuck is happening and why can't I just* shoot her!

And through it all Cindy noticed one curious thing. The noise from the confrontation hadn't elicited a response from the dog or the children.

It was just the two of them.

Where are they? Even if the dog was locked in the base-ment, he'd be barking. And the kids, especially the little one, would have cried out or something. But there's nothing, no other sounds, just the two of us and—

I'm just going to let my dog fuck her.

With a renewed burst of energy and anger Cindy opened her eyes and surged forward, screaming, "You bitch!" She squeezed the trigger, and the sound of the gunshots weren't as loud as she thought they'd be. They were eclipsed by the sudden pain she felt shooting through her chest, digging deep within her. She almost blacked out and for a brief moment she thought she was falling, but then her last remnant of consciousness was the image of Diana's shimmering, melting visage standing in front of her, grin-ning. She felt the pain in her chest explode and as she looked down she saw Diana's arm sunk into her ribcage. Diana grinned, blood and saliva dribbling down her chin. The shock raced forward and her last thought before she died was, *Mary!*

PART II

CONFLICTS

CHAPTER NINE

The phone call that came the following morning was nothing short of heart-breaking. Elizabeth took it in the kitchen as her mom dished out scrambled eggs and sausages for Gregg and the kids, and the minute she heard her father's tone of voice she felt a vice squeeze her heart. "Honey, I have some bad news. It's . . . it's Cindy . . ."

Oh my God, she's finally done it, Elizabeth thought, feeling the sadness come. *She's finally gotten herself killed in a drunk-driving accident or OD'd or something.*

She headed toward the front of the house toward the stairs so the rest of the family wouldn't see her expression. "What happened?"

"The police are still trying to sort it out," her dad said. He sounded incredibly aged; it was probably the shock. "She broke into Ronnie's house last night and tried to kill Diana and the kids."

"What?"

"She must have been high on something," Jerry continued. "Diana said she was hallucinating. She tried to talk Cindy out of it, and then Cindy just collapsed and stopped breathing. Diana tried CPR and Rick called 911 but it was too late. They . . . they think it was a heart attack."

The laughter of the kids in the kitchen brought the sadness to the surface and Elizabeth felt the tears come, but not so much for Cindy; she'd grieve for her ex-sister-in-law later. The sadness she felt was for her niece, Mary.

"Is your mother there?" Jerry said, his voice soft. "I should talk to her."

"Just a minute," Elizabeth said. She set the phone down and sat on the steps, fighting hard to compose herself. *Stop thinking about her, just stop thinking about Cindy for a minute. Pull yourself together. Get Mom over here, build up some strength for Mary because she's going to need it. Then maybe later you can cry your heart out.*

She felt a calmness settle over her, and she took a deep breath. Then she called her mother to the phone.

The next week passed in a blur. Elizabeth found it hard to concentrate at work. It was a good thing she taught at the high-school level; the students she worked with were good kids, independent and smart, and she rearranged her lesson plans to give them as much study time as possible, shoving her lecture and workshop time to the following week. She needed the quiet time the kids would spend reading or writing papers so she could sit at her desk and think about what had happened. During breaks and lunch, she talked to Mom on her cellular phone, catching up with the latest news and helping out with the funeral plans.

It was Laura who had told Mary her mother was dead. After she'd gotten off the phone with Jerry, she and Elizabeth had stood in the entry hall hugging each other, crying, and Gregg had asked what was wrong. Elizabeth had told him they'd be right back. Even Eric seemed to sense from the tone in her voice that everything was *not* all right. Mom had said, "I'll tell her." Then she'd gone to the kitchen and taken Mary's hand and led her to the family room where

she'd sat down with her on the sofa and told her granddaughter that her mother had died.

Everybody had cried at the house that day. Even Gregg,
who had been the first to show intolerance toward Cindy's
lifestyle and drug and alcohol abuse, had gotten teary
eyed. Understandably, Mary had taken it very hard.

She'd wanted her daddy.

They'd all gone to the house. Jerry was there, looking
glum. The police had still been at Ronnie's house, and later
that afternoon Ronnie and Diana showed up with Rick and
Lily. Ronnie's face was puffy from lack of sleep; his blond
hair was tousled, and he hadn't shaved. The weight he had
put on in the years following Mary's birth had dropped
from his frame in the past few months, and Elizabeth
thought the weight loss made him look unhealthy. Elizabeth gave her brother a hug, and he held her tightly. "I
didn't . . ." he began, stammering, and she could tell he
was fighting hard to keep his emotions in. "I didn't want her
to . . . d-d-d-*die!*"

"I know," Elizabeth whispered, and she allowed her
brother to weep onto her shoulder.

The story slowly emerged that week, starting that Sunday afternoon when Diana related the experience in a
still-shocked tone. They continued to learn more through
the investigation and the autopsy. The more Elizabeth
tried to process the information, the more the events that
were being chronicled and filed in all the official reports
bothered her.

On the evening of Saturday, October 23, Cindy had
driven a vehicle owned by her latest boyfriend, Scott Anderson, to Ronnie's neighborhood and parked at the curb.
A few neighbors reported seeing the vehicle. Diana reported not being aware Cindy was watching the house.
She'd stayed up till one-thirty, then went to bed. Ronnie
had been due to come home from work at two-thirty or
three A.M. Before she'd gone to bed, Diana had put Himm-

ler in the basement because lately he'd been soiling the carpets in the living room at night. That explained why the dog hadn't woken the household when Cindy broke in.

Diana was in bed no more than thirty minutes when she heard the sliding-glass door open. She'd known instinctively it wasn't Ronnie returning home—he always used the front door. She'd gotten out of bed and was about to head into the living room when she ran into Cindy Baker.

"She had a gun," Diana said, recalling the incident with a shaky tone, her hands clutching a can of Diet Pepsi that she sipped intermittently during the narrative. "And she was wearing gloves and had a ski mask pulled over her face, but I knew who it was. I turned on the light and she jumped and pulled the trigger. The shot blasted a hole in the wall. I started talking to her, tried to tell her she didn't want to hurt anybody, and by then the kids were up. Lily was crying, and Rick looked shocked. I didn't want her to hurt the kids, so I kept trying to calm her down."

According to the preliminary autopsy report, Cindy's bloodstream contained traces of marijuana and opium, enough to suggest intoxication. Elizabeth didn't realize people still smoked opium—she knew heroin and morphine were derived from opiates and they could produce hallucinations. The lead detective surmised that Cindy was as high as a kite when she broke into the house. Her ex-boyfriend, Ray Clark, stuck by his story that Diana had still been making threatening phone calls to their apartment in the days prior to their split, a charge Diana vehemently denied. A check with the phone company and further follow-ups on the boyfriend's story strongly suggested that the phone harassment in the month preceding this incident had never occurred. True, Diana had admitted that Cindy called the house a few times in the early months of her moving in with Ronnie, and that she had gotten carried away and called her back to engage in some mean-spirited verbal cat-fighting, but she never called Cindy unless she had to. The phone records proved this, but Ray stuck by his story that Diana had still been harassing Cindy. When asked if Cindy was drinking or using drugs during this time, Ray had waffled. "She had a few drinks and smoked a little, yeah. So what?"

This dovetailed with Cindy's behavior at the house. Diana stated to the police and the family in the following week that Cindy appeared to be on something. "She was saying crazy things," Diana said. "She didn't actually threaten to kill us, but . . . she was just being so weird, saying things that didn't make sense. She took the ski-mask off at one point and I could see her pupils were dilated, her skin was pale. She was definitely tripping on something."

Diana had continued trying to talk Cindy into putting the gun down when she'd suddenly fallen to the floor and gone into convulsions. Diana had kicked the gun away and screamed at her son to call 911. She'd dropped to the floor and tried to stabilize Cindy, who appeared to be having some kind of seizure. "I tried CPR, but I didn't know if I was doing it right," she'd said, her brown eyes reflecting a sense of sadness, something Elizabeth had never seen before in Diana. By the time the EMTs arrived, Cindy was dead.

The official cause of Cindy's death was cardiac arrest. Ronnie and Diana were questioned repeatedly by Lancaster County detectives, and when all the factors were considered—Ronnie's divorce from Cindy and subsequently winning temporary full custody of Mary; Cindy's continuing slide into alcohol and drug abuse; her further broken relationships with other men, including her bearing another child with Gary Swanson and their break-up; her spotty employment record; her reputation at the Cocalico Tavern as a brawler; comments from friends and family that she always turned on the women Ronnie dated; and her continued feelings of resentment and anger toward Ronnie and Diana—the results were clear that she'd been heading to an early grave for a long time. Her actions the evening of her death were attributed to a final episode of desperation fueled by drugs and coupled by their hallucinatory effects. The strain had a final catastrophic effect on her heart, and she'd collapsed. When the EMTs arrived they'd found Diana bent over Cindy desperately trying to revive her, but it was too late.

Cindy's family, of course, was devastated. Her brothers had been trying to get Cindy help for years now, to no avail. In the days following Cindy's death, Mary sought refuge at her maternal grandmother's house, probably in an attempt to be closer to her mother. She'd been teary and crying all that Sunday, and while she'd wanted her daddy, she'd also told Laura that, "I don't want to spend the night at my house." So she'd stayed with Andrea, Cindy's mother, and was shuttled back and forth from there to Jerry and Laura's while funeral arrangements were made.

Elizabeth helped out her parents and Andrea Shull with funeral arrangements, and on Thursday morning, October 28, four days after her passing, Cindy was eulogized at the Stouffer's Funeral Home and Chapel in Mountville. The service was attended by Cindy's immediate family, Jerry and Laura, Elizabeth and Gregg, Ronnie and Diana, several of Cindy's ex-boyfriends, as well as Gary Swanson and his and Cindy's son, Jason. Mary did well during the service. Some of Cindy's friends showed up, leather- and denim-clad biker types with long hair and tattoos, standing forlorn and silent through the service. Ronnie and Gary Swanson had exchanged quiet words together at the rear of the chapel, commiserating the loss of a woman they had loved then left due to her psychological imbalance. Some of the other guys there appeared nervous, out of place. A brief viewing followed the non-denominational service, and Mary had cried as she stood in front of her mother's casket. Elizabeth felt herself collapse emotionally as the little girl cried, "Mommy!"

Laura had gently escorted Mary away from the casket and sat with her in the front pew of the chapel, holding her as she cried.

And when Elizabeth stepped up to Cindy's open casket

and gazed down at her, noting her calm, almost peaceful visage, she suddenly felt that something wasn't right.

You weren't supposed to die, Elizabeth thought, gazing down at her ex-sister-in-law. *I mean . . . God forgive me . . . we always thought you'd kill yourself somehow. I know that's a horrible thing to think, but we did. You were a train wreck waiting to happen. I suppose I would have been able to accept this news if you had simply died at home from a drug overdose or pulled a Bon Scott and choked on your own vomit during an all-night drinking session. But . . . breaking into Ronnie's house with a gun? I mean, I know you were probably tripping but . . . it just doesn't add up. Why did you go over there?*

Elizabeth realized she had been standing at Cindy's casket too long when she heard her mother say, "I'll be outside with Mary." Elizabeth looked up and saw that the funeral home had emptied out. Casting one last look at Cindy, Elizabeth gave a silent prayer for her former sister-in-law and followed her mother and niece outside.

Cindy remained on her mind throughout the graveside service.

And the more she thought about what had happened, the more she realized that she didn't like the way it all added up.

She cast quick glances at her brother and Diana behind her dark shades during the graveside service, studying their faces and postures. Their features were downcast, forlorn expressions of grief. Ronnie looked visibly strained, worn out. Mary stood beside him, between her father and grandmother. Elizabeth tried to read her brother's face. His emotions seemed genuine enough, but there was something missing. It was as if his real emotions were locked away somewhere and a false Ronnie had sprung up, wearing a mask to show grieving mourners so they wouldn't notice anything was unusual. Diana had that look too; she looked saddened, but it had the veneer of falsehood. It wasn't real.

Diana hated Cindy, Elizabeth thought as the minister concluded the service, and Ronnie and Gary stepped forward to drop roses on top of the casket as it was lowered into the ground. *She's obviously faking her grief. And Ronnie . . . I think he'd be more open in his grief if Diana weren't there. He'd be trying to comfort Mary more.*

She and Gregg drove back to her parents' house for the wake, each staring silently out the window. Finally Gregg said, "I feel so bad for Mary."

"I know. So do I."

"Your brother doesn't look so good."

"He doesn't," Elizabeth agreed. "He looks like shit."

They were heading up 222 toward Reamstown, the afternoon sun shining bright and warm. "It still seems weird that this happened," Gregg said.

"I know." Elizabeth wanted to talk about it, but she didn't know what to say. She still wanted to think her thoughts through before talking to Gregg about it.

Gregg beat her to it. "I can't believe Cindy would have done something like this," he said. "That wasn't the Cindy I knew."

It felt like a revelation, as if for the first time Elizabeth realized she wasn't alone in the world. It felt like a tremendous weight had been lifted from her shoulders. "No, that wasn't the Cindy we knew. She might have been a fuckup, but she wasn't the type to break into people's houses and try to hurt them."

Gregg nodded. He had gone into the office this morning and left at ten to make the service. He was wearing his blue suit and white sport shirt. "Even the drug thing doesn't add up. I know you can hallucinate when you're on coke and stuff—"

"They found opium in her system."

"That can produce hallucinatory effects. I mean, you can trip when they give you morphine at the hospital, and opium is the pure thing. I still don't buy that it produced hallucinations powerful enough to send her over the edge like that."

"I don't either." Elizabeth tried to think of a way to broach what was on her mind to Gregg. "In fact, I think there's more to what went on than we know about."

"Well, obviously."

"Remember when Mom told us about the time Cindy told her that Diana was threatening Mary?"

"Yeah, the sick pedophile shit?"

"Exactly. Mom didn't believe her. She thought Cindy was making it up to cause trouble for Ronnie. I thought the same thing, but now I'm not so sure."

Gregg looked at her. "You're serious?"

Elizabeth nodded. "Yeah, I am." She looked at her husband as he turned his attention back toward the road. "It was easy to believe she'd make something like that up. She was an alcoholic and a drug addict, and she was very jealous of Ronnie. She was also lying on job applications and stealing from employers. She wasn't Mother Teresa, I'll be the first to admit that. So when you take that into consideration, when she starts spouting those kinds of accusations, it was easy to dismiss them. Nobody believed her because she was a fuckup, and she had already proven to my folks and everybody else that she'd pull crazy shit to get her own way." Elizabeth paused, still trying to collect her thoughts so she could make some kind of sense. "But one thing you've got to admit . . . even if she was a fuckup, she loved Mary dearly. She adored that child, and she tried so hard to be a good mother despite the custody ruling and the divorce and all that. And I don't believe that Cindy would have made up such an ugly story involving the harm of her own child just to get back at Ronnie."

Gregg nodded. "Yeah, you're right. I was thinking the same thing."

Elizabeth was feeling better now that she and Gregg were talking about this. The Reamstown exit was coming up and Gregg got off. "She went out of her way to be with Mary," Elizabeth continued. "If she just would have gotten some help for her addictions . . ." She stopped, momentarily stricken with grief again, then continued, "I believe she would have gotten help eventually. She had reached rock bottom, and I think she would have bounced back. I really saw that chance. And even though she was an addict, even though she was fighting those demons, she really did try to be a good mother. You could see it in her face whenever she was at Mom's visiting Mary. You could see it in Mary's behavior whenever Cindy was around. Mary loved being with her mother, and she missed her. Ronnie did the right thing when he filed for full custody. I don't think Cindy would have done anything to intentionally hurt Mary, but you saw the kind of people she was hanging out with. He needed to keep Mary away from Cindy at that point."

Gregg was silent as they pulled into the development where her parents lived. The funeral services had taken a lot out of Elizabeth, and there was still the wake to think about. "I do have a theory," she said.

"And that is?"

"I think Cindy went over there to protect Mary."

They were cruising down her parents' street and Gregg glanced at her, eyes wide with shock. He pulled up to the curb in front of the house and turned off the ignition. "Protect her from Diana?"

"Yeah." They sat in the car for a moment. "Think about it. Let's assume that Cindy was telling the truth to Mom about the threats and harassing phone calls Diana was making. According to Mom, it began in August and started getting uglier well into September. That's when Diana allegedly threatened to have Mary beaten and tape the screams to sell to pedophiles."

"That's sick," Gregg said.

"I know." Elizabeth sighed. The thought of something like that happening to Mary—to *any* child—was horrifying. "So let's assume Cindy was telling the truth. After all, she *did* call the police to report the harassment."

"She called the police a lot, and they never did anything about it because they pulled the phone records," Gregg said matter-of-factly. "They were able to prove Diana never made those calls."

"Let's not put that in the equation for now," Elizabeth said. "Let's assume the police never pulled the records. Let's pretend they just ignored Cindy's accusations."

Gregg opened his mouth to say something—to protest perhaps—then closed it. He nodded. "Okay. I'm listening."

"Assume Cindy not only got those calls from Diana, but she also called the police and they did nothing. Maybe they were tired of hauling her into jail for assault and drunken driving and being under the influence of drugs or disturbing the peace or whatever. Small-town cops don't have a lot of patience for people like Cindy. And when something legitimate *does* come up, you can call it the cry-wolf syndrome."

"Wouldn't they be obligated to follow up anyway?"

Elizabeth shrugged. "Probably. But forget about that. Maybe they were going to follow up, but they just never got around to it."

"This sounds like one of your novels."

Elizabeth slapped his arm lightly. "It sounds like the last film you were in."

Gregg laughed.

"Wouldn't you feel frustrated if the police didn't take you seriously that somebody was threatening Eric?" Elizabeth asked.

"Not desperate enough to try to kill somebody."

"That's you, though. We're talking about Cindy, and in order to understand her you have to think like her. Cindy tried to get help and get somebody to believe her and nobody did. Even my parents dismissed the allegations, and of course Ronnie backed up Diana. The phone calls and the harassment continued, as well as the escalation of threats against Mary. Cindy was scared—Mom admitted that much when she told me about it two weeks ago. Cindy was upset that nobody was taking her seriously, and she was afraid for Mary's safety. It made her more desperate. And because she was the type of woman who took things into her own hands, it was easy for her to decide to do the only thing she could think of to protect her daughter. Eliminate the threat."

"So she went to Diana's to kill her because she thought Diana would eventually carry out her threat?"

"Sure. Put yourself in her shoes. If somebody were calling us, saying that they were going to abduct and rape our son, and the police refused to do anything and nobody would believe you, and you knew who was making those threats, what would you do?"

Gregg looked grim. "I guess when you put it that way . . . I'd do the same thing Cindy did."

They sat in the SUV for a moment. A car passed by and pulled up to the curb in front of them. Elizabeth's uncle Harold and aunt Tina stepped out of the car. "We should probably make our appearance."

"Yeah," Gregg said. He opened the driver's-side door and stepped out.

Elizabeth got out and joined her husband. "We'll continue this discussion at home," she whispered.

Aunt Tina waved to them, and Elizabeth and Gregg waved back. The two couples met at the driveway and headed into the house together.

CHAPTER TEN

The wake that afternoon was a blur.

Laura Baker and Andrea Shull had ordered a lunch spread from a local caterer, and the dining room table was laid out splendidly with different meats, bread, mustard and mayonnaise, lettuce and sliced tomatoes, cheeses and two different salads. There were soft drinks and punch, coffee and tea, and plenty of beer in the bar downstairs.

People from both sides of the family extended their condolences to both Ronnie and Gary who, for the first time they'd known each other, were spending time together hanging out, talking, drinking beer. Elizabeth revised her opinion on Ronnie's physical appearance from this morning. He didn't just look like shit—he looked almost dead.

The more she looked at him, the more alarmed she was by his appearance. There was a period of five years following his marriage to Cindy when he had put on considerable weight. His lean, muscular frame had turned to flab, and he'd gained sixty pounds, most of it in his belly, chest and face. He'd become less active physically, and with the chores of raising a daughter and settling down, he didn't run around anymore, participate in the sports he'd once been involved in, and he'd kicked his cocaine habit. He was by no means obese or terribly overweight; he'd simply put on more pounds than he should have.

Now he looked almost cadaverous.

Elizabeth watched him from across the room as he talked with Gary. His once plump face was now thin, almost bony. The suit he'd worn at the funeral fitted him loosely, like it was two sizes too big. There were dark circles under his eyes, and his skin looked dry, parched. It looked like Ronnie had lost eighty pounds in the last two months, which couldn't be healthy. She looked over at her mother, who was bustling about, making sure people had food and drinks. Mom had never said anything to her about Ronnie losing so much weight. Surely her mother would have been the first to voice concern that Ronnie had lost such an unhealthy amount of weight so quickly.

By contrast, Diana looked ravishing.

Diana stayed by Ronnie's side throughout the wake. Gone was the too-thin frame, the bony cheeks of a skinny white-trash girl who smoked too many cigarettes and drank too much diet soda. Her once frizzy black hair with the multitude of split ends was now full of body and shine. It hung to her shoulders, shimmering in its cleanliness. Her skin was smooth, unmarred by blemishes and acne. Her face had filled out, revealing attractive features. Her body had filled out as well, accenting a curvy figure. She looked like she had stepped out of a fashion magazine with her new body, her well-tailored outfit, her black heels.

Elizabeth watched Diana, who appeared engaged in conversation with people with the same depth that Ronnie was. She held Ronnie's hand, always the faithful companion. Mary spent most of her time with Elizabeth and Gregg, picking at her food.

Ronnie approached Mary a few times during the wake. "Hey, honey, why don't you come with Diana and me for a minute." Mary went to Ronnie reluctantly, but she always wound up back with Elizabeth and Gregg. Elizabeth paid close attention to Ronnie and Diana and the way they interacted with people. On the surface, everything looked fine. But there was an undercurrent of dread, a soft whisper that suggested things weren't so right.

It gave Elizabeth a bad feeling.

At two-fifty P.M. Gregg suggested it was time to start heading home. Eric got out of school at three-thirty. Elizabeth and Gregg began making the rounds, saying good-bye to everybody, and Mary hovered near them. When they got to Ronnie and Diana, Elizabeth gave her brother a hug. "We gotta go. If you need anything, give me a call. Please." She looked into his eyes, hoping he could read the seriousness in her face. He looked empty, drained.

"Yeah, I'll give you a call," Ronnie said.

As an afterthought, she hugged her brother again. She felt his arms encircle her limply. She kissed his cheek, then leaned forward quickly and whispered in his ear: "If you're afraid to give me a call, stop by the house on your way home from work. We're here to support you." She kissed him again and stepped back, giving him a weak smile. "Go home and get some sleep."

Ronnie nodded. She couldn't tell if what she'd said registered. "Yeah, I think I will."

To Diana: "And when you get home, feed this boy," Elizabeth said, trying to interject a joking tone. "He needs to put some meat on his bones."

Diana chuckled, her arm encircling Ronnie's waist. "He works so much he hardly ever eats at home anymore."

"Seriously," Elizabeth said, clutching Ronnie's hand. "If you want to talk, call me anytime."

"I will," Ronnie said, almost dismissively.

"We'll have to have you guys over at the house some time," Diana said. "We can do dinner, and the kids can play in the basement or something."

"That would be fun," Gregg said.

Mary was practically glued to Elizabeth's leg. When she

bent down to give her niece a hug, Mary held on to her tightly. "Please don't go," she whispered into Elizabeth's ear.

A shiver of fear went down Elizabeth's spine. Mary sounded petrified. "You'll be fine," she whispered back. "If you want, you can come spend the weekend with me and Uncle Gregg again, okay?"

"I want to go with you *now!*" Mary whispered, more urgently.

Elizabeth bit back her emotions. *She's just affected by everything that's happened in the past week with her mother. She'll be okay.* Taking Mary by the arms, she looked into her eyes. "We'll see you tomorrow. You can come to our house and have a slumber party with Eric. He'll like that." She looked up at Ronnie and Diana, who were within earshot and who had no doubt heard some of the exchange. "Would it be okay if Mary spent the weekend with us? She had a great time with Eric the last time she was over."

"Maybe Lily can come, too," Diana said.

"We'll see," Elizabeth said, standing up. She wasn't going to go there; Diana could push her mother around, but she couldn't pull that shit on her.

Mary looked like she was going to cry, but she held it in. She wiped her eyes. "I'm going to miss you," she said.

"She's not going away forever," Ronnie said, some of that old crankiness returning. "If you want to spend the weekend with your Aunt Elizabeth, stop crying."

Mary nodded, holding back the tears. Elizabeth bent down and swept her niece up in a hug. She kissed her and whispered, "Everything will be okay, honey. I'll see you tomorrow."

Mary nodded, her eyes closed.

Elizabeth took Gregg's hand. "We'll see you guys later," Elizabeth said.

"Bye," Diana said.

Laura looked up from the kitchen as Elizabeth and Gregg headed toward the front door. "You leaving, Elizabeth?"

"Yeah, we gotta pick up Eric."

"You want to take some food home with you?" Laura headed toward them and gave Gregg a quick hug as they made their way to the front door together.

"We can pick it up later," Elizabeth said, glancing at her watch. "We've really got to get moving."

"Well thanks for coming," Laura said, hugging her daughter. Elizabeth hugged her mother as Gregg opened the front door and stepped out. Elizabeth and Laura stepped outside and when Elizabeth was sure they were out of earshot, she pulled her mother aside.

"Mom, why didn't you tell me that Ronnie had lost so much weight?"

"What?"

"Ronnie! He looks horrible! You didn't tell me he'd lost so much weight."

Laura frowned. "What on earth are you talking about?"

Surely she has to see it, Elizabeth thought. "He's lost a ton of weight," she said. "When Diana moved in and we had that cookout in the backyard that day, he was at the weight he'd been maintaining the past five years, and today he looks like he's lost sixty pounds. He looks sick, Mom. Did you not notice?"

"Don't be silly, Elizabeth. So he's lost a little weight. Big deal."

Elizabeth couldn't believe what she was hearing. Her mother looked serious—she knew when mother was joking about things, and this wasn't one of them. Mom honestly didn't see anything wrong with Ronnie. "So you honestly don't think Ronnie looks sick?"

"Well of course not! He looks fine."

Elizabeth was about to protest the matter, to keep the argument going to make her mother realize that Ronnie was obviously *not* all right, but then dropped it as a thought came to her. "Well, maybe I just haven't seen him in a while," she said, changing the subject to take advantage of her thought. "But you and Diana did a really good job with the catering. The food was great."

"Thank you, honey," her mother said, putting her arm around her. "Diana really did a good job. She's been a real help to me this week in getting Cindy's wake arranged. I don't know what I could have done without her."

Elizabeth tried not to let her shock show. She'd intentionally mentioned Diana instead of Andrea to see if her mother would notice; Andrea had worked closely with Mom with the preparations, yet Diana had not been at the house all week. She quickly hugged her mother. "We gotta go. I'll call you later."

"All right, honey."

Standing in the doorway behind the storm door, watching them, was Diana.

Elizabeth turned and began walking to the car. She heard her mother go back into the house, but she could still sense that Diana was standing at the front door watching her leave.

She didn't want to turn and look back.

Gregg was waiting for her at the car. Elizabeth slid into the front passenger seat as Gregg started the car. "Let's get out of here," Elizabeth said, looking straight ahead.

Gregg looked at her and frowned. "You okay? What happened?"

Elizabeth shook her head, her face stony. Gregg made a U-turn and drove the car down the street and out of the cul-de-sac.

"Something happened," Gregg said as they headed south on 272 towards Lititz.

"Did you get a look at Ronnie?"

Gregg snorted. "Yeah, he looked like shit."

"Thank God you said that." Elizabeth felt like she was going to faint. *I'm not going crazy; it's not just me.* "I asked Mom why she hadn't told me that Ronnie had lost so much weight and she had no idea what I was talking about."

"*What?*"

"You heard me. She doesn't think there's anything wrong with him! She thinks he looks fine!"

Gregg glanced at her quickly. "You can't be serious. I mean, given the fact that she sees him a lot more than we do, I can understand a slight weight loss wouldn't faze her but . . . he looks like he's dropped sixty or seventy pounds in the past three months."

"I know," Elizabeth said. "And Dad acted as if there were nothing out of the ordinary. He would have said something before today if Ronnie had dropped so much weight. Did you notice Diana?"

"Yeah."

"What did you think?"

"She looked nice. In fact, she looked pretty damn good."

"Total opposite of what she looked like when she first moved in, isn't she?"

"You got that right," Gregg said, looking concerned. "I don't understand how they can't see that."

"Neither can I. And there's another thing that's really got me weirded out." She told Gregg about the exchange she had with her mother outside and how her mom had praised Diana to no end for all the help she claimed she'd been. "It's almost like Mom's done this complete reversal in her stance on Diana. You know Diana hasn't done shit to help my folks, especially this past week."

"I know. We've been over there every night this week. You've been helping your mom arrange the service and the wake for Cindy the whole time. I don't think I've seen Diana do much of anything."

"So why is she behaving as if Diana walks on water now?"

Gregg shook his head, his features set and serious. "I don't know. But it doesn't sound right. The past month your mom has been growing disenchanted with Diana and has been more vocal about it. Why suddenly change her tune now?"

"She wouldn't do it to be politically correct in a time like this," Elizabeth said. "Especially when we were out of earshot like that. We've talked about Diana and Ronnie enough when they weren't around, even when they were upstairs or something and we were whispering about them to each other. A wake surely wouldn't stop her."

Gregg glanced at her. "You really think your mom's changed her tune?"

Elizabeth sighed, at a loss for words. She felt confused and scared. "I don't know. I really don't know."

CHAPTER ELEVEN

In the following weeks, Elizabeth paid close attention to what her mother said about Diana. She also paid attention to how they interacted with each other.

Before, Laura had tried to be friendly to Diana but then stopped caring about being nice when Diana seemed indifferent in her effort to include her in the family. Now Laura was going the extra mile to make sure her son's girlfriend felt like she was part of the family. Pictures of Rick and Lily appeared on the refrigerator, sharing space with Eric and Mary in one of those refrigerator magnets emblazoned with the phrase, *I Love My Grandchildren*. Elizabeth bit back the sarcasm that wanted to leap out when she first saw that. The few times Diana was at the house when Elizabeth dropped in to pick up Eric, she was chatting with Mom in the kitchen like they were old friends. And while Mom acknowledged Elizabeth, there was something different about her tone of voice and behavior. It was as if all her attention were being diverted to Diana, and it was being done unwillingly.

The first weekend after Cindy's funeral, Elizabeth made

good on her offer to have Mary sleep over at the house. But when she called her mother to make the arrangements, Laura said that Diana was looking forward to having Mary and Lily spend the weekend with her. When Elizabeth told her mother that the invitation wasn't extended to Lily, Mom got huffy. "I don't see what the problem is, Elizabeth," her mother said. "Lily *is* Mary's sister now."

"No, she's *not!*" Elizabeth shot back, feeling suddenly angry at her mother for letting Diana manipulate her.

"Well I'm sorry for the misunderstanding," Mom said. "But I was led to believe that the sleepover was for both the kids, not just Mary."

Elizabeth was furious. "*Bullshit,* Mom! I told you the day after the wake."

"Well I must've forgotten. What am I going to tell Diana?"

"You're not going to tell Diana anything," Elizabeth said. "I'm calling myself."

When Elizabeth called her brother's house, Diana answered the phone. Elizabeth had waited ten minutes before making the call in an attempt to calm down. "Just calling to let you know I'll pick up Mary at six," she said.

"I'll have them ready," Diana said. She sounded indifferent, in a hurry.

"Oh, Diana? This invitation was for Mary only. I'll be picking *Mary* up, not Lily."

The pause on the other end of the line spoke loud and clear: *How dare you say that!* When Diana managed to speak she sounded annoyed. "I'm sorry to hear that. Lily was looking forward to spending the weekend with your family. This will crush her."

"She'll get over it," Elizabeth said. *God, I sound like a bitch, but I don't give a fuck.*

"I'll have to check with Ronnie," Diana said. "He was led to believe that you were taking the girls, so we made plans this weekend."

I'll bet, Elizabeth thought. "Well, check with him, then

call me back," she said, the urge to hang up resounding strongly.

"Okay," Diana said, bored.

An hour later Diana called. "If you're not changing your mind about having Lily over, we're going to cancel our plans. Ronnie says he'd rather have you take both kids for the weekend."

Since when did my stupid brother become my lord and master? Elizabeth's true feelings came to the surface. "Well obviously we don't think alike because I don't want Lily all weekend. Just forget about it!" She hung up, suddenly angry at herself for letting her emotions get the better of her as she burst into tears.

Gregg had already come home from work, and he came downstairs as soon as she started crying. Eric was in the basement playing air hockey with one of the neighbor's boys. Elizabeth told Gregg what had happened and gained control of herself. "I hate that bitch," she said, sniffling.

"I'm glad you stuck up for yourself," Gregg said, leaning against the kitchen counter. He looked concerned when Elizabeth told him about the exchange. "We don't need to be kissing Diana's ass the way your folks have been."

"I know, but I feel bad for Mary," Elizabeth said, sniffling back tears. "I feel like I'm letting her down."

It turned out not to be a very good weekend.

Laura seemed different in the week following Cindy's funeral and wake. Elizabeth wanted to talk to her, but Laura was distant, almost cold. On Monday when she picked up Eric, she was about to mention the spat she'd had with Diana, but her mother beat her to it. "I heard you and Diana got into a bit of an argument."

Elizabeth stiffened at the sound of her mom's voice. Eric was washing his hands in the bathroom after having come inside from playing in the backyard with Mary and Lily. Jerry had raked the newly fallen leaves into a big pile for the kids to jump in, and Eric had dead leaves and mulch all over him. "What did she tell you? That I got upset with her because I didn't like how she was trying to push her kid on me?"

"She said you were clearly upset about taking Lily for the weekend."

Elizabeth felt herself growing angry. She felt light-headed. Her mother's tone was the one she used when she was trying to be the stern disciplinarian. It was the tone that used to preclude a stronger reprimand from her father that was usually more devastating. "She obviously didn't pay attention to the part in my original proposal when I suggested that *Mary* come spend the weekend with us. Where she might have heard the syllables that pronounce what sounds like *Lily* in that sentence is beyond me."

"You don't have to be so sarcastic," Laura said in a clipped tone. "Lily and Mary were very disappointed they didn't spend last weekend with Eric."

Eric emerged from the bathroom at that moment, and Elizabeth used the opportunity to take her son's hand. "We've gotta go," she said. She picked up Eric's book bag and started ushering her son out of the house through the garage. "We'll see you tomorrow."

"Fine." There was dismissal and disappointment in her mother's voice.

Elizabeth held her rage in check all the way to the car. She didn't want Eric to see her like this, but she couldn't help it. The minute they were in the car, she slammed her fist against the dashboard. "Dammit!"

"Mom?" Eric's eyes were wide. He looked frightened.

"I'm okay," Elizabeth said quickly, trying to calm down. "I'll be okay . . . just . . ." *Just leave me be for a moment.*

Eric looked at her, understanding the silent communication that passed between them.

When Elizabeth calmed down she turned on the car. "I don't want to talk right now, okay? Do you want me to put the radio on?"

Eric nodded. He looked concerned. "Okay."

They drove home to the sound of classic rock and roll coming out of the speakers.

That evening Elizabeth told Gregg about what happened. "Your mom sounds like she's really trying too hard to get on Diana's good side," he said. "It might be a good idea to just lay low on her for awhile and see if she comes to her senses."

"At this point I don't even think I can talk to her," Elizabeth said. They were in the kitchen putting away the dinner dishes. Eric was sitting at the dining room table doing his homework. "I'm just so angry right now."

"I know," Gregg said. He began stacking the dishwasher. "When things ease up a bit, maybe the two of you can talk without letting your anger get out of control."

Elizabeth was on the verge of saying, *Don't you think I have a right to be angry at my mother? Are you on* her *side now?* Those thoughts came to her quickly, so naturally, that she almost voiced them, but she held her tongue. "I guess we'll see how the rest of the week goes."

Elizabeth decided to pick up Eric from school after work rather than hang around the office when her classes let out. She wanted to avoid the trouble at her parents' house, and she didn't want Eric exposed to any negative vibes. The rest of the week passed without incident. With the exception of a brief conversation with her mother Tuesday afternoon when she told her she'd be picking up Eric after school for the rest of the week, Elizabeth had no contact with her parents. Her mother's tone was clipped and hurried, as if she didn't care she wouldn't see Eric during the week. Elizabeth didn't want to get into it again with her mother, so she kept the conversation short. *Maybe Gregg is right,* she thought. *Maybe I should give her some time and space and she'll come to her senses.*

The next two weeks were spent with little communication between Elizabeth and her parents. After work she picked Eric up from school and, if she didn't take him along on shopping errands, they went straight home. Elizabeth would prepare supper while Eric played outside with his friends, and after supper Elizabeth and Gregg spent time together in the living room. Elizabeth wrote after nine P.M. for about an hour or so, and on weekends she put in two hours a day. Thank God she was starting a new novel; her publisher already had another novel in preparation for publication, and Elizabeth knew if sales from the last two books were good, they would want another. Getting her mind into a completely different world was also a great release; once she was in the world of her own creation, it was like relaxing with a martini after work. The social interaction she engaged in with her fellow writers via e-mail also helped. It reduced the stress from a hectic day.

The three of them took in dinner and a movie one late Saturday afternoon. Gregg remarked that fall was retreating rapidly. "It already feels like winter," he said. The high temperature that day was forty degrees, and it was supposed to dip down to the twenties in the evening. That morning the front lawn had a fine bed of frost.

Elizabeth got through both weeks by putting her family and her work first. The days flew by.

Her mother didn't call once during the entire two weeks.

Gary Swanson was getting off work at the lumber yard where he was employed as a foreman when he saw the skinny guy who had been at Cindy's funeral and wake leaning against his car.

Gary squinted in the late afternoon sun as he approached the car. It was chilly, and it had rained earlier that morning. He was in his early thirties, with a stocky build. He had a buzz cut and sported a goatee. He was wearing a denim jacket over a red-checked flannel shirt, blue jeans and brown work boots. As he approached the car, the skinny guy looked at him and stepped forward. "Gary?"

"That's me," Gary said. He approached his car warily. He was pretty certain the guy was an acquaintance of Cindy's. He remembered seeing him at the funeral and the wake that had followed at Laura and Jerry Baker's house. He hoped it wasn't one of her drug dealers coming to collect money. "What can I do for you?"

"Was wondering if I could talk to you for a minute?"

"What about?"

The guy looked nervous, embarrassed even. Gary pegged him as a worn and weathered twenty-five. He had collar-length brown hair and wore faded denim jeans, a long sleeve T-shirt, an insulated denim jacket and boots. A dirty baseball cap sat on his head. "I don't think we had a chance to talk much at the funeral service." The guy held out his hand. "My name's Ray Clark. Cindy and I were friends."

Gary shook Ray's hand. Ray's grip was firm, an honest handshake. Gary felt some of the wariness leave him. "Just friends?"

"Yeah, just friends. We used to hang out together at the Cocalico Tavern. I let her move in with me for a while after she broke up with Carl Eastman till she could get back on her feet."

Another one of Cindy's fuck buddies. What else was new? "She wasn't living with you when it happened, though," Gary said. "What happened?"

"She met a guy at the Cocalico," Ray said. "Scott Anderson. He's in Lancaster County Jail now on parole violation because of what happened."

"Oh yeah? How so?"

"The gun she used was one he'd taken in a robbery a few years ago. Cops traced it. He was on parole for possession of heroin when all this happened and, well . . . it really fucked him up."

"Guess it did. So what do you want to talk about, Ray?"

Ray looked around quickly. He seemed embarrassed. Scared. "You heard the whole story of what happened that night, right?"

"Yeah, Ronnie told me most of it at Jerry and Laura's," Gary said. "Cops told me some the day after it happened, too. Why?"

"They told you Cindy broke in the house and that she was high on dope, right?"

"Right." Gary fished for his pack of cigarettes in the front breast pocket of his flannel shirt. He extracted one, got it lit with his lighter. He regarded Ray calmly. "That's what happened. Didn't surprise me a bit. She was getting crazier and worse in her behavior the past few years. She tell you why I left her?"

Ray opened his mouth, then shut it. He looked embarrassed. "Yeah, but . . ."

"But what? What did she tell you?"

"She told me she got fucked up one night and threw a telephone at you while you were arguing and that it hit your son instead," Ray said. "She told me all about it, and she said she felt bad about it but—"

"Let me tell you something about Cindy," Gary said, feeling the anger and resentment that had been building up in the past year since the breakup come to the surface. "I did everything I could to help her. We all did. Ronnie Baker didn't even divorce her until she had been living with me for two full years. You know how that makes me feel sometimes, knowing I had hurt him and cheated on him by committing adultery with his wife? You know how that made me feel when I finally sobered up?"

"No," Ray said, clearly at a loss for words now. Whatever he had wanted to talk about to Gary seemed forgotten now.

"It made me feel less than a man," Gary said. He took a drag on his cigarette, regarding the younger man who was looking more nervous as the minutes ticked by. "Made me feel like a goddamn piece of shit for neglecting myself and my son, and I got two DUIs, and I did time for attempted murder ten years ago. I feel bad about that too, but I was too fucked up even after that to get help. To tell you the truth, after I did my time I got worse. Guess I felt guilty for almost killing James Short in that fight, and I was on a mission to slowly kill myself. When I did get my shit together, it was *my* choice to finally get sober, and Cindy didn't want to get on the wagon with me. I didn't push it. I asked her if she would stop drinking and partying for the sake of our son, but she said she didn't have a problem. I used to say that, too, so I thought she'd eventually come to her senses." Another drag on the cigarette. "Obviously she didn't. Her addictions got worse. We started fighting about it all the time and the more sober I stayed, the more I started to fear for Jason. When she accidentally hit him with the phone, that was the last straw. She knew goddamn well why I packed up and left, but all she could think about was herself. All she could do was beg me to come back, that she needed me and Jason back in the house, but when I told her Jason and I would come back only on the condition that she stop drinking and get some help, she refused. I washed my hands of her then. I filed for full custody of Jason because I didn't trust her for shit to be with him by herself, especially when she started hanging out at the Cocalico Tavern more. Bunch of low-life fuckheads is all that hang around there."

There was no flinch or flicker of embarrassment on Ray's face at that. Gary smoked calmly, feeling the tension ease as he blew steam. "When I met Ronnie Baker at the funeral, I asked him to forgive me. I never knew him that well before all this happened. Always thought he was a dumb shit for letting Cindy go the way he did, but—"

"So you knew Ronnie before all this happened?"

"A little." Gary took another drag. The few remaining members of his crew were leaving the warehouse, and amid the crunch of gravel beneath booted feet was the sound of cars and pickup trucks starting and driving through the rough driveway. "I knew who he was, had a nodding acquaintance with him because he used to drop by our place with Mary, but that was it."

"How did Ronnie look to you at the funeral?"

"Like shit."

"Don't you think that's unusual?"

Gary was about to ask what Ray was trying to get at, but

then it dawned on him. The last time he had seen Ronnie before the funeral was when? Last spring? He'd looked fine then. Normal. But at the funeral he'd been . . . well, almost sickly.

He remembered vaguely thinking Ronnie had lost a lot of weight in the four or five months since he'd seen him when they shook hands and talked quietly at the Baker house. Gary had still been stunned by all that had happened, and he'd been tired and buzzing from too much caffeine. Ronnie had looked like he'd lost a lot of weight, and his face had looked very thin and haggard. There had been dark circles under his eyes, and his skin had looked yellow. Gary hadn't thought much of it because he had probably been going through the same range of emotions—rage, sorrow, worry for his kid, wondering if he could have done something to prevent this.

"No," Gary said, feeling a little unsure of his answer. "I don't think it's unusual, considering all that he's gone through. I probably looked like shit to him, too."

"Did Cindy ever tell you about the harassing phone calls she got from Ronnie and Diana's house?"

This was something new. He'd never heard this. Cindy hadn't talked to him much in the four months before her death, even though he still tried to keep the communications open. When he did talk to her, all he could ask her about was the people she was with and if she was working. That usually pissed her off. "No, she didn't. What's this about?"

Ray told Gary about the harassing phone calls from Ronnie's new girlfriend. He detailed the increasing frequency of the calls, Cindy's initial reactions to them, and the police investigations into them. "Most of them were pretty bitchy," Ray said. "You know, chicks cat-fighting and shit. It was almost like Diana was baiting her, you know?"

Gary nodded. He knew very well what Ray was talking about. The more Cindy drank, the easier it had been to draw her into fights.

"The cops always dismissed our complaints, though," Ray said. He had lit his own cigarette and was smoking it as Gary finished his. "They kept saying that we couldn't prove the allegations, that they'd have to go to the phone company and it was a big process. They said it was better if we just let it drop and ignore the calls if they kept coming. Besides, there wasn't much they could do about harassing phone calls."

Gary nodded. He had a sick feeling that there was more to this story than harassing phone calls.

"They stopped for a while," Ray said. "There was some shit going on with Cindy and . . . well . . . I asked her to move out. She kept getting into shit, you know what I mean?"

Gary nodded and lit another cigarette. "That's been the cycle of her life the past three years."

"Right before she moved out, she claimed Diana had called again. I wasn't there when she called, but I was just getting home when Cindy started heading out. She had found the gun I keep in my closet and was going over to kill Diana."

This interested Gary. While Cindy had sometimes become violent when she drank, he'd never known her to be so angry with somebody to the point of deliberately wanting to kill them.

Ray brought the narrative to a close, and at the mention of the threats Diana made to Ronnie's daughter, Gary flinched. "You serious?"

"Damn right, I'm serious."

"Cops know about it?"

"The cops don't give a shit. Cindy told them about it twice, and they dismissed it, just like all the other times."

Gary finished his cigarette and threw the butt on the ground. "Shit." He had a sick feeling in his stomach. Ray looked like he had seen a ghost. The younger man was pale, his eyes wide with fright. "You were never around when those particular calls were made?"

"No." Ray looked embarrassed, as if he resented not being around to witness the threats against Mary. "Of all the calls Diana made, the ones where she threatened Mary were what really drove Cindy wild." He paused, licked his lips. "Tell you the truth, I'd've been ready to kill the bitch myself."

Gary nodded, stuffed his hands in his denim jacket pockets. Cindy wouldn't have made up a story like that. Much as she had been a fuckup, she would *never* have made a disparaging remark against either of her two children, even in jest. She had been fiercely protective of Jason and Mary; he could believe that threats leveled against Mary would have driven Cindy to violence. "So you think she went over to the Baker house to kill Diana because of these threats. Is that it?"

Ray nodded. "Yeah."

"Fuck." Gary took out another cigarette, lit it, smoked.

"Remember when I said the cops didn't pay attention?" Ray asked. Gary nodded, looking out at the hill toward Ephrata. "Well, the first few times this happened, the cops kept threatening they'd go to the phone company and pull the phone records, see who was telling the truth. Back in October they finally did. Guess what they found?"

"Diana never made the calls," Gary said, calmly smoking.

"Yeah."

The two men looked at each other, and Gary felt light-headed. He felt his skin tingle. "They pulled records on the first few incidents she reported?"

"No. But they told us if she kept calling they *would* pull the records, and if they showed she made those calls, they would have her arrested."

"But obviously Cindy did call the police again," Gary said. "When Diana threatened Mary, right?"

"Right. And the cops didn't do anything. They just threatened to take her to jail."

Gary smoked his cigarette. He felt scared and nervous, and for the first time in a long time he craved a drink.

"I'm sorry to have to . . . you know . . . spill all this shit on you," Ray said. "But I thought you should know."

"I'm glad you told me," Gary said, turning to Ray.

"What are you going to do?"

Gary took a drag on his cigarette. "Fuck if I know."

CHAPTER TWELVE

Thanksgiving was going to be hell.

Elizabeth had been dreading it ever since the fight with Mom, and the closer the weekend came, the more she felt the need to try to mend the wounds that had been opened. She called one afternoon after school, and while her mother sounded happy to hear from her and seemed like her old self, Elizabeth caught the vague sense that she was not sincere in her efforts at being nice and talkative. She'd mentioned this to Gregg that evening in bed. "She's probably still a little mad, but give her time," he said. "She'll get over it."

The following day Elizabeth swallowed her pride and called her mother from school. Would she and Dad like to do something for dinner that evening? Mom said she was making beef and noodles and invited them over. She sounded a lot better, too, like her old self. Elizabeth felt better at the sound of her mother's voice. "Eric and I will be over around three."

That afternoon was nice, but it was still awkward. Elizabeth expected Mom to have the kids, and she had Lily, but

Mary wasn't there. "Mary is involved in an after-school project," Mom said when Elizabeth asked her about it. They sat
at the kitchen table with the *Lancaster News* and that
week's *People* magazine spread out before them, the beef
simmering in a pot on the stove. Eric and Lily were in the
living room playing some electronic game that whirred
and buzzed. "Diana says she's really into it. It's the school
play."

"Really?" It reassured her to hear Mary was participating
in after-school activities. At least it got her out of the house
and away from Diana.

Dinner would have been uneventful had it not been for
the subtle change in behavior Elizabeth noticed in her
mother. During dinner, Lily didn't say a word and picked
listlessly at her food. Elizabeth peppered her mother with
gossip. Her father listened, grunted and nodded, made a
comment every now and then about what was going on in
the news while he ate. Eric ate heartily, tried to participate
in conversation with his mother and grandmother and was
rebuffed twice by Laura. She wasn't overtly rude, certainly
not enough to attract attention if a casual observer had
been watching them, but it was enough to register with
Elizabeth. Eric noticed, too, and he ate the rest of his meal
in silence. Elizabeth tried to pretend she hadn't noticed,
and she continued talking, paying attention to her mother.
She noticed Mom was colder and harsher with Eric than
usual.

By contrast, she treated Lily the exact opposite. She not
only showered the little girl with praise for "eating real
good," she used the tone of voice she normally reserved for
Mary and Eric. She spoke to Lily as if she were her own
daughter or grandchild.

Elizabeth tried not to let this bother her, but it did. On
one hand, it was part of her mother's nature to make
friends feel like they were family. For Mom to treat Diana's
children well was something that had come naturally. It
was part of Elizabeth's personality as well; she'd gone out of

her way to be nice to Diana and her kids, to be friendly and make them feel welcome. And while Diana had not been outright rude, she'd not been very friendly either. Her kids had been worse. Mom had noticed this as well, had talked about it with Elizabeth numerous times, had confided to Elizabeth that she didn't think much of Diana and she wondered what Ronnie saw in her, but ever since Cindy's funeral she'd done a quick about-face.

So much that Elizabeth got the faint underlying feeling that her mother preferred Diana's company over hers.

She brought this up to Gregg that evening. Gregg listened as Elizabeth related her and Eric's evening at her mother's, and then he said, "You're mom is really stuck between a rock and a hard place, honey. You know how she is. She wants everybody to get along. She doesn't like confrontation. She's trying to make the best out of a situation that she doesn't agree with. Think of it this way: Picture us twenty years from now when Eric brings home a girlfriend you might not like."

"Gregg!" Elizabeth scoffed, resenting the implication but quickly understanding where he was getting at. "This is *different!*"

"How different? We don't like Ronnie's girlfriend. Your parents don't like her, but obviously Ronnie thinks the world of her and has moved in with her. Ronnie's your mother's son, her youngest child. She loves him and wants him to be happy. So she swallows her pride and smiles and makes nice to Diana for the sake of her son. She does that because she loves him. She might not like his choice of women, but he *is* an adult and she has to accept that. She'd be doing herself and your family a bigger disservice if she were to express her dislike of Diana."

Elizabeth picked up the paperback she was reading and got into bed. "I hate it when you sound reasonable."

She didn't pick Eric up from school that week. Things went back to normal, to the way they were before. Eric went to his grandmother's immediately after school, and

Elizabeth picked him up on her way home. Lily was always at the house, but Mary was never around. Her mother seemed fine, her old self, and everything appeared normal with the exception of Mary's absence.

Elizabeth asked Eric about this the Tuesday before Thanksgiving as they drove home.

"When was the last time you saw Mary?" Elizabeth asked casually.

There was a long silence. Out of the corner of her eye she caught a glimpse of Eric frowning slightly. "Maybe . . . since after Aunt Cindy's funeral."

Over two weeks. "She's never in the car with Diana when she drops Lily off?" Elizabeth tried to keep her voice casual.

"Nope."

"Diana drops Lily off every day?"

Eric nodded. "Sometimes Lily's already there when I get there."

"What do they do? Does Lily play with you?"

"Sometimes."

Elizabeth sensed the hesitation in his voice. "Do you not like playing with her?"

"Not really," Eric admitted, looking sheepish.

"What does Grandma do? I'm sure she finds time for Lily."

"They usually take naps together," Eric said.

Elizabeth felt her flesh crawl at the thought as Mary's story came to mind. She thought of what Mary had seen in her father's bedroom as he lay sleeping, that shapeless mass of flesh attached to his slumbering form like a giant leech. Elizabeth tried to control the tremble in her voice. "How often does this happen?"

"Every day."

"What do you do? Where are you when this happens?"

"A lot of times I'm outside with the Becker twins when Grandma tells me she's going to lie down with Lily for a nap."

Elizabeth nodded, her imagination running. *Why is this bothering me so much? Why am I letting this get to me when it isn't any of my business?* "Does Diana come in the house?"

"Sometimes," Eric said. "She never says anything to me. She just comes in and drops Lily off. She and Grandma talk for a little bit, and then she leaves."

"Where does she go?"

Eric shrugged. "Grandma always says she goes shopping or runs errands or has stuff to do at the house."

For a stay-at-home mom with loads of free time courtesy of my stupid brother, she sure dumps her kids off with Mom every chance she gets, doesn't she? The thought that Diana had shacked up with her brother in order to take advantage of him had occurred to her months ago, but she'd dismissed it, part of her still wanting to give the woman the benefit of the doubt. The more Elizabeth was hearing about Diana from her mother and Eric, the more she was beginning to believe that Diana didn't care about Ronnie and Mary, or even her own kids. She just wanted somebody to pay her bills, feed and clothe her kids and, thanks to Mom, she got free babysitting as well. Why keep the kids at the house when Mom would watch them all day for free with no complaints?

And then there was the affect this was having on Mary. The psychological stress was putting Mary over the edge. Following Cindy's death, the subject of what Mary was alleged to have seen in the master bedroom had been brushed under the table. Elizabeth had tried to bring it up, but Laura always dismissed it, attributing it to a case of Mary's overactive imagination. Elizabeth wanted to believe this, and logically she *did* believe it. But part of her also wondered if there was something more to the story, and she kept her ears open for the slightest chance of anything weird that was even remotely related. She also paid close attention to reports from Laura regarding Mary.

When she asked her mother how Ronnie was, the response was always the same. "Oh, he's fine!"

Elizabeth learned for herself the day before Thanksgiving.

* * *

Elizabeth was sitting at her desk in Room 145 while her fourth-period class—American literature—was silently absorbed in the assignment she had handed them yesterday: reading chapters twelve through fifteen of Hawthorne's *The Scarlet Letter*. She was giving them until Monday to read the chapters and compose a critical analysis. They were being tested on the novel in two weeks, and they were already ahead of schedule when it came to their discussions of the book.

When the lunch bell rang, her students closed their books, put papers into notebooks and filed out of the room. Elizabeth called out, "Happy Thanksgiving, class!"

A couple of her students smiled and wished her happy Thanksgiving. Elizabeth smiled and waited for her students to empty out of the room. She had forgotten to pack her lunch this morning; normally she ate lunch in her room while reading a book, but today that was out of the question. She was starving, so she gathered her purse up and was just about to head outside when her cell phone rang.

She scooped it out of her purse and her eyes lit up when she saw Ronnie's name in the LED screen. She hit the green Receive button. "Hello?"

"Elizabeth." Her brother's voice sounded tinny, as if he were far away. "It's Ronnie."

"Hey, what's up?" Elizabeth felt suddenly excited to be talking to her brother.

"I'm on my way to work." Ronnie sounded good; he sounded normal, and Elizabeth wondered if everything was okay now. "I was wondering if you had time for lunch today so we could talk?"

"You caught me just in time," Elizabeth said as she headed out of her room. She closed and locked the door behind her and headed to the teachers' parking lot. "I was just on my way to lunch."

"I'm heading toward the school now," Ronnie said. "I'm on Mannheim Pike."

"There's a McDonald's there," Elizabeth said. "Is that okay?"

"That sounds good. See you there."

As Elizabeth drove to the McDonald's three blocks from the school, her mind raced. It had been over three weeks since she'd seen Ronnie, and she was sure Diana had told him about the fights they'd had regarding letting Lily tag along with Mary when Elizabeth invited her niece over a few weekends ago. She'd expected Ronnie to be angry with her about that, but he hadn't sounded the least bit mad. Instead he had that tone of voice that suggested he was on the verge of unloading all his guilt on her. She wondered briefly if he had been thinking about her invitation to call her. She wondered if he had been mulling this over and finally decided to take her up on it, but had to do it outside the house lest Diana overhear their conversation. Catching up with her on his way to work would provide the perfect opportunity.

She saw Ronnie pull in to the McDonald's parking lot ahead of her and made a left-hand turn, following him in. She raised her hand, hoping he'd see her in his rearview mirror, and he did. He pulled in to the next available parking slot and she pulled in to one two cars down from him. She turned the engine off and got out. Ronnie had already gotten out of his pickup truck and was standing at the rear of her car. He looked the same way he did when he'd finally gotten off coke: sheepish, a little guilty and a *what-the-fuck-was-I-doing* look.

"Hey!" Elizabeth said, forcing a smile. "How you doing?"

Ronnie glanced at her quickly, and she could tell there was something wrong. He was still thin and sickly looking, even more so than when she last saw him. He was wearing his blue denim jacket and a pair of faded blue jeans and a baseball cap. His long hair blew in the chilly wind, and his hands were thrust deep into his jacket pockets. "Shit, I must be crazy to have come here," he said.

"Ronnie, what's the matter? You look sick. Do you feel

okay? I told you at the wake that if you ever wanted to talk, I'm here. I want to help you."

"I know," Ronnie said. He looked at her again, and there was that look of shame once more, as if he were afraid to talk to her for fear she would chastise him for something he had done. In a way they had been through this before when Ronnie had gotten off coke. Elizabeth had been the first person he had come to talk to, and he'd been nervous then. He looked nervous now.

"Are you doing coke again?"

"No!" The quickness of his answer told her he was telling the truth. "No fucking way." A pause. "Sometimes I wish I was, though."

"Is that it?" Elizabeth said, wondering now if that's what his problem was all along, that he was relapsing. "Because if you're having trouble staying off coke, it's okay. It's nothing to be ashamed of. I mean, you fall off, you get right back on the wagon, okay?"

"It's not that," Ronnie said, rocking on his heels. He was shaking, nervous. "Shit, I don't know how else to explain this to you."

Elizabeth opened her mouth to answer but found she couldn't—she didn't know *what* was wrong, and she didn't want to keep pressuring him. She felt her resolve shatter as her last hope—that he'd had a cocaine relapse vanished. "Ronnie, I'm your sister. I want to help you."

Ronnie took a deep breath and looked down at the ground. He seemed to be drawing into himself, as if to ward away the cold. Around them cars continued past to the drive-through. High school kids cruised past, blaring rap and heavy-metal music from car stereos. When Ronnie looked back up again she saw he had tears in his eyes. "I can't help it," he said, his voice shaky. "God help me, Elizabeth, but I just can't help it."

Now Elizabeth felt a sudden surge of fear. She reached out and touched Ronnie's arm in an attempt to comfort him. "You can't help what, Ron?"

"I can't *help myself!*" He was crying, and he wiped his eyes with the back of his hands. "I . . . I . . . keep trying to end it, but I can't . . . she's too *strong*, and—"

Elizabeth felt her entire body go numb. "Is it Diana?"

". . . and I'm scared for Mary . . . I love her so much and—"

Elizabeth gripped Ronnie's shoulders. "Is Diana hurting you or Mary?"

This seemed to snap Ronnie out of the spell he was in. He shook his head and took a deep breath, taking several steps back. "Elizabeth, I'm . . . I'm sorry I even bothered you . . ." He was retreating back to his truck.

"Ronnie!" Elizabeth stepped forward after him.

Ronnie turned and headed back to his truck. "I've gotta go. I'm already late for work."

"Ronnie!" Elizabeth caught up to him at his truck and tried to get him to stop. He brushed past her and climbed behind the wheel. "Ronnie, I can help! If you're afraid for Mary, I can get her out of there. I can get you *help!* I can—"

Ronnie started the car and looked at her. His blond hair seemed thinner, brittle. And the baseball cap . . . Ronnie had never worn baseball caps before now. She wondered if his hair was falling out. His stubbled face looked dry, his hands weathered. This was not her brother. This was not Ronnie Baker, the happy-go-lucky ex-drunk coke-fiend she had come to love since he settled down with Cindy Shull almost ten years ago.

"I can't help it," Ronnie said, starting the truck and crying.

"Cut the bullshit," Elizabeth said. She pounded the driver's side window. "Open the fucking window!"

Ronnie rolled down the window. His hands were shaking on the wheel. He had his head down, his eyes closed, and it looked like he was gasping for breath.

Elizabeth felt scared again. Seeing him behave like a junkie jonesing for a fix was driving the spike of fear into her veins. "Ronnie, are you okay? Are you sick?"

Ronnie shook his head. He took a deep breath, composing himself. Elizabeth waited, trying to stay calm. She didn't want to drive him away now. She wanted to get it through his thick skull that she was going to help, she was going to do whatever it took to help him and Mary.

"Ronnie?"

Ronnie took another deep breath and looked up. He appeared in control again, as if he had fought off whatever spell had come over him. He didn't look at her when he spoke. "Whatever happens, know this, Elizabeth. I love you and Mom and Dad, and I love Mary more than the world itself."

"Ronnie, you're scaring me!" Now she couldn't help it; hearing him say that sounded like Ronnie was giving her advance warning of his impending suicide.

"I'm sorry I'm scaring you, but I can't help it." He turned to her, his green eyes alight with fear. "I love Mary, and I would never do anything to hurt her. Okay?"

"Ronnie, let me get you help!"

"I *want* help," Ronnie said, and she saw his hands shaking again. *It's drugs,* she thought. *It's got to be drugs. He has to be doing something to keep him working those brutal hours.* "I want to . . . I want to . . . but . . . she's stronger than anything I've ever done. Stronger than coke. . . . stronger than booze . . ."

"If Diana's hurting you—"

". . . but I can't *help it* . . . I *want her,* Elizabeth! I wanted her so *bad* and then . . .

Elizabeth stopped, not knowing what to say and unable to tear her gaze from her brother. "What's she doing to you?"

Ronnie looked at her with pleading in his eyes. "If I could get rid of her I would, but she's got me . . . she's got me good. And I can't—"

"Kick the bitch out!" Elizabeth said, practically spitting the words out with a sudden burst of anger. "Go home and kick her fucking ass out the door—"

"I *can't!*" Ronnie suddenly wailed. He pounded the dashboard with his fists. "I can't, I can't, I can't!"

"Why not!"

Ronnie stifled back a cry, his head bowed down again. Then, in a small, weak voice. "You wouldn't understand."

"Try me." Elizabeth was begging him to do anything it took to keep him away from Diana Marshfield. If she'd had the strength to drag him out of the pickup truck, she would have. "Please!" she said. "Let us help you. I'll bug out early from work, you can come home with me. You can—"

Ronnie raised his hand to stop her and shook his head. He put the truck into reverse with his other hand, and Elizabeth felt the vehicle lurch. "I can't, I just can't, and I've gotta go. I'm gonna be late for work." And then just as suddenly as he had unleashed this barrage of emotions, he was backing out of the parking spot and driving away. Elizabeth was too stunned to yell at him to come back. She stood at the empty parking spot, trying to control the flood of anger and fear that was racing through her, threatening to overtake her.

Ronnie alternated between crying and being incredibly angry at himself as he wound his way to Route 30. He hadn't meant to rile Elizabeth up like that, but he'd needed to talk, and she was the only one he could turn to. He shouldn't have tried to reach out and ask for help in the first place; he had no idea how deep he was hooked.

With his stomach churning, threatening to make him sick and pass out, he managed to get back onto Mannheim Pike. He tried to control the shaking in his hands, but he couldn't. The more he tried to fight it, the harder it became to control his urges, his undying desire to take pleasure from Diana's sensuous nature.

He was heading north on Mannheim Pike, the opposite direction from which he wanted to go, but that was of no concern to him now. He had to get into a less populated area, and he had to do it quickly. He would have preferred to just go home and give Diana a quick fuck, but he had to be at work in thirty minutes. This would have to be a quickie. He made a right down Brenner Road, the first road that looked like it was far off the beaten path, and pulled over to the side. Pausing quickly to scan the neighborhood for anybody who might be watching, he put the vehicle in park, picked up his cell phone and hit speed dial. With his other hand he unbuttoned his jeans and extracted his raw penis.

Diana answered on the third ring. "Hello."

"It's me," Ronnie said, his pitiful attempt at getting help gone. Hearing Diana's voice had obliterated that now. *It's just one more time,* he thought as he began stroking his penis. *Just one more time, just a quickie and then no more.* "I'm so horny for you."

"Are you at work?"

"No, I'm in my truck."

A throaty chuckle, sexy in its timbre. "You naughty boy!"

"That's it, talk to me like that!" Ronnie's voice panted as he jerked himself off. He didn't even feel the irritation of the raw skin of his penis as he stroked himself rapidly. "Talk to me like that, make that sucking sound you make when you suck my dick."

"Mmmm . . . like this?" A slurping sound, loud, purringly feminine, made goose bumps down Ronnie's spine.

"Yes, yes, keep doing that!"

And as Ronnie jerked himself off with Diana over the phone he was in another world, a world far away from the one he had struggled to build with his daughter, one he had hoped to live in with humility and respect. And as he came quickly in a shuddering gasp, the guilt crashed into him again. He leaned against the steering wheel, struggling to hold his emotions in because he didn't want Diana to know he was losing his mind.

CHAPTER THIRTEEN

They arrived at her parents' house shortly before noon on Thanksgiving day, and as Gregg pulled the Saturn up their street, Elizabeth saw that Diana's Chrysler was already parked in the driveway. "Looks like the princess is here already," Elizabeth muttered.

"Now, now," Gregg said as he pulled in behind the Chrysler. "Be nice."

"I will, but if that bitch is rude I will *not* be polite," Elizabeth said.

Elizabeth had been up all night talking to Gregg and thinking about what had happened yesterday at lunch. She'd called Gregg from her cell phone in her car and told him about it; in fact, she'd canceled her last class and went home sick. "I tried to get him to talk to me but he wouldn't. It was like he *wanted* to but . . . but it was like he was in denial over something."

"He's got to be using again," Gregg had said. She'd heard him sigh over the phone, heard the squeak of his chair as he shuffled in his cubicle at work. "This sounds more serious than we thought. We need to do something. An intervention or something."

"Oh no," Elizabeth had said, shaking her head. "We did that with him twelve years ago when he was strung out on coke, and that was a disaster."

"I'd suggest having a professional present when you do this one," Gregg had replied. "I'm sure if you call AA or NA and tell them what's going on, somebody will volunteer to help out."

"What about Diana?" Elizabeth had said. "I think she has a lot to do with this."

"So do I, but I think we need to deal with her role in this at another time. The first thing is to confront Ronnie with his problem and get him help. If Diana's around and objects, fuck her!"

Elizabeth had smiled. The sound in Gregg's voice then, so filled with righteous anger, had been inspiring.

She had picked up Eric at her mother's, telling her quickly what had happened with Ronnie. For the first time in months, Laura had looked concerned for her son. "Maybe I should call him at the plant," she'd said, heading for the phone.

"Maybe we should wait until tomorrow," Elizabeth had said, the plan formulating in her mind haphazardly, coming out as it was being born. "If the time and opportunity presents itself, we should bring it up to him at dinner."

"I think that's a good idea," Laura had said.

Elizabeth hadn't mentioned or alluded to Diana being the problem, and she hadn't told her mother everything Ronnie had said. She was afraid her mother would overreact and defend Diana. If Ronnie were using coke again, the key was to get him help. Only then was there a possibility that he might see Diana with new eyes and do something about it himself.

As they got out of the car Gregg said, "Let's see what happens."

"I know," Elizabeth said. Eric was silent. They'd told their son that Uncle Ronnie was having some troubles and that they might have to talk with him about it—just the grownups—and Eric had nodded and said he understood. It was amazing how perceptive Eric was at only nine years old.

They entered the house to the welcome aroma of baking turkey and stuffing, the warm smells of cooking and burning candles bearing an autumn scent. Jerry was cheerful and smiling, dressed in blue jeans and a long-sleeve red plaid shirt. "Hello! How you guys doing today? Hope you brought your appetites!"

In a way it was very much like Thanksgiving dinners of the past, except for one thing: Ronnie wasn't there.

Diana was sitting at the kitchen table with Mom, chattering away, and Elizabeth felt Gregg react visibly to Diana's appearance. She looked ravishing in tight black jeans, a white blouse with the top three buttons undone, revealing deep cleavage. Her hair and makeup were perfect. Elizabeth couldn't believe it—if she were a guy, she would've had a hard on. Diana was that sexy and alluring.

Rick, Lily and Mary were playing in the living room. Eric joined them, and Elizabeth smiled when she saw her niece. Mary looked up from her spot on the sofa where she was sitting with a book, and smiled and waved. The expression on the little girl's face was not only one of recognition and happiness at seeing her aunt, it also bore a hint of relief, as if she were thinking, *Thank God you're here.* Mary looked back down at her book, and Elizabeth paused for a moment. Something about Mary wasn't right. She seemed a little too withdrawn, as if she were afraid.

She was about to go talk to Mary, see how she was doing, when she heard her mother's voice. "Elizabeth! I was just telling Diana about that recipe you have for Shoo-fly pie. Where did you say you got it again?"

Elizabeth told her, the words tumbling out of her mouth, and they spent the next twenty minutes or so talking about cooking. Jerry and Gregg were in the living room, watching a game and discussing sports; the kids were in the living room, either playing or reading books; and Elizabeth tried to join in on the conversation with her mother and Diana, but her mind kept wandering between Mary and her brother.

Gregg went down to the basement and brought up sodas and beer, and Elizabeth poured a Dr Pepper for herself. She was standing by the kitchen counter, munching on potato chips. Diana had gotten up to refill her glass with Diet Pepsi and Mom was at the stove, dressed in faded blue jeans and a red sweater, tending to the meal. "So where's Ronnie?" Elizabeth asked.

"He's in bed," Diana said, her tone of voice bearing a slight tinge of sympathy. "He worked a double shift last night and didn't get home till four. He's exhausted. He said he might come by later this afternoon."

From the living room, she heard her father mutter. Elizabeth couldn't tell what he said, but she guessed immediately it was a response to Diana's explanation of why Ronnie wasn't present. Mom didn't say anything, as if it were a normal occurrence for Ronnie to skip out on Thanksgiving with his family because he was too busy working. Elizabeth shrugged and took a sip of her Dr Pepper. "He sure works a lot. Too much work for so long isn't such a good idea. He should look into cutting back on his hours. Don't you worry about him driving home from work so late at night when he's tired?"

"I'm not worried," Diana said casually. "Ronnie's a tough guy. When he's at home he gets plenty of rest."

"I hope so," Elizabeth said. Then, before she could stop herself, she continued. "I suppose it's easy for him to sleep during the day when the kids aren't home. How long has it been since he's seen Mary?"

She glanced into the living room quickly and caught a brief glimpse of Mary, who was looking up from her book toward the dining room eagerly. She'd been listening to the conversation and now she turned away almost fearfully, as if afraid of being caught eavesdropping.

"He'll see Mary tonight," Diana said. Her dark eyes were riveted on Elizabeth. She was smiling, but it wasn't an honest smile. It was manufactured civility, and beneath it Elizabeth could sense the mask of disapproval and hate simmering. "He does work hard, but he's doing it for his family. It's a big sacrifice for a man to take on as much as Ronnie is doing so his children can have a mother to come home to after school. That's something most children these days don't have. Know what I mean?"

I know what you mean, you bitch, Elizabeth thought, immediately recognizing the barb for what it was—a direct stab at her own working condition. She let it roll off her back and continued, keeping her voice calm and level. "Well, as his sister I worry about him. All that work and hardly any time off . . . it could drive him to do things he probably shouldn't be doing. He should take it easy."

"He'll be fine," Diana said. Her false smile widened, became more forceful.

"And what have you been up to lately?" Elizabeth asked, feigning a change of subject. "You working now or . . . ?"

Her father muttered again, louder this time. "That'll be the day."

It was clear Diana heard Jerry's response. She glanced back at Jerry with such a look of distaste that Elizabeth felt like slapping her (*how* dare *you look at my dad that way when he's only reacting to the fact that you're a lazy* bitch!), but she held back. That look said, *Say one more thing about me and I'll fuck you up.* Diana turned back to Elizabeth and smiled sweetly, her entire demeanor false. "No, I'm not working. At least not yet. And what about you? I hear you actually had a book published! Is it available in bookstores?"

If the question had come from anybody else, Elizabeth wouldn't have been offended; since most people were only aware of brand name authors like Tom Clancy and Stephen King, she didn't fault them for having never heard of her. She wasn't offended that this particular barb came from Diana, but she could tell it was intended to be insulting. Elizabeth smiled. "Yes, it is, but since you don't read, there's no sense in me telling you which store you can pick it up at." *Do you even know how to read?*

Diana's smile remained in place but her eyes were smoldering pits. Laura turned away from the stove, and Elizabeth saw from the look on her mother's face that she didn't approve of the conversation Elizabeth was baiting Diana into. *And I don't give a fuck,* Elizabeth thought. *For once in my life I don't care what my mother thinks.*

The rest of the hour prior to dinner being served was civil, but there was an undercurrent of tension. Gregg sensed it as he came into the kitchen to munch on snacks. He glanced at Elizabeth quickly. She caught his eye, then turned away. Eric was sitting on the sofa with Mary, showing her how to play a Game Boy, and Lily was hovering near them. Rick was sitting by himself playing another video game, looking sullen. Mary looked like she was trying to flinch away from Lily every time the little girl got near her, and Eric seemed to notice this; several times Elizabeth heard him say, "This game is a little too hard for you to play with, Lily. Why don't you try one of those other ones over in the toy box?"

Diana heard Eric and turned around. "Mary, let Lily play with you and Eric!"

"Mommy!" Lily wailed, her face pouting.

"Mary . . ." Diana's voice was stern, authorative.

"Okay." Mary's voice was so soft, so subdued, that Elizabeth barely heard it but she could detect the defeat and fear in it. Eric looked puzzled and a little annoyed. He glanced at his mother, and Elizabeth met his eyes. *Just do what Diana says,* Elizabeth thought, nodding at her son. Eric understood the silent communication and sighed. *We'll talk about this later.* She traded glances with Gregg

again, and then her silent reverie was broken by Laura calling everybody to the table for dinner.

As usual, the food was excellent. The turkey was moist
and seasoned perfectly; the stuffing was scrumptious. The
corn and mashed potatoes melted in your mouth. There
was warm bread, sweet potatoes and cranberry sauce. Elizabeth helped her mother with the drinks, and conversation
centered on the food and past years' Thanksgivings. Diana
gave an anecdote or two about Thanksgivings in Ohio. Elizabeth paid special attention to them as Diana talked. "My
mom comes from a big family, so we'd usually have two
turkeys and a ham," Diana said, her tone now more jovial
and friendly but still bearing an underlying hint of conden-
sation. "And my ex-husband came from a big family. Every
year we would take turns going to each other's parents' for
Thanksgiving. My ex mother-in-law ran a large resort hotel
outside Cleveland, so she always had the best spread on
the table. Perfect china, perfect silverware. It was like eating
at a five-star resort hotel at her place. Of course, she hated
it every time we came over because Rick always found
something to break and—"

On and on it went. Elizabeth ate and listened, paying
more attention to Diana than she had in the past four
months. Diana didn't seem to notice and rattled on. Laura
carried most of the conversation with her, but her father
piped in as well, along with Gregg. The more Elizabeth observed her parents, the more she realized that something
was wrong.

Mom had slipped back into that body-snatcher persona;
it almost seemed like her mother's mind and will had been
zapped by the evil entity Elizabeth imagined Diana to be
and was replaced with a puppet-mom who nodded and
spoke the right things, the kind of things only Diana would
approve of. Dad didn't fare much better, but Elizabeth
caught the faint hint of disapproval in his demeanor. Gregg
caught the vibes at once and glanced at Elizabeth again.
Diana's kids picked at their food and were mostly silent

during the meal. Eric dug into his food ravenously, shoveling it in like it was the last thing on earth to eat, and Mary ate quickly. Elizabeth's eyes lit on her niece, and Mary looked back briefly. *I'm scared,* those eyes seemed to say.

Elizabeth finished her meal and helped her mother clear the table. "That was great, Laura," Gregg said, leaning back in his chair. "Once again, you put on a fabulous dinner."

"Diana helped quite a bit with this meal, folks," Laura said, carrying plates of turkey to the kitchen counter. "She helped make the stuffing."

I doubt it, Elizabeth thought as she picked up empty glasses. *She's so stuffed with bullshit, I doubt she'd have the strength to turn her attention away from the cigarettes and the Diet Pepsi she drinks all day. Besides, isn't this the woman who doesn't cook for her own kids? What the hell is she doing suddenly helping prepare Thanksgiving dinner?*

Gregg and Jerry headed back to the living room to reclaim their respective spots in front of the TV. Rick and Lily went back to the living room to mope, and Eric went to the bathroom. Elizabeth helped her mom and Diana clear the table, and then she picked up her own glass. She was out of soda and still thirsty. "I'm going down for a refill," she said, heading toward the basement door. "Anybody want anything?"

There was no answer, so she shrugged and headed down the stairs to the basement.

Once in the basement she made her way toward the bar, heading to the refrigerator. She had just opened the refrigerator door and was rummaging among the bottles of Rolling Rock and the liter bottles of Pepsi when she heard footsteps scamper toward her. She turned around and was surprised to see Mary.

Her niece ran up to her and clutched the side of her leg. She immediately started crying, and as Elizabeth bent down to calm the girl down she could tell Mary was trying to control her emotions. "Mary," Elizabeth whispered, trying to soothe her down. "What's the matter, honey?"

"Take me home with you," Mary said quickly between sobs. Her face was hot and wet with tears. "Please! L-let's *leave* . . . nh-nh-*now!*" She started sobbing again.

"Mary, honey," Elizabeth said, her arms around her niece, trying to comfort her. Her mind was racing back to almost a month ago when her mother had called that Saturday morning and told her Mary had spent the previous evening at their home and made those wild accusations. "Shh. It's going to be okay."

"Just take me," Mary said, her breath hitching as she fought to control her sobs and the volume of her voice. "K-kidnap me or something . . . just . . . take me away from them!"

Elizabeth felt the skin along her arms erupt in gooseflesh. The intensity of emotion in Mary's voice was too great to be coming from such a young child. Elizabeth instinctively held her niece close to her for protection. "It's okay, Mary, you'll be safe. I'll take care of you."

The door to the basement opened, and footsteps sounded on the stairs.

Elizabeth felt Mary stiffen in her arms; she felt her stomach contract as the footsteps grew closer. Mary's face scrunched up as she fought to hide her emotions. "They never leave me alone!"

This last exclamation from Mary, spoken with such heartfelt emotion, sparked anger in Elizabeth. She stood up quickly and, grabbing Mary's hand, she led the girl to her father's workroom. She opened the door quickly and pushed Mary through. "Stay there," she whispered quickly, then shut the door before Mary could respond. By now the footsteps had reached the bottom of the stairs. Elizabeth spun around, already knowing who she was going to meet when they rounded the basement family room.

Rick and Lily entered the basement family room, Lily's eyes glancing around as if searching for something. Rick looked bored, but there was an undercurrent of something else working there, something malicious. "Could you please go back upstairs?" Elizabeth asked.

Rick looked at her with an expression that seemed to say, *You think you can tell me what to do?* Lily ignored her and tried to walk around Elizabeth toward the door she had shoved Mary into a moment before.

"I don't think so," Elizabeth said, placing herself in front of Lily. She was furious. "You aren't allowed down here at all. Now go upstairs!"

"We can go anywhere we want," Rick said. It was one of the rare times the boy spoke, and if she hadn't been so angry she would have felt a tremor of fear at the sound of his voice. It was so . . . *wrong*. It was as if he were speaking while chewing a mouthful of rocks at the same time.

"No, you may not," Elizabeth said, and she had to stand her ground as Lily tried to get around her again. The little girl tried to dodge past her to get to the door that led to Jerry's workroom, and this time Elizabeth had to grab her to hold her back. She was a little too forceful, and Lily stumbled back slightly. Elizabeth felt her hands go cold at the brief contact between them, and she tried not to let her surprise and fear show. *She's cold,* she thought. *So cold.* There was also the sense that Lily's flesh was slimy, as if she weren't even human. "Get the hell out of here," she said, the fear making her incredibly defensive.

Lily glanced back at Rick briefly, who nodded. "Come on, Lily," he said. The two kids headed toward the stairs; they glanced back at Elizabeth as they ascended the staircase, as if they were waiting for the opportunity for Elizabeth to turn her back on them.

Elizabeth watched them go up the stairs, heart pounding in her chest, and when the basement door closed, she bolted toward her father's workroom and Mary came to her quickly. Elizabeth swooped her up in her arms and held her as Mary cried openly now. "Shh, calm down, honey, it's okay, they're gone, they're gone, I've got you and nobody's going to hurt you. It's okay, I'm going to take care of you."

She repeated this mantra as Mary cried into her shoulder. Elizabeth held her niece, trying to soothe her and calm her own racing nerves. Then she heard another set of footsteps on the stairs.

Elizabeth tensed, hoping it wasn't the kids again, but these footsteps were heavier, those of an adult. She whispered to Mary, "It's okay, it's not Rick and Lily. Just be quiet." She stood up and Mary held on to her as Elizabeth approached the partly opened door to see who was coming down the stairs.

Diana walked past the door on her way behind the bar, presumably to fetch another can of Diet Pepsi.

Elizabeth turned to Mary quickly. "Shhh, it's Diana. Be quiet."

Mary quickly hitched in a sob and tried to hold her breath.

Diana turned toward the door and saw Elizabeth and Mary. She frowned. "Everything okay?"

The anger came out again, so sudden and huge that Elizabeth had a hard time holding it back. She glowered at Diana as Mary cowered against her. "Everything's fine."

Diana stepped forward, a Diet Pepsi in her hand, a look of phony concern on her face. "Are you sure? Mary, you okay honey?" She took another step closer to dad's workroom.

"Everything's fine!" Elizabeth said through gritted teeth. "This is none of your business!"

Diana barely flinched. She looked a little surprised maybe, but not too much. She looked toward Mary, who hid her face against Elizabeth's stomach. "Everything will be okay," she said, her voice all fake concern and affection. "I know you miss your daddy, but you'll see him tonight when we get home. He's looking forward to seeing you. I know he is. He just hasn't seen you for so long because he's been working. That's why you're upset, right?"

She was talking to Mary, but the question was directed at

Elizabeth, who felt a burning in the pit of her stomach. She felt like a rabbit cowering in its burrow as a snake slithered by looking for food.

"Mary?"

Mary nodded once, keeping her gaze downcast and away from Diana. Elizabeth glanced back up at Diana. "She's just upset that her father couldn't be here," she said, the words coming quickly. "That's all."

Diana stood there for a moment as if considering this. Then, as if she were satisfied with this answer, she nodded. "Everything will be okay. Your dad will be home tonight. He'll be very happy to see you. Now why don't you come upstairs and play with Lily and Rick."

Elizabeth bristled at the suggestion. *Now why don't you come upstairs and play with Lily and Rick.* There had been no mention of Eric. Not, *Why don't you come back upstairs and play with the kids.* It was as if Eric weren't even in the equation.

"I'll take her up," Elizabeth said, meeting Diana's gaze.

Diana studied her for a moment, and Elizabeth forced herself not to drop her gaze. She tried to be strong in the conviction of her promise to take Mary upstairs, and it must have worked. Diana nodded, then turned and headed toward the stairs.

Elizabeth pulled Mary close and whispered in her ear. "I'm going to go upstairs and tell them you'll be up in a minute, that you're in the bathroom. I want you to slip out through the sliding door and make your way around the side of the house to my car. The car is unlocked, so open the back door and crawl in and lay down in the backseat. I'm going to get Gregg and Eric and we'll be out in less than five minutes. Whatever you do, don't get out of the car. Do you understand me?"

Mary nodded, her lips trembling.

"Okay." Elizabeth gave Mary a kiss, then stood up, motioning Mary out the workroom. "Let's go."

As Mary headed toward the sliding-glass door that led to

the concrete back patio, Elizabeth headed toward the stairs. She paused briefly at the half bathroom situated beneath the stairs to turn on the light and close the door so it appeared occupied, and then she headed up the stairs.

She immediately crossed the kitchen to the living room, ignoring Diana, who gazed at her from her seat at the kitchen table. Gregg was sitting in the plush red easy chair. She leaned close and whispered in his ear, "Please don't make a fuss, but we have to go. Now!"

Gregg looked at her in surprise, the implications of the sudden change of plans evident on his face. He must have immediately sensed something was wrong; whatever he was going to say in protest never made it out of his mouth. "I'll explain on the way home," Elizabeth whispered again. "We're not going to say goodbye, we're just going to get up and go. Meet me at the car." Hoping Gregg would do exactly what she asked, she headed to the living room to find Eric.

Eric was playing with one of the electronic Game Boys. Rick was sitting next to him, peering over his shoulder.

Elizabeth stepped over Lily, who was sitting on the floor in front of Mary's toys, and plopped herself on the sofa next to Eric. Knowing there was no other alternative for prying her son away from Rick without raising some sort of alarm, she went for the direct approach. "Honey, I need you to come home with me real quick."

Eric and Rick looked up in surprise. Eric looked surprised that they were leaving. Rick frowned. "Going home already?"

Elizabeth tried to smile to reassure the older boy, but she knew it was a false smile he would see right through. "I forgot something at home, and I don't want to drive back and forth by myself," she explained. "We'll be right back."

"But, Mom!" Eric protested as Elizabeth took the Game Boy out of his hand and pulled him off the sofa. She didn't even bother to get their coats; her purse was on the end table by the front door and as she passed it, dragging Eric behind her, she plucked it up with her free hand and slung it over her shoulder. She opened the front door and was just stepping outside when she heard Diana call out. "Where are you going?"

"We'll be right back," she said, ushering Eric ahead of her out of the house and slamming the door behind her.

"Get into the car," she told Eric. Elizabeth noticed with relief that Gregg had reached the car—he'd probably exited quietly through the garage door—and was already getting into the driver's seat. Elizabeth steered Eric toward the backseat, saw that Mary was hunkered down behind Gregg, and slipped into the front passenger seat. "Let's go," she said.

"What the hell is going on?" Gregg said, his voice high and scared. He started the car and had barely gotten it warmed up when the front door opened and Diana peeked out. Rick's face peered out from beneath her right arm and Elizabeth said, "Drive!"

Gregg backed the car down the driveway, and as they drove past the house and down the street, Elizabeth noticed Diana and Rick had taken another step onto the front porch and were watching them leave. Elizabeth felt their eyes light on her as if they were looking directly at *her*, and she turned away, feeling a creeping sensation along her spine and the back of her neck.

From the backseat Mary's voice came, full of fear. "Are they following us?"

Gregg jumped. He glanced back into the rear-view mirror as he made a left on Fir Lane then a right on Douglas, which would lead to Denver Road. "What's Mary doing back there?" he asked. He glanced at Elizabeth quickly, the look of confusion and fear quickly giving way to anger.

"Please just drive home, and I'll explain everything."

"They're not following us, are they?" Mary asked. She was still hunkered down in the backseat and Eric, who had barely been able to climb into his seat and buckle up when Gregg had backed the car up, was looking at his cousin in surprise.

Elizabeth glanced behind them. "They're not following us," she said. "They probably don't know you're gone yet." She turned to Gregg. "Get us home."

"What the hell is Mary doing back there, and why is she here without her parents' knowledge?" Gregg asked. He glanced from the rear-view mirror to the road in front of him, and Elizabeth knew that if she didn't explain quickly she would lose her credibility.

"Diana is not her parent!" she snapped. "Her father hasn't known what's been going on at that house for months and her mother is dead, so just drive and listen."

As Gregg drove them home through Lancaster County's back roads, Elizabeth told him about their encounter in her parents' basement. And for the first time since Mary and Laura had come to their home for the weekend, when Laura had told them Mary had seen a shapeless, shifting monstrosity fused seamlessly with Ronnie's sleeping form in the master bedroom, she told Gregg her true feelings of the situation. "This is far more than Mary reacting psychologically against all she's been through," she said. "There's something wrong with Diana and her kids. I don't know what it is, but I can feel it." She glanced in the rear-view mirror into the backseat at Eric and Mary, who was now sitting up, her face still red from crying but now looking calm. "The kids feel it too. Don't you?"

And while she had never spoken of her feelings with her son, Eric met her gaze and slowly nodded.

Gregg saw the exchange and, still looking stunned, his face showing the strain of wanting to do what was right and trying to be rational, stayed silent and drove.

CHAPTER FOURTEEN

When they got to the house, Elizabeth made sure Eric and Mary were inside before she closed the garage door. Gregg had already gone in with the kids, and as she stepped into the mud room that led to the kitchen she called out, "Eric, take Mary upstairs to our bedroom. We can talk up there."

Gregg stood in the kitchen while Elizabeth went around the house checking the windows and doors. She could feel his gaze on her as she drew the drapes closed. "Jesus, Elizabeth, what the hell is going on?"

"Can you set the alarm, please?"

Gegg started, his features puzzled, then registered the implications of what she was asking him to do. She could feel her stomach grow tight, and she wondered if she should go to the basement to check the windows there. She felt cold, the hairs along her arm standing on end, and she was shaking.

The tension had grown so thick in the house since they'd entered that it felt like they were walking through molasses.

Gregg had stepped away from the kitchen to cross over to the entryway to engage the alarm, and Elizabeth felt a little relieved he hadn't used this opportunity to argue the matter. Gregg could be overly analytical when it came to emotions, but she could clearly tell he was letting his instinct take over his rational side. There'd been times in the past when he'd tried to be too rational and they would argue over the stupidest things. Thank God that wasn't happening now. Because if it was, if he had decided to be pig-headed about this, they could be—

The phone rang. The sudden sound made her jump.

"Don't answer it!" she yelled. She took a moment to catch her breath, then went to the phone in the kitchen.

She looked at the LED readout.

The call was coming from her parents' house.

Gregg was standing in the breakfast nook. "Your folks?"

Elizabeth nodded. "Is the side garage door locked?"

"It's always locked."

"What about the basement windows?"

"They're locked."

"Let's go upstairs." She led the way upstairs and motioned down the hall toward her office. "Can you go around the bedrooms and make sure the drapes are closed? I'm going to make sure the kids are okay."

Gregg started down the hallway to her office, which was the only second-floor room over the garage. The remaining three bedrooms were on the opposite end of the house.

Elizabeth went down the hall to the master bedroom, where Eric and Mary were waiting for her.

She had left the drapes wide open when they'd left this morning, but Eric had probably either heard her closing the drapes downstairs or had felt the instinctual need to do so, and they were now all closed against the afternoon sun. Mary was sitting on the edge of the bed. Elizabeth nodded at Eric and mouthed "Thanks," then went to the master bathroom. "You guys thirsty?"

Mary said, "Yeah."

Elizabeth checked the windows in the bathroom and went back into the bedroom. Eric had joined Mary on the bed. The kids looked scared, but they also looked relieved that they were safe, that Elizabeth was doing everything she could to keep them that way. "Would you like water? Soda? Lemonade?"

"Do you have any punch?"

"I have fruit punch."

"I'll have some punch."

"Okay. Eric? You want anything?"

"A Coke."

Gregg entered the bedroom. "Drapes are all closed," he said.

"Are you thirsty?" she asked him.

"A little."

"Then come downstairs and help me get us some drinks."

Gregg gave a quick glance around the room, as if to assure himself everything was all right, nodded at Eric, then joined Elizabeth.

When they returned a few minutes later bearing drinks, Elizabeth felt the clock ticking; they had to act fast because something was going to happen. She didn't know what, didn't know why she felt this unnerving feeling something was going to happen. Therefore, she needed to cut to the chase and get to the bottom of what was going on. She looked at Eric. "We're going to be talking about some pretty intense stuff, Eric. If you want to stay, you can stay. If you think you won't be able to handle it and you'll be scared, that's okay; you can go to your room. Just don't open the drapes or go downstairs. Okay?"

Eric shifted uncomfortably on the bed. He took a sip of Coke. "I can handle it," he said.

"What Mary says does not leave this room," Elizabeth said, looking at him sternly.

Gregg sat down on his side of the bed, back against the headboard. He had gotten a beer for himself. Elizabeth had gotten a Dr Pepper. Mary sipped from a glass of punch Elizabeth had poured her. "So," Elizabeth said, looking at

Mary. "Grandma told me a few weeks ago about the night you saw that thing in your daddy's bed . . . the weekend you spent with us. Remember?"

Mary nodded, chugging punch. She finished, released a deep sigh. Her mouth was stained red from her drink. She looked more relaxed now that she was away from Diana.

"Grandma told me all about it," Elizabeth said. "I told Uncle Gregg later." She glanced at Eric. "Your cousin doesn't know what I'm talking about, but he's a smart kid. He'll figure it out as we talk."

"What thing did you see in your dad's room?" Eric asked, looking interested.

Elizabeth leaned toward Mary. "Your grandmother thought you'd had a bad dream, that you might be reacting in some way because of . . . the situation at your house, not seeing your daddy. Is that right? Did you have a bad dream?"

Mary shook her head vigorously. "No!"

"So what you told Grandma that night was the truth?"

Mary nodded just as vigorously.

"What happened after that?" Elizabeth asked. "In the weeks that followed? I know it's been hard for you because of what happened to your mommy, but . . ."

"It got her, didn't it?" Mary whispered. She looked like she was going to cry again.

Elizabeth glanced quickly at Gregg, whose gaze seemed to say, *Take it easy*. She shifted around on the bed and tried a more gentle approach. "I don't know, honey, but I believe you even if Grandma doesn't. And we want to help. We love you, and we don't want anything to happen to you. If you can tell us anything that . . . well, anything that you can remember about the last few weeks, that would really help us out a lot."

Mary began slowly, repeating the story Laura had told her three weeks ago. As the story spun out, she seemed to get her bearings on it and was able to skip right through without crying. Eric listened, his eyes growing wide; he occasionally cast questioning glances at his parents as if to seek their confirmation that what Mary was telling them was really true. Gregg rubbed Eric's shoulders as Mary brought the story to its conclusion.

"What's happened during the last few weeks?" Elizabeth asked. "Eric told me you had signed up for some after-school thing. Was that what you were really doing?"

Mary looked ashamed. She bowed her head slightly. "I lied," she said, her voice almost a whisper.

Elizabeth glanced at Gregg quickly. "It's okay, honey. You won't get into trouble. We won't tell anybody."

Mary sighed, looked back up at her aunt. For a seven-year-old, she had the composure of a much older child, one who has been through a lot. "After that weekend . . . especially after my mommy died, I didn't want to go back to my house, but there was no place left for me to go. School was the best part of the day for me. I started dreading the three o'clock bell. The first few days after I spent the weekend here, Diana would pick me up and we would go to Grandma's because of Mommy." Elizabeth nodded, understanding what she meant; Cindy's funeral had been planned that week, and Diana had picked the kids up from school and brought them to the house where the family was gathering every day. "Then at night I'd have to go to that house. I'd go straight to my room and go under the covers and pretend to sleep so Lily wouldn't bother me, but I could always feel her watching me. Sometimes I would sit in the bathroom and I'd be afraid to come out, but then Diana would yell at me to come out, to go to my room with Lily and then I would." She started crying again and Elizabeth immediately rubbed her shoulder lovingly, soothing her. "I just kept trying to go through it, and then after Mommy's funeral, I thought the best thing to do was just to stay away from the house as much as possible. So I lied and told Diana that I signed up for an after-school play and some other things and that Grandma had signed the paperwork. At first she didn't believe me, and I panicked, but then I remembered there really *was* an after-school play going. So that day at school I signed up. I had Mrs. Sweet, my teacher, call Grandma to get permission. I also signed up for girl's gym. So in a way I had signed up for stuff, but I lied to Diana about how long it lasted. They were supposed to get out at four and five, but I'd stay out till six and seven, sometimes even later."

Elizabeth didn't know whether she should hug her niece or scold her for taking such risks. She wanted to do both. "Didn't the school know you weren't being picked up?"

Mary shook her head. She gave a little smile. "My friend Tina Walker was in girl's gym, and I rode home with her every night. She lives a few blocks from us, and at first her mom wanted to drop me off at my house. I made her go to Grandma's instead. Grandma and Grandpa were surprised to see me, but I told them Diana wasn't home when I got to the house and I didn't have a key." She smiled wider. "I got to stay till ten o'clock that night!"

Elizabeth couldn't help it; she grinned. "What did you do the rest of the nights?"

"I had Tina ask her mommy if I could eat supper at their house because my parents were working late," Mary said. "At first Tina's mother wasn't sure and she said no. I was expecting that, so when they dropped me off at the house, I went in through the door in the side of the garage. I'd wait until they were gone, and then I'd slip out and head toward the end of the street where the creek was. I'd hang out down there and—"

"You went to the creek by yourself at night?" Gregg exclaimed, his voice rising in surprise.

The sudden shrill of Gregg's voice startled Mary, and she got that ashamed look again. "I only went there because I didn't have anywhere else to go!"

"How long did you stay there by yourself, honey?" Elizabeth asked, gently coaxing the little girl back into her narrative.

Mary took a sip of punch and shrugged. "I stayed there

till it got too cold to stay outside. Maybe eight o'clock. Then I'd walk home."

"And Diana never knew where you were?"

Mary shook her head. "A lot of times when I came home, she was the only one at the house 'cause she'd leave Lily with Grandma. So that was neat. That was why I signed up for the activities, so I wouldn't be forced to be with Lily every day at Grandma's. Sometimes I'd even wait until I knew Diana was in the bathroom or the bedroom or something, and then I'd sneak in. Or sometimes I'd time things just perfectly and I'd get home when she wasn't even there!" She grinned again. "That was the best!"

Elizabeth smiled at her niece, then took a sip of her Dr Pepper. She held up her hand, one finger up. "Hold that thought, please." She stood up and went to the windows to peer outside. She still had that anxious feeling; they'd been home twenty minutes already, more than enough time for Diana or Mom to have arrived at the house by now if they'd gotten in the car and driven over immediately after they had left. "So you've spent the last three weeks staying out till seven, sometimes eight P.M. on school nights, then you'd sneak into the house. When would Lily get home?"

"Lily would get home around nine. By then I was taking a bath. I'd take my time, too." Mary grinned again.

"And what was it like the rest of the night?"

Mary got that look of dread in her features again, the same look she had when she first told them about seeing the shapeless thing attached to her father. "Lily would always be hanging around me," she said. "If I wanted to read a book or watch a cartoon, she would always be there. Every time I wanted to do something by myself, Diana would make me do it with Lily. Even if I wanted to go to bed early she made Lily go to bed *with* me."

"And Rick?"

"If Lily wasn't around, she made Rick be with me. On weekends if I wanted to go to Tina's house, or if she came over and we wanted to go play in the backyard or something, Diana always made one of her kids go with us. They never left me alone!"

The phone rang again. Elizabeth ignored it and nodded at Mary to continue. She was about to launch into it again when Gregg said, "Are you sure maybe Diana just wanted Rick to watch you to make sure you didn't hurt yourself?"

Elizabeth turned to Gregg, the beginning of a frown on her face. Mary turned to him too, her features bearing annoyance. "She always made me be with Lily or Rick. She never let me be alone!"

Gregg shook his head, and Elizabeth recognized the look coming over his face; he looked like he wasn't buying any of this. "I'm sorry, but I just don't see what the fuss is. I don't like Diana or her kids either, but—"

"She's stronger now," Mary said, her face solemn, grave. "Ever since Mommy died, she and Rick and Lily seem . . . *stronger*. More in *control*."

"Jesus Christ!" Gregg protested. He rose to his feet. "This is ridiculous! I'm not going to—"

"Gregg, shut up and sit down!" Elizabeth roared, and the intensity of her voice shocked her. The kids jumped, surprised at the tone of her voice. Even Gregg stopped in mid-tirade. He turned to her and she could tell that he knew he had overstepped his bounds. "You're like the blonde with the big boobs you're always raving about in horror movies; you know, the ones who always go into the room when everybody knows the freak with the knife is waiting. You're acting just like that, so just shut up and sit down!"

Gregg took a sip of his beer. He looked confused, not sure of what to do with himself. Eric looked out of place too, as if he didn't know what to make of this sudden sense of conflict between his parents. Elizabeth nodded at Mary. "Go ahead, Mary. What happened? Did things go on as you described them until today? When's the last time you saw your daddy?"

At the mention of her father, Mary got teary eyed. "I haven't seen Daddy since . . . since Mommy's funeral." She wiped her eyes with her fingers and started sobbing. Elizabeth reached out and held her. As Mary cried, she met Gregg's gaze, and he seemed to understand the seriousness of the implications. Even Eric looked disturbed by what Mary was insinuating. He had moved from his side of the bed to be closer to his father, and as Elizabeth soothed Mary with meaningless words, she tried to grasp at the last straws of rationality that refused to leave her. *He's slipped off the wagon again. Diana knows it and is shielding Mary from it. Maybe—*

"I hate it there!" Mary cried. "I hate it! There's never any food in the house, and it's messy. Diana never cleans anything, she never makes supper, she doesn't do *anything*. She doesn't talk to me, she doesn't even talk to her kids. I've never even seen her talk to Daddy!"

Elizabeth didn't know what to say. She looked at Gregg, knowing she had to wrap this up soon; her mother had probably left messages on their voice mail. She'd have to call them back, would have to at least get Mary back to her parents' house soon.

"There's something wrong with them," Mary said. She wasn't crying anymore, but her eyes were still red, her cheeks wet from tears. "They're weird. They also seem . . . different!"

"Different how?" Gregg asked softly.

"I don't *know!*" Mary cried. She was obviously growing frustrated at her inability to effectively express herself and she knew it. "My daddy's never around, he's always working. I would try to wait up for him, but I kept falling asleep. One time I tried to peek in their bedroom before I went to school. This was before I saw that thing attached to him. Diana was getting ready to take us to school, and she'd already put Lily in the car. I pretended that I had to go to the bathroom, and when I thought they were gone, I went out and tried to go into their room, but Rick caught me. He . . . he wouldn't let me in and said my daddy was asleep and he . . . he *touched* me—"

"He touched you?" The first thing Elizabeth thought was that Rick had touched her inappropriately.

"He touched me and it felt. . . . it felt *creepy!*" Mary shivered, rubbed her arms as if she were cold. "Him and Lily . . . they feel . . . slippery . . . like they're slimy!"

"Slimy?" Gregg asked.

"One night I could sense Lily watching me," Mary continued, not breaking her stride. "I would try to stay awake for as long as I could and would only let myself go to sleep when she went to sleep first. But then some nights I'd wake up and Lily would be in the bed with me and she'd be all over me, like her arms and legs would be wrapped around me like she was hugging me, only . . . she *wasn't* hugging me." She started crying again, and Elizabeth didn't know what she could do to calm her down. Mary's crying seemed to be both a great emotional release and a venting, and the best course of action was to let it run its course. "I'd push her out of bed, and it would hurt . . . it was like my skin was burning, like a Band-Aid was being ripped off my body. Then I'd be awake and start crying and Diana would come in and try to get me to go back to sleep, but I'd get sick and I'd either throw up in the bedroom or I'd run to the bathroom and be sick."

"How often did this happen?" Elizabeth asked.

"Two, maybe three times."

"Your daddy never knew about it?"

Mary shook her head, still crying. "The second time it happened, Diana kept me home from school and she kept Lily away from me for a few days. I . . . I liked not having Lily around me . . . it almost made it worth it to not be forced to be with her. I stayed at home and watched TV all day, and Diana made me take a nap after lunch and . . . I n-n-never saw my daddy when he woke up, got breakfast and left for work!" She buried her face in Elizabeth's breast again and sobbed uncontrollably.

The three of them looked at each other; Gregg, Elizabeth, and Eric. There was the silent understanding that they knew something was very wrong, that this wasn't a simple matter of family dysfunction. Even Gregg seemed to have come around to this conclusion. He got up and peeked out the window quickly and returned to the bed. He silently drank his beer as Elizabeth calmed Mary down.

"It happened again maybe a week ago," Mary said, rubbing her face. "When I started feeling better, Diana started making me be with Lily again. And I'd still try to stay awake until Lily was asleep, but I always felt so tired in the morning. I was so tired I could hardly do anything. I even fell asleep at school a few times. Sometimes after school I'd go to Tina's and fall asleep in her bed while we were in her room watching TV."

"When you were sick and Diana kept Lily away from you," Gregg asked, his voice gentle, "where did Lily sleep? Did she sleep in your room with you?"

Mary shook her head. "No, she didn't. I don't know where she slept. I . . . I think she slept with Diana and my daddy, but . . . I'm not sure."

"What about Rick?" Eric asked.

"He has his own room," Mary said, "but I never saw him sleep in it. Every time I went to bed he was always watching TV."

The phone rang again, and Elizabeth stood up slowly. "It's probably my mom again."

"Are you sure you should answer it?" Gregg asked.

"I'll see who it is on the caller ID." She turned to Mary. "You okay, honey?"

Mary nodded. She took a big drink of punch. "I'm okay," she said. "I'm tired, my throat hurts a little, but I'm okay."

"I'm going to go downstairs and check our voice mail for messages," Elizabeth said. "I'll be right back. Gregg, will you stay up here with the kids?"

"Yeah."

She went downstairs, pausing at the living room window to peek outside but saw nothing suspicious. The phone stopped ringing, and she went to the kitchen and punched the text messages button on the caller ID read out. Sure enough, her mother had called five times in the past thirty minutes. Elizabeth picked up the receiver and checked her voice messages.

"Honey, it's your mom," Laura said, her voice sounding normal, like the mom Elizabeth had always known. "I was just wondering if you saw Mary before you left. We can't find her anywhere, and Jerry and Rick are checking the backyard and the neighborhood. Diana's worried sick and—"

I'll bet, Elizabeth thought, listening to all the messages. The next two calls were hangups. The fourth was Laura again, her voice more desperate, definitely more worried, and it was genuine. "Mary's missing, honey, we can't find her. When I get off the phone with you I'm calling the police."

Mom's terror and worry were evident in her tone of voice, and Elizabeth knew she had to talk to her mother now. She dialed the number and it was answered on the first ring. "Elizabeth, is Mary with you?"

"Yes, she's with me," Elizabeth said, her mind trying to come up with a story quickly. "She wanted to come with us, so I let her. Sorry."

"Oh, thank God, I'm so relieved," Mom said. "We were so worried. Diana was just beside herself and—"

"I'm sorry," Elizabeth said. "I wanted the company, and I should have said something, but Mary was upset and—"

"Upset? Why was she upset?"

Elizabeth was quickly growing confused. She shouldn't have taken Mary so quickly, so suddenly, but at the time it was the only thing she could think of to get her away from Diana and talk to her openly without fear of reprisal. Her mom was still in Diana's camp; at least that was Elizabeth's impression, and she didn't want to upset her. "She's just upset at . . . at everything," Elizabeth said, making up excuses on the spot.

"Didn't you even think to tell us you were taking her? We've been so—"

There was a sound on the other end, background voices, and then Diana's voice came on the line. Stern, angry, authorative. "What the hell were you thinking, taking Mary without my permission?"

For a moment a part of Elizabeth was afraid and wanted to back down. "I . . . don't know," she said. "I wasn't—"

"Bring her back here and do it *now!*"

Then suddenly all the anger that had been building up broke to the surface and whatever confusion and fear Elizabeth had felt was gone. "Bring her back and do it now? Who do you think you are?"

"I'm Mary's parent, and you took her without my permission!"

"You're *not* Mary's parent!" Elizabeth yelled. "You don't give a *shit* about her and you know it!"

There was a pause on the line. Then Diana's voice started breaking down into sobs. "How can you *say that?*"

That stopped Elizabeth. It sounded like Diana was crying. *Maybe I'm wrong,* she thought. *Maybe she isn't the monster I think she is, maybe they're not the things Mary is making them out to be.* Elizabeth could hear her mother in the background talking calmly to Diana. She heard Diana's voice as she tried to hold back her tears, and then she felt her resolve crumble. *My God, I screwed up. I kidnapped my niece and—*

Through sniffles, Elizabeth heard Diana tell her mother, "I'll be okay. Why don't you go out and tell Jerry and Rick that we found her."

"All right, honey," Laura said. There was the sound of Mom's footsteps retreating.

"Diana," Elizabeth said, feeling a sudden sense of shame at having caused so much anguish. "I'm sorry. I didn't know . . . we . . . we just forgot something at the house and Mary wanted to come along and—"

"Bring her back now, or I'll castrate your son and stuff his cock up your ass." The sudden emotion, the breakdown and tears that had been in Diana's voice a moment before were now gone. In its place was pure evil.

Elizabeth's voice froze. An icy grip throttled her. "What did you say?"

"Did I stutter? Are you as deaf as Cindy was?"

At the mention of Cindy, Elizabeth felt cold. She tightened her grip on the receiver. "I'm not bringing Mary back."

"You will," Diana said, her voice a low purr that was both seductive and cunningly evil. "You'll bring her back now or—"

"Or what?" Elizabeth said, her voice rising, panicking now, the fear still there but helping to spike the anger that had momentarily retreated. "What the hell can you do? You aren't Mary's legal guardian. You have no legal claim to her, so fuck you!"

And then she slammed the phone down.

She stood at the kitchen counter, hand still on the receiver, her heart pounding. She felt dizzy.

Diana's voice . . . it had still been her, had still had that smoky tone of cigarettes and booze, but it had changed as soon as her mother left the room. It had changed into something unnatural, something un-human.

Bring her back now or I'll castrate your son and stuff his cock up your ass.

And Cindy . . . what did she mean by Cindy being deaf? As if she had made a similar threat to Cindy.

The hairs on Elizabeth's arms stood up on end as it hit her: *Cindy hadn't been intoxicated when she broke into Ronnie and Diana's house. Yes, she had broken into the house and tried to kill Diana but . . . maybe it's true that Diana threatened Mary.*

And knowing Cindy, she wouldn't have taken that lying down. She would have been driven to do something about it.

But she would have called the police. Surely she would have told Ronnie—

Well, maybe Ronnie wouldn't have listened. In fact, it was more likely Ronnie had rebuffed her. And with Cindy's criminal record and her reputation as a drinker and brawler, any reports to the police would have fallen on deaf ears. Mom hadn't thought Cindy was serious when she told Elizabeth about the harassment incidents prior to Cindy's death. *And who would have back then?* Elizabeth thought. *Cindy was a drunk, a fuckup. And Diana is the kind of person who would have taken advantage of that.*

Elizabeth stood at the kitchen, her heart trip-hammering in her chest.

The intensity in Diana's voice reverberated in her mind.

The guttural tone—

—*the evil.*

Elizabeth rushed upstairs, not knowing what they were going to do, but knowing they had to get moving, get a plan in action, and do it fast.

CHAPTER FIFTEEN

They argued about what to do. Elizabeth wanted to pack some things and go somewhere, anywhere, as long as it was far away from Lancaster County, and she wanted to take Mary with her. Gregg was the voice of reason; it was clear he believed her, and she told him everything down the hall in her office while the kids waited for them in their bedroom. His eyes grew wide when she related what Diana told her she would do to their son, and if it wasn't for that, he might not have been totally won over to her corner. As it was, he still tried to play devil's advocate in the situation, suggesting the possibility they would be arrested and charged with kidnapping. Still, she pressed the issue with Gregg. "Diana is not Mary's legal guardian," she reiterated. "If they want to get her, they'll have to come here with Ronnie. In fact, I insist that Ronnie come get her. After what happened yesterday, I want to see him."

Gregg stared out the window that overlooked Elm Street. Elizabeth was sitting in her chair, back turned to the blank computer screen. Gregg turned around. "She's probably on her way over here."

"You're probably right."

"Let's get in the car and go to his house."

Elizabeth felt the fear twist in her stomach. "And do what?"

"For one, if Diana and your mother are heading over here, and I think they or the cops will be soon, we'll avoid them for awhile. It'll buy us some time. Two, if we head to Ronnie's house, we can see for ourselves what the situation is, and we might be able to talk some sense into him."

"Buy some time?"

"If Diana left your mom's house to come over, she'll be here in five or ten minutes," Gregg said, leaning against the windowsill. "It'll take us thirty minutes or so to get to Ronnie's. Diana isn't going to know how to get to our place unless your mother is with her, and your mom knows the back roads. We can bypass them by taking 222 and getting off in Denver and heading toward Adamstown. By the time Diana and your mom get back to the house, we'll be at your brother's. Worst-case scenario is even if Diana calls the police, they can't do anything to us because Mary is your niece and she *did* come with us willingly and we brought her back to her father. Cops won't want to get involved in a domestic situation anyway."

"I don't know if I feel good about leaving Mary with Ronnie," Elizabeth said, worried.

"I don't either, but we can at least see what the situation is at the house before making that decision."

"What if Ronnie isn't there? What if we can't find him?"

"Why wouldn't he be there?"

Because maybe he isn't Ronnie anymore is what she wanted to answer. The more she thought about it, the more her imagination started to run away with her, and when she took Mary's account into the situation it sounded like a horror movie. Like Diana was some kind of vampire or succubus, draining the life out of everyone around her. Instead of answering, she shook her head. "I don't know . . . I'm just scared about what we might find."

"So am I. But we'll have the cell phone with us. At the first sign of anything dangerous or weird happening, we get the hell out of there and call the cops."

Elizabeth looked down the hall toward the bedroom. "I'm so worried for her."

"I know," Gregg whispered. He approached her and touched her shoulders. "So am I."

The clock was ticking. They had to get moving, had to do something. Elizabeth nodded and stood up. "Let's do it."

When they pulled up in front of Ronnie's house twenty-five minutes later, Elizabeth was struck by how barren it looked.

The one-story brick ranch had been built on the corner of a quiet cul-de-sac, a new development of homes that were mostly finished. Another development a few blocks over had been completed a few years before, and the lot behind Ronnie's had been bought and a new house was to be erected there next spring. The neighborhood was well-populated and full of activity, but Ronnie's house looked like one from a movie: alone on a barren Midwestern field, desolate, secluded from civilization. Elizabeth looked out the passenger window at the house as they pulled up to the curb, and she shuddered as she noted the yellowing lawn, the drab appearance. The garage door was closed and the curtains were drawn shut, giving the appearance that nobody was home. Ronnie's black Ford Explorer was in the driveway. He was there, at least.

From the backseat, Mary started crying.

Gregg turned off the ignition and looked at the house, then at Elizabeth. "You want to go up?"

Elizabeth nodded and swallowed. She had thought about it on the drive over, knew Gregg had mulled it over as well, and having her walk up to the house and knock on the door, gain entrance into the house and talk to Ronnie was probably the best course of action. Of course she would hightail it back at the first sign of any weird shit. If she could see Ronnie, assess the situation, talk to him openly about what was going on, she'd have a firm grip on which to base her next decision.

And if he seems fine, if he's just tired from all the over-work and stress, then what? Do I just hand Mary over to him, knowing what I know about Diana?

What exactly do *I know about Diana?*

And for that matter, what does Ronnie know about Diana?

It was time to find out.

"I'll be fine," she said as she opened the door and stepped out.

She headed up the walkway to the front door. Pausing for a moment, she glanced back at the car and rang the doorbell.

Waited.

She rang the doorbell again, then leaned forward and tried to listen for any sounds emanating from within.

Nothing.

She frowned. No, there wasn't exactly silence. She definitely sensed a presence, but it wasn't anything she could discern. It wasn't as if somebody were lying in wait on the other side of the door. The feeling was almost like—

Like that of an animal—or some*thing*—waiting for her to come in.

She thought of Himmler sitting in the dark house calmly as she stood outside. And while the image would normally be threatening, ominous, it didn't scare her.

But something else did scare her, though. It was the thought, the feeling, that the presence she felt waiting on the other side of the door wasn't Himmler at all, but something else.

She whirled toward the car, momentarily panicked. Then Gregg held up his hand, holding something. She realized it was the cell phone and she ran to the car, wanting to get away from the house, feeling she was being watched, and as she stepped into the car Gregg asked, "What happened?"

"Nothing. He didn't answer," Elizabeth said. "But something's there. I can feel it."

"Something?"

"It's that *thing!*" Mary cried. She was huddled against Eric, who had his arm protectively around her, his face worried. "That thing's in there, and it's got my daddy!"

"His car's parked in the driveway," Gregg said, licking his lips nervously. "Call him." He held the cell phone out to Elizabeth.

Elizabeth took the phone and hit the speed dial button for Ronnie. The phone rang once, twice, three times, then—

"Hello?" The voice on the other end was groggy, weak, and slightly raspy.

"Ronnie?"

"Hello?"

"Ronnie, it's Elizabeth. Are you okay?"

"Elizabeth?" She could tell it was Ronnie now, but he sounded weak, disoriented. "Where are you? What's—"

"I'm in front of your house. Are you okay? I rang the doorbell a few times, but nobody answered."

"Feel horrible."

"You feel horrible?"

"Yeah." His voice was weak, raspy.

"Do you feel sick?"

"Yeah. Tired . . ."

"Where are you?"

"In bed."

"Can you walk?"

"Yeah." There was muffled coughing on the other end, and then he came back on the line, still sounding weak. "Hold on."

Elizabeth glanced at Gregg, the earlier paranoia she had felt about Diana draining the life out of him now dissipating. Ronnie was sick, and judging from his condition a few weeks ago and yesterday, he was deteriorating. He probably had fallen off the wagon, was using drugs, maybe cocaine, maybe heroin. He was doing something, had to have been doing something to get him through the stress of working all those double shifts every day with no days off, dealing with Diana not working and doing nothing in the house, dealing with her lazy kids, not being able to see his daughter, then dealing with Cindy's incompetence and addictions. Elizabeth actually wished her brother *had* fallen off the wagon and slid back into drug use. It would be better for him if that were the case rather than what her paranoid, fantasy-addled imagination had dreamed up. "Ronnie, you okay?"

"You outside? I'll unlock the door."

"Okay." She looked at Gregg, feeling the tension shift. "He's going to unlock the door. I'm going to see what the situation is."

Gregg nodded. "Does he sound like he's been using?"

"Yeah. I hope that's the case." She stepped out of the car, handed the phone back to Gregg and headed back to the house.

When she reached the front door she heard the lock disengage. She pushed the door open, letting light into the room. At first she didn't see Ronnie because it was so dark inside, but as she took a step inside the first thing that struck her was the closed-in, musty smell of the house. It felt like the place had been closed off for a few months. She held her breath, then stepped into the living room.

A couch flanked the right side of the living room, and there was an easy chair beside it, in the far right corner. The entertainment center sat opposite the sofa, and beyond the living room the dining room and kitchen lay in darkness. She could make out the odor of rotting food and garbage, the lumps of trash stacked up on the kitchen counter and the dining room table amid piles of clothes. The brightness that had been evident when Ronnie and Diana first moved in—the decorative furnishings, the toys that lay in the living room, the pictures—had been stripped away so the house was devoid of life and essence. There was no longer any sense of warmth or personality in the house. Elizabeth had been in homes that were hardly cleaned, that were perpetually sloppy due to laziness or lack of time for proper house cleaning, but there had always been a ray of life within those dwellings. Ronnie and Diana's house was missing such life. Elizabeth gritted her teeth, disgusted by how fast the house had gone downhill and the sloppy living conditions they had allowed the children to live in, and then she saw Ronnie.

Ronnie lay slumped on the sofa. It was hard to get a good look at him in the dark. His body odor hit her the moment she crossed the threshold and she blanched. "Ronnie," she whispered, bearing the stench and striding forward. He was slumped on the sofa, and at first she thought he was wearing white sweat pants and a white long-sleeved t-shirt stained with colored splotches; that's how pale his skin was. The tattoos only made the whiteness of his skin stand out more. When she got a closer look and her eyes adjusted to the darkness, her heart lodged in her throat and she almost screamed.

Ronnie lay naked on the sofa, breathing fast and heavy. His eyes were riveted on the ceiling. While yesterday he had looked even more cadaverous than he had at Cindy's wake, seeing him nude only reinforced that. He had shrunk to a shriveled wraithlike *thing*. His hair had started to fall out, revealing bits of mottled scalp. His skin had become baggy, wrinkled where the fat and muscle had shrunk. His cheekbones and chin were more pronounced, his eyes sunken, haunted. His arms and legs were sticks covered with folds of cracked skin; his stomach had grown slightly sunken in, his ribcage had become very prominent, his hands brittle sticks.

And they were moving.

At first Elizabeth couldn't get her mind around it. She had been on the verge of telling him she was calling 911, he had to get into a hospital, and then she had been distracted by the fluid rhythmic motion his right hand was making over his groin and his frenzied breathing. Drool ran down his chin amid his raspy breathing. It wasn't until she realized with shocking clarity what he was doing that she pieced together what he was saying.

"I just need her, I need Diana, I need her to come home, I need her, I need her, I need her, I need to fuck her, I need to fuck her, I just have to fuck her now, *now, now, now, NOW!*"

Ronnie was masturbating.

She turned away in shock and embarrassment, but not before getting a brief glimpse of his withered stalk of a penis, red, raw and bloody from overuse. Despite Ronnie's obvious deterioration, he was fully erect.

Elizabeth forced herself to stay calm despite the rising sickness she felt. "Ronnie, you need help."

"I just need Diana to come home," Ronnie said, between gasps. "Where is she, why isn't she here?"

"Ronnie," Elizabeth said, not knowing what to do. She was confused, scared for her brother, afraid for Mary and at a loss. "Ronnie, I'm here to help you. Gregg and the kids are here, we're going to take you to the hospital, you'll be okay, you'll—"

Ronnie shook his head, still stroking himself. "I just need Diana, I need Diana, I need Diana . . ."

He repeated this litany, and Elizabeth realized her brother had gone off the deep end. Whether drugs had caused his mind to snap or what, he was beyond help, beyond having any sense talked into him. Swallowing her pride and the disgust she felt, she was about to reach down and attempt to scoop him out of the couch when she felt the presence of something watching her from the master bedroom.

Himmler's red eyes glowered and Elizabeth felt her heart leap in her chest. She had no idea how long the animal had been watching her, but it almost seemed the creature knew what she was doing and disapproved. For a moment she remained frozen, poised over the sofa and her brother, the massive canine hidden in shadows, and then she felt the paralysis slowly leave. Himmler wouldn't attack if she just backed up right now and got the hell out of the house. That was the ticket. If she left the house, she would be allowed to leave, but if she tried to help Ronnie, tried to get him off of the sofa, she knew the dog would lunge at her and she would never make it out of this house alive.

Himmler growled and took a step forward. She heard something squishy, as if it was slithering forward. Another odor erupted, something rotten and foul.

And Elizabeth knew, despite all her attempts at rationalizing everything that had happened thus far, the creature she thought was Himmler, what she thought was a normal rottweiler, was not a dog at all, but some unnatural creature.

Her temporary paralysis broke, and she bolted for the door. She flew through it, not knowing if Himmler was on her tail, not hearing Ronnie as he continued to beat off and chant that he just had to fuck Diana, and she was down the steps and running down the walkway and across the front lawn, throwing open the door to the car and diving into the front seat and she screamed, "*Drive! Get the hell out of here, just go!*" and Gregg started the car and threw it into drive, pealing away from Ronnie's house. She wasn't aware of the kids in the back screaming and crying, wasn't aware of Gregg's panicked voice as he kept asking her "What happened? Is he all right? Did he hurt you? What happened?" She wasn't aware of any of this until later; the first thing she became aware of was her own crying, which brought her to the stark reality of what they were now facing.

CHAPTER SIXTEEN

She told Gregg what she saw as he drove out of the development toward 222. Mary was crying, and Elizabeth wished the girl didn't have to hear this, but it was all coming out of her. She had to tell Gregg, had to convey to him the horror of what she had seen in that house. He had to know how bad the situation had gotten. "We've gotta call the police," he said.

Elizabeth was furious. "I can't believe that bitch let it go this far," she said.

"Who said she let anything go that far?" Gregg said, his eyes on the road. "For all we know, she encouraged it."

Elizabeth pulled out the cell phone and took a deep breath. In the backseat, Mary and Eric were crying. Elizabeth turned around, her composure under control. "Mary, honey, everything's going to be okay. I'm going to call the police and have them send an ambulance for your daddy, okay?"

If Mary heard her she gave no indication. She cried as Eric held her.

Elizabeth was just about to call 911 when she thought

about Diana and her mother. "We can't release Mary into Diana's custody," she said.

"So what are we gonna do?"

"I'm going to call 911, but no way in fucking hell is Mary going back to that house," Elizabeth said. She dialed 911, and when the operator came on Elizabeth said, "I just left my brother's house on 232 Severn Lane in Reinholds. He needs an ambulance. He's had a nervous breakdown, and I think he's going through a psychotic drug episode."

The 911 operator asked for her name and Elizabeth gave it to her. When she was finished making the call she hung up and leaned back in the seat, eyes closed, hoping the authorities made it to the house before Mom and Diana did.

When they pulled up to the house, Laura Baker was grateful to see her son's pickup truck parked in the driveway. Diana cursed under her breath and turned off the ignition. "I'll be right back," she said, and in one fluid motion was out of the car and heading toward the front door.

Which was wide open.

Laura was about to get out and follow Diana to the house, but something made her stop.

Something was watching her.

Laura remained in the front seat of Diana's Chrysler, frozen, afraid to come out. On the drive to Elizabeth and Gregg's house, Diana had ranted and raved about what a bitch Elizabeth was, about what a brat Mary had been lately, how Ronnie was going to ground her for the next six months when she got home, and Laura had nodded silently, agreeing with her. But at the same time a small voice inside her had been appalled at how Diana had blatantly slammed her granddaughter and daughter in front of her, and another part of her was disgusted with herself for not protesting. Something had kept her from doing this, though. It was some force that kept her silent and meek, that kept her in her place. And as she sat there, she'd felt ashamed for allowing herself to be manipulated like this.

Laura watched as Diana went into the house and shut the door. Laura stared at the front of the house, noticing the barren lawn, how drab and dingy the house had become in the last few months. She wondered why she hadn't paid attention to it before.

It was like an awakening. She had been spending so much time and effort trying to like Diana and her kids, trying to get Jerry to accept them, trying to get Elizabeth to give her a chance, she supposed she had gone overboard. She'd spent so much time trying to see the good in Diana that she had refused to see the negative.

Now the negative was staring her straight in the face.

Elizabeth and Gregg hadn't been at their house when they'd pulled up. Laura had followed Diana to the front door, had tried to take command of the situation when they arrived, and told her she would do the talking, but Diana was having none of it. When it was clear nobody was home, they had gone back to the car, but instead of heading back to Laura's house, they had come straight to Ronnie and Diana's.

Diana had been silent on the drive to the house.

Laura noticed with rising alarm that she was looking at a different person. It was Diana Marshfield, the woman her son had brought home five months ago, the woman with whom he had fallen in love on the Internet and had moved out from Ohio to start a new life. Physically, it was her.

But something inside her was wearing a costume, a mask with Diana's face and body on it.

And that something was ugly and foul, and although Laura couldn't actually *see* it, she could sense it.

And the thing had burned with a blinding hatred and rage over Mary's disappearance.

This is too much, Laura thought. *I'm letting my imagination get to me. I'm letting Elizabeth's feelings influence me too much. Diana is not . . . she's not as bad as she's been made out to be. She really isn't!*

Laura waited in the car, wondering now if her opinion on Diana had been wrong all along. She had tried to accept Diana and her kids as part of the family, had tried not to show favoritism between her own grandchildren and Diana's children because she didn't want them to feel they were left out. She'd wanted Diana to feel at home and welcome. And as her mind quickly retraced the last five months Diana and her kids had lived with Ronnie, she noticed some disturbing trends that hadn't been evident until now.

There was the extreme work hours Ronnie was putting himself through. Laura realized with alarming clarity that this was unlike Ronnie, who in the past had avoided overtime as much as possible. Ronnie had never been much of a worker anyway and would take every opportunity to call in sick or take a vacation. He'd gone through so many jobs in the past twenty years she'd lost count, and when he was married to Cindy he'd never put himself through so many extra hours. True, he'd gotten a little more serious about money when Mary was born, but he never worked overtime like this, even when Cindy didn't have a job. Ronnie didn't need this much overtime, even with the added expense of a mortgage and two additional kids to pay for.

The reason she felt he had to work so much overtime was because of all the expensive gifts he showered on Diana. She'd come across credit card receipts in the room he shared with Mary when they were still living at the house— one for eight thousand dollars for a matching gold bracelet and necklace studded with four-carat diamonds, the other for a two thousand-dollar custom engagement ring. Since then, Laura had seen Diana bearing more gifts from Ronnie: designer clothes, new furniture for the house, new electronic gadgets. And it was still going on as far as she could tell. She wouldn't be surprised if he was over twenty-five grand in debt because of her.

Then there was the matter of Mary being out of control lately. Normally Mary was a very amiable child, but in the past two months she had been not only sullen and withdrawn, she'd been rebellious. Diana had related the arguments they'd had. She just didn't understand why her father had to work so much, so she took it out on Diana and Lily. And then there was the matter of that episode the weekend of Cindy's death and—

Laura frowned, remembering that weekend. It had been unlike Mary to have such vivid, horrible nightmares. Until just a few minutes ago she believed Mary had made the episode up as some sort of psychological rebellion against what was going on at home, but the more Laura thought about it, the more she was beginning to believe that perhaps there was some truth to the story.

Then there was the random weirdness that had gone on in the neighborhood in the weeks following Diana's moving in. Himmler lunging at the neighbor boy being the most prominent, and then the final violent episode of Cindy meeting her untimely demise in the house on the very weekend Mary called, crying that she had seen a bloblike monster attached to her father like some sort of leech.

And as Laura remembered these incidents one thing stood out clearly: Diana and her kids seemed to thrive on the growing violence and mayhem around them. They seemed to be . . . more alive, more vital, more powerful.

When Ronnie had brought Diana and her kids to the house for the first time, Laura hadn't thought much of her. She'd thought Diana was too skinny, with frizzy hair and not much of a personality. Her kids hadn't been memorable either. They had slowly started to come around, though, and as Laura retraced the events that had occurred in the neighborhood, she tried to pinpoint their gradual physical improvement: Ronnie started working the double time, and Diana's hairstyle became nicer and the kids less sullen; more overtime for Ronnie, and Diana's thin frame began filling out; followed by even more overtime from Ronnie and a complete reversal of demeanor for Diana. It had quickly accelerated from there, especially after Cindy's death. In the past month Diana had taken center stage in the household. She was more vibrant; her hair now shimmered with life and bounce, and her body displayed a curvy, seductive figure. Laura had to admit, Diana was stunningly attractive now. The kids had become more outgoing, with Rick getting into after-school sports and becoming more verbally abusive toward Ronnie. Lily had become bolder and more aggressive, following Mary around everywhere and not leaving her alone. It seemed that even though the house Ronnie had bought was in his name, Diana and her kids ruled the roost there.

I can't believe I'm letting myself think this way, she thought, trying to rationalize it. *But no, I'm not letting my imagination run away with me. I'm suddenly seeing things from an outsider's perspective. No wonder Elizabeth's been upset about what's been happening. She's been seeing it for what it is. Diana's been taking advantage of Ronnie and Mary the entire time she and her children have been living here.*

It reminded Laura of an old movie she had watched one afternoon with the kids in the late seventies. She remembered the name of the film—*The Godsend*. In the film, a couple who had been trying to have a child met a young unwed pregnant woman. The woman was desperate; she had been kicked out of her home and had no place to live. The couple took the woman in and she gave birth to a healthy baby boy at their home. Shortly after, she disappeared, leaving the infant behind. The couple searched for the woman to no avail, and eventually adopted the baby. The baby grew up, and the older he got, the more bad luck fell on the couple until they realized the child was the cause of the bad luck. And as more unfortunate incidents occurred, the child got stronger.

Laura didn't remember how the couple managed to get away from the child's malevolent influences, but she did remember the end of the film perfectly. They were walking through a park and saw a young couple talking with a pregnant woman. As they walked by they noticed she was the same woman whom the main characters took in. She caught their gaze, recognizing them, and smiled knowingly.

Laura didn't know why she was suddenly reminded of this film, and she was trying to think of an explanation when she heard sirens approaching from within the development.

She looked in the rear-view mirror as the sirens grew louder. She glanced at the house, wondering what was taking Diana so long and where Ronnie was. Then she saw the unmistakable red swirling lights of an emergency rescue vehicle turn down the street, siren turning off in mid-whoop. A police car followed, and Laura wasn't surprised when the vehicles stopped in front of Ronnie's house.

Laura got out of the car, a feeling of dread spreading through her. A second police car approached from the other end and parked across the street. She looked toward the house and was relieved to see Diana come out, shutting the door behind her. She stepped off the porch and looked surprised as she saw the ambulance and police cars. She frowned as she approached the car. The EMTs began assembling their gear and Diana met them at the end of the driveway. "What's going on?"

Laura approached Diana, wondering what this was about. A police officer approached Diana, who stood at the end of the driveway. "We got a 911 call that there was a man suffering a psychotic drug episode here," he said.

"You're kidding," Diana said, looking confused. "There's nothing wrong, everything's fine."

Another officer approached and Laura knew Elizabeth had made the call. She wasn't going to volunteer that information, though. "Can we go in and take a look, ma'am?" The officer asked.

"Well, sure," Diana said, leading the officers to the front door. Laura watched as she unlocked the door, and she heard Diana ask the officers where the call came from. She heard one of the officers say the call came from a cell phone, confirm that the call didn't come from within the residence, and then they were stepping inside the house.

Laura could only stand outside in breathless suspense, wondering what was going on, hoping that something would happen that would make the paramedics take Ronnie to the hospital and take Diana to jail. A police officer approached her and asked if she was related to the woman who lived there and Laura told him she was her son's girlfriend. "Is that your son's truck in the driveway, ma'am?"

Laura nodded. "Yes."

The two officers who had gone into the house came out followed by Diana, who closed the front door behind her. They walked down the driveway, and one of the officers said, "Everything's fine. False alarm."

Laura felt slightly dismayed, but she also felt glad that everything was all right. She asked Diana, "What happened? Who called 911?"

"We don't know, ma'am," one of the officers said. He was young, with a military-style brush cut and rugged looks. "We'll try to put a trace on where the call came from. Calling in a false 911 report is some serious business."

"So everything's all right? Where's Ronnie?"

"He's in the living room watching TV," Diana said, shrugging her shoulders. "He's fine."

Laura looked at the officers. "Everything's fine?"

One of the officers nodded. "Everything's fine. He's watching TV. Nothing to worry about."

Diana headed back to the car. She appeared to be already dismissing the incident.

Laura climbed into the front seat quickly, still not able to believe the police weren't doing anything. The ambulance and police cars were already pulling away, and as Diana started the car Laura asked, "Diana, are you sure everything's okay?"

"Everything's fine."

"I want to see Ronnie!" The urge to see her son was suddenly overwhelming.

"Laura," Diana said, turning to her. Her features softened, her hazel eyes twinkling. Laura was suddenly struck with how radiantly beautiful Diana really was; her skin was flaw-less, her lips were a healthy red, her eyes deep and pene-trating, her hair shimmering and clean. "Ronnie's fine. Honest, he really is. He's tired and he's just hanging out a little bit. He was watching TV when we showed up, and he said he was going to take a shower and come to the house later in the afternoon for pie and ice cream."

Laura didn't know whether or not to believe her. "I'd just like to see him for a minute."

Diana sighed and Laura could tell she didn't like the di-rection this conversation was going. "Do you really think Jerry is going to be okay with Lily and Rick by himself for much longer? You know how he is just watching Lily."

Lily isn't his granddaughter, Laura thought. She knew what Diana was talking about, though. Jerry's patience with Diana's kids had been short lately.

"We should probably find out if Mary is back at the house," Diana said. She put the car in gear and headed out of the neighborhood.

"We could call," Laura said.

"What?"

"Your cell phone." It had suddenly occurred to Laura that if she could get hold of Diana's cell phone she could try calling Ronnie. "Give me your cell phone, and I'll call the house and see if Elizabeth and Mary are back."

Diana passed the cell phone wordlessly to Laura.

Laura dialed her home and waited until Jerry picked up. "It's me. Is Elizabeth back yet?"

"Not yet." Jerry sounded funny. "I'm just sitting here with the kids."

"We're on our way back. I'm going to call Elizabeth at home and on her cell and see if I can get her."

"Okay. I'm just sitting here with the kids."

There was something odd about Jerry's voice. It sounded like he was forcing himself to sound casual. "We didn't find them at Ronnie and Diana's house."

"I know, honey," Jerry said, and now Laura could clearly

detect the tinge of fear in his voice. "I'll wait here for you with the kids."

And then Laura understood what Jerry was trying to tell her, and gooseflesh erupted over her arms as Mary's voice came to her. *They never leave me alone!*

The kids were sitting with Jerry in the living room.

They weren't leaving him alone.

Knowing Jerry, he'd probably already tried to convince them to go outside and play. He'd probably gone about his normal routine of reading a book, watching the game and fiddling in the basement. And Diana's kids had probably stayed at his side the entire time.

Watching him.

"We'll be home soon," Laura said, then hung up.

They were heading toward Reamstown already and Diana was driving like a bat out of hell. "You going to try Elizabeth again?"

"Yes," Laura said, dialing the number and already knowing she wasn't going to get an answer.

Nobody picked up the phone at Elizabeth's house.

"I'm going to try her on her cell," Laura said.

She called Ronnie's house instead.

The phone rang once. Twice. Three times.

It was picked up on the fifth ring.

She barely recognized the voice on the other end as Ronnie's. He sounded like he had just run a marathon. His voice was panting, out of breath. "Diana?"

"Hello, honey," Laura said, pretending she was talking to Elizabeth. "I'm glad I got ahold of you. Is Mary still with you?"

"Diana? Where are you, why wouldn't you climb on me when you came in? I'm ready, I'm hard and ready and waiting, just waiting for your hot pussy—"

Laura held back the gasp that wanted to come out. A cold spike of fear stabbed her heart. She felt suddenly afraid for her son and knew he was in serious trouble and that Diana was aware of it and didn't care. She knew then that Diana had walked in on something horrible and was hiding it from her. But if that were the case, why didn't the police see it? Wouldn't they have done something if they had sensed something was wrong? "Wonderful," she said, forcing herself to go along with her impromptu script. "I'm sure everything will be okay."

"Please, where are you where are you where are you?" Ronnie panted. Laura could hear something in the background, something that had a rhythm, as if he were slapping himself.

"Yes, we're heading back to the house. We'll meet you there."

"The house? What house? You're still at my fucking mother's house!"

"Yes, we're heading over now. We'll be there in about ten minutes. We'll see you there."

"I want to see you with my dick in your ass!" Ronnie screamed and Laura hung up, shuddering at the sound of her son's voice, at his language. She felt embarrassed at having caught a glimpse into her son's sexual life, and she felt afraid for his mental state. He had sounded disturbed, on the verge of a mental breakdown. He needed help.

"So they're heading to the house?" Diana asked, a hint of eagerness in her voice.

"Yes," Laura said, her mind already racing at trying to come up with another story to explain Elizabeth and Mary's absence.

"Good," Diana said, her voice low and threatening. "I can't wait."

Laura remained rigid in the passenger seat of Diana's car, more frightened than she had ever been in her life.

Her son needed help. He was in grave danger. She didn't know the full extent of what had been going on at that house, but she knew that Diana was responsible.

She knew now without a doubt that Mary's story from last month had to be true. Fantastic as it was, grotesque as it sounded, Mary saw something she wasn't supposed to have seen. If Diana realized this, Laura didn't know, but she felt Mary knew Diana and her kids were not who they said they were. She also felt Ronnie was blinded by his love for Diana and had refused to see her for what she was.

All she could do now was look out the window at the flashing countryside as they sped toward the house, hoping Elizabeth was doing what she thought she was doing.

Protecting Mary.

CHAPTER SEVENTEEN

They argued about it all the way home and once there, Elizabeth ordered Eric to go into the house and pack. "Get whatever clothes you have that don't fit you," she said, following him into the house. "Mary's going to need something to wear for the next few days."

Mary and Gregg followed her into the house, and Mary darted up the stairs after Eric. Elizabeth went into the kitchen and began placing bowls on the floor next to the half-filled bowls of cat food. She reached into the cupboard and pulled out a package of cat food and began filling the bowls.

Gregg entered the kitchen. "Elizabeth," he said.

Elizabeth whirled around, trying to fight back the anger. "Don't talk to me, okay? If you're not going to get it, just shut up!"

"I'm just asking you to be reasonable!"

"And what's reasonable, Gregg? Letting Mary back into that house?"

"Kidnapping her isn't the answer, either," Gregg said, standing his ground.

"I suppose if it were Eric you wouldn't have any trouble kidnapping him, would you?"

Halfway home they'd gotten into an argument about what they were going to do with Mary. Elizabeth was adamant that she wasn't releasing Mary back into Diana's custody. Diana had Mom wrapped around her finger now, and while normally in a situation like this Mom would have gladly taken Mary, now Elizabeth wasn't so sure and she wasn't taking any chances. She was going to let the authorities and proper medical personnel handle her 911 call, and she was sure Diana was going to come up with some bullshit story to explain Ronnie's physical and psychological condition. If things worked the way they should, Social Services might intervene and take Diana's children and start an investigation; until that happened and Mom came to her senses, she was keeping Mary. She mentioned this to Gregg, who promptly disagreed. He said they should call her folks as soon as they got home. "Whatever happens, your mom should probably take Mary," he'd said. Elizabeth had countered that Diana would be forceful in trying to claim her and that's when the argument had started. The kids had listened in the backseat in silence, their faces wide and terror stricken.

"Will you at least call your mother and tell her Mary is safe with us?" Gregg said. His face was open, honest, pleading. He also looked worried. "I'm concerned for her too, Elizabeth. Really, I am. I'm also all for insisting we keep her until things are sorted out. I think once the police see Ronnie's state, Social Services will allow Mary to stay with us anyway."

Elizabeth sighed. For once Gregg was speaking reasonably. "You're right. I'll give her a call."

She picked up the phone and pushed the speed dial button for her mom's house.

Her father answered the phone.

"Hi, Dad. Is Mom there?"

"She and Diana should be back any minute." Her dad's

voice sounded different. Hollow, false. "I'm sitting here with the kids."

"Can you tell Mom that Mary is with me?"

"I will, dear. I'm just sitting here with the kids."

Mary's voice echoed in her mind. *They never leave me alone!* Christ, were Lily and Rick sitting in the living room with Dad watching him? Not letting him out of their sight? "Mom told you they were coming home?"

"Yes."

Elizabeth's heart pounded. She'd called 911 almost thirty minutes ago. Even though the development was in the sticks, the volunteer fire department—which had a para-medic van—was less than two miles away. The first unit on arrival would have shown up within a few minutes. Even if her mother arrived at Ronnie's house minutes after that, she'd still be there. So why was she on her way back to the house? "Dad, I called the police."

"Did you?" her father asked, and now Elizabeth could tell that something was *definitely* wrong. It sounded like he was being evasive, as if he didn't want somebody on his end to hear what they were talking about. "I'm glad to hear it."

"If Mom went to Ronnie's, she would have told you about the police being there," Elizabeth said, gripping the receiver tightly. "Ronnie isn't well, and I called 911. I saw him, Dad. Mom didn't say anything about the police being there?"

"No she didn't, honey."

That decided it for her. "I'll be right over." She hung up the phone.

Gregg peppered her with questions. "What's going on? What happened?"

She told him quickly as she grabbed her purse and headed for the door.

"So why are you going over there?" he asked. Gregg looked scared now as he followed her out to the car.

"Because it's time to cut through the bullshit and give Mom and Dad some tough love," Elizabeth said. They walked to the driveway, where her car was parked. With the exception of some long-haired guy pulled over in front of their house looking at a map with the engine of his car running, the neighborhood was deserted.

"Take the kids and go to that bed and breakfast we went to last summer near the Poconos. I think it was called the High Suites. Park the SUV in front of the room you take, and I'll meet you there later tonight."

Elizabeth opened the driver's seat of the car and slid inside. She started the car and rolled down the window as Gregg stood uncertainly outside.

"I won't be gone long," she said. "I'm going to Mom and Dad's and I'm going to get to the bottom of this."

"What about Mary?"

"Take her. If Diana pushes this, I'll make the police go back to Ronnie's house and see for themselves what's going on. They might not have been able to see what was really happening, especially if Diana beat them to the house. She might not have let them inside, and I did make the call anonymously. This time I'll push the issue."

For the first time since the incident started Gregg looked genuinely scared. Looking at him, Elizabeth was swept with a sudden feeling of love for him that was overpowering. Gregg looked nervous, uncertain. His voice trembled. "Be careful, honey."

"I will," she said. He leaned forward and kissed her quickly, and then she was backing down the driveway and heading out of their development toward her parents' house.

Ronnie couldn't take it anymore.

He'd stroked himself until he was raw and bloody, and he couldn't come. He needed Diana to come.

He'd awoken this morning with a raging hard-on and a need to give it to Diana, but she wasn't there. He had lain in bed listening for any sounds, but the house had been silent. He'd called out for her, but received no response.

And he'd been too tired to get out of bed and find her.

Through it all, his body and soul screamed to give themselves to her.

To fill her up. To fuck her.

He'd lain in bed, the need strong and pulsing through his veins, and he could barely stand it. Then the phone rang.

He'd hoped it was Diana and he picked up the receiver and called her name. He'd started stroking himself immediately; maybe just hearing her voice would satisfy his urges, would feed his addiction of her. All he needed was Diana, all he needed was to fuck her, and if he could just see her or hear her he'd be temporary satiated.

He hadn't recognized the voice on the other end of the line and he kept asking Diana to come home, to come home and fuck him, and then the line was dead and he continued to lay in bed, crying for her, and then the next thing he was aware of was the doorbell ringing.

What happened next was a blur. He thought his sister came in. He remembered her voice, remembered seeing a fleeting image of her, but he'd been too involved with wanting to fuck Diana. Since yesterday when the need for Diana had been so strong that he'd begged off his meeting with Elizabeth and left abruptly, and this morning, he'd been torn between succumbing fully to Diana, letting her feed his addiction of her, and making one last attempt at getting help.

But he couldn't . . . Diana's touch, her caress, her voice, her body . . . being with her was intoxicating. When he was with her it was the best high he'd ever had. And the more he had her, the better he felt. He had to have her more to maintain that feeling. He recognized this now as part of his problem—he remembered the cycle of addictive behavior from his therapy sessions when he entered rehabilitation for cocaine addiction over a decade ago. He recognized the patterns.

This was worse than any drug, though.

Now he knew how heroin addicts felt.

Ronnie cried, but he wasn't aware of it. He wished he hadn't gotten himself into this mess. He wished he hadn't met Diana, but he couldn't help it. He had been lonely—he'd always had a girlfriend; always. And when he'd broken up with Linda he had been restless. He'd had his family, he'd had Mary—whom he adored dearly—but he was lonely for that missing piece in his life. He had grown tired of the bar scene, and there was no telling when he would run into Cindy, so he had gone on the Internet, not even thinking he would meet anybody and then Diana came into his life and he thought he was so lucky to have found her.

Only he wasn't lucky. Oh, she was charming, all right. She was sexy, she was sweet, she said and did all the right things . . . she made him feel so good when they were together . . .

: . . but the more he had her, the more he had to *have* her. And the more he had her, the more he abandoned his common sense. He did everything he could to make her happy because he didn't want her to walk out on him, not now, not after she had given him a taste of her, and he realized he couldn't bear to live without her.

She'd hooked him.

And he couldn't tear himself free.

In a brief respite from his obsession with Diana, he'd called Elizabeth yesterday on his way to work. He had been thinking about it for a while, and the only way he would be able to talk to her is if he were away from the house. He could tell Elizabeth knew something was wrong, and he'd tried to formulate the right words to properly explain it, but then he'd thought about Diana and all bets were off. The urge was just so strong—he couldn't resist. It had made him physically ill just to be away from her. He had to have some kind of contact with her, even if it was just hearing her voice. He'd told himself he would call her, hear her voice, then he would redeem himself by calling

Elizabeth again that evening on the way home from work. He just needed a quick fix—

(a quick fuck)

—and then he would be fine. He would be satisfied and of his right mind, and he could think rationally and tell Elizabeth he needed help.

Instead he had driven straight home after work like a zombie and fucked Diana till he passed out.

That was the last thing he remembered until the door-bell rang.

He remembered suddenly being in the living room, sprawled on the sofa. And he *did* remember Diana, or at least he thought it was her. Maybe he'd been dreaming. He could have sworn she'd come in, and his need to fuck her had been so strong he'd ejaculated the moment she'd walked in the door. But then she'd left and he'd screamed for her to come back and he felt himself falling into an end-less sea of despair. It felt like coming off his cocaine addic-tion twelve years ago, how the constant craving had been so bad, and without having blow around to feed his crav-ing he'd been irritable and sick. This was how he felt now that Diana was being withheld from him, only it was a thousand times worse.

The next thing he remembered was the telephone ring-ing, and he had sprung at the phone again like a drowning man reaching for a life vest. He'd yelled, "Diana!" into the receiver and began begging her to come home, telling her he needed her. He'd been so wrapped up in his fantasy, was so into it, that it wasn't until the phone call ended that he realized that the voice on the other end was his mother's. It hadn't been Diana at all.

And when he realized it was his mother, he'd become enraged. He was suddenly sober with clarity, the burning need to see Diana not entirely gone—that would never go away—but still pulsing in the back of his mind. All he could think about was the last six months of bitching and carping his mother had leveled at him. Mom never had anything nice to say about Diana or her kids; in fact, she'd done everything she could to wreck their relationship. He could tell she didn't approve of Diana, that she'd talked his father and sister into not liking her. She'd always protested whenever he asked her to watch Mary and Lily, and she seemed to resent Diana's kids. She'd become selfish and never had a good thing to say to him since Diana and her kids moved in with him. She never even invited them to the house for dinner. The bitch.

What was worse was that she *knew* how much this relationship meant to him. As fucked up as things had become, he still loved Diana, and his mother knew this. He just wanted everything to turn out right. She knew how much he loved Diana, and she knew he had to work all those hours to pay for the house and the bills. She knew that it was important for him to maintain a solid family life; that Diana was to stay home and take care of the kids and the house; that he was to provide the financial means necessary for this. He wanted Mary to grow up with a mother. Cindy hadn't been much of one lately, and now Mary had not only a mother, but a new brother and sister! She was able have a stable home with a mom who wasn't fucked up every afternoon, and with a little sister to play with. Rick would be a great older brother for her in time. Sure Ronnie was working a lot now, but that wasn't going to last forever. You had to make sacrifices to get what you wanted. Mom and Dad had always bitched and complained to him about that before. In fact, that was one of the things they used to ride him about all the time, that he never worked hard and wasn't serious about the future.

Well, now he was. And now he was finally serious about the future, his life, and most importantly his child, they were doing everything they could to derail him.

Goddamn them!

When the phone rang he'd been hoping it was Diana and he'd gotten a little carried away at first, screaming that he wanted to fuck her in the ass, but he didn't even realize it was his mother until after she'd hung up on him, and then he became furious.

He'd sat on the sofa, nude and sweaty, the rage coursing through him. All he could think of was his mother and how she and his father had always fucked up everything in his life. They'd always told him what to do, what to say, how to act and how to dress. They'd never understood him, never liked any of his friends and never encouraged his natural interests or talents. In fact, his father had done everything to discourage him from pursuing a career in music when he'd developed an interest in high school. He'd wanted to go to college and be a sound engineer, but his father had said, "What the hell are you going to do with a job like that?" Just because his father had the same hum-drum boring ass fucking job for twenty-five years he'd hated with a passion didn't mean *Ronnie* had to. His mother had backed Dad up on it, though, and Ronnie had broken down and entered trade school to be a computer programmer—which he'd flunked out of. No wonder he was a fuckup. Everything he tried to do on his own, his parents had put their grubby paws on it and ruined it for him.

And now they were trying to ruin his life with Diana.

Ronnie rose to his feet, feeling a sudden surge of strength flow through him. He stomped into his bedroom, slid into sweatpants and a dirty T-shirt and rummaged in the top bureau of his dresser where he kept his Smith & Wesson 9mm. He checked the clip; it was full. He stuck the gun into the waistband of his sweatpants and grabbed the keys from the dresser and headed out the door. The cold concrete against his bare feet didn't even register as uncomfortable; he was too enraged to pay attention.

He got into his truck, started it up and backed down the driveway.

This was the last time his parents were going to meddle in his life.

He loved Diana.

He needed her.

They were not going to fuck up his life anymore.

When they got to the house, Diana led the way inside and nodded at Rick and Lily, who were sitting on the sofa in the living room across from Jerry. Laura went into the kitchen, and Diana could sense the woman was confused and growing aware of what was going on. Laura had always been easy to maintain a good solid grip on, but that hold had broken this afternoon, thanks to Mary. And Elizabeth. In fact, thanks to Ronnie's sister things were slipping away fast. Her life here with the new host was spinning rapidly out of control, and Diana felt it was time to shift gears quickly and adapt to the situation.

"Are they back yet?" Laura asked Jerry.

"Not yet," Jerry said. "They'll be home soon."

Diana didn't say anything; she just sat down at the kitchen table, her mind racing. If Elizabeth was coming with Mary, that would solve all her problems. Everything else was already set in motion, and she began to rein in her extensions. Rick and Lily, who had been sitting rigidly on the sofa across from Jerry, now sank down a little farther in their seats. Diana feigned normalcy and said, "Ronnie will be here soon and when he gets here, everything will be okay."

"I'm sure it will," Laura said. Diana could hear her putting plates in the dishwasher. "I'm glad Elizabeth is bringing Mary home. It's probably time we had a talk."

"I agree," Jerry said from his chair. "It's about time we had a family discussion. Maybe we should call Ronnie."

Diana didn't respond. There was no need to. It was almost over.

Ronnie was coming home.

She had gotten a nice long run of nourishment from Ronnie and his family, but Mary had proved to be tough, even with Lily around to siphon off her. Ronnie had proved to be essential—he was so eager to give, so satisfying in so many ways, just like the others—but his daughter was even sweeter. She was so sweet, so innocent. It was always nicer when there were two different sources to feed from; the lust of a young man or woman feeding the primal need, and the newborn innocence of the uncorrupted. Mary represented that latter part, and taking the soul and life force from the young represented a source of energy worth five adults.

Draining them slowly made their energy last that much longer.

The groundwork had been laid for Ronnie's end weeks ago and she tapped into that now, to bring it to pass. She still wanted Mary, though, and she believed she could finish her. Cindy was dead, and her family was scattered across the country; they'd barely known their granddaughter. And after today Mary would have nobody. When it was all over, it would be Diana and Mary (and her extensions Lily, Rick and Himmler; mustn't forget them). She could apply to the State Social Services Department to be Mary's foster parent. Surely they would take into consideration the fact that Diana had been like a mother to the girl for the past five months. She knew she would see Mary before she was taken by the state—that was all she would need, just to see her. She'd let her extension, Lily, do the rest, let Lily get her hooks in the little girl. One little hook, and that connection would be permanent. Soon Mary would begin to cry for Diana the way Ronnie was yearning for her now.

Now she had to play her role. She smiled, easing into it effortlessly. "I'm sure when Ronnie gets here we'll all have a nice family talk," she said.

She gave the communication to her extensions: *Perk up, not much time left.*

Lily and Rick straightened up slightly on the sofa as if they were balloons suddenly filling with air. They became more animated as the life came back into them.

The Diet Coke Diana had been drinking before she and Laura left for Elizabeth's was still on the table. She picked it up and took a sip, not noticing or caring that it had grown warm.

Laura stacked dishes in the dishwasher.

Jerry sat in his chair looking nervous, keeping his gaze turned away from her extensions and out the sliding glass window.

Diana took another sip of coke and smiled.

Soon.

Laura knew something was wrong, knew it in her bones, but she didn't know what to do. The only thing she could think to do was wait for Elizabeth to arrive. She trusted that Elizabeth would cut to the chase and confront Diana with everything. And even though Laura was bothered by a lot of things, was confused and scared by what had happened today, she couldn't articulate her feelings. She knew Elizabeth would fix it, would get right to the root of the problem. Elizabeth knew what was going on, and her patience had run out with Diana and Ronnie.

Please, Elizabeth, she thought as she rinsed dinner dishes in the sink and placed them in the dishwasher. *I know you think something's wrong, you've been bothered by Diana and her kids for weeks now and I'm just sorry I didn't listen to you sooner. I hope you get down to business when you get here, because I know if you do, it'll snap me out of my state of confusion and maybe rile me up. And once I get riled up, once I have you backing me up, I think we can get to the bottom of whatever bullshit has been going on around here.*

"So what was Ronnie up to when you went in the house with those policemen?" Laura asked, trying to sound naturally curious.

"He was just watching TV," Diana answered.

"Just watching TV?"

"Yep."

"How's he been lately?"

"Fine."

"Fine?"

"Yeah, fine."

"Has he been eating right?"

Diana gave Laura a look of annoyance. "Of *course* he's been eating right!"

Laura shrugged as she finished placing glasses in the top level of the dishwasher. "Last time I saw him, he looked like he'd lost an awful amount of weight in a short period of time. He didn't look good."

"He's fine," Diana said.

"Are you sure? You know, come to think of it, I haven't seen Ronnie since Cindy's wake. Haven't even heard from him since then, either. That's odd for Ronnie. I used to hear from him at least once a week."

"He's been working," Diana said, and Laura could feel her eyes on her smoldering with hate as she answered. "He works second shift and half of third shift at the plant. You know that."

"I know, and that's not good for him. I'm concerned for his health."

"You know," Diana said, and something about the tone of her voice made Laura stop what she was doing and look at her. Diana had straightened up in her chair; she looked more animated and bold, in control. "I think Ronnie's right. He's been complaining to me about things, you know."

"No, I don't know," Laura said, turning away from the dishwasher and facing Diana. The kitchen counter separated them and Laura glared at her, feeling the sudden anger surge through her. "I don't know anything anymore since you've moved in."

"Oh, is that how it is?" Diana said, her voice rising and there was venom in it. There was real anger in that tone of voice.

Now we're going to get into it, Laura thought, and a part of her was thrilled with this. *Let's have it, baby.* "Is that how what is?" Laura asked, feeling more bold herself and not in the mood to put up with Diana's attitude.

"Ronnie always said that you and Jerry always bossed him around," Diana said, accusatorily. "That you never approved of his life. That you're always trying to tell him what to do and how to live. And then I come along and give him happiness and what do you do? You try to get between us."

"Oh, is that right?" So this was where it was going. Laura couldn't believe she was hearing such horseshit.

"Yes, that's *right!*" Diana snapped. Her cheeks were flushed. She stood up, livid with anger. "Admit it, Laura. You don't like me and you don't like my kids. You don't like the fact that your son is seeing me, that he loves me, and you're just trying to ruin our relationship."

"Maybe I am," Laura said.

Diana's mouth opened in shock.

The sight made Laura want to burst out laughing. She couldn't believe she was hearing this, but she also knew Diana was serious. The woman was deranged. She was a mental case, and her son had gotten mixed up with her. Ronnie had always thought with the little head more than the big one, and she supposed she couldn't blame him entirely for that. He was a man, after all. But to have let Diana get away with taking advantage of him for so long was something so unlike her son, she knew she had to put her foot down at some point and stop it. His relationship with Diana was not only affecting his life and health, it was affecting Mary greatly. If he didn't see that, he was a fool. Laura was going to step in for her granddaughter's sake. If he didn't care for that, they would take it up in private, away from Diana. Ronnie was an adult and whatever he wanted to do with Diana was fine with her, so long as it didn't involve Mary. And if Diana thought she was going to interfere in her protection of Mary, then she had another thing coming.

Out of the corner of her eye, Laura noticed Lily and Rick sitting wide-eyed and nervous on the sofa. Jerry looked surprised by the argument as well. He had turned in his chair to watch the exchange and everybody seemed poised on the brink of war, as if the fight were going to get worse. Laura could feel it too, and she supposed in a way their premonition was right. It *was* going to get worse. Elizabeth was due any minute, and now that Laura had already gotten the ball rolling and was pissed off beyond belief, her daughter would be more than happy to jump in and have Diana for breakfast. *You don't fuck with us Baker women,* Laura thought, glaring at Diana. *You think I'm a tough bitch, you ain't seen nothing yet. Wait till Elizabeth gets here.*

She heard a car pull in to the driveway.

Here it comes, she thought.

"I kind of figured that," Diana said, not breaking her gaze from Laura's face. "I knew you didn't have his best interests at heart, even though I tried not to believe it."

"Honey, I think it's the other way around," Laura said.

The slam of a car door outside, feet running toward the porch.

Diana's anger had driven her toward the counter so that the two women were almost standing nose to nose on each side, yelling at each other. "I *dare* you to say that to Ronnie's face!"

"You don't have to dare me, I'll be honored."

The front door burst open. Both women turned toward the door.

Ronnie lurched into the room.

The first thing Laura could think of when she saw him was, *Oh my God, he looks awful! Christ, I can't believe Diana was keeping this from me, what in the goddamn hell is wrong with her?*

Laura only had a brief moment to register that the man swaying on unsteady feet in her living room was a crude caricature of her son. He was rail thin, with open sores along his face and pale tattooed arms. His long hair was greasy and hung limp against his shoulders; it was falling out in clumps, and his scalp revealed patches of raw skin.

His clothes were dirty, and Laura noticed his stench right away. "Ronnie," she said, all the fight draining out of her at the pitiful sight of her son.

Then she saw what Ronnie held in his right hand . . . a black gun.

He raised the gun at her and pulled the trigger.

When the bullet hit her, it felt like she had been punched in the chest. The force of the shot pushed her back into the stove, and she looked at her son dumbfounded as he staggered into the room, his eyes wild. She could hear Jerry's voice, panicked and trembling. *"What in the goddamn hell is going on here?"*

And then all hell broke loose as Ronnie continued shooting.

Ronnie's pickup was in the driveway when Elizabeth pulled up to her parents' house. She swung the car in and parked beside it, hoping Ronnie was okay. She wondered what it had taken for Ronnie to get over whatever state he'd been in when she saw him at his house, to actually get past that and drive to Mom and Dad's. Mom and Diana must have been able to get Ronnie help. That might explain why the truck was there—maybe Mom had driven it to the house. Maybe they'd taken Ronnie to the hospital or something. She turned off the ignition and saw Diana's car parked at the curb in front of the house. Nope, Diana was here. Maybe they were all inside.

With that thought in mind, Elizabeth took a deep breath, preparing herself for the big showdown, and got out of the car.

It hit her the minute she stepped in the house. It was quiet. Too quiet. She walked through the living room toward the kitchen, wondering where everybody was. Then she stumbled right into the bloodbath.

Her father lay sprawled on his side between the dining room and the family room, the left side of his skull blown open.

She screamed and turned toward the kitchen. That's when she saw her mother.

It looked like Mom had been shot multiple times. There was blood spattered against the microwave and the kitchen counter, and it was smeared all over the floor in large puddles. Mom lay propped up against the oven, her head dangling over her shoulders lifelessly.

Two shots rang out, and Elizabeth jumped and let out a scream. She whirled around just in time to see Diana fall back against the sofa in the family room, a bullet hole in her forehead. Lily and Rick lay slumped on the sofa, idiotic grins on their faces, their eyes glazed, the fronts of their shirts drenched in blood.

"Ronnie!" Elizabeth screamed.

Ronnie turned to her slowly. He still had the gun pointed at Diana and now his finger closed on the trigger, which clicked on an empty chamber.

Elizabeth dove into the living room toward the front door but slipped in a puddle of her father's blood. The fall sent her skidding along the floor.

She heard the sound of a clip being inserted into the gun just as she started to get to her feet to make another attempt at running for the front door.

"Elizabeth!" Ronnie's voice was compelling, commanding. His tone made Elizabeth hesitate for a fraction of a second. She turned around, five feet from the front door as Ronnie approached the living room.

He looked the same as he did when she saw him at the house. No, he looked *worse*. Elizabeth's stomach turned to lead and she froze. She was so scared, so petrified, that she didn't know what to do. Her brain kept telling her to get the hell out, to leave, but her body wouldn't obey the commands. It was like there was a short circuit somewhere between her feet and brain. She was just making the connections of what had happened—Ronnie coming over in his psychotic state and blowing away their parents—when a flicker of movement from the family room caught her eye.

"Ronnie," Elizabeth said, her voice trembling. *Diana or one of the kids must still be alive, oh my God—*

"Fucking bitch always got what you fucking wanted," Ronnie said. He chambered a round, pointed the gun at her, and that's when her paralysis broke. Elizabeth turned and started running toward the front door. Her life literally flashed before her eyes—she'd always read about that happening in books and had thought it was a cliché. Everything seemed to slow down and she saw Gregg, saw them getting married, remembering what it was like when they were dating and they would sneak off together to make love every chance they got because she was so in love with him, and he with her, that it was simply magic; she remembered their early days when he was a struggling actor, she a struggling writer, both of them working unsatisfying day jobs to make ends meet and working collectively on their dreams at night, and she remembered feeling pride and happiness when she first saw Gregg in *Voyeur,* which had won such accolades at Sundance, and she remembered holding her first published novel in her hands, feeling like she had truly given birth to something special; then she remembered holding Eric when he was a baby and feeling even happier, feeling so in love with this little human being, knowing it was the most special thing she and Gregg had ever created, more than her fiction, more than his playing various roles as an actor, and there were the bad times, the uncertainties, the arguments, and she felt bad that Gregg had given up his art but she didn't care, he still had the rest of his life to get back into it; they still had a chance to make things better, they loved each other, and then she was thinking how wonderful it was going to be to grow old with Gregg and watch their son grow into a man. All these things went through her mind in a fraction of a second as her legs propelled her toward the front door, and then she heard the shot and it sounded like a clap of thunder. She heard it explode behind her and then she felt a fist crash into her back, pushing her to the floor. Then time sped back up again and she was slammed into the ground hard, her face hitting the carpet and her breath went out in a *whoosh*. She tried to get up and turn over, tried to take a breath, but it hurt. She was able to turn over once and she knew she was shot, knew she was bleeding now, knew she was in trouble. But still she found the strength to rise up and begin crawling toward the door and then Ronnie shot her again.

The bullet tore through her shoulder, breaking bone. It threw her to the floor again, and this time Elizabeth cried out in pain. Then she saw them.

They had gotten up from the sofa and seemed to be floating over to the living room.

Diana, Rick and Lily . . . they were alive.

They were looking at her.

They were looking around at the carnage in the house.

They didn't seem to be bothered by their wounds. In fact, their wounds appeared to be mending themselves.

Diana was looking at Ronnie and smiling.

The kids were motionless, but they weren't dead.

They were very much alive.

And they were feeding off the violence and misery around them.

She knew this was happening as Ronnie stood over her and pointed the gun at her again. She saw how Diana's smile grew wider in anticipation, as if awaiting some tasty meal. When Ronnie shot her again, putting bullets into her abdomen and chest, she felt that Diana was somehow feeding off what was going on, that it was making her stronger. That she was saying, *Yes, Ronnie, shoot her, kill her!*

She also sensed that Diana was in total control of him. That she was *making* him do this.

Elizabeth's mind clung to this certainty as she lay on the living room floor trying to breathe, blood pouring from her wounds. She didn't feel pain—she knew it was the shock—

and maybe that was good. Not feeling the pain kept her mind clear, brought everything into focus. It confirmed everything right down to the end.

The last thing Elizabeth Weaver saw before she blacked out was Diana and her kids standing at the threshold of the living room, their grins wide and eager, feeding off the violence as Ronnie put the gun into his mouth and pulled the trigger.

PART III

'TIL DEATH DO US PART

CHAPTER EIGHTEEN

For the most part, Gregg Weaver tried not to think of the repercussions as he drove north on the Pennsylvania Turnpike heading toward the Pocono Mountains. He'd quickly packed a bag with three days' worth of clothes for himself and Elizabeth, and Eric had packed some things for himself and Mary. Then they'd thrown them into the Blazer and set off. Mary had asked if they were going away and Gregg had said yes, they were going to the mountains for the weekend but everything would be okay. At this point the kids sensed that what was happening was serious and Mary, in particular, was in danger. Despite this, Gregg noticed a sense of calmness settle on Mary's face. She appeared to relax, as if she knew everything was being taken care of. And in a way Gregg supposed things *were* being taken care of. She had found a pair of adults who not only listened to her but believed her (and a part of Gregg still wanted a rational explanation for all the weird shit he had witnessed), and probably just knowing that and being in their protective custody was enough for her to relax and finally get some rest.

This rubbed off on Eric too, and he settled in the backseat and watched the scenery flash by as they drove.

The kids might have been less anxious since this whole mess started, but Gregg was going batshit. He had to flip the cruise control on and keep the Blazer at a steady sixty-five miles per hour because he found he had a lead foot when he was nervous, and twice he was surprised to see their speed creeping up close to ninety. The turnpike was no place to be picked up speeding, so Gregg eased up and tried to keep his eyes on the road and his mind off the possible repercussions of what he and Elizabeth were in the process of doing.

They'll have a full-blown argument at the house, he thought, noting it was probably taking place right now. *They'll be a lot of yelling and screaming and Diana will probably get pissed and leave. Maybe Ronnie will show up and it'll be one big slam-down mad fight between all of them. Whatever it is, the cards will finally be laid on the table. If Ronnie doesn't get it through his thick skull today that Mary has been neglected, at least the seeds will be planted in his mind. If that's the case, I'll probably wind up driving back down again tonight if Elizabeth calls and tells me to come home. But if not, I'm guessing she's going to suggest to everybody that Mary stay with us for the weekend to keep her out of the war path. Ronnie will probably be a belligerent fool and protest, but I think Laura will see the wisdom in this and back Elizabeth up. Hell, Elizabeth will probably just tell Ronnie that if she has his daughter they could leave Diana's kids with her folks for the weekend and they could go out and party it up. He'll respond to that. Laura might not like it, but she hasn't liked a lot of things that have gone down in the past four months. One more weekend of babysitting Diana's kids for the weekend surely won't hurt her.*

This was the mantra Gregg repeated to himself on the drive up. After mulling it over for thirty minutes, he began to feel a little better. Finally, he put the radio on and turned it down low. "You guys doing okay back there?" he asked, glancing into the rear-view mirror at Eric and Mary. They looked fine; they were relaxing, looking out the window. "Anybody need a bathroom break?"

"When will we be there?" Eric asked.

"Another hour." He'd called ahead to the B&B from the cell phone and was able to secure a room, so things were set on that end. He'd left a message on Elizabeth's voice mail and told her this, leaving her the room number for when she showed up later. "Your mom will be up later tonight, so maybe when we get there we can get some supper if you're hungry."

"That sounds good," Eric said.

"Sound good to you, princess?" Gregg directed this to Mary, who glanced at him.

"Yeah." She nodded.

"Great!"

Gregg felt better having lightened the mood somewhat. The kids had something to look forward to. Now if only he could shake off this new feeling he had, the one that had settled into him suddenly, making him shiver and his skin break out in gooseflesh.

He tried not to let it show as he drove up the Pennsylvania Turnpike to the Poconos.

They reached the bed and breakfast a little after six P.M. It was much colder in the mountains, and the kids stayed in the Blazer while Gregg checked them into their room, which was on the other side of the rambling three-story structure. The B&B was large enough to accommodate a dozen guests and had seven bedrooms, each one with its own bath. There was a large and spacious den with a stone fireplace, a formal living room, a large country kitchen and a huge dining room. There was a restaurant down the road, and when Gregg returned to the car after getting the keys to the room he asked the kids if they were hungry. "I'm starved!" Mary said. Eric nodded eagerly.

"Let's get some grub then," Gregg said.

They drove to the restaurant and the kids had hamburgers and french fries, and Gregg had baked chicken, mashed potatoes and vegetables. The restaurant was cozy, with a large fire blazing in a stone hearth in the middle of the room. The floor and walls were polished oak, giving the restaurant a dark, rustic look. Twice Gregg checked his cell phone to see if Elizabeth had called and left any messages; she hadn't. "Are you going to call Mom?" Eric asked.

"Yeah, I'll give her a try." He pressed the pre-programmed speed dial button for Elizabeth's cell phone and let it ring.

It went right to voice mail.

Frowning, Gregg hung up. "She isn't answering."

Eric's eyes widened with panic, and Gregg picked up the phone again. "Let me try the house, see if she's gotten home yet." He dialed their house and when the voice-mail system picked up Gregg left a message. "Elizabeth, when you get this message give me a call on my cell. Bye."

"Try Grandma's," Mary said. She had picked up on Eric's mood and looked worried. Though both kids were tired and Mary had been through the emotional wringer today, they were wired and alert, ready for anything. Mary put her fork on the table. "Maybe they're still at Grandma's."

Gregg nodded, his thumb poised over the keypad of the cell phone. He didn't know why, but he had a bad feeling about calling his mother-in-law's house. He didn't know why, didn't know where this feeling came from, but it was strong and persistent. The minute he thought about calling them, his gut clenched; he'd felt the same way when he was a kid and had to walk home from school in the fifth grade, dreading to walk past the alley on 135th Street knowing that Andy Williams, the neighborhood bully, was always hanging around, but there was no other way home—he had to go home this way or risk being seen by his mother from their second-floor apartment, which overlooked Van Ness Boulevard as he crossed the busy intersection. She'd forbidden him to cross the busy street and had instructed him to walk home through the various back streets so he'd be safer. But routes less traveled by car always meant more kids were about, and where there were kids, there were bullies, and Andy Williams had been the toughest. Gregg had been terrified of him and—

"Dad?"

Gregg started, looking at his son. Eric swallowed, not breaking his gaze. "Call."

Gregg nodded, then started dialing.

"Mr. Weaver?"

Gregg looked up, finger poised over the Send button.

He didn't recognize the man who approached their table. In fact, he didn't remember seeing the man in the restaurant, but he was here now, standing beside their table and leaning close so he could speak in a low voice to them. The man was thin with shoulder-length blond hair and a beard. He wore thin wire-frame glasses and was dressed in stone-washed blue jeans and a gray knit sweater. His features were slender, sensitive and intelligent. The man leaned forward, ignoring the kids. "Mr. Weaver, I need to speak to you. It's extremely urgent. Can we go outside?"

"Who are you, and how do you know my name?" Gregg felt stricken with terror; he'd never seen this man before in his life. *How does he know my name?*

"It's about Diana and her kids," the man said. "Please." The man took a step back, as if he were confident this would be enough information to get Gregg to come with him.

"What do you know about them?" Gregg asked, his voice rising. He couldn't help it, couldn't control himself, and he didn't care. He could feel his emotions rising, and he was suddenly very scared for the kids and for Elizabeth.

"We can't talk here," the man said, leaning forward again to speak in a lowered tone. "I've already paid your bill. Please, take the kids and we'll talk outside."

Gregg opened his mouth, but he didn't know what to say. He looked at Eric, who seemed to tell him, *Let's go with him, he's safe.* Mary looked afraid. She had sidled up to Eric on their side of the table and was now glued to him.

Gregg took a quick glance around the restaurant, then back at the stranger who remained at their table. "What . . . how . . . ?"

"Not here," the man said, stepping back to let Gregg out of the booth. "Let's go back to your room at the High Suites."

The thought that they'd been followed didn't sit well with Gregg. It made him more scared and angry. "What the god-damn hell is going on?"

"I understand you're upset," the man said, leaning closer again so he wouldn't have to raise his voice, the tone seeming to implore Gregg not to make a scene. "When I first encountered it, I was upset too. But I've been following it across the country for the last three years, and now it's here and your family is in danger." He glanced at the kids, and Gregg understood that meant the kids were in danger. "If you continue to resist here, I will be forced to explain my-self further, and if I do that, it might upset them." He motioned ever so slightly to the kids with a tilt of his head, and Gregg understood the implications clearly. What this man had to tell him was not only true, it was going to upset the kids. He wanted to get them out of the restaurant, maybe get them back to the High Suites so he could put the kids in the room and he and the stranger could talk in private outside.

Gregg nodded, understanding what the man was getting at. The man nodded back. "Good." He stepped back and Gregg silently stood and beckoned for Eric and Mary to slide out of the booth and follow them.

They left the restaurant and the man indicated the parking lot. "My car's out there. Why don't I follow you back to your room?"

On the drive back Eric asked, "Dad, who is that guy?"

"I don't know," Gregg answered. He was nervous, scared as hell, but something told him to trust this man, whoever he was.

"I'm scared," Mary said. She was beginning to cry.

"It'll be okay," Gregg said. The words sounded false to him. "When we get to our room I'll have a talk with him. You guys will stay in the room with the door locked. Is that understood?"

The kids nodded, and while he said this to make himself feel better, it didn't.

Instead the feeling of dread he'd felt when he first started trying to reach his wife back at the restaurant was coming back stronger than ever.

CHAPTER NINETEEN

When they reached the High Suites Bed and Breakfast, the man parked in the slot next to the Blazer and got out. Gregg parked in a spot directly beneath the window of their room. He waited by his car while Gregg ushered the kids to the room. "Keep the door locked," he whispered to Eric as he let them in. "Double bolt it. You hear anything weird, you hear me yell or scream or anything, call 911. Got it?"

Eric nodded, his eyes wide, filled with tears. Gregg got the kids in the room and waited until the door shut and the locks were thrown up. Then he went back to the parking lot where the bearded long-haired man was waiting between their vehicles.

"Okay, what's going on here?" Gregg asked, surprised at the sound of his voice. He'd expected to sound afraid because what happened back at the restaurant scared the hell out of him. Instead he felt a sudden rush of anger, and he could tell it came out in his voice. "Who the hell are you, and why have you been following me?"

"I'm sorry about what happened back there," the man said, and for a moment he looked like the bearer of bad news. Something flickered across his features briefly that bordered on sorrow, then was quickly gone. "I have some bad news for you, and I want to help, and I didn't want to cause a scene back in the restaurant."

"Bad news? What bad news?" Gregg's heart raced. He felt his knees go wobbly. He had a feeling the bad news had to do with Elizabeth, that something terrible had happened. "It's about Elizabeth, isn't it? Diana's done something to her."

The man opened his mouth as if to answer, then hesitated, as if he had been in Gregg's situation before and was unsure how to proceed. "I wasn't lying when I told you I know about Diana. I know all about her, and I can help. What happened to your brother-in-law Ronnie . . . something similar happened to me three years ago."

"Is Elizabeth all right?" Gregg blurted out.

The man's face appeared to fall, as if the weight of all the bad news had finally broken it. "I'm sorry, Mr. Weaver. Your wife and . . . her family . . . they're dead. They're all dead."

The news was so sudden, yet so *wrong,* that Gregg didn't know if he had heard it right. Elizabeth dead? That was impossible! No fucking way. She was a strong woman. She was tough. She would have gotten the hell out of the house if Diana had gone bugshit. Christ, she was so pissed off at Diana she would have stopped her clock before anything could happen. How could she be dead?

"You're lying," he said, hearing his voice crack.

The man opened his mouth, then shook his head. "I'm sorry, Gregg. But it's true. Diana made Ronnie kill them."

Gregg still couldn't believe what he was hearing, but as he listened to the stranger's voice, something about his tone and demeanor convinced him the man was speaking the truth.

And then the enormity of it hit him fully, and he sank to the ground so fast, he almost fell. He caught the side of the Blazer and leaned against the vehicle, closing his eyes. He felt dizzy and empty. "No," he said, his voice strangled. "It can't be."

The stranger's voice was low. "I'm sorry."

Elizabeth couldn't be dead. She simply *couldn't* be. Gregg couldn't accept his world without her. It was too sudden, too final. Elizabeth Weaver, his wife, simply couldn't be dead.

But she was. The dread he'd felt earlier at the restaurant when he had been trying to call her on the cell phone . . . the bad feeling he'd had . . . it must be true.

"Oh my God," Gregg moaned, trying to hold the sudden grief and emotion inside him. Despite no evidence to the contrary, he knew what the stranger had just told him was the truth. "Oh my God, it just can't be."

The stranger remained silent, head bowed. The bearer of bad news.

Gregg felt a tightening in his chest. This just couldn't be *happening!* Elizabeth was supposed to meet him this evening at the High Suites. She was on her way up this very moment! She—

Gregg pulled his cell phone out and pressed the speed-dial button for his in-laws' house. It was an act of desperation; if a familiar voice answered the phone he'd know everything was okay, that the stranger was lying and he would know how to proceed from there. But if the phone simply rang or if it was picked up by a cop—

It was picked up on the third ring. "Baker residence." The man who answered was unfamiliar to him.

"Is . . ." Gregg began, the question dying in his throat. In the background he could hear voices mingling together. It sounded like men talking, and it sounded far busier than it should have.

"Can I help you?" Now the voice sounded more official.

Gregg pressed the hang-up button. The suddenness of what had happened, what the stranger had asked in that official tone, now hitting him full force.

His wife was dead.

So was her family.

Diana made Ronnie kill them. The stranger's words

echoed in his mind. *Diana made Ronnie kill them . . . made Ronnie kill them . . . made Ronnie . . .*

A part of Gregg wanted to break down and sob, wanted to pour his heart out and mourn. But he also knew he couldn't do that right now. As much as he wanted to, he couldn't mourn Elizabeth right now, but oh God how he wanted to. The hurt was coming on hard and strong and he had to get a grip, had to get a hold of himself and be strong for not only himself, but for Eric and Mary. And in doing so he had to push aside his grief and face up to the nightmare that had been thrust into his life. He had to do this because Elizabeth would have done it. Because Elizabeth *had* done it, and it had cost her her life.

Gregg looked up at the stranger, barely feeling the tears streaming down his face. "How? How do you know . . . how can this . . . ?"

"I was parked in my car down the street from Jerry and Laura's when I heard the shots," the man said, his voice still bearing a tinge of sorrow. "I followed Elizabeth from your house; I knew she was heading to her parents'. I was parked in front of your house when you two came out. I had my window rolled down and had a street map out and pretended I was lost. That's how I learned where you were going."

Gregg remembered now. The long-haired guy parked at the curb in front of their home, looking at the street map.

"So I followed Elizabeth to her parents'," the man continued. "I didn't suspect anything was wrong, but I heard the shots a moment or two after she stepped inside the house. I was hoping they weren't what I thought they were. There were several, and then I saw somebody from next door approach the house and walk up to the front door and peer in. I heard her scream and run back to her house and I knew what'd happened immediately."

Now Gregg couldn't help it. He started to cry. The harder he tried to hold it in and be strong, the harder he sobbed and the more his chest and throat hurt from the exertion of emotion.

"I feel horrible," the man said. He knelt beside Gregg and touched his shoulder gingerly; Gregg barely felt it. "I'm sorry."

Gregg cried for a moment and he finally was able to hitch his sorrow back in with a deep breath and wipe his eyes. He looked back toward the room he had rented for himself and the kids. Two silhouettes were at the window peering out. Gregg nodded toward them and waved them back. *It's okay, go on, it's okay.*

The kids retreated back into the room, away from the window, and Gregg buried his face in his hands. He didn't want the kids to see him like this. He hoped they hadn't heard him crying. If they had, he was going to be in for a rough night.

Wait a minute. . . . that was an understatement. He was *already* in for a rough night. He was in for the worst night of his life.

Gregg took a deep breath, the cold mountain air searing his lungs. He badly wanted a drink right now more than anything in the world. "I don't know what it is, but I have a very strong feeling that you're telling me the truth. And it's not just because of what you say, about knowing my name and knowing about Diana and Ronnie. It's a feeling I have. I can't explain it, but . . . the feeling I have and . . . calling Laura's house and hearing that . . . I don't know who it was—"

"The police, probably," the man murmured.

Gregg looked at the man. "What the hell is going on? Who are you, and how do you know so much?"

"I'll be glad to tell you," the stranger said, and then he held out his hand and Gregg looked at it for a moment, his mind blank at first. Then he took the stranger's hand and, with his help, rose to his feet.

They sat in Gregg's Blazer with the engine running for a while so they could get some heat. Gregg had begun to shiver the minute they climbed into the car and once he got the engine cranked, the long-haired man flipped on the heater. "Supposed to be in the high teens tonight," he said, rubbing his leather-gloved hands together. "I'm surprised you didn't feel it before."

"So am I," Gregg said, hugging himself. His mind still refused to believe that Elizabeth was gone.

"My name's Don Grant," the man said. "And . . . what I have to tell you may sound . . . well, shit, it sounds like something out of an *X-Files* episode or a Stephen King novel. But it all relates to Diana and how she ensnared Ronnie Baker so quickly."

"Ensnared," Gregg muttered, shivering, slowly warming up. "You got that right."

Don looked at him. "She moved in quick, didn't she? You've known Ronnie how long? Ten years, maybe more? He never fell for a woman this fast before, has he?"

Gregg shook his head. "He used to run around with a lot of different women. Then Cindy came along and . . . well, he settled down a little bit. They had Mary, they got themselves a nice little townhouse, and then she started fooling around with somebody."

"Gary Swanson?"

"Yeah." Gregg felt tense. "How do you know all this? I mean . . ."

Don held up a hand to stop him. "It's a long story, so I suppose I should start at the beginning. All I ask of you is one thing. Keep an open mind to what you are about to hear. Okay?"

Gregg nodded, his heart thudding in his ribcage. He didn't think it would be tough to do that. With everything that had happened in the last twenty-four hours, he didn't think it would be difficult at all.

When Don Grant began telling his story, it sounded to Gregg like a typical case of adultery.

Married professional couple lives in Los Angeles. They are married to their careers, are active in their church, but their love life begins to fizzle. Don didn't realize it was hap-

pening until he began to suspect his wife, Lisa, was having
an affair. "I don't know why I started having suspicions," he
said. "We were devoted to each other. We were very active
in our church. We were very Christian. The thought of having an extra-marital affair certainly never crossed my mind,
and in the beginning of our relationship, Lisa and I made
vows that we would be together forever. Then things just
got hectic . . . you know . . . jobs, both of us trying to finish
our degrees. We were so busy that it was hard just to
arrange a quiet evening to have dinner together. We became strangers in our own house, and I kept trying to
mend things, but every time I tried, she had something
come up in her schedule, or every time she tried to get
something going, I had something come up. We never put a
stop to what was going on in our lives. It wasn't until I . . .
well, I guess you could say I wised up . . . it wasn't until *that*
happened when I realized Lisa was having an affair."

For the first few months, it was merely suspicions. Don
tried talking to Lisa, tried getting her to cut back on her
hours at school and work, but she refused. When his suspicions became stronger, he started snooping around in her
belongings while she was absent from the apartment, or
through her purse when she was in the shower or asleep.
That was when he found the sheet of paper with Lisa's
lover's name and phone number written on it.

"I knew it wasn't the name and address of a colleague,"
Don said. "It was like some lightning bolt of knowledge
zapped me and said, *That's the guy who's fucking your wife.*
I just *knew.* And I was enraged."

He tried asking Lisa who the man was—Bruce Miller was
his name. Lisa said he was a friend from work. "But the way
she said it, the way she said he was just a 'friend' told me
there was something more going on between them than
mere friendship. She didn't even try to evade anything or
change the subject. It was like she didn't care."

Don started following Lisa, and that's when his suspicions were confirmed. "I followed her one night after work.

She was supposed to have a class at Long Beach State, but she went to his apartment instead. I watched her go up to the complex and I sat in my car the rest of the evening, just watching the apartment complex, and crying my heart out because by then I really knew. And knowing that she was betraying me, cheating on me so blatantly, tore me up."

He confronted his wife the following morning with evidence of her infidelity. "I told her I'd followed her and asked her where she had gone the night before. She said it was none of my business. As if she were daring me to ask her again, but at the same time rubbing it in my face, you know? Like, 'Yeah, I'm fucking around, but so what? What are you going to do about it?' "

Lisa continued to deny she was having an affair, but at the same time she toyed with Don. It was as if she felt no shame in cheating on her husband, that she was *glad* he knew, but wasn't going to do anything to stop the relationship or hide it from him any longer. Gregg listened, wondering how this related to Diana and Ronnie and what had happened today. Why the hell should he care that Don's wife had fucked around on him? The more Don relayed the story, the more Gregg wondered where this was leading.

"After a while she began taunting me with it," Don continued. He was looking out the windshield of the Blazer at the High Suites Bed and Breakfast in front of them. "It was like she knew that this was tearing me apart emotionally. I tried everything to keep us together. I asked for advice from my pastor, which didn't help. I asked her to go to marriage counseling, but she refused. I went into therapy myself just so I could talk to somebody about this because I couldn't talk to my friends, couldn't talk to my family. I'd have felt ashamed to do that at the time; I didn't want anybody to know we were having trouble. I felt embarrassed. So I went to a professional therapist. I needed to come to some kind of . . . some kind of grip with what was happening."

In the meantime, Lisa became more obsessed with her new lover. She quit school and began cutting down on her work hours, but the time she gained they could have spent with each other—by this time Don had quit school as well—was spent with her new lover instead. She began seeing the man openly now, no longer seeming to care she was committing adultery or that her husband was being tortured emotionally as he saw her carrying on with another man.

And the more Don was hurt, the more he became enraged.

"I began to get obsessed with Lisa," he said, glancing quickly at Gregg. "I was never the kind of man to become obsessed with a woman. I was never a violent person. *Never!* But the more I thought about her, the more I imagined her with this other guy doing the things we used to do together. Her opening up to him emotionally and sexually. I began to imagine him exploring every inch of her body, doing things even Lisa and I had never done before. Then I imagined her *liking* it and . . . it just sent me into a *rage!*"

It was then when he began to think about killing his wife.

"The guy was actually calling her at our apartment now," Don continued. "Sometimes I'd answer the phone and he wouldn't even hang up. Bastard was bold. He'd come right out and ask for Lisa, and I don't know what made me do it, but I'd hand the phone over to her like I was some puppet on a marionette's strings. It was like he was controlling me, laughing at me while I screamed inside from rage and anger over what he was doing to me . . . to *us*. And then Lisa would get on the phone and get all giggly and . . . sexy-talking the way she used to do with me when we were dating. And she'd do this right in front me! With me in the goddamned apartment! During the last week or so of our marriage, he'd come to the apartment while I was there!"

That had proven to be the last straw. Don had spent the last month of their marriage in turmoil, entertaining fantasies of killing his wife and her lover, and while he was secretly appalled by it, another part of him kept urging himself to do it. Don buried his face in his hands, his long

hair framing his shoulders as he spoke. "These thoughts I
was having were just killing me. I mean . . . I was a good
man. I'm *still* a good man. I'm a Christian, I believe in God
and Jesus Christ. Lisa and I were both believers, were both
very active in the church. We didn't think anything could
penetrate our faith and our lives, that God would protect
us. And then . . ." His voice quavered slightly. "Then *this*
happens and suddenly I'm thinking things I've never
thought before, never thought I'd have the desire to feel,
and they *scared* me! But they also spoke to me so strongly,
they were so persuasive that I couldn't resist their beckon-
ing. The more I let those voices in, the more I began to believe what they were telling me. And before I knew it I had
convinced myself that the only way to put an end to the
whole mess was to confront them, just follow Lisa to
Bruce's apartment, force my way in and kill them. But I'd
kill *him* first. I'd let her watch me shoot her lover because I
wanted to see the look on her face when I did it. Then I was
going to kill her."

So he bought a small-caliber pistol at a gun shop in
Hawthorne. He was in a fog when he did it, picking the
weapon out hurriedly, not caring what he bought, just so
long as he had a gun. The mandatory three-day waiting period he had to endure before picking up the handgun
didn't change his mind. Then after he picked the weapon
up, he simmered for two days. During that time he quit his
job suddenly, withdrew what little money he had in his personal savings account, as well as all the money in their
joint checking account. "Then I followed her to Bruce's
house one morning," he said, looking back up into Gregg's
face. "And I did it. I watched her walk into the complex and
I waited for a few minutes, and then I got out and followed
her. I got his apartment number from the mailboxes outside, went through the courtyard to his apartment and
knocked on the door. He answered the door wearing a pair
of slacks and his shirt was unbuttoned and I . . . I shot him
in the chest and he fell back into the apartment." Don swal-

lowed, and Gregg listened closer to the story, riveted now. "I shot him a few more times, and then I went into the apartment, and Lisa started screaming for Bruce. The sound of her voice just ripped my heart out. She sounded like the love of her life had just been wrenched away from her, and hearing that . . . well, part of me got a thrill out of hurting her like that. That kind of fueled me, kept me going, and I turned to her and yelled something—I don't remember what—and then when I turned back to plug another couple shells in Bruce, I saw that he was laughing at me! And he was starting to get up."

Gregg felt all the spit in his mouth run dry. "He stood up? You mean . . ."

Don nodded. His eyes looked haunted. "Yeah. He was still shot, but he was getting up. I could see the blood staining the front of his shirt. In fact, his shirt had been unbuttoned, and I could see the wound in the center of his chest. I'd shot him at close range, but the fucker was *laughing* at me. And then as I stood there in shock, the wound started to heal, and he began to change."

Mary's words danced in Gregg's head. *I saw it change, and there were different shapes in it and some of the shapes were faces, Diana's face and Lily and Rick's face and—*

And then it was a shriveled demonic-looking thing that had no sex and was as old as time. And it was laughing at Don. But that wasn't the worst of it. The worst was the look of surprise and joy that had come over Lisa's face at seeing her lover wasn't hurt. And then she had rushed forward and embraced it, hugging it, seemingly not even aware of the monstrosity she was embracing.

Then she'd kissed it square on the lips. Don had been frozen in shock and fear and a sense of sickness as their tongues danced, hers healthy and vibrant, Bruce's gray and diseased looking, probing her mouth, tasting her, sucking her in.

"I lost it then," Don continued. "I fucking lost it and bolted out of the apartment. I don't even remember making it to the car. The next thing I remember, I'm tearing down Redondo Beach Boulevard doing eighty. I got myself under control and back to the speed limit. I was entering Gardena, so I pulled off into a cul-de-sac and parked the car, and then I got the shakes so bad I felt like I was going to pass out. I didn't even think about the possibility of the cops chasing me or anything. Didn't even think somebody had called the police. I just lost it. All I could think about was Lisa kissing that . . . that *thing* that had been Bruce and she didn't *care!* It was like . . . she knew, but she didn't see it, you know? It was like he had fooled her, he had ensnared her and trapped her, and she *knew* what she was doing was wrong, *knew* he was so bad for her but she didn't care anymore because she was *addicted* to him, the way junkies know heroin is bad but they do it anyway because they can't help it; their bodies scream for the relief it gives them. That's the way it was with Lisa. And I knew right then that it was not only over, she was dead. This thing had gotten her, sucked the life out of her, reduced her to this junkie addicted to the physical pleasures it gave her. It fed off not only her need, but the emotion that came from the repercussions of our relationship. All the anger, hurt and resentment I felt when I found out about the affair . . . it *knew* this would happen and it had played Lisa right along, *knowing* it was going to get this out of me because it wanted *that*, too. And . . . and it *fed off it!*"

Gregg immediately saw the parallels between Don's story and what had happened with his brother-in-law. "Did your wife get . . . did she get sickly looking?"

"Yeah, she did," Don said, and he reached out and gripped Gregg's arm. His eyes looked wild and scared. "She'd started losing weight, lost interest in eating. She was nowhere as bad as Ronnie, though."

"You saw how Ronnie got?"

Don nodded. He released Gregg's arm and slumped back in his seat. "I didn't even think about it till later," he said. "Until after I left. And when I came across the others, when I did my research into it and read about others who had been affected, it was only then I thought back to Lisa and what it was doing to her."

"What *is* it?" Gregg asked, both horrified and enthralled now. "Is it . . . some kind of vampire?"

Don straightened up and held his left hand up to Gregg, palm outward, finger raised. "We're getting ahead of ourselves here. Let me finish. I promise I'll answer all your questions, just . . . let me finish."

Gregg nodded, settling back in his seat. He took a quick glance at the room he had booked for himself and the kids tonight and saw the two silhouettes in the window again.

"After I calmed down, I checked into a cheap motel in Torrance. I was afraid to go over to the apartment, but I finally got the courage and drove by about an hour or so later. There were no cops around." He looked at Gregg. "It was like it had never happened. I had shot a man multiple times in the middle of the morning and there were no cops, no nothing! Part of me actually wished the place was swarming with cops when I drove by, but there wasn't. That's when I knew my mind hadn't been playing tricks on me, and I suppose that's when I really knew Lisa was gone." Don took a deep breath, as if composing himself for what was to come, then let it out in a whoosh. "So I spent the next few weeks watching them.

"I had quit my job, of course, but I had some money to live off from our checking accounts," Don continued. "I hoped the cops would find me, that Lisa would call them to complain I had stolen the money out of our checking account, but that never happened. So I started following them around. Bruce was still Bruce. That thing that I had seen him turn into . . . I didn't see that. But every time I saw him I knew what I was really looking at now. I wasn't looking at a man, I was looking at an indescribable thing I had no name for. It also seemed to recognize when I was around. I always kept the car parked half a block from the apartment, far enough away so nobody would notice, but every time they came out of the building, Bruce would look up the street toward where I was parked and . . . it almost seemed like our eyes locked. Like he knew I was there and knew right where to find me. I'd look away, bend down over the dashboard to hide, but I knew it was too late. He knew I was there, but he never did anything; he never nodded or gestured toward me. But he knew . . . he *knew*."

"What about Lisa?" Gregg asked.

"Lisa didn't recognize me," Don replied. "She looked lost, glassy-eyed, like an addict. And she was an addict, in a way. She was addicted to Bruce, to this *thing*. And when I saw her that first time after bursting into that room . . . it must have been two, maybe three days later . . . she'd gone downhill fast. It looked like she'd lost twenty pounds, her clothes barely fit her, and she clung to Bruce like some street-corner hooker hanging on to a pimp. And . . . I gotta tell you, Gregg, when I saw her that first time, I couldn't control myself. I fucking broke down in the car and wept like a baby."

Gregg's mind went back to Cindy Baker's wake and how horrible Ronnie had looked that day . . . and how vibrant and alive Diana and her kids had become.

"I knew I couldn't help her," Don continued, looking out the windshield. "I knew there was nothing I could do. I tried calling her parents one night to see if they could do something, but her mother's got problems of her own and her dad—well, shit, her dad's an asshole. Always fucking working, so I couldn't count on them. I knew I would hate myself if I didn't try to do something one last time, so one day I followed them to the Del Amo Mall. I knew Bruce could sense I was there, but I didn't care. He never looked back, never gave any indication he was aware I was following them, but he didn't have to. The only way I can explain it was I felt that he knew I was there. But I was still as discreet as possible.

"I followed them around for an hour. At one point, Lisa split up from him and went to the bathroom. Bruce actually helped her to the door that led down the service hall to the restrooms. I thought he was going to wait outside for her, but instead he darted into a clothing store a few doors down. I was around the corner from the mall, near the south food court, and I looked down the mall to where Bruce had gone, but I couldn't find him. I saw an opportunity to do something, so I hurried over to the restrooms. They were at the end of a long service hallway that served several of the businesses. Bruce had escorted Lisa right to the door of the hallway, had waited till she had gone into the ladies' room, then left. This was my chance.

"I made it across the mall and dived down the hallway. When I got to the ladies' room I hesitated for a moment, wondering whether I should go inside. It turned out I didn't have to; Lisa came right out. She almost bumped into me."

Don frowned at the memory. "I was standing right in front of her, and she didn't even recognize me, didn't even say anything. I took her by the shoulders and said, 'Lisa, Lisa, it's Don, it's me honey, it's okay.' And she . . . she acted like . . . like a zombie. She didn't even react. Didn't yell, didn't try to get away. It was like she was indifferent to me. And as I looked at her I noticed two things—one, her physical condition had deteriorated rapidly, and two, I could see his hold on her and her complete dependence on him. She was completely addicted to him.

"I said her name several times, and she didn't respond. And then I noticed this aura about her just around the same time she started warming up to me. Her face, which had been slack and unresponsive, suddenly came to life. It was like . . ." Don shuddered, closing his eyes, head bowed. "God, it was awful. It was like watching a rag doll suddenly come to life. It wasn't *natural!* And she had this aura about her . . . this real strong aura of sexuality that was like being around a whore in heat. I could smell it, I was drawn to it, but I also knew instinctively she was already marked and she wouldn't respond to me even if I tried to seduce her right there. She would respond sexually to one man and one man only. Bruce Miller."

Don buried his face in his hands, and as he wrapped up the narrative his voice began to tremble and break. "I was still carrying the .22, and I had it in my pocket that afternoon and . . . Oh God, please forgive me." A sob escaped his throat. "But . . . when I saw how hopeless it was . . . how bad off she was, I just knew she wasn't going to make it. I *knew* she was a lost cause and I *knew* she was suffering. She had this need to satisfy by being with Bruce, but he was sucking the life out of her and it was *destroying* her, but she was *enjoying* it. And at the same time it was *killing* her and . . . and . . . I couldn't stand by while she *suffered* like this!" Don was crying quietly now, and Gregg held his breath, already knowing the outcome. "So I shot her. I didn't even look around to see if anybody was there, I just shot her. I shot her in the head, and she fell to the floor and . . . and I just started walking down the hall toward the exit, trying to act casual about it and . . . and even now when I think back on it, I still remember the look in her eyes when she went down." He looked at Gregg with tears in his eyes. "Whatever hold he had on her was gone and . . . it was like she was *thanking me* . . . she was *thanking* me for taking the pain away and setting her free."

Gregg didn't know what to say. Don's story was so powerful, so disturbing. He was stunned.

Don sniffled, wiped away his tears. "Some fucking husband I am, killing his wife when she needed him the most. I didn't think of that till later, when I was miles away from L.A. I was lucky to make it out of that parking lot."

"Nobody saw you?"

Don shook his head, looking back out the window. "It was like I was on auto pilot. I knew what I had to do, and my body just reacted. I shot her and just started heading out the door. It happened so fast, within seconds. The exit was maybe ten feet away. I went out the door, and I just walked out to the parking lot as calmly as can be. The gun? I stuck that in my jacket pocket before I hit the exit door. By the time I got to my car I knew I was safe. I didn't think about who might have seen me or could be watching me. I tried not to draw attention to myself. I drove away, and I don't even think the cops had shown up yet, although I'm sure by then somebody had found Lisa and was calling 911."

They were silent for a moment as Gregg thought about this. He glanced at the room again. The silhouettes remained.

"I just drove," Don said, his voice sounding tired. "I made it to the 91 freeway and headed out to Riverside, then found the 10. I went east. By nine that evening, I was on the outskirts of Phoenix, and I pulled over at a Motel 6. The next day I left, and that afternoon I stopped in El Paso, Texas."

He wrapped it up. He had ditched the car in Juarez, Mexico, trading it in for a cheap Buick. Then he drove northeast into New Mexico, settling in outside of Carlsbad. He found a little apartment and got a job working at the Caverns, a popular tourist spot located in the Carlsbad National Park. "Of course, before I did that, I went into Mexico and got some new ID." Don smoothed his hair back from his forehead. "I knew I couldn't stay in the U.S. under my own name. And Juarez was the best place for a gringo like me to get anything: new social security number, new identity. American money can go far down there."

There had been no witness to Lisa Grant's murder, which was reported all over Southern California, but her husband was being sought for questioning. Don kept on top of the story and laid low, working his job as a janitor in the Caverns; cleaning up trash dropped by awestruck tourists and bat shit off the floor of the well-worn paths that snaked their way into the immense caverns. A job like that made it easy for Don to change his appearance pretty fast. "Places like that, jobs like that, they don't care if guys grow their hair long," he said. "Long as I was doing my job, they didn't care."

A year later a very different-looking Don Grant took a week vacation and drove to Los Angeles. Only his name wasn't Don Grant anymore. It was John Lowe.

The first place he went to was the apartment complex Bruce had lived at. Bruce's name was no longer on the mailbox, but Don remembered his last name: Miller. During his week in Los Angeles, with the aid of a cellular phone, a laptop computer and a ton of determination, stealth and brawn, he tried to track down Bruce Miller by way of his last residence and got nowhere.

The landlord of the apartment complex wasn't much help—she just confirmed that Bruce had once lived there.

Neighbors were a little more helpful. One man said that Bruce just "up and moved out" one day. This man, who Don paid a visit to (he told the man he was a private detective— even showed him a fake badge he had procured especially for the trip; it worked!), indicated Bruce had been a quiet neighbor, had kept to himself, and he didn't think much of him until he was suddenly gone one weekend. "It was like he was never here," he told Don.

The few people at the complex that would speak to Don reported the same thing.

He knew better than to try to look into Lisa's death, but he did it anyway. He had done pretty well in grieving for Lisa in the year that had passed, and when he finally looked into her death from a different perspective, he began by contacting her old friend from work, Connie Washington. He was able not only to convince Connie he was a private detective, he was also able to get most of the information he needed over the phone. Good thing Lisa was attracted to stupid friends; Don had seen more raw intelligence in the eyes of frogs.

According to Connie, the police were still looking for Lisa's husband. They'd learned that Don had bought a handgun a few weeks before the shooting. Ballistics tests from the spent rounds found at the crime scene matched the weapon Don had purchased. They'd also learned that she'd been having an affair with another man. Further-more, they'd questioned this other man—Bruce Miller—and his neighbors. And while Bruce Miller denied any role in Lisa's death, a few of his neighbors swore they'd seen Don at the apartment complex one morning a week or two before his wife's murder, running out of Bruce's apartment looking terrified, holding a gun. Prior to that there had been loud yelling and arguing followed by what sounded like gunshots. Bruce later dismissed what happened as some "personal mess."

But the circumstantial evidence against Don was great, and he was officially charged with the murder of Lisa. Don had felt a brief stab of fear when Connie told him this but it quickly went away. "What about Bruce Miller?" he had asked. Connie hadn't known much about Bruce. Lisa had never talked about him much (at this, Don had silently screamed at her, *You bitch! You fucking* knew *she was fucking around!*). Don was afraid he wasn't going to learn about Bruce unless Connie let something slip.

"She told me one time he was from the Midwest," Connie had said. "Denver or somewhere near there. He was mar-ried once and had lived there. Then after the divorce he moved to L.A. That's about all she told me about him."

And that was all Don had needed to jump-start his inves-tigation.

He paid a sketch artist he met in Venice a hundred bucks to draw a likeness of Bruce Miller that he recalled from a memory. It was as good as a snapshot. He made photo-copies of the sketch and, armed with that, he went home to Carlsbad, New Mexico.

Three months later he took a long weekend and traveled to Denver, Colorado.

Nine months later he was able to find out by combing through every available source of public records and a few follow-up phone calls that Bruce Miller had, indeed, once lived in Denver.

Only he hadn't left behind a divorced wife.

He'd left behind a dead one.

Hannah Martinez had been young, vibrant and beautiful when Bruce Miller swept her off her feet one day in May of 1992. Just twenty-one, she had met him at a popular nightclub. She'd gone home with him that night, moved in with him the following week, and within a month they were married. Her parents had been surprised at the speed of their relationship. They also hadn't approved. It had been very easy for Don to convince Hannah's still grieving father that he was a private detective investigating a case involving Bruce Miller when he called him. The poor man had been a chatterbox. The more her parents expressed their disapproval of Bruce Miller, the more Hannah defied them. Bruce soon quit his job so that Hannah could support him while he "pursued other interests." When her parents asked her what these other interests were, she told them Bruce had always wanted to be an artist and needed time away from the corporate rat-race to devote to his art.

Hannah's father thought that was not only stupid and foolish, but crazy. Don related a story familiar to Gregg— Hannah had worked two jobs to support them and pay all the bills. Bruce had always wanted sex, and all Hannah did was cook, clean, do the laundry and work to support them. It drove her ragged and she started deteriorating. The more her parents protested, the less they saw of her because she was always working to pay the bills. On the few occasions Hannah's mother, Anita, was able to speak to her daughter by phone Hannah sounded like a different person. "Like a junkie," Hannah's father had told Don. Hannah's entire focus had become centered on Bruce and on making him happy.

Meanwhile, Bruce was not only indifferent to Hannah's downward spiral, he seemed to thrive on it. His physical appearance changed—the skinny man Hannah had brought home that first time had filled out into a muscular, well-groomed man who sparkled with an energy and charisma that was frightening. He had become handsome, bearing a perfect body that looked like it got plenty of time at Gold's Gym. He even became more likeable to her parents. Hannah's father began to question whether he had been wrong to condemn his daughter's new husband so openly. He questioned it right till the end when Bruce suddenly demanded a divorce from Hannah and left.

The news shattered Hannah. Before her parents realized it, Bruce had left Denver, and Hannah was an emotional wreck. They tried to get their daughter support, tried to get her to talk to them, but she wouldn't open up.

Five days after Bruce left her, she hanged herself in the condominium she'd shared with him.

"Poor man was still crying about it when he told me this," Don said, looking out the window. "To him, it was like it happened yesterday."

"I don't doubt that," Gregg said. "To lose a child like that . . . I don't ever want to have to go through something like that." He turned back toward the window and saw that the two silhouettes were gone. "Which reminds me," he said, glancing at his watch. "We've been out here for two hours, and I have a feeling we could be out here the rest of the night with all you have to tell me. I've really got to get in and make sure the kids are okay, and then I guess I should get some sleep."

"You're right," Don said, smoothing back his hair from his face. "I'm sorry I've kept you up so late."

"It's okay," Gregg said, sighing. Despite all that had happened, despite hearing the bad news and knowing it was true, he felt a strange sense of calm. "I'm glad I'm hearing this. Frankly I'm . . . well, I'm reeling from it all. I don't know what to do, and I know I need to hear more. No, I *have* to hear more."

Don looked at him. "You believe me?"

"Yeah," Gregg said, nodding. "I believe you."

A sigh of relief from Don. "Good. I was afraid that all my work, all my research, everything I had put myself through to reach you and get in touch with you, would be in vain."

"Before I go in and we call it a night, I do need to know two things," Gregg said, turning to Don. "And please be honest with me."

"I've been honest with you the whole time," Don replied.

Gregg saw no guile in those blue eyes, and he knew he could trust Don. "Did you have any idea that what happened today was going to happen?"

"I was afraid that something like it *might* happen," Don answered. "That's why when I found out where it was and who it had latched on to, I came out here as quickly as I could and tried to learn everything about Ronnie and his family."

"You keep referring to Diana as an 'it.' What are we dealing with here? A vampire? Some supernatural creature that can change shape?"

"I think it's a succubus."

"A what?"

"A succubus," Don said, hugging himself; it had grown suddenly cold in the SUV, and Gregg could see the mist rising from Don's mouth as he spoke. "Or something like a succubus."

"What's a succubus?"

"They're usually described as mythical creatures," Don began, hunched over against the cold. "The various vampire legends are thought to have evolved from the Lilith myths. Are you familiar with Jewish lore?"

"A little. Isn't Lilith supposed to be, like, Adam's first wife?"

Don nodded. "According to some versions of ancient Hebrew myth, Lilith was actually the original woman and Adam's first wife. She was described as a woman of great beauty, with long flowing black hair. Unlike the subservient Eve, Lilith demanded to be treated as her husband's equal. She especially disagreed with Adam about taking a position beneath him during intercourse, and it was this battle that led to Lilith storming out of paradise. Adam was outraged, and insisted that God make her come back. Lilith refused, and for her sins of independence, she was demonized and cast out. After that she was given a variety of names: Night Hag, Queen of the Vampires. Her most notorious role was as the queen of all succubi."

"Diana's a vampire?" Gregg said. He couldn't believe he was hearing this.

"Not a vampire. Something different. A succubus. There's a big difference."

"What's the difference?"

"After Lilith was banished, God created Eve. Lilith wasn't about to let Adam live on in bliss. Some myths suggest Lilith was the demon that tempted Eve with the apple in the Garden of Eden. It's even been suggested that she transformed Cain, influencing him to murder his brother. This drove Adam to celibacy, and he began to feel the pangs of manhood. His separation from Eve left him wide open and vulnerable to his ex-wife. Lilith came to Adam in his sleep, teasing him with horrific, erotic dreams. She took him every night, sucking the life force out of him as she carried him to sexual climax. Legions of demons were born to Lilith from these couplings, and she released these children, the lilim, upon the earth—succubi and incubi."

"Incubi?"

"The male counterpart. In fact, some myths state that they're shape-shifting creatures, that they can change their form at will. The more I read about the various myths, the more I began to form my own opinions. It took me a long time to piece everything together. I think I was fully convinced of what I was dealing with when I found records that went back to . . . well, shit, I found records that went back to 1872 or so and—"

"1872? You mean this thing has—"

"It's probably older than that," Don said, cutting Gregg off, speaking quickly. "I can show you—I brought some disks that contain pdf files of newspaper clippings and copies of official documents, all of it verifying my research. How before it was Bruce Miller it was a woman named

Heather Wilson who lived in Seattle, and then it was a woman named Tonya Williams; then it was a man named Stephen Billings, then a man named Jesse Rodriguez, then a woman named Julie Magby. The more I began to trace all this, to connect the dots, the more I began to believe, and then—"

"So you're not shitting me?" Gregg couldn't believe this. "My brother-in-law's girlfriend is really—you *really* think she's some supernatural *thing?*"

The look on Don's face was one of pure terror—he looked like a child who was suddenly told that Santa Claus doesn't exist, that the whole thing was just a fairy tale. "I thought that . . . that you were accepting this—"

"I am," Gregg said, feeling the adrenaline rush again, his mind spinning as he tried to process the impossible. "I just . . . I guess I just don't know how to take it."

"I understand," Don said slowly, more carefully. "Hearing this for the first time can be traumatic. I don't think I would have handled it very well either if I had learned all this in less than two hours."

Gregg glanced at the dashboard clock—it was now after midnight. "Listen, I believe you. I just . . . I have to think about this for a moment. I have to process it. And I have to get to the kids. They're going to have a thousand questions, and I don't know what to tell them."

"Don't tell them anything," Don said. "Don't make a hard night even harder."

Don's words made sense, but when he got into that room and had to look at his son and see Elizabeth staring back at him, he hoped he didn't break down. He sighed, closed his eyes and took a deep breath, slowly exhaling. He did this again to relieve the pressure. "Okay," he said.

"I'll get a room down the road," Don said. He opened the passenger side door of the SUV. "You have a pen, paper?"

Gregg patted his shirt and jacket pocket automatically, then reached for the compartment between the seats. He found a blue pen and a scratch pad amid change and com-

pact disks and handed them to Don. Don jotted a number
down, tore off the paper and handed it to Gregg. "My cell
phone. Give me a call tomorrow morning. We'll . . . we'll
talk more then."

"What are we going to do?" Gregg asked, putting the pen
and pad back in the compartment. He put the piece of paper with Don's cell phone number in his breast pocket. "Especially with the kids. I have to tell them something."

"Be vague," Don opened the door and leaned out. "But
don't tell them what happened today. Not now. Later . . .
yes . . . but not now."

"Wait!" Gregg called as Don turned to leave. "One more
question."

Don had the door open and his right foot planted on the
ground. The cold night air bit into the interior of the Blazer.
Gregg licked his lips and shivered. "Did you know that Elizabeth would die?"

Don shook his head. His eyes looked haunted, as if he
wished he had gotten here sooner. "No. That's why I came
here. I only found out about its new identity—Diana
Marshfield—a week ago. I've been in Pennsylvania for two
days. I was going to follow you home from your Thanksgiving dinner and tell you about Diana tonight, but . . . I was
too late." His features were sad, everything about his demeanor telling Gregg what he spoke was the truth. "I'm
sorry I didn't get here sooner. I'm really sorry."

Gregg nodded, feeling a sting at the back of his throat.
His eyes grew blurry with tears. He looked down at the
floor, willing himself not to cry. "It's okay," he said, feeling
his throat hitch. "I'll be okay. I'll call you tomorrow."

Don nodded, hesitated for a moment, then got out of the
Blazer and closed the door.

Gregg didn't watch him leave. He sat in the Blazer and
took deep breaths, trying to control his emotions. He
couldn't collapse now. He didn't know how he was going
to keep up the illusion in front of the kids that nothing was
wrong, but he had to try. He had to be strong for them.

Gregg remained in the Blazer long after Don Grant left. He banished all thoughts of what had happened from his mind. He didn't want to entertain it because to do so would be facing the concept of a life without Elizabeth. Instead, he told himself that Don was wrong, that he had just assumed that Elizabeth was injured during Ronnie's rampage. She was okay, she was fine, and the police were trying to contact him now. Elizabeth wasn't dead; she was hurt, probably in the hospital, but she wasn't dead. Don was mistaken; after all, he hadn't actually seen her get killed, he'd merely heard the gunshots. It was only speculation that everybody but Diana and her kids had been slain. Don had only reported what he'd heard and feared, which was a very human trait.

She isn't dead, she isn't dead, Gregg repeated to himself. He kept telling himself this as he sat in the Blazer, head bowed and eyes closed. He thought of all the things he and Elizabeth hadn't done together yet; their plans for retirement, settling into a large single-story ranch home they would build in the country; watching Eric grow into manhood; enjoying the grandchildren he might produce. So much left to do.

She isn't dead!

He kept telling himself this as he finally got out of the Blazer and slowly walked to the room. He felt a little better, but he was still troubled, as if somewhere deep down inside he knew that what Don Grant told him was really the truth.

The trick was not to let that truth out this evening. Just let it hide back there, thrown under the rug.

Don't even entertain the notion.

The kids were asleep on one of the two queen-sized beds in the bedroom. Gregg watched them sleep, keeping the bad thoughts at bay as he noticed Eric and Mary had gotten into their pajamas. They slept side-by-side, deep and untroubled.

Gregg undressed down to his underwear, checked the

heater and thermostat, then lay down on the second queen-sized bed. He pulled the covers over his lanky frame, noted the time: almost one A.M. The kids would wake up by seven; he was sure of it.

He spent most of the night gazing at the ceiling, fighting back the tears and sobs that threatened to carry him down a deep well of grief.

CHAPTER TWENTY

When Don Grant met them at the restaurant the following morning for breakfast, Eric and Mary glanced up as if expecting him to answer all their questions. They'd peppered Gregg with questions the minute he'd woken up, and Gregg was vague with his answers. *Yes, Mom is okay. No, I don't know what happened at the house. He says his name is Don Grant and that he knew Diana Marshfield a long time ago. No, I don't know why Mom hasn't called me, but I'm sure she's okay.* He could tell Eric sensed he was lying, and normally the boy would have confronted him with it. Mary would have, too. For some reason both children seemed to understand that there was a reason for his vagueness, that they would learn soon what was going on but that now wasn't the time for Gregg to tell him, so they fell silent. Gregg welcomed it; he'd barely gotten any sleep last night and could barely think straight.

"What's on the menu today?" Don asked, sliding into a chair.

Gregg nodded at the carafe sitting in the middle of the table. "All the coffee you can drink."

"Good," Don said, picking up the carafe and pouring a cup. "I need it."

Gregg had called Don an hour ago and told him he was taking the kids to breakfast. Don suggested that he check out of the High Suites and head back to Lancaster County with the kids. Gregg admitted he was thinking of doing that very thing. "We'll talk about it after breakfast," Don had said before they hung up.

Now in the warm comfort of a country restaurant with the smell of coffee and pancakes and scrambled eggs, the clatter of silverware and dishes amid the background murmur of other patrons conversing and waitresses taking orders, Gregg quickly introduced Don to the kids. He thought Mary would ask Don about Diana, or that Eric would ask him about his mother, but they didn't. They nodded quietly at Don and went back to looking at the table. A waitress quickly appeared and took Don's order: scrambled eggs and ham with hotcakes. She jotted it down and Don asked, "How'd you sleep?"

"Okay," Gregg lied. He took a sip of coffee.

"You guys hungry?" Don asked the kids.

They nodded. Mary looked up at him shyly. Don smiled at her.

They made small talk, skirting the subject of what they'd discussed last night. Gregg could tell Don was trying to put the kids at ease by talking about the places he'd been and people he'd met, like he was trying to portray himself as some worldly traveler. He looked the part with his long hair and neatly trimmed beard. He reminded Gregg of a slightly bookish country-rock singer; a Travis Tritt or a Johnny Van Zant, or the kind of guy who would drive an eighteen-wheeler for a living. All he lacked was the black cowboy hat.

Gregg had ordered for himself and the kids ten minutes before Don arrived. Their waitress emerged bearing their breakfast, and they dove in the minute it hit the table, providing a welcome reprieve from awkward silences.

They ate quickly, not talking much. Gregg asked for the check, which he paid, and thirty minutes later he was stowing their luggage in the back of the Blazer. Don was waiting for him at the side of the vehicle. The kids had already been buckled in the backseat. Gregg closed the door and turned to Don. He gestured toward the rear of the Blazer. "Well?" he asked, his voice low.

Don nodded. "I take it they don't know yet?"

"No."

"Good." Don was speaking in a low tone. He seemed to understand that the kids were straining to listen to what the two men were talking about. "I think the only sensible thing to do now is for you to go back home and . . . well, face the music. It's the only thing you *can* do if you don't want the cops looking for you."

Gregg nodded, stony. He was still relying on his defense mechanism that Elizabeth was still alive to keep him from breaking down.

"You okay to drive?" Don asked.

"Yeah," Gregg said. "I'm tired, but I'm okay."

"Tell you what. I'll follow you, just to make sure you make it back okay. I'd drive you back myself but . . . I have my reasons for not wanting to draw attention to myself. I haven't talked to a cop in over three years. Haven't even had a traffic violation, and I want to keep it that way. You understand?"

Gregg nodded, sighed. "Yeah."

"You sure you aren't drowsy?"

"I'm tired, but I'm not drowsy," Gregg said. "I can make the drive. I've got plenty of CDs in the car to keep me awake."

"Okay. I'll follow you back to make sure you're okay. I'll only follow you as far as your development, and then I'm getting a motel room in the area. Hang on to my phone number and call me later when you can."

"What are we going to do?" Gregg asked. They were still whispering. Gregg could see Eric craning his head around, watching them.

"The cops will want to question you," Don said. He made a slight gesture toward the SUV. "You might want to do a little prepping with the kids. Do they know anything?"

"Not about last night, but they know that Diana and her kids aren't normal."

Don's eyebrows raised in surprise. "Really? You'll have to tell me about this later. Do they know enough that you can convince them to tell the police a story other than what they've experienced?"

"Yeah," Gregg said, remembering Mary's reluctance to tell him and Elizabeth what was going on because even at the tender age of seven, she realized an adult wouldn't believe a story about the creature she'd seen in her father's bedroom. "They'll want to know where Diana and her kids are, what happened. I . . . I can hold them off on the truth for as long as I can, but—"

"For now, tell them to stick to this simple story," Don said, lowering his voice even further so that Gregg had to step closer to hear him. "It's close to the truth. Diana was neglecting Mary and her own kids, and she was neglecting Ronnie. There was disagreement between Ronnie and Diana over money, and Ronnie was running himself ragged with all the overtime. There was also friction between your in-laws and Ronnie because of this, and it all came to a head yesterday. You took the kids out of the house because you didn't want them exposed to what you were thinking was going to be a heated fight. You can also say that your mother-in-law told you to take them somewhere for the weekend. Diana might try to dispute it, but it'll be her word against yours. Elizabeth was going to meet you later, and you had no idea what happened. That's why you came down this morning, because you hadn't heard from Elizabeth all evening."

"I tried calling," Gregg said, remembering the calls he'd made. "She must have had her cell phone turned off or something. Won't they try to trace any calls I might have made?"

"Don't worry about that," Don said. "Don't even mention you made any calls. If they ask . . . tell them the truth. It's going to be best that you stick as close to the truth as possible. All you know is that Elizabeth stayed behind to help her family sort out this mess. Okay?"

Gregg nodded, feeling the lump in his throat. He took a deep breath to calm himself down. "Yeah. I can do that."

Don regarded Gregg calmly, then patted his shoulder. "You'll be fine. Let's take this one step at a time. Get home, get the kids taken care of. Make sure they're safe. Do what you have to do to take care of your family. Then call me."

Gregg nodded, then went to the driver's side of the Blazer. He hesitated a moment, then climbed in, hoping the kids didn't see the troubled look on his face.

"What's going on?" Mary and Eric asked in unison.

Gregg saw their scared faces, eyes wide as saucers. Gregg started the engine, noted that Don had gotten into his rental car. He took a deep breath. "We're going home," he said. "I'll tell you in a minute. Let's get on the road first."

"Is Mom okay?" Eric asked. He was looking at Gregg, trying to meet his father's gaze in the rear-view mirror.

Gregg refused to look his son in the eyes. He couldn't. "She's fine, son," he said, looking straight ahead as he put the Blazer in reverse. He glanced behind him to check for oncoming traffic, looking past the kids at the parking lot. "She's okay. We'll talk when we're on the road."

He caught a glimpse of Eric's face, though. It was a flicker of understanding, of acceptance that his father was keeping something from him. That he was keeping something from him because he didn't want him to cry. Eric took a deep breath and looked out the window, not looking toward the front of the Blazer as Gregg steered the vehicle carefully out of the parking lot and onto the main street, heading toward home.

CHAPTER TWENTY-ONE

They faced the nightmare the minute they returned.

It started when Gregg pulled up in front of their home and saw the police car waiting at the curb.

The dread settled in his system as he got out of the Blazer. A police officer got out of the waiting cruiser and approached him as Gregg told the kids to stay in the Blazer. He met the officer at the curb, where his nightmare was confirmed.

Somehow he held up long enough to usher the kids into the house. The officer followed him inside after radioing in that Gregg Weaver was home with the kids. Gregg asked the officer if he could have a moment alone with the kids and was granted permission. Gregg ushered them upstairs to the master bedroom, and by the time they got there both children were in tears. It was as if they already knew what Gregg was going to tell them, as if they had been silently expecting this, hoping what they were feeling wasn't true.

He let them cry, and he cried a little bit with them. He quickly gained control of his emotions and whispered to them. "We need to stick to what we talked about on the way home. Okay?"

The kids nodded. On the drive back they had listened raptly as Gregg told them that Don was here to help them get rid of Diana Marshfield and her kids—he made that up on the spot, hoping to give the kids a glimmer of hope to counteract the horror they would face later this afternoon. He'd told them that no matter what happened they weren't to tell any adult of what they'd talked about the day before, that Diana and her kids were monsters. Mary understood immediately and she nodded. Then he told them that if they were questioned, they could answer truthfully, so long as they did not reveal what Mary had confided to them yesterday afternoon. Tell them Diana was uncaring, that she didn't take care of the house or her own kids, that Ronnie was ignoring Mary. Tell them all that, but don't tell anybody about the monster part. Nobody would believe them.

The kids nodded, sniffling, Eric still crying. The kids understood; they weren't immune to the fact that adults wouldn't believe them. Gregg gripped his son's shoulders, their foreheads touching. "It's going to be okay, son. We'll get through this." The words rang false to his ears. He didn't know *how* they would get through this.

Within thirty minutes, a team of detectives were at the house, questioning the three of them downstairs in the living room. Gregg sat on the sofa with Mary and Eric on each side of him, his arms around both children. The kids were still crying, and the detectives were as gentle as possible in their questioning. Elizabeth's aunt Debbie arrived fifteen minutes later, her weathered face showing the strains of the past twenty-four hours. Debbie was Laura's younger sister, who lived in nearby Berks County. Gregg rose from the sofa and embraced Debbie. "I can't believe this has happened," Debbie said softly into Gregg's shoulder. Gregg was still stunned; he looked at the detectives over Debbie's shoulder, and they rose to their feet. A man about Gregg's age with thinning blond hair, said, "We'll be outside."

After that the floodgates opened. The house was a constant parade of Elizabeth's aunts, uncles, cousins and their children. They all streamed in slowly as the hours passed, many of them staying into the night as they traded information and grieved together. Through it all, Eric and Mary stayed at his side constantly.

Shortly after Debbie arrived at the house, Elizabeth's cousin Tracy and her husband, Keith, arrived. While Tracy kept the kids occupied in the family room, Gregg led Debbie upstairs to the guest bedroom down the hall from the other bedrooms and she told him what had happened.

According to Debbie, the police were still investigating. So far all the testimony was coming from Diana and her kids, who had survived the massacre. There was additional eyewitness testimony from the neighbors, Chuck and Susan Finlay, who heard the shots. It had been Susan who ventured outside to investigate the noise. She had discovered the bodies and ran screaming to her house to call 911. Between Diana and the Finlays, the police were able to discern the following:

Sometime between 2:30 and 3:00 P.M, on Thanksgiving Day, Ronnie Baker had driven to his parents' house armed with a loaded Smith & Wesson 9mm pistol and an extra clip. He had arrived at the house and started shooting when he walked in. He shot his mother first, in the kitchen. Then he had shot his father, who had risen from his chair in the family room. Diana and the kids had screamed, and he'd started shooting them when something made him stop. "Diana said he just froze, like he heard something," Debbie said, dabbing at her eyes with a tissue. "He was in the family room and the front door opened. He . . . he waited until Elizabeth was in the kitchen before he came out of hiding. She . . . she saw her mother lying there in the kitchen and . . ."

Ronnie had shot his sister in the back as she fled to the

front door. And while Diana admitted that she hadn't actually seen Ronnie kill his sister, she'd heard at least two additional shots. There had been another pause, then a final shot. That had been Ronnie blowing his brains out.

The only survivors were Diana Marshfield and her kids.

The sound of the shots had aroused the curiosity of Susan Finlay. She saw Elizabeth's body lying in the living room amid a puddle of blood when she ventured over to investigate, then ran to her house screaming. Two 911 calls were logged to the Reamstown Police, one from Susan, the other from inside the house itself. Diana had made that second call. When the first unit arrived, they found Diana trying to revive Elizabeth. Diana had been bleeding from a shoulder wound. And while both her children were still cowering in the corner, covered in blood, they had escaped serious injury.

Diana had been hysterical. She admitted that there had been some strain between Ronnie and his parents lately, that she had argued with them about her relationship with their son that day. The 911 call that had been made earlier requesting help at Ronnie's house was finally traced back to Elizabeth's cellular phone, and Diana was asked why Elizabeth would make such a call. Diana didn't know. All she knew was that Ronnie's parents had been putting their son under a lot of pressure to end their relationship and he must have exploded because of it. But she had no idea he would snap so violently.

"I went to the house last night after I got a call from the police," Debbie said. She and Gregg were sitting on the twin bed that flanked the north side of the guest room. Debbie had related the incident between tears and now she was relatively calm, the finality of everything large and heavy. Aside from wearing her graying hair short, she bore a strong resemblance to Laura, and had a thick Pennsylvanian Dutch accent. "I saw Diana being questioned by detectives. She was hysterical. Just hysterical."

"What about the kids?" Gregg asked.

"I didn't see them. I don't know where they were."

The police tried getting in touch with Gregg, to no avail. Elizabeth had never programmed Gregg's cell phone number into her phone—she'd had it memorized—so there had been no way to call him. There was some initial worry that Gregg was injured or that Eric and Mary were in danger, so a bulletin had gone out to the State Police with the Blazer's make and license number. Diana didn't know why Gregg was absent, and Debbie told him that the investigators wanted to speak to him about his absence. Gregg saw this opportunity as a way to explain the story he had worked up. "I think I can talk to them now," he said, taking a deep breath.

Debbie stood up with him. "Then let's go."

Holding hands, they walked downstairs to the living room.

The rest of the day was a blur. Gregg was questioned by a detective named Kurt Newsom. He told Kurt that Elizabeth had been concerned for her brother and they'd argued with Diana at the house during Thanksgiving dinner about her relationship with Ronnie. Elizabeth had asked Gregg to take Eric and Mary out of the house because Mary was getting very upset, and Laura suggested Gregg take them to a weekend retreat to give them time to play and just be children for once. Elizabeth was going to help sort things out at the house, but they had already planned to meet up at the High Suites B&B that evening. He had tried calling her several times on her cell phone and couldn't get through. Then he got worried so they drove back this morning.

Kurt didn't pepper him with questions immediately, but he did probe gently. "Why did Elizabeth make the 911 call?"

"We drove over earlier to see why Ronnie hadn't shown up because we didn't believe Diana's story that he was tired, and Elizabeth said he looked like he'd been using drugs again. She thought Diana was covering up his drug use—that's part of the reason why she and her mom started arguing with Diana."

A female detective questioned the kids in the family

room. Mary told her that her grandmother and aunt didn't like Diana, and they were arguing about it. She was afraid her daddy was sick. Eric said his grandmother had asked his dad to drive the kids to the Poconos for the weekend; he knew Grandma wanted them out of the house because she didn't want them to see the argument. The kids were teary-eyed, crying, and the female detective was gentle in her questioning. She compared notes with Detective Newsom, and then they left.

At one point during that long horrible day, Diana Marshfield showed up at the house with Lily in tow. Despite her ragged appearance, left arm in a sling from the flesh wound she had apparently received, Gregg could see the vitality flowing through her, more so than yesterday. It was as if the murders had sparked her energy. Her look of fatigue and mourning was a mask; he knew that, could tell instinctively she was faking her emotions, but gave no indication he did. Elizabeth's family members acknowledged her silently as she walked into the house and approached Gregg.

"I'm sorry," she said, her large brown eyes downcast.

"Me too," he said quickly, not looking at her.

"If I had known . . ." She began, and then looked down. "How's Mary?"

"She's fine."

She sighed. "Good." She looked around the family room. "Where is she? I'll take her home."

"She is home," Gregg said firmly, feeling a sudden wave of rage flare inside him. *How dare she come in and try to take a child that isn't hers!*

Diana turned to Gregg, looking as if she had been slapped in the face. "Excuse me?"

"She's not your daughter," Gregg said, trying to control the anger in his voice. "She never *was* your daughter. You can't take her; she's with family now."

"Family . . ." Diana's face reddened. "In case you didn't realize, Mr. Weaver, Mary's legal residence is at 232 Severn

Lane in Rienholds. Just because her father's gone doesn't mean—"

"You haven't legally adopted her," Gregg countered. "You have no claim to her. She's not your child." He wanted to add, *So get the fuck out of my house.* But he held his tongue.

"Bullshit! Ronnie and I were devoted to each other, and he was devoted to my kids like they were his own! We were a *family!*"

"Oh yeah?" Gregg said, looking up as Elizabeth's cousin and another woman walked in. He suppressed a grin. Thirty minutes before Diana showed up, the Department of Child Welfare and Social Services had arrived to talk to Mary and the family and determine temporary custody status for Mary. Tracy had kept the kids occupied in the family room basement while Gregg, Debbie, and another cousin of Elizabeth's, Brenda Wandrei, talked with the social worker. Gregg had been crossing the living room to head to the bathroom when he'd seen Diana arrive. "Well, I beg to differ," he said. "Besides, I think the decision has been taken out of your hands."

The social worker was accompanied by Debbie and Brenda. She was a short thirty-something woman with a slim build and dark hair. "So what's the verdict?" Gregg asked.

"Mary will stay with me for a few weeks," Brenda said, noticing Diana but barely acknowledging her.

"Brenda's going to take me to her house, so I can finish the verification process," the social worker explained to Gregg. "Then it's a go. Temporary custody until we can get all the proper paperwork in order and you and Debbie can do the appropriate follow-up."

Diana was listening with a look of shock. "You're taking Mary away from me?"

The social worker turned to Diana. "I understand you were Mary's father's girlfriend?"

"Yes, and Mary lived with us and my two kids," Diana

said. "My daughter looks up to Mary like a sister." She put her arm around Lily, who pouted silently. "You can't take her out of the house; you'll be breaking up the family."

"From what I've been able to determine, Mary's family is with these people," the social worker said. Her demeanor was complete business.

Diana looked like she was going to argue further, but then she held up her hands. "Fine," she sputtered, clearly frustrated. "Let Brenda have temporary custody while I get things cleared up at the house. When temporary custody's over, she's coming back home. Who do I need to speak with about this?"

The social worker's voice was polite with an icy undertone. She handed Diana a business card. "Call the 800 number on my card if you really want to pursue this. They'll help you out."

"Fine." Diana took the card and, grasping Lily's hand, whipped around quickly and headed out the door with Lily in tow.

The four watched them leave. Gregg was the first to break the silence. "I don't want Mary back in that house again." He could barely control his voice. Brenda put a comforting hand on his shoulder.

"From what you've told me, I don't either," the social worker said, her eyes on Diana as she climbed into her Chrysler and drove away. She looked at the three of them. "In all seriousness, Diana doesn't have a chance. She has no case. Ronnie lived with her for five months, and both of Mary's natural parents are dead. Her only living relatives in the state are you, and I sincerely doubt that if Diana should seek custody her case would even make it to the review board for consideration. In fact, I'm tempted to look into the way she handles her own children."

"That might be a good idea," Debbie said.

The social worker glanced at Brenda. "Shall we go?"

"Yes." Brenda slung her purse over her shoulder, and the two women left.

When Brenda came back later that day to pick up Mary, Gregg pulled her to the side. "Don't let her out of your sight," he whispered. "Don't let her talk to Diana or her kids."

"Don't worry," Brenda said. "Julie and I talked about Diana on the way to my place. There's no way she's getting Mary."

"I'm serious," Gregg said, feeling himself crumble. "Diana wants Mary, she—"

And then Debbie was there, her calm voice soothing, encouraging him to hush, just hush, they'll take care of everything, Mary was going to be safe. Gregg allowed himself to be led away by Debbie and be taken care of. It was easy to do. Elizabeth's entire family had all sprung into action, working together like a well-oiled machine. They were like disaster-recovery workers; they knew exactly what to do, when to do it, and each of them knew their place in the process and worked at it without having to be told what to do.

The following day was worse, when Gregg found himself alone in the bedroom he shared with Elizabeth. He woke up at four A.M. after having only gotten a fitful two hours of sleep. Eric was down the hall in his bedroom, and the house was silent. Gregg sat up in bed, feeling the weight of loneliness and loss crash down on him, and he wept.

The next few days were a blur of funeral arrangements, talking to more detectives and the constant parade of Elizabeth's family. Somehow they kept the reporters at bay. Elizabeth's Uncle Glenn and Aunt Grace spearheaded the funeral arrangements. Gregg went through a parade of emotions in the three days leading up to the funeral for Laura and Jerry Baker; anger, dismay, grief. He spent a lot of time away from the house at Brenda and Donald's place in Leola with Eric and Mary. He couldn't stay at his own house. The constant activity, the police presence were all weighing heavily on him, and he couldn't deal with it.

He did a lot better when he was away from the house with Eric and Mary. They needed him, and he and the rest of the adults did everything they could to tend to the children first and foremost. His employer asked no questions when Gregg called to say he was taking the rest of the year off to deal with what happened—he had vacation time and his employer had a generous benefit policy that allowed for temporary leave of absence.

Through all the planning and grieving, somebody was always with the kids talking to them, watching TV with them, playing with them, encouraging them to talk and cry and confront their feelings. For the most part it worked.

At some point during those first three days, Gregg called Don Grant late one night and gave him a quick rundown on what had happened before bursting into tears. "I'm here whenever you need to talk," Don said. "Twenty-four seven. I ain't going anywhere."

Hearing that gave Gregg some confidence, some solace that he wasn't in this by himself. True, he had Elizabeth's family. He had his own family, too; his parents and his sister and her husband had flown in from California when they'd heard about the tragedy, and Gregg insisted they stay at the house. They pitched in with the rest of Elizabeth's family in arranging the funerals and taking care of Eric and Mary. And then, before Gregg knew it, the first funeral was upon them—Jerry and Laura's, at the First Presbyterian Church in Adamstown.

Gregg kept Eric and Mary close to him as they sat in the first row of the tiny chapel, which was overflowing with people. He didn't look up to see if Diana Marshfield had shown up with her kids, although later that day Tracy reported she had. Gregg hadn't stayed at the service very long—he was helping Tracy with the final touches of Elizabeth's memorial service, which was being arranged with the help of Elizabeth's friends—Brad Campbell and some of the other local writers she had hung out with, some of whom were flying out from as far away as California to attend. Eric had wanted to help on that, too. Ronnie's service was being arranged by Debbie and her husband, Chris, who had politely but firmly rebuffed Diana's offers of help in making arrangements. "She seems like a lost confused soul, but I don't care," Debbie said to Gregg one evening at Brenda's, shortly before he left with Eric to return to the house. "I don't like her and I know that's not a very nice thing to say, especially at a time like this. And it's not my place to make judgments on the relationship she had with my nephew, but—"

"You don't need to explain yourself," Gregg said, understanding perfectly. He hugged Debbie tightly.

The night before Elizabeth's memorial service, Don Grant called. "Diana is still in the area."

"Yes," Gregg said. He looked out his bedroom window at the darkened street below. It had rained the night before, and the evening temperatures had plummeted to the teens. Already he could feel the first chill of winter in the air.

"I notice she didn't stay long at Jerry and Laura's funeral," Don said. "And I doubt she'll attend the memorial service for your wife. She *will* be at Ronnie's, though, to try to convince your family she's not the monster she really is. Your family doesn't know what she is, but they know she isn't right . . . is that correct?"

"That's correct," Gregg said, leaning back in bed. He was nursing a glass of bourbon on the rocks, which was the only thing that was helping him sleep at night. "They have been cold toward her, but they haven't excluded her entirely yet."

"She'll try the pity angle on them at Ronnie's funeral," Don said. "She'll have Rick and Lily with her. You're going to need to watch Mary closely and not let her out of your sight."

"I plan to."

"No, I mean it," Don said, and Gregg detected the seriousness in Don's tone and shivered. "I've been observing her the past few days and I was really hoping she would have left town after being rebuffed by that social worker.

But she hasn't gone away. She hardly comes out of that house. She's planning something."

"What's she going to do?" Gregg asked, feeling frightened.

"She wants Mary," Don continued. "When she got into Ronnie's life she struck gold. She was not only able to sustain herself from Ronnie's lust for her and the chaos the relationship caused, she was able to insinuate herself into Mary's life. Mary represents all that is good and pure, and to engulf that is like taking down two or three adults. It's more energy, more life. The last time she—*it*—was able to devour a child was—"

"Stop it!" Gregg said, closing his eyes, the words *devour a child* resounding in his head like a horrible refrain.

"—five, maybe six years ago." Don paused briefly. "That wasn't the first, either. It's usually difficult for it to latch itself to a single man or woman with a child of Mary's age, especially if they place their children above themselves, but Ronnie was different. He already had problems and—"

"I'm sorry," Gregg said, heart pounding. "But I can't listen to this right now."

Don stopped. "I'm sorry," he said. "I shouldn't have gone on like that."

"It's okay," Gregg said, feeling the tears spring to his eyes. "I just—"

"Tomorrow's a big day," Don said. "So is the next day. Just remember to keep Mary with you all the time."

"Do you think Diana will try to take Mary?" Gregg blurted.

"If she can get her alone, yes," Don said. He lowered his voice. "And . . . Gregg? I don't mean to be nosy, but . . . you might want to emphasize this point to Brenda. I know they live out in the country and people leave their doors and windows unlocked in the summer out there but . . ."

Gregg felt his heart freeze. "Is Mary in danger out there?"

"Brenda just needs to be careful," Don said. "More careful than she's ever been before with a child. That's all. I mean. . . . I don't mean to be nosy or anything, but—"

"I'll speak to her," Gregg said. "In fact, I'm calling her right after I get off the phone with you."

Which he did. But before he picked up the phone to call Brenda, he went to the dresser, where he had placed the bottle of Jack Daniels, and refilled his glass.

Brenda Wandrei listened to Mary's end of the conversation as she spoke with Gregg on the phone. It was late—close to eleven P.M.—and Gregg had sounded drunk when she answered the phone, but it wasn't her place to judge. He was going through a lot—they all were. And when he asked to speak to Mary, she'd readily passed the phone over to the little girl.

"Yeah, I know," Mary said, nodding solemnly. Mary was dressed in a pair of pink pajamas, but she hadn't gone to bed. They had stayed up and watched *Shrek* and were now watching the Disney Channel. Nobody could sleep.

"Uh-huh," Mary said, glancing at Brenda. "I know . . . everything's okay . . . uh-huh . . . no, I haven't seen her . . . uh-huh . . . yeah . . . well . . . um . . . yeah . . ."

Brenda heard the TV click off in the family room and she cast a glance as her husband, Donald, walked in the kitchen. He looked tired, and his thinning gray hair was tousled and uncombed. He was wearing his plaid flannel robe and the bunny slippers she had bought him ten years ago. He mouthed, "Everything okay?"

Brenda nodded, and Donald knew from her expression that it was Gregg on the phone. He motioned toward the living room and Brenda knew he and their kids were going upstairs to bed. That was fine. She would sit down here with Mary until she was finished talking with Gregg and then she would talk to him a little herself, after which she'd usher Mary upstairs. For the past four days Mary had been sleeping in her daughter Amy's room, which was right next to the master bedroom. It was a good arrangement. Brenda had been able to hear Mary last night when she had woken up from a sound sleep, the sound of a nightmare-induced scream ready to burst from her lungs. Brenda had been able to rush in and head off that scream at the pass every time.

". . . yeah . . . I know . . ." Mary said, her eyes glancing at Brenda. "You want to talk to Brenda? Okay." She handed the phone to Brenda.

"Everything okay?" Brenda asked Gregg.

Gregg didn't answer right away. She heard him take a sip of something, and this confirmed the suspicion he was drinking. "No, everything isn't okay," he said.

"What's the matter?" Brenda asked, trying to keep her voice calm. Mary was still in the kitchen, still watching her with those large, luminous eyes.

"Can you do me a favor?"

"Sure, what?"

"I know you don't lock your doors out there much but . . . can you lock them tonight? The windows too?"

"We've been doing that since the day after Thanksgiving," Brenda said, knowing where this was leading.

"I know."

"Is Mary still standing there?"

"Yep."

"Has she said anything about Diana to you?"

"Just that . . . you know."

"That she doesn't want to go back?"

"Yep."

"And that's it?"

"That's it."

"Tomorrow's going to be tough for me," Gregg said, and Brenda could hear him take another sip. She heard the faint sound of ice cubes clinking. "I may . . . I may not have my full . . . you know . . . I may not be totally aware of what's going on around me tomorrow and . . . well, I need you to really keep an eye on Mary."

"You don't have to worry," Brenda said. "Donald and I are—"

"I'm afraid Diana may try to abduct her," Gregg said. The stark accusation was so sudden, so brutal in its clarity, that

Brenda started. "I'm not shitting you, Brenda. I have every reason to believe Diana is going to try to get her. That's why I'm being such a paranoid bastard with you about locking your doors and windows. You probably think I'm completely fucking nuts—"

"No," Brenda said quickly, not wanting Mary to learn too much of what they were talking about from this end of the conversation. She gestured at Mary. *Go in the living room!* But Mary remained in the kitchen at the table, looking at Brenda as if she were trying to listen in to both ends of the conversation. "I don't think that at all."

"You're about the only person I can trust right now with Mary," Gregg said, taking another sip of his drink. "Don't let her out of your sight tomorrow. Don't let Diana or her kids near her, even if there are other people around."

"Okay."

"I mean it, Brenda. I don't want *any* of them around her."

"And I said everything will be fine! Trust me, I understand completely."

Gregg paused. "I wish we could talk more, but I don't want to freak Mary out. She's still standing there, isn't she?"

"Yes," Brenda said, not looking at Mary.

"You don't want to scare her either?"

"That's right."

"You believe me?"

"Yes."

"Okay." She heard Gregg sigh. He took another drink. "I don't think Diana would know where to find you anyway. She and Ronnie never came out to your house, did they?"

"No, they never did."

"Did Ronnie have your phone number or address?"

"I doubt it."

Another sigh. She could tell he was chilling out. "And you're locking the doors and windows. I'm . . . I'm sorry for being like this, Brenda, but . . . I'm going to feel a lot better when Diana and her kids are out of this state and away from here."

"I know. I feel the same way."

Another sigh, another sip of the drink. "Shit, it's late and I can't get to sleep," Gregg mumbled. "Listen . . . I'm sorry I bothered you."

"You aren't bothering me," Brenda said, turning to Mary and gesturing for her to go upstairs. Mary retreated to the doorway of the living room and the kitchen and stood there, waiting. "Everything will be fine," Brenda said. "Don't worry. I'll make sure things go as we talked about."

"Okay," Gregg said. "Thanks."

"Get some sleep, Gregg," Brenda said. "You want us to pick you up tomorrow morning?"

"That would be nice. Yeah, come by and get us."

"We'll be over at about nine."

"Nine it is. We'll be ready."

"Okay. Goodnight, Gregg."

"'Night."

She hung up the phone.

"Is Uncle Gregg okay?" Mary asked.

Brenda nodded. "He's okay. He's just very troubled now and very sad."

Mary still had that look on her face, as if she were afraid. "Am I safe here?"

Brenda tried not to let the unease she felt show on her face. She smiled and ruffled the child's hair. "You're fine here, kiddo."

They headed upstairs. "Is Diana going to be at Aunt Elizabeth's service tomorrow?"

"She might," Brenda said.

"I don't have to sit with them, do I?"

"No. You don't have to. I take it you don't want to."

They paused halfway up the stairs, and Mary turned around to face Brenda. She shook her head emphatically. Brenda gave her an encouraging smile and leaned forward. "Well, you don't have to. You stay with Donald and me and don't even look at them. If they try to talk to you, just ignore them."

"That won't be rude, will it?"

Brenda shook her head; not replying when you were spoken to was a lesson probably courtesy of Laura, who had mostly raised Mary. "No, it won't be rude. In fact, it may give Diana and her kids the message that you don't want to be with them and they'll go away."

Mary appeared to accept this; she nodded, her shoulders seemed to relax from the tension. "Okay," she said. She turned and headed the rest of the way upstairs.

Brenda tucked Mary in bed with Amy, who was already fast asleep. She kissed Mary's forehead. "You get some sleep. I'll be right down the hall if you need me."

"Okay. 'Night, Brenda."

"Goodnight, sweetie."

Brenda left the room, keeping the door open, and entered the bedroom she shared with Donald. After brushing her teeth in the master bathroom, she climbed into bed and stared at the ceiling for twenty minutes before sleep claimed her.

Outside the Wandrei home, Diana Marshfield ran her fingers over the glass panes of the French doors that led off to the back deck to the living room, trying to find a way in. She had been outside in the darkness, listening to what was going on inside for hours.

Her clothing obscured the shifting mass of flesh of the Lily and Rick appendages as she worked at feeding them, preparing them for their appearance tomorrow.

CHAPTER TWENTY-TWO

The following evening Don Grant came over to the Weaver house. He arrived well after the rest of the household—Eric, Gregg's parents and his sister, Tina, and her husband, Jack—had gone to bed. It had been a long day.

Gregg had been sitting in the kitchen waiting for Don for fifteen minutes when he saw the car pull up outside. He stood and went to the side door and let him in, closing and locking the door behind him. "We can talk in the basement."

Don nodded and Gregg led him through the kitchen and the living room to the rear of the staircase that led to the second floor. He opened a door and switched on a light, revealing a set of stairs that descended to the basement. He trumped downstairs, and Don closed the door behind him.

The Weavers had a partially finished basement. It ran almost the entire length of the house, except for the garage, and consisted of a family room, a bar set into the northwest corner near the fireplace, and a rec room, where a pool table sat. The rest of the basement was unfinished, yet dry,

and served as storage. Gregg approached the bar and
brought down a bottle of Jim Beam. "Drink?"

Don shook his head. "None for me, thanks. A Coke will
do if you have any."

Gregg produced a can of Coca-Cola from the refrigerator
and handed it to Don.

When Gregg finished preparing his drink and took a sip.
Don sat on one of the four barstools that lined the ma-
hogany bar. "It was a nice memorial service."

Gregg nodded. "Yes, it was." The memorial service had
breezed by amazingly fast, although it lasted approxi-
mately three hours. Jointly arranged by Tracy and her husband, Keith, with a few of Elizabeth's writer friends who
lived in the area, the service had been held in the basement of a Quaker church in Ephrata. The room had been
bursting with people, some of whom traveled great dis-
tances to pay respects to Elizabeth, many of them writers
and former and present students. Gregg had sat in the front
row with Eric, feeling a sense of pride and love as people
went to the front of the podium and spoke eloquently of
Elizabeth; of her kindness, her wit, her affection and love
for her family and friends. Her acquaintances at school recalled a dedicated teacher; her students regarded her as
more than an instructor, somebody they could confide in.
Her friends in the writing community showered her with
praise, giving nods to her work, but reflecting that the
woman behind those words was the one they had come to
value most of all. Gregg had sat through the service, feeling
that he should be crying but not doing so. Instead he felt
an overwhelming sense of gratitude that he had been fortu-
nate enough to have met and loved such an amazing
woman.

He hadn't been aware that Diana Marshfield and her
kids were at the service until Brenda approached him during the wake that followed. "She's here, and she's like a fish
out of water," she whispered. "Donald's with Mary now, but

Diana hasn't been near her. I think she knows we're keeping an eye on her."

Gregg had nodded. "Good."

"I've let two of Elizabeth's friends know to keep an eye on her," Brenda continued. "Geoff and Brad. They're keeping watch."

"Thank you," Gregg said.

Gregg had been vaguely aware that Don Grant was at the service. He'd caught a glimpse of Don out of the corner of his eye during the service. Don had been seated toward the back, and during the wake Gregg brushed by him at the refreshment table. "Come by the house this evening after eleven," he'd said. "I need to talk."

Don had nodded, refilled his punch glass, and drifted back into the crowd.

And now he was here.

And he had a haunted look on his face . . . as if he had seen a ghost.

"I noticed that Diana left shortly after the wake started," Don said.

"Yeah. Geoff told me he watched her get in her car with her kids and drive off."

"You did well today," Don said, sipping his Coke.

"Yeah, I did," Gregg said. He seated himself two stools down from Don, both men facing each other, elbows leaning against the bar top. "I kept thinking I was going to break down, but I didn't. I guess part of me still can't believe all that's happened."

Don nodded. "That's natural. I went for almost three months before everything hit me."

"Did you?"

"Yeah." Don took a sip of Coke and set the can down on the bar. "You did a great job in keeping Mary away from Diana."

"Was it enough?"

"I don't think so."

"You saw her?"

"Yeah." Something in his face flickered. He looked bothered by something.

"Did she see you?"

"I don't think so. With all those people, I probably didn't register."

"She indicated before that she was married to a man in Ohio before Ronnie. Did you know this?"

"I found out a few days before I learned of her new identity."

"Was she . . . did she look the same?"

"I don't know," Don said. He sighed, brushed his long hair back from his forehead. "I lost track of it for a while. I learned about the Ohio case just recently."

"But it was similar?"

"Very," Don said, nodding. "The guy she was with was a mechanic named James. They met over the Internet, same as Ronnie. She moved in with him, same as Ronnie, and—"

"Her kids," Gregg interrupted. He took a sip of Jim Beam. "What about her kids? Were they with her?"

Don shook his head, his blue eyes boring into Gregg's. "When she moved in with James Whitman she was childless. Rick and Lily and the dog came with her when she moved out here to be with Ronnie."

Gregg's mind tried to process this. "So where'd she get them?"

"I think you need to hear the rest," Don said, settling forward, his voice lowering a little. Gregg hunkered forward and for the next forty minutes he was lost as Don spun a tale that was so unreal, so terrifying, that he could barely remember to breathe.

Don had started researching demons and the occult when he moved to Carlsbad, New Mexico.

"My faith demanded it," Don explained. "I was still looking at this from a Christian perspective. The thing I saw that had taken my wife, what I experienced . . . the only way I could rationalize it to myself was that it was something demonic, something evil. So when I got my head on straight, I started reading books. I'd drive to El Paso or Roswell for the weekend and go to every used book dealer I could find and purchase everything I could lay my hands on that had something to do with the occult and demonic possession, the spirit world. I was looking for answers, and I had to try to find something that explained what I had experienced."

And while he had researched he went high tech. With the money earned from his job at the caverns, he bought a computer and got on the Internet. "I started going to message boards devoted to the occult just to see what was out there. It took a while, but I finally got acquainted with people online. The more I read, the more confident I felt in my research, and pretty soon I was able to ask the kind of questions that were formulating in my mind. It was around this time I discovered hundreds of cases that were similar—no, thousands! You'd be amazed, Gregg, really amazed. I found stuff going back over a hundred years, things that—"

"A hundred years?" Gregg asked, incredulously. "You mentioned this the other day. About stuff that went back to the eighteen hundreds and that Diana was—"

"Sorry, I'm getting a little ahead of myself," Don said. He took a sip of his Coke. "Basically here's the gist of it. I mentioned a few days ago that Diana was a succubus . . . remember that?"

Gregg nodded.

"And I told you the basic rundown of succubi and incubi, right?"

"Yeah, they're, like, sex demons."

"Very much so," Don answered. "Like I said before, the general belief is that succubi are female demons that visit men in their sleep and incubi are male demons that visit women. They're said to come to people in their sleep and invade their dreams, and the person they visit imagines consorting with a beautiful woman or a handsome man, but it's really the demon they're having intercourse with."

"Kind of like that movie *The Entity*," Gregg said.

"Yeah," Don said, nodding. "I saw that. One of the many fictional pieces I viewed during my research. Supposedly the book and the film were based on a true story."

"Really?"

"Oh, yeah. Happened back in the seventies. Woman was repeatedly raped by the incubus. There was also the presence of other activity, mostly poltergeist, but—"

"So the incubus in that case was invisible?"

"Apparently."

"Why isn't Diana invisible?"

"You got me, buddy."

"So you're saying Diana is a succubi."

"Succubus." Don corrected him, and then leaned forward. "She's—*it's*—definitely a succubus. Only here's where most of the general myth and folklore written about them have it wrong . . ." Don's voice was a whisper. "They're actually *both* . . . like hermaphrodites . . . like those frogs that can change from male to female at will to suit their reproductive needs. In fact, there are some myths that claim the incubus and the succubus are one and the same and that they can change their form at will while preying on us."

Gregg's eyes widened. "Diana . . . she was that guy Bruce . . . the one that . . ."

"Yes," Don said, his voice level. "You got that right, buddy. The same thing that's fucked up your family killed my wife. You better believe it."

Gregg was barely aware he was holding his breath. He couldn't tear his gaze from Don's blue eyes, which were now blazing with an intensity that was a little frightening. Gregg looked away, feeling a shiver race through him. "Jesus, this is fucking unreal. Are you *sure?*"

"As sure as you are that Diana is responsible for the downfall of your wife's family," Don said, his eyes locked on Gregg's. "You *are* confident she's responsible, right?"

"Yeah," Gregg said, his mind racing. "I can't explain it, but yeah, I know she's the cause of all this."

"Remember when I told you about tracking Bruce back to Colorado?"

Gregg nodded.

"I tracked him all over," Don said. "It took a while, but I did it. I tracked him back till around 1872 or so. I just kept following the dots, using public records I found at libraries and archives, newspapers, police blotters, the Internet, everything I could get my hands on. I documented forty-one different identities it used and was able to get photographs from some of them. What I've discovered is fucking amazing, Gregg. Amazing and scary as shit on shinola."

"What was she before she was Diana?" Gregg asked, feeling his voice break. He was scared, but also angry. "How did you . . . how did you trace Bruce Miller to Diana Marshfield?"

"After Bruce Miller disappeared, he re-emerged as Tracy Bogart in Lakeland, Florida," Don said. Gregg drained his glass and poured himself another as Don laid out his case. "Tracy moved in with a young phone executive named Albert Fowler. Albert hanged himself eight months later, leaving a suicide note saying he couldn't live without Tracy. She cleared out of town that week. She moved to St. Louis, Missouri, and became a young middle manager named Marc Anderson. As Marc Anderson, he wooed a young woman he worked with named Grace Finlay. She moved in with him, they got married, and a year later she was found dead in her bed. She had gone from a healthy woman to skin and bones at seventy pounds. It was like she'd been sucked dry of everything inside her. Know what she was found holding?"

Gregg shook his head.

"A dildo and a photo of Marc," Don whispered. "She'd been . . . using it up to the point she died."

The image burned itself in Gregg's mind. Ronnie's sudden downfall came to mind, how he had gone from being overweight to a rapidly dwindling man who looked like he was back on the cocaine wagon. He thought about how quickly he'd moved in with Diana, how at Elizabeth's parents' house Ronnie had been all over Diana like a lustful teenager.

"She changes to suit her needs," Don continued. "She thrives on all kinds of things, but one of the things that she lives on is sexual appetite. She feeds off it. It makes her stronger, so that she's able to . . . I don't know how else to describe it . . . but it's like she plants something inside her victims that makes them obsessed or addicted to her. The more the victim becomes sexually obsessed, the more they feel the need to be with this monster. When my wife was in the throes of its power, there was nothing I could do to stop her. When I saw her right before I . . . before I saved her . . ." Don's voice lowered to a shaky whisper. "She had a look of desperation in her eyes. She looked like a junkie who couldn't help herself but who somehow knew what she was doing was killing her. . . . But she couldn't help herself . . . she had to have him, had to keep going back to him." Don took a deep breath and closed his eyes.

Gregg waited, his mind recalling the past five months, remembering Ronnie's gradual decline, his withdrawal from his family, his need to give everything to Diana above everything else, his slow physical deterioration.

Don opened his eyes, seeming to compose himself. "When it's finished it moves on. Many times it just takes everything it can, and the person it leaves behind is so far gone they die a few days later, often from starvation."

"Starvation?"

"Yeah. They no longer think about food. All they think about, all they crave, is sex with it. They stop bathing, stop taking care of themselves . . . that's when they're totally on the downhill slide. By then it's already planning its escape, and many times it's already tapped in to its host's family and friends. It feeds off them, too."

"How?" Gregg was finding this fascinating.

"Through the misery and emotional anguish created in the wake of what is happening to their loved one," Don answered. He took another sip of soda. "Think about it. One or two months after Diana showed up to live with Ronnie, what happened? How did Elizabeth's parents feel about her?"

"They didn't care much for her."

"And Elizabeth?"

"She hated her."

Don nodded. "And that caused friction between Ronnie and his parents. The more they disapproved, the more he got into her, so to speak."

Gregg nodded, taking a drink of bourbon and sighing. "Yeah, that's exactly how it happened."

"It feeds on that," Don continued. "The more havoc it can create in its host's family or its immediate living area, the more negative energy it has to feed on."

"So it feeds on the negative energy it creates?"

Don nodded. He swallowed the last of his soda and put the glass down. "Very much so. Take Ronnie's ex-wife for instance."

"You know about Cindy?"

"Oh yeah. Remember, I told you I did my research before I came out here. I know all about what happened to Cindy."

"Diana killed Cindy, didn't she?" Gregg's heart was racing, everything clicking together.

"Diana created great strain between Ronnie and Cindy," Don explained. "She took on the role of the new girlfriend very easily, and she used it to make Cindy extremely jealous."

"Cindy claimed Diana made threatening phone calls," Gregg said, remembering the incident vividly. "She said Diana threatened to hurt Mary."

"And Cindy called the police, but there was no proof, right?"

Gregg nodded. "And it kept happening. And Mary . . . she hated living there. Said Diana was . . . not only a cold person, but . . . that her kids were . . ."

"Her kids," Don said, leaning back slightly, rubbing his bearded face. "Damn, how to explain that."

"What *are* they? Are they really *her* kids?"

"I'll answer that question, but let me get back to Cindy," Don said, shifting on his stool for a more comfortable position. "The reports I read indicate she died of a heart attack in Ronnie's home, correct?"

Gregg nodded. "Yeah, she had broken in. She was armed, too."

"Cops think it might have been drug-induced, that she was tripping or something."

"Sure. With Cindy that would have been very believable."

"Diana used Cindy's addiction problem against her," Don said. "That's what this thing does; it uses people's weaknesses against them. In Cindy's case, it was her drug addiction and her love for her daughter. By threatening Mary, it pushed Cindy's buttons. It knew Cindy's story wouldn't be taken seriously. And it continued pushing those buttons until Cindy reacted the only way she knew how, by striking back."

"So Cindy did break into the house to kill Diana?"

"Oh yes," Don said, nodding. "And Diana knew it. And while I don't know what went on in that house that night, I can hazard a guess as to how Cindy came to die of a heart attack and why the police would think it was drug-induced. For one, Diana knew that by having Cindy break into the house, she would create the illusion Cindy was doing it under the influence of drugs—she already had that manipulative trick up her sleeve. But we have to ask ourselves, what really triggered that heart attack, if that's indeed what it was? Last I heard, the jury was still out on that."

"I guess," Gregg said, sipping his whiskey. "Tell you the truth, I haven't really paid much attention to Cindy's case lately."

"My guess is when Cindy got into the house she saw Diana's *true* self," Don said. "And seeing it drove her mad; it was such a great shock that it triggered whatever it was that killed her."

"Do you think Diana did all this—taunted Cindy—to make her come over so she could kill her?"

Don nodded. "Yeah, I do. It's . . . unusual in that before it never did this. Before, it just used to live off the man or woman it had taken up with. But I've noticed that in the last few cases it's reached out beyond its victim. It's always created havoc and misery among the victim's family, but the last few cases . . . well, it's manipulated things and situations that have led to other people's deaths."

Gregg's mind was racing. "I remember Laura saying something about Cindy telling her ex-boyfriend Gary about the threatening phone calls Diana was making. And that she had a roommate, some guy that was apparently around when some of the calls were made."

"Really?"

"Yeah. Now that we're talking about this I'd kinda like to talk to them."

"I can understand why you would, but I'd advise against it."

"Why?"

"You think they'd believe all this?"

"I don't know," Gregg said. He drank the rest of the whiskey. "But they were close to Cindy . . . they had to have known something . . . suspected something."

"Maybe," Don acknowledged. "But for now let's get away from that. You asked about Diana's kids . . ."

Gregg looked up at Don. "Yeah, her kids. Tell me."

Don rummaged in a knapsack he had brought with him from his rental car. He brought out a sheaf of papers and glanced at Gregg. He looked like he was hesitating. Gregg read the nervousness on his face and nodded for him to continue. "First I have some pictures to show you." He passed the folder to Gregg, who took it and opened it.

The photo on the top of the stack was of a dark-haired man with a slim, muscular build. It looked like he was at a family picnic. He was standing on the side of a picnic bench, holding a cigarette. His face was perfectly centered, as the photographer caught him engaged in conversation with somebody off camera. "Who's that?"

"That's a man named Ron Doyle," Don said. "This photo was taken in 1972. Two years later he met a young woman named Nancy Padilla in a single's club and took her home. Eighteen months later he was dead, and Nancy cleared out." He motioned to the photo. "The first time I laid eyes on Bruce Miller *that's* who I saw. This same exact face, same build. When I found this photo during my research—which had led to Nancy Padilla—I was shocked."

Gregg looked at him with confusion.

"Ron Doyle was one of its victims," he said. He looked hesitant again. "Flip down to the next photo."

In this one, a younger Don Grant was with a pretty, dark-haired woman wearing a blue sundress at an amusement park. They posed with somebody dressed in a giant purple bunny costume. Don's face beamed with happiness; his hair was short, and the woman radiated life and joy. "That's me and Lisa," he said. "Two years before she was taken from me, in happier times."

Gregg wasn't listening. He was looking at the photo of Don and his late wife with numbing horror.

The woman standing next to him was the splitting image of Diana Marshfield.

"You see?" Don asked.

Gregg nodded, his heart thumping hard. "That's Diana."

"No," Don said, his voice lowered, more gravelly with a slight tinge of anger. "That's my wife, Lisa. That thing . . . that fucking *thing* . . . even though I tried to save her, it still . . . it was still able to absorb enough of her to . . . to use her essence. To masquerade in her face, her body."

Gregg understood completely. He stared at the photo in numb silence. "What about the kids?"

"It's only had children twice in all the times I've been able to document its path, but I have no doubt there have been more. The first time I found was back in the 1940s. It moved in with a woman named Alice Peterson who lost her husband in World War II. Alice had a twelve-year-old son named Donald." He paused, looking at Gregg. "That's the first time it had a child." He flipped through the photos to an old black-and-white snapshot and turned it faceup to Gregg. The photo depicted a boy with close-cropped dark hair and freckles, smiling into the camera. It was the splitting image of Diana Marshfield's son, Rick, that sullen boy who barely spoke a word.

Gregg understood the implications perfectly with dawning horror. "It . . . whatever it did with Alice . . . it did the same to her son?"

Don nodded. "Taking Alice's son gave it so much energy that the next documented evidence I found of it wasn't until the 1970s . . . '71 maybe. It worked its way through maybe half a dozen identities and switched back and forth between sexes. Around 1980 or so it married a single father of a six-year-old girl."

"The girl looked like . . . was . . . Lily," Gregg said, feeling his mouth go dry.

Don nodded. He arranged the photos in the folder and put them on the bar top. "That kept it going until 1997, when it emerged in Iowa. It went from there to Colorado, then to Pasadena, California, where I had my encounter. It was still feeding off the energy from the little girl and—"

"So what are they?" Gregg asked. "Lily and Rick, I mean? Are they . . ."

"They're part of it now," Don said. "The souls of children act like a powerful battery. When that power is drained it can use their essence, sort of use them as an extension of itself."

"So Lily and Rick are really a part of Diana?"

"Yes."

"What about the dog? Does it feed on animals?"

"It can emulate animals to a certain extent. Enough to

fool us. But children?" Don's bearded face looked grave. "If it can find an adult host with a child, the better."

"And that's why it wants Mary?"

Don nodded. "Like I said, it's had other children," he continued. "Sometimes it uses Lily and Rick to help insinuate itself into its host's life. It works especially well with recently divorced people with children or people who've lost their spouses. They're lonely, they're vulnerable . . . a lot of people like that let their guard down, don't even think about who they're letting into their lives. And especially now with the Internet and people meeting in chatrooms and stuff . . . it's like the sexual revolution of the '60s and '70s . . . the field is ripe with hosts. It can gorge itself."

"So it controls Lily and Rick?"

"They're a part of her," Don explained, his fingers tracing patterns on his soda glass. "She can detach them from herself and they're wholly independent of her, but she controls them."

Gregg tried to remember how Rick and Lily carried themselves. He shuddered at the memory. They had been such sullen, uncommunicative children. He had initially thought their dull, almost glazed expressions were because they were bored, unimaginative children. Perhaps dumb. In light of what Don was telling him now, he was beginning to see them for what they really were. "So what do we do?" he asked. "How do we stop it?"

Don sighed. Once again there was that look of defeat, of sorrow, in his face. "I don't know. That's why I'm here . . . to see if we can brainstorm something together. I've been thinking about this by myself now for three years and . . . I don't have all the answers." He looked at Gregg. "I need somebody to help me with this. I want to destroy it."

Gregg met his gaze, his resolve strengthening. "I'm in."

They clasped hands. And to Gregg it felt like he was enlisting in battle.

*   *   *

Mary was dreaming that her daddy was calling her name, and she fought sleep. She tried to look for him, tried to follow his voice as it echoed through the vast blackness of her mind. "Mary . . . Mary . . . Mary . . ."

She fought the blackness of sleep and the more she climbed out of it, the more audible her daddy's voice was. It reverberated in her ears, his voice musically clear. "Mary . . . wake up, honey . . . come on . . . wake up . . ."

Mary opened her eyes and saw her daddy.

He was crouched down on the side of her bed, leaning over her. For a minute she was so surprised she almost let out a scream. Her daddy placed a finger to his lips to quiet her, then touched her gently, his fingers trailing to her lips. "Shhh . . . it's okay . . ."

"Daddy?" Mary said. She had intended to whisper, but was so surprised that her voice was louder than expected.

"Shhh . . . don't wake your cousin up." Her daddy gestured to Amy Wandrei, who was sleeping soundly next to her.

Mary blinked, fighting weariness. Was she dreaming? She had to be. Her daddy was dead; they were having his funeral in two days. True, she hadn't actually seen his dead body, but everybody had been crying, and her aunts and cousins were telling her something bad had happened and he had died, so it must be true. She knew something bad happened; nobody would tell her outright what *had* happened, and the police had asked her a lot of questions, so it must have been really horrible. Mary had cried, knowing in her heart her daddy was not coming home, so this must be a dream, it must be—

Her daddy leaned closer to her and touched her face gently with his hands.

Her skin tingled at his touch, obliterating her fatigue.

"Daddy?" She sat up in bed, feeling her chest constrict, the happiness and joy building in her.

Daddy put a finger to his lips. "Shhh," he whispered.

All thoughts of her daddy being dead were replaced

with the knowledge—the *proof*—that he was *here*. He was *alive!* She could touch him, she could see him! He was *alive!*

But another part of her, something rational that was quickly evaporating, spilled to the surface, parting through the overwhelming joy she was feeling. "What are you doing here? We thought you were dead! What happened? Are you okay? Are—"

Daddy covered her mouth, making that *shh*ing sound again. He looked around cautiously, and Mary felt her heart leap in her chest. In her excitement she'd been loud. They stood still for a moment, listening to the silence of the house. Mary was certain that Brenda had heard her, and she waited for the inevitable footsteps to come down the hall to the room she was sharing with Amy, but they didn't. Daddy's fingers were over her mouth, silencing her, and Mary felt such happiness at their touch, at their sandpapery texture, that she didn't care they were cold. It was cold outside, once he was in the house for a while he would warm up.

Her daddy leaned so close to her that she could almost feel the bristle of his lightly bearded face. His long hair tickled her face. "I'm fine, honey," he whispered, and she could feel the air of his breath. "I'm okay, and I'm here to take you home."

"How did you get inside?" she asked, not able to stem the flow of tears now. The past five months of longing to see her daddy—to be taken into his loving embrace, protected and cared for by him—was overwhelming her. "Brenda locked up the house because she didn't want Diana to come get me," she said, her voice cracking. "You're not going to take me back to Diana are you?"

Daddy's fingers pressed lightly on Mary's mouth again, quieting her, and he shook his head. "No, honey, I'm not. Diana's gone. I'm here now. It's just going to be you and me, honey."

And then Mary's happiness overcame her completely,

and she fell against her father, her face buried in his chest, trying to contain the sobs. Her daddy held her, whispering. "It's okay, honey. Shhh. Don't cry. We don't want to wake everybody up, okay? I don't want to wake anybody up and cause a fuss."

Mary didn't want to wake anybody up either. Already she could feel herself relaxing in her father's embrace, calm in the knowledge that he was here to take care of her.

"Everything's going to be okay," Daddy whispered, kissing the top of her head. "We'll go back home and it'll just be you and me. Okay?"

Mary took a deep breath, containing her crying. She didn't want to wake everybody up, but shouldn't Brenda know that her daddy was alive? She looked up at him, her face wet with tears. "What about Brenda and Donald?" she whispered.

"They'll be okay," Daddy said. "I left a note for them on the table. They'll understand that in the face of what happened to your grandparents and your aunt Elizabeth that I had to come get you. They'll understand how important it is that you had to be alone with your daddy."

Mary nodded. Of course they would understand. Her daddy had probably explained everything in his note to Brenda, and in the morning he would call and everybody could come over to the house and learn everything. She would learn everything, too. In fact, she already knew that somehow the police had made a mistake. They just *thought* her daddy was dead. He had woken up in the hospital and had gotten out and come out here as soon as he could. That's what happened.

And now he was here, and he was her daddy again . . . not that crude imitation of a daddy he'd been when Diana and her kids lived with them. He had started out as her daddy when Diana moved in, but the longer she and her kids were at the house, the more Daddy became less and less of himself until it felt like he was a different person. Toward the last month or so, she hadn't even seen him. But now he was here and he was better, and he had gotten rid of that nasty woman who had taken her daddy away, and they could go away together and be a family again.

"What about Mommy?" she asked. She knew her mommy was dead, but was still having a hard time trying to accept that fact.

"I don't think Mommy will be able to come with us," Daddy said, looking sad.

The finality of her mother's death hit her. She nodded, the tears streaming anew.

Her daddy hugged her closer. "Come on. Let's go home."

Moving quietly, Daddy helped her out of bed. They paused at the doorway to the bedroom. The house was silent. Daddy led Mary to the kitchen, and she wondered fleetingly if she should change out of her pajamas. They reached the side door that led out to the driveway, and Daddy lowered himself so that he was facing her at eye level. "My car is parked across the road there. You'll be fine in your jammies. We'll go home and get some rest together, just you and me. And in the morning everything will be fine."

Mary nodded. She felt good that her daddy was back. She felt happy. Despite all the horrible things that happened in the past month, this was the best day of her life. Her daddy was alive and he was back!

"Okay," Daddy whispered, standing up and taking Mary's hand. He unlocked the door and opened it, then reached down and scooped Mary up in his arms. "Snuggle against me. It's cold outside."

Mary wrapped her arms around her daddy, closing her eyes as she felt the tears of happiness overwhelm her again. Her daddy carried her outside, closing the kitchen door softly behind him, and by the time she was safe inside his car—well, not his truck exactly, but the Chrysler Diana drove, which she knew Daddy had bought for her so maybe he really *had* kicked her out—she was crying again, only this time she let the sobs break through. She was so happy and brimming with love for him, that she just couldn't contain her joy. And as her daddy started the car and slowly drove down the lonely country road away from Brenda and Donald's house, Mary told herself that she was never going to be separated from her daddy ever again. They were going to be together forever and ever.

Forever and ever.

CHAPTER TWENTY-THREE

The ringing of the phone jolted Gregg Weaver out of a light sleep.

He hadn't slept well at all, and the jarring of the telephone finally drove away the sleep that had eluded him for most of the night. He peeked at the clock on the nightstand by the bed. Six-thirty A.M. Don Grant had left the house at two-thirty, and Gregg had come straight upstairs and gone to bed, where he had lain tossing and turning and catching brief snatches of sleep ever since. He sat up quickly as the phone brayed a third time and scooped up the receiver. "Yeah?"

"Gregg, Mary's gone!" Brenda's voice was loud, trembling with fear and panic.

"What?" Gregg sat up, the shock of the news and Brenda's terror-stricken voice providing a jolt to his system. "What do you mean she's gone?"

"She's gone!" Brenda wailed, her voice quivering in sobs. "I just went in to check on her and she wasn't in bed. I've . . . I've checked the whole house and she's *gone!"*

Gregg's mind was racing in panic. "Did you call the police?"

Brenda was sobbing so loudly that he couldn't hear her response. There was a sound on the other end of the line, and then Donald's voice came on. He sounded scared, but his voice was more level. "I've looked all over the house and she's gone, Gregg. The police are on their way."

"Is there any sign of a break-in?" Gregg asked, his heart pounding.

"There's none." Donald paused, and Gregg caught a sense of hesitation in his voice. Brenda cried in the background, and he could hear their kids' excited voices. "Something was here last night, Gregg," Donald's voice was a shaky whisper.

"What do you mean, *something?*"

"I went outside to look for her and saw . . . hell, I don't know how to describe it." Donald sounded like he had seen a ghost. "Outside on our back deck where the shrubbery and the grass grow up against it . . . near the French doors that open out onto the patio. There's a big patch of dead grass and vegetation there and . . ."

Donald hesitated and Gregg tried to fathom what he was getting at. Of course the grass and vegetation would be dead. It was fall. Winter was officially three weeks away. What the hell was he talking about? "What is it, Donald?" he asked, trying to sound gentle but persuading.

"There's a trail," Donald said quietly. "That leads from the road and through our yard around the side of the house to the back deck. It stops near the window, as if somebody were looking into our house." He paused again, and Gregg could hear him licking his lips. "The yard has been yellow anyway, but this path is . . . well, the grass is actually *white!* The bushes near the back deck are white and when I touched them they just fell apart. And . . ." Gregg heard him gulp. "There's this . . . ah shit, there's this *shit* on them that's like. . . . grease . . . or *slime* . . ."

Diana, Gregg thought, his heart freezing in his chest.

"This shit wasn't there yesterday," Donald said. "We keep our garbage cans right outside off the back deck, and I put some trash out yesterday and the wind had blown some newspapers along the side of the house. I was over there yesterday afternoon and this shit wasn't there!"

"Okay," Gregg said. He closed his eyes and pinched the bridge of his nose, his mind racing. *I've gotta call Don, tell him what happened, we've gotta go to Ronnie's, see if she's taken Mary there, we've gotta—*

"I called the police the minute I realized the house was broken into," Donald said.

"How do you know somebody broke into the house?"

"That slimy greasy shit . . . it's caked all over the doorknob of one of the French doors on the back deck." He paused again, and Gregg could tell Donald was preparing for what he was about to tell him next. "And there's a small puddle of it just inside the house, in the family room on the other side of those doors . . . and there's some in Amy's bedroom beside the bed Mary was sleeping in."

Gregg thought about the thing Mary had claimed to have seen attached to her father in the master bedroom. The shapeless, slimy thing that had undulated and changed, the faces that were inside it moving around. It had come to the Wandreis' house in its natural form somehow and changed once inside. The question was, what had it changed into?

"Did you tell the police that Diana took her?" Gregg asked.

"No. I just told them we had a break-in and that Mary's missing." He paused, spoke something to Brenda, then came back on the line. "Police are here now."

"Tell them Diana Marshfield broke into your house and took Mary," Gregg said. "Have them send a squad car there. It's a Reinholds address, 232 Severn Avenue or something like that. I'm leaving right now for Diana's."

"Gregg!" Donald said, but Gregg hung up.

The silence was deafening.

He could feel the blood pounding through his veins.

I've gotta call Don, he thought, reaching for his wallet for the card with Don's cell phone number on it. He punched the number in, and it was picked up on the fourth ring. Don sounded groggy, but quickly woke up as Gregg hurriedly told him what happened. "I'm going over there now," he said, quickly slipping his tennis shoes on over stockinged feet.

"I'm staying not that far from you," Don said. "The Sunset Motel on 272 near the turnpike. Is that too far out of the way?"

"It's on my way to Reinholds. I'll come get you."

"I'll be outside," Don said.

Gregg hung up, grabbed his wallet and car keys from the nightstand and slipped out into the hall. He treaded downstairs quickly, thought briefly about waking his parents to tell them where he was going, then decided not to. He didn't have time to provide the explanation they'd demand, and he didn't have time to scrawl down a note. He let himself into the garage, got into the Blazer, started it, opened the garage door and started backing up before the garage door was fully open.

When they pulled up to Ronnie Baker's home forty-five minutes later, the first thing he noticed Diana's Chrysler parked in the driveway. Gregg saw another car parked three houses down with two men sitting in the front seat. One of them looked vaguely familiar. He pulled into the driveway of a house on the other side of the street and did a three-point turn, heading up the opposite end of the neighborhood. He wanted to approach the house from the rear, so Diana didn't see them.

He pulled to the curb and killed the engine.

They sat in the car for a moment, looking at the house.

"Think she's home?" Don asked. He'd been standing beneath the awning of the motel when Gregg arrived and had climbed into the vehicle wordlessly when Gregg pulled up.

"It looks like it," Gregg said.

Don looked nervous. He licked his lips, ran a shaky hand through his hair. "Much as I don't like facing her, I think we should go up and ring the doorbell."

"Me too."

They got out of the car and walked toward Ronnie's house.

The men who had been sitting in the parked car got out.

The closer the four men drew together, the more recognizable one of them became to Gregg. He made the connection as they drew within five feet from each other on the sidewalk. "Gary?" Gregg asked the taller of the two men, holding out his hand.

"Yeah," Gary Swanson said, shaking Gregg's hand. "Good to see you again, Gregg." Cindy Baker's ex-boyfriend looked tired, as if he had been up for the past twenty-four hours. He was wearing a denim jacket over a red flannel shirt, blue jeans and brown work boots. He glanced at the smaller man, who was wearing a black leather jacket over a blue flannel shirt, and had a stubbled face and longish dirty-blond hair. "This is Ray Clark. He was Cindy's roommate."

Gregg shook Ray's hand and introduced Don, who nodded politely. Gregg cast a quick glance toward the house, then back at the other men. "How long have you guys been sitting out there?"

"All night," Ray said, and the way he said it made Gregg's veins freeze. The smaller man had the wide-eyed look of one who has just seen the unthinkable; a tree pulling its roots out of the ground and walking, or a dog speaking Italian. Gary Swanson didn't look much better himself.

"I think we need to talk," Gary said.

"Yeah," Gregg said, turning to Don. "I think that's a good idea."

The four men headed toward Gary's car, which Gregg saw was a blue Toyota hatchback. Gregg and Don squeezed into the backseat, and the first thing Gregg noticed, besides the mass of papers and wadded-up fast food wrappers and bags, was the sweet smell of marijuana. He said nothing, however, as Gary and Ray shut the doors and turned their attention to Ronnie's house. "What do you guys know?" Gary asked.

"What do *you* know?" Don asked.

Gary turned around, his eyes lighting on Don's for a second, then on Gregg's. "I know Ray and I saw some weird shit here last night. That's why we're still here. We've been talking about it since one, two o'clock this morning."

"You've been sitting here all night?" Gregg asked, trying to hide his amazement. "I'm surprised the neighbors didn't call the cops."

"I'm sure some of them are thinking of doing so now," Gary said, glancing around the neighborhood before turning back to Gregg and Don in the backseat. Ray was sitting in the passenger seat, half turned around so he could get in on the conversation. "But I'm guessing the cops are already on their way over. Am I right?"

"Yeah," Gregg said, his heart pounding. *He saw something,* his mind screamed. "Elizabeth's cousin Brenda called them. I told them to send somebody over here because Mary's missing. Diana took her last night."

Gary and Ray glanced at each other, then looked back at Gregg and Don. "How do you know that? Did you actually see Diana take her?"

"No, but Donald and Brenda's home was broken into and Mary's missing. Diana's already threatened to take her." Gregg couldn't contain himself anymore. "You saw her last night, didn't you? You saw her pull up to the house with Mary."

Gary and Ray traded worried glances again, and this time Gary shook his head. "No. We didn't see Diana at all last night."

Gregg wanted to explode; in fact, he was on the verge of exploding in Gary's face yelling, *Bullshit,* when Ray diffused the situation. "He's telling the truth. We didn't see Diana last night. We saw Ronnie."

"What?" Gregg looked from Gary to Ray, trying to read the expressions in their faces.

"It's true," Gary said, nodding, trading another glance with Ray. "I kid you not, man. We were both sitting here last night, talking about what we were going to do. We came over here last night to have a talk with Diana about . . . certain things. Anyway, we were sitting here talking about what we were going to do when we see Diana's car pull into the driveway, only it wasn't Diana driving. We thought it was, and we were going to wait until she got out of the car, but it was Ronnie."

"Ronnie?"

"Yeah."

Gary and Ray were telling the truth. Gregg could feel it, could see it in their faces. They were not lying, as much as he wanted to believe they were.

Gregg hadn't looked at Don, but he could sense the other man sitting in the seat beside him, silently soaking this all in. Gregg's mind was still trying to come to grips with it. "You saw Ronnie last night. My dead brother-in-law."

"Yeah," Gary said, swallowing. "It was Ronnie. We weren't seeing things. I know you smell weed in the car, but we didn't start smoking till after we saw that shit."

"What did he do?" Don asked.

Gregg glanced at him and saw that Don had taken a keen interest in this story. He was leaning forward, elbows on his knees, totally absorbed.

"He went around to the passenger door and opened it," Gary said. "There was a kid in the front seat. I couldn't see who it was at first, but when they got to the front door of the house I caught a glimpse. It was Mary."

"Mary. Mary and Ronnie."

Gary and Ray nodded.

"And Mary was . . . she was okay?"

"Yeah," Gary said, trading another glance with Ray, who shrugged. "She looked okay to us. I mean . . . everything looked *normal,* you know? I mean . . . if you hadn't known that Ronnie died last week, you would have looked at the two of them coming home last night and thought nothing of it."

"So it didn't look like she was being forced against her will?" Don asked.

"Not at all."

A squad car pulled up to the house and parked at the curb.

Gregg started, glancing at Don. "Will you stay right here?"

Don nodded. "Yeah."

"You going in?" Gary asked, as Gregg climbed out of the backseat.

Gregg nodded and motioned for Gary to roll down his window. "Take Don back to his motel. He'll give you the directions. I'll meet you over there as soon as I can. He can explain everything there."

Don glanced at Gregg, looking nervous, and Gregg nodded to him. "They might be able to tell you things I wasn't able to tell you. Especially Ray. He was present when Cindy got some of Diana's phone calls."

"Yeah," Ray said, nodding. "I was there all right. Bitch was out of her fucking skull."

"We'll be fine," Gary said. He started the car and pulled away from the curb.

Gregg crossed the street and started heading toward Ronnie's house.

The cops had already exited their vehicle when Gregg approached them. "Hi," he said quickly. "My wife's cousin Brenda Wandrei put in the call about the kidnapping."

One of the officers looked to be about Gregg's age, with thick dark hair. "Yeah," he said, "You're the girl's guardian?"

"Brenda is," Gregg said. "I'm her uncle."

The second officer, younger, blond, well-built, said, "Mr. Weaver?"

"That's me," Gregg admitted.

The first officer radioed in on his two-way that they were at the house. "You want to come with us to the front door, or would you like us to do the search?"

"I'll come up," Gregg said, joining the officers as they made their way up the driveway to the front porch.

The older cop rapped on the door. Gregg felt light-headed with nervous tension as they waited. He glanced around at the front porch. The house looked in worse shape than he had ever seen it. When Ronnie and Diana moved in last June it had been brand new, bearing fresh paint and clean woodwork along the porch. The lawn had been freshly seeded, the driveway was smooth, and the interior smelled of new paint and carpet. Now the paint outside was fading, the driveway was riddled with asphalt chunks, and the windows were dirty. The grass was long and dead. It looked like nobody had lived there for quite some time.

It was as if the life had been sucked right out of it.

The officer knocked on the door again, and Gregg sensed somebody's presence before he heard footsteps. There was a pause and then the door was opened. Diana peered out, looking curious. She was wearing a long T-shirt that reached the top of her thighs, and she looked as if she had just woken up. Her features were flawless; she looked beautiful. Gregg found it hard to keep his eyes off her figure. "Can I help you?"

"Diana Marshfield?" The older cop asked, his tone brisk and businesslike.

"Yes?"

Gregg resisted the urge to leap forward and yell at her, throttling her by the throat. The younger cop was standing close to him, probably to keep him back, so Gregg let the police handle things. The older cop said, "Your boyfriend's daughter, Mary Baker, was reported missing this morning. Can we come in?"

"Sure." At the mention of Mary being reported missing, Diana appeared to wake up. She saw Gregg and looked a little surprised, but tried to hide it as they came into the house. Diana closed the door as Gregg took a quick look around the living room. It was a mess. "What happened?" Diana asked. "When'd this happen?"

"Would you mind telling us where you were last night, Miss Marshfield?" the younger cop asked.

"I was home all night with my kids. Why?"

At first Gregg hadn't noticed the kids, but now he saw that Lily was huddled on the sofa, morosely watching TV. He didn't see Rick anywhere. "Where's Rick?"

"Probably in his room," Diana said. She turned toward the hallway that led to the two bedrooms. "Rick! Hey, Rick! Get out here!"

Rick came in a moment later, his face vacant and expressionless as his muddy eyes went from his mother to the cops. "What's up?"

"Mind if we have a look around?" The older cop asked, already strolling around the living room toward the dining room.

"What for?" Diana's rising voice hinted at panic and anger. "I was home all night. What the hell is going on?"

"Nothing's going on, ma'am," the younger cop said, inserting himself in front of Diana. "We just want to check things out. The Department of Social Services has it on record you were considered a threat to Mary Baker and might try to abduct her, so we're just following up."

"*What?*" Diana looked angry. It was the most genuine emotion Gregg had ever seen on her. "You've got to be kidding?"

"It's not a big deal," the older cop said, poking around the kitchen. "If you were home last night, you were home. As long as you can prove it, you're fine. We just have to do this as a sort of process of elimination."

Diana turned to Gregg, her eyes blazing. "You think I kidnapped Mary?"

Gregg couldn't help it; his emotions got the better of him and he fought to hold back his fear. "Where is she, Diana?"

"I don't have her!"

"Then you won't object if we look around the house?" The young cop said.

"You have a search warrant?"

"No, but I can be back later this morning with one if you want."

"Fine!" Diana huffed, heading to the dining room. She picked up a pack of cigarettes on the computer desk and lit up. "Look around. Knock your socks off. She ain't fucking here."

The older cop nodded at his partner and they split up. Gregg joined the older cop, heading toward the master bedroom while the younger cop went into the two kids' bedrooms. Gregg's heart raced, his mind constantly whirling with paranoia. He dashed into the master bathroom and looked in the bathtub and shower stall, checking the cabinets under the sink. He heard the cop opening drawers and closet doors. Finding nothing in the bathroom, Gregg entered the master bedroom. "Did you try under the bed?"

The cop shook his head. "Not yet."

Gregg threw back the covers of the bed and looked underneath the king-sized water bed. Aside from a few boxes, it was empty.

It took them twenty minutes to search the house and through it all Diana fumed and smoked cigarettes, standing at the computer desk, her face glowering with rage. Lily and Rick sat on the sofa unmoving, looking unfazed by it all, as if they couldn't comprehend what was happening. Gregg's eyes lit on them briefly and thought back to what Don had said about them. *They're extensions of her and she controls them like puppets.*

His skin broke out in gooseflesh at the thought.

The three covered every room in the house, checked every closet, looked under the beds, in cabinets and under tables. While the younger cop looked in the garage, Gregg led the way to the basement, but there was nothing down there except a few toys and the wire mesh of Himmler's pen.

The dog wasn't in the basement.

"Wonder where the dog is?" Gregg asked, mostly to himself as he tried to calm the fear that was rising. They weren't finding Mary anywhere and he was starting to panic.

"They have a dog?" The cop asked.

"Yeah, a rottweiler."

"Maybe he's outside. He have a doghouse?"

"I don't know."

"Let's check."

They tramped up the stairs and when the cop asked Diana where the dog was, she huffed. "I had him put up for adoption a few days ago."

The cop nodded, seeming to accept this. Gregg felt the skin along his arms erupt in gooseflesh at the implications. She had already reined in that third extension. She had no use for it anymore. He was about to respond to that when the second officer appeared from his search in the bedrooms and motioned them over.

They reconvened in the living room. Diana regarded them with scorn. "So did you find her?"

Gregg ignored the sarcastic remark; part of him wanted to believe everything Don had told him wasn't true, that Diana was really innocent of kidnapping Mary and could never do such a thing, that she was not the creature he'd made her out to be. But another part of him knew Don was not only telling the truth, but Diana had taken Mary while assuming Ronnie's physical shape. She had the girl hidden somewhere. Gregg could feel Mary was very close to them, and the frustration of not being able to do anything without having the two cops place him under arrest was threatening to crumple him. He took a deep breath to calm his nerves and headed toward the door, feeling tears well in his eyes. Behind him the older cop told Diana, "Thank you, ma'am. We appreciate the cooperation."

Gregg felt Diana's eyes burn into his back as he left with the two policemen, and he risked a glance back at her. Her blurry form was barely recognizable behind his tear-filled eyes, and as he looked back at her he couldn't help feeling afraid and scared. He looked away quickly, mentally chastising himself for letting her see how vulnerable he was. He tried to ignore her watchful glare as he walked with the cops to their patrol car. The older cop opened the driver's side door and turned to him. "I think it's very doubtful that Miss Marshfield took your niece, Mr. Weaver."

"I know it seems that way to you—" Gregg began, feeling his throat hitch.

"It does seem that way to us," the older cop said, putting on his sunglasses. The early December sky was clear and the sun was shining. A brisk wind blew cold air from the north, ruffling Gregg's hair and jacket. "That doesn't mean we're not going to keep a watch on her. I'll get in contact with the Social Services Department and report on our search and have them come out. They'll want to take a more thorough look at the situation."

Gregg felt his hope rise. "Really?"

"Yeah." The cops got into the squad car and started it up. The younger cop rolled down the window, and Gregg leaned forward so they could continue their conversation. "I can try to have somebody come down this afternoon. They'll probably request to have us conduct another search. We have to follow up on any leads we get resulting from our investigation at the Wandrei house."

"Great!" Already Gregg felt a little better, but he wouldn't feel safe until Mary was found.

"In the meantime we'll put out an Amber Alert, get the state police involved. Don't worry, we'll find her."

"Thanks."

The cops waved and the car pulled away from the curb. Not wanting to risk another glance back at the dead façade of Ronnie Baker's house, Gregg Weaver headed back to his own car, once again feeling vulnerable and sick. He was racing against the clock to save Mary Baker's life.

CHAPTER TWENTY-FOUR

Gregg Weaver didn't go straight home; instead, he headed toward the Sunset Motel, where he had told Gary and Ray to take Don Grant.

On the drive over he called his house from his cell phone. His father answered, sounding worried, and Gregg quickly told him Mary Baker was missing and he had slipped out of the house this morning to comfort the Wandrei family and provide information to the police. "I didn't want to wake anybody," he said. "And I had to get out of the house quickly."

"What's going on?" his father asked. "Do they have any clues?"

"Not yet," Gregg replied, knowing he'd have to wrap the conversation up quickly or his father would keep him on the phone forever by asking him a thousand questions he couldn't possibly answer. "But they're working on it. Can you keep Eric at the house with you today?"

"Sure. What are you going to do?"

"I'm helping out here, and I'm heading out to breakfast

right now," Gregg said quickly. "Listen, I have to go. I'll have my cell on if you need to reach me, okay?"

"Okay," his father said, and Gregg felt briefly relieved when they hung up. Knowing he had most of the day to brainstorm the situation with Don, Gary and Ray, Gregg headed to the Sunset Motel.

Gary's hatchback was parked in the slot in front of Don's room, and Gregg got out of the car and knocked on the door. Ray answered, his eyes bloodshot but alert. Gregg came in and the other guys jumped up, excitedly asking what had happened. Don looked worried and concerned. A hush of silence fell across the room as Gregg told them about the search, how Diana had been seething with anger, how he had been freaked out by the kids' demeanors. Don Grant beat him to the punch line. "You didn't find Mary."

"No," Gregg said, the finality of the situation weighing heavily on him. "But she was there. When we were searching, I swear I could sense she was somewhere in that house."

"Where else could Diana have hidden her?" Ray asked.

"Lot's of places," Don said. He picked up a Styrofoam cup of coffee from a Turkey Hill market and took a swig. "I take it you didn't search the attic?"

"No," Gregg sighed. "Maybe when Social Services stops by we can perform a more thorough search."

"We might not have time for that," Gary said.

Gary's knowing tone piqued Gregg's interest, and he turned to Don. "You tell them everything?"

Don nodded. "Yeah."

Gregg turned to Gary and Ray. "You believe him?"

"Fucking A," Ray said. Gary nodded. Both men, though obviously tired, their eyes bloodshot from lack of sleep and dope smoking, looked like they had been reanimated, probably with caffeine, judging from the large Styrofoam cups of coffee around the room.

Gregg's stomach rumbled. "I'm hungry, and I need some coffee. Can we head out and get a bite to eat?"

"I could use some food, too," Gary said, standing up. "I got the munchies."

"Anyplace we could go where we could eat and have privacy?" Don asked.

Gregg glanced at Gary and Ray. "Does the Silk City Diner sound okay to you guys?"

They nodded and headed outside, piling into Gregg's Blazer for the short trip down the road to the diner.

Fifteen minutes later as they ate farm-fresh eggs, hashbrowns, bacon and sausage, hotcakes, orange juice and coffee, Don brought Gregg up to speed. He had given Gary and Ray a simplified version of what he'd told Gregg over Thanksgiving weekend and last night. Gregg was surprised to see the two men had not only filled in the blanks themselves, but they accepted the story readily. A grin cracked its way across Gary's features. "I may not be the smartest man in Lancaster County, but I believe what I see," he said. "And Ray and I saw some weird fucked-up shit last night. We were up all night talking about it, trying to come up with plausible explanations, and we couldn't come up with any. Ray had come to me shortly after Cindy was killed and told me about his suspicions to me, so he'd had plenty of time to dwell on this."

"And what was that?" Gregg asked between mouthfuls of food.

"Right after Cindy died, I tracked Gary down and told him about all the phone calls we got at the apartment," Ray explained. "The ones from Diana."

"I just assumed Diana was egging Cindy on for a fight," Gary said, stabbing a piece of sausage with his fork. "It was pretty easy to goad Cindy into a fight."

"The thing was," Ray resumed, "nearly every time we called the cops on Diana, they would trace the calls with the phone company and the report would say Diana never made any calls to our apartment."

Gregg nodded. "I'm sure you thought she was using a cell phone."

"Sure," Ray said, taking a sip of coffee. "But the phone company went through all that shit. The more we pressed the issue, the more the phone company denied Diana was making those calls, and then the cops would bring up Cindy's criminal record. I knew then that Diana was trying to set Cindy up."

"What about the threats Diana allegedly made to Cindy about hurting Mary?" Gregg asked.

"She told me about those," Ray said. "She'd get upset every time that happened. Not that I don't blame her, but I saw the pattern. I tried to talk some sense into her, make her see Diana was just talking bullshit, but it wasn't doing any good."

"So you went to Gary after Cindy was killed," Gregg said, working on his eggs. "When you heard Cindy was dead, what did you think?"

"When I heard what happened I knew it wasn't an accident," Ray said. "I knew Diana had killed her."

"Even though the police were saying she had a heart attack in Ronnie's house and Diana had tried to revive her?"

Ray nodded. He was picking at his food listlessly. "I didn't believe that shit for one second."

They were silent for a moment. Gregg thought about this as he dug into his food.

"Ray came to my work a few days after Cindy's memorial service and told me everything," Gary said quietly. "I was still stunned by what had happened. I . . . I believed what the police had told me." He glanced at Don. "It's like I said, if you had known Cindy it would have been easy to believe she had been whacked out on dope and broken into Ronnie's house."

"So you believed the official version?" Gregg asked, finishing his eggs and wiping his mouth with a napkin.

"Oh yeah," Gary said. He had sucked down an entire

stack of pancakes and was leaning back in the booth. "I mean . . . you knew Cindy, Gregg. You saw how fast she was going downhill."

Gregg nodded, digging back into his food. "Yeah, I know. I thought the same thing myself."

"I was afraid for Jason," Gary said. He took a sip of coffee. "When I heard the news I . . . well I cried. I wept like a baby. I was so sorry it had happened and I mourned for her. I really loved her, and I was just so sorry she had thrown her life away like that. But another part of me was . . . I don't know . . . sort of glad that . . . that she wasn't around anymore to be a danger to my son." Gary looked sheepishly around the booth. "I know that probably sounds like a pretty shitty thing to say about the mother of your child and the woman you used to love."

"It doesn't," Gregg said, leaning forward. "I would have felt the same way too."

Gary nodded, eyes downcast. "Yeah, well it still made me feel shitty. I was stunned by it all. So stunned I didn't really reflect on how bad Ronnie looked at the wake. I just figured he was as shocked as I was. Then . . ." He motioned to Ray. "When Ray showed up at work and started talking to me, something that . . . something in what he was saying told me he was telling the truth."

"Why's that?" Gregg asked.

Gary looked up at him. "When he told me about the phone calls he and Cindy were getting, it was the first I'd heard about them. I didn't know what to think. When he told me that the last phone calls Diana made were threatening Mary, that she expressed wanting to do physical harm to her . . . well . . . I just knew right then what happened at Ronnie's house wasn't an accident."

"I think I told Gary because I wanted some kind of reality check on what I was feeling," Ray said, picking at his own food. "I thought I was going crazy thinking the shit that was going in my head."

"Cindy loved her kids," Gary said. "She may have had her

problems, but she loved Jason and Mary to death. When Ray told me everything that happened between her and Diana, I knew right then Cindy had gone over to the Baker house to protect Mary."

"So you believed she went over there to kill Diana?" Gregg asked, his voice low.

Gary nodded. "Kill her, beat the shit out of her, warn her . . . whatever. Yeah, I think she went over there because of those phone calls. She did it because she was scared for Mary, and nobody would believe her."

Gregg finished off his breakfast, his mind racing. "Did you try contacting Ronnie?"

"Yeah, lots of times," Gary said. "I called him every day for like, over a week. He was never home."

"Diana always answered?" Gregg asked.

"Yeah."

"Then what happened?"

"Then . . ." Gary began, and from the way his voice dropped Gregg knew they were coming to the present. "I heard about what happened at Jerry and Laura's Thanksgiving evening," he said, his voice low. "When I heard Diana and her kids were the only ones who survived and that you and Mary were missing . . . I knew something was up."

"He called me that night," Ray said quickly. Between the two of them Gregg learned the rest, which was simple. For the next two weeks Gary and Ray were constant companions. They traded notes on Diana Marshfield, they cruised by the house hoping for a glimpse of her. Gary tried to get more information on the investigation into Cindy's death, which had officially been closed, and he also tried to learn more about the massacre at the Baker house.

Gregg was surprised to hear Gary and Ray had attended Elizabeth's memorial service. "Thank you," he said following their condolences on his loss. "I had no idea you guys were there. I was pretty out of it that day."

"Ray noticed something about Diana at the service," Gary said, nodding to Ray. "Go on, tell him."

Ray licked his lips, looking nervous. Gregg watched them, noting Don Grant's expression. Don looked like he had heard this before; his calm blue eyes reflected acceptance of their story and understanding. Instant camaraderie. "When I first met Diana back in June, maybe July, she was real skinny. Her hair was lifeless and dull and she looked . . . well hell, she looked like shit. But when I saw her at Elizabeth's memorial she looked like a different person. In fact, I barely recognized her. Her hair was the same color and a little longer but it looked real . . . I don't know . . . real *lively.* And her eyes were different, her posture . . . she was just . . ."

"She looked energized perhaps?" Gregg asked.

Ray nodded. "Yeah, that's the right word. Energized. She looked damn good. When I first met her I thought she was kinda a white-trash dog, but when I saw her at Elizabeth's memorial service I couldn't believe I was looking at the same woman. She looked damn fine."

"You were sexually attracted to her?" Gregg asked.

"Hell yes!" Ray looked embarrassed by his answer. "I mean . . . if I had no idea who she was before and she walked into a bar, I would've hit on her."

"We talked more about it on the way home," Gary continued. "We went to my place and went on the Internet and researched all kinds of shit. I had seen a movie once where this guy falls in love with this woman and she totally seduces him, sucks him in, drains the life out of him."

"Succubuses," Ray said.

"Right," Gary said. "Succubuses"

"Succubi," Don corrected.

"Huh?" Gary looked at Don, confused.

"Forget it," Don said, and to Gregg it looked like he was fighting back a grin. Gregg held back his own grin with a cough.

"Anyway," Gary resumed. "I finally found the movie—it was some cheapo horror flick. And anyway, the thing in the movie was a succubus, a female demon that comes to men in their sleep, seduces them and drains the life right out of them."

"We researched the fuck out of that shit," Ray said, looking proud. Gregg wondered if this had been the first thing he had researched in his entire life; if he had kept company with Cindy Baker it probably had been.

"Most of what we found on the Internet was shit," Gary said. "Lots of occult-related sites, stuff about demons, lots of Satanism stuff. They seemed to treat succubuses like it was a myth."

"I even went to the library," Ray offered. "I found a book that told us some stuff."

"Yeah, Ray found this great book about the occult that had a pretty good section on succubuses and incubuses—you know, the male ones."

Gregg nodded at Don. "Did you tell them what you told me?"

Don nodded.

"Yeah, he told us that shit," Ray said, looking disturbed. "It's like even the stuff in the books have it all wrong. Like they don't even know that succubuses and incubuses are the same thing."

Gregg fought the urge to correct their grammar, and he fought the urge to laugh out loud. "So what happened then?" he asked, the beginnings of a grin cracking his face.

Gary didn't appear to notice. "Last night we got together and started talking and before we knew it we were driving over to Ronnie's. We were still not . . . we still didn't want to believe the occult shit we were reading. I mean it was crazy, you know? So we decided to drive over to Ronnie's house and go up to the front door and talk to Diana."

"We were going to offer our condolences," Ray said, looking solemn. Gregg nodded, getting the message of their underhanded attempt to check things out last night.

"Exactly," Gary said. "We were going to offer our condolences, see if she would talk to us. We thought if we could do that we'd see what was going on."

"Only when we got there nobody was home," Ray resumed. "So we parked down the street and waited."

"We were there maybe forty minutes," Gary continued. He fingered the rim of his coffee cup. "We were just talking, when Diana's car pulled into the driveway."

"And that's when you saw Ronnie," Gregg murmured.

Gary and Ray nodded. "At first our theory kinda got blown out of the water," Gary said. "We started thinking maybe she was a witch or a Satanist or something, bringing people back from the dead like zombies."

"Or causing dead people to be possessed so they come back," Ray said, his features grave.

"That's the same thing, dumbass," Gary said.

Ray looked like he was going to protest, but Gregg waved it off. "Did Don tell you how it lives? How it gets its energy?"

They nodded. "He told us everything on the drive back to his motel room," Ray said. "And after seeing what we saw, it kind of confirmed what we were already finding out for ourselves."

"He told you how it gets its greatest energy from the souls and life force of children?"

They nodded.

Gary looked nervous. "When he told me that . . ." He glanced at Don, and for the first time Gregg saw fear in his eyes. "It . . . it made me think about something I had almost forgotten at Cindy's memorial service. And when I remembered, it scared the shit out of me." He glanced at Ray. "In fact, I don't even think I told you."

"What?" Ray asked.

Gary drew a deep breath, took off his baseball cap, and looked around the diner as if afraid he would be overheard. "Well . . . you remember how packed Jerry and Laura's place was that day, right Gregg?"

Gregg nodded.

"I was standing in the living room in the corner, just . . . just kind of lost in my own thoughts. Trying to deal with it. I had already talked to Ronnie for quite a bit, and we had a good talk. Diana had been there, but I didn't even register her. She just wasn't there to me. And . . . well, shit, that day was such a blur that I don't remember who all else I spoke to after that, but at one point Diana walked past me and caught my eye. She smiled and came up and touched my arm." He put his right hand on his left forearm. "And . . . I could tell on the surface it was meant to be a gesture of support, but . . . the look she gave me and . . . her touch . . . it was brief and real subtle, but there was this undercurrent of sexual desire. She told me she was sorry for my loss, and she said that if I ever needed to talk I could call her or see her anytime. And . . . and when she told me this I got this flash . . . you know that feeling you get when you meet a woman you're really strongly attracted to for the first time and the tension is just real strong? I felt that for like a second. And she felt it . . . it was like she *knew* I felt it. And she rubbed my arm, smiled and then I started getting a boner. And even though I was wearing slacks and I casually crossed my legs and tried to think other thoughts, I knew that she was aware of . . . you know . . ."

"Your raging hard-on?" Ray asked. He chugged the rest of his coffee.

Gary didn't even give Ray the benefit of a retort. Instead he swallowed, his face pale. "Like I said, it only lasted a second or two and she was gone. But I felt it, I know she felt it, and Ronnie was there the whole time and he didn't even notice. When they left, I told myself I was imagining things and a minute later people were coming up to me again, saying they were sorry and stuff, and I forgot about it."

"Did you think about her since then?" Gregg asked quietly.

For a minute Gary didn't answer. He looked down at the dregs of his coffee cup. The booth was quiet. Then, in a soft voice, Gary said, "Yes. I have. Sometimes I fantasize about what it would be like to go to bed with her. One night I was feeling horny and started thinking 'bout her and I . . . I jacked off." Gary looked embarrassed and frightened when he related this last part. Gregg also detected a hint of guilt in his eyes. "And that's why I'm scared." He looked up at them, and the fear in his face was evident. Gregg knew where it stemmed from. "I'm not afraid for myself. I'm afraid for my son, Jason. She knows I have a little boy. She knew Cindy and I were living together, that . . . that . . . you know."

Gregg nodded, laying a hand on the other man's arm. "I know, Gary. I know."

Gary took a deep breath, composing myself. "It just hit me when Don told us."

It had also hit Gregg, but not in the same way. During Gary's story he turned things over in his mind, listening, absorbing, analyzing. When Gary told them about Diana touching him and how that had made him feel, the idea caught a spark.

Gregg looked up, his nerves racing. He knew *exactly* what to do.

"I've got an idea," he said.

Gary, Ray and Don stopped talking and looked at him. Don recognized the look in his eyes and his face paled. "You're not serious," he said.

"I am," Gregg said, feeling better about the idea the more he turned it over in his mind. "And it's the only way. But we can't discuss it here. Let's go back to the room." He pulled out his wallet and slapped down two twenties for the bill, which still hadn't arrived, and slid out of the booth, grabbing his jacket. "Come on, time's awasting."

"What are we gonna do?" Ray asked, confused.

They followed Gregg out of the diner.

CHAPTER TWENTY-FIVE

When Gregg started explaining his plan on the short drive over to the Sunset Motel the first thing Gary said was, "You gotta be shitting me! You actually mean you're going to try to—"

"Don't argue with me!" Gregg said, his mind set. He pulled into the parking lot. "Just hear me out."

Once in the room, the protests began. Gregg held his hands up, pleading for them to quiet down. "We don't have time to argue! The sooner we can do this, the better chance we have of saving Mary. Just hear me out, okay?"

The three men looked at one another, shrugged, then turned to Gregg, nodding.

It took Gregg ten minutes to explain his plan. By the time he was halfway through, Gary, Ray and Don were nodding. They still looked frightened, but there was also a glimmer of hope, as if the solution Gregg had just offered them might work. There was still plenty of unease in their expressions, and Gregg understood why. It was the first part of his plan that was causing it, and it made him nervous too. But he knew he could pull it off.

He'd done it before.

"When do we do it?" Ray asked.

"Now," Gregg said. "We'll get some stuff together, whatever you guys can find—baseball bats, guns, chainsaws, whatever it takes to kill this thing. Then we head over and do it."

"Um, earth to Gregg?" Gary jerked a thumb toward the slightly opened window. "In case you haven't noticed yet, it's *daylight* outside. People will see us! Or was getting caught for breaking and entering and attempted murder part of the plan and you just didn't want to tell us?"

Gregg winced. Gary was right, but he also felt it was imperative they act soon. The thought of forcing Mary to spend another minute alone in that house with that thing was driving him mad with worry. "We've got to get Mary out," he said.

"How did Diana look when you went into the house with the cop?" Don asked.

"Same as she always does, only pissed off."

"No, I mean did she look tired at all?"

Gregg frowned, turning to Don. He tried to remember. "I don't know. She was very hostile, very angry. It was hard to tell."

"Do succubuses sleep?" Ray asked, looking genuinely interested.

"You think she's tired?" Gregg asked.

"From what I've been able to tell in my research, it *does* recharge its batteries after a feeding." Don rubbed his chin thoughtfully. "I think it would be safe to say she would be safe during this time. It wouldn't be able to drain its victim completely within one day anyway, especially a child."

"Why's that?" Gregg asked.

"A child's life energy is more potent. Stronger. It would be like you trying to chug a pint of Jack Daniels in an under an hour. You'd pass out halfway through the bottle if you were a social drinker. The vitality of a child affects them the same way."

"So it might take a few days for her to completely take Mary?"

Don nodded. "Yes."

"But you're not one hundred-percent sure."

"I'm very positive," Don said. "Almost one hundred-percent sure." He looked at Gregg, his features serious. "You're going to have to trust me on this, Gregg. I think it's a foolish idea, and I also think it's brilliant. But we can't do it today. We'll have to wait until tonight when it's dark."

"You think it'll work?"

Don nodded, trading glances with the other guys. "Yeah. I think it'll work."

That confirmed it. He was going to do it.

Gregg turned to Ray and Gary. "Will you help?"

"What do you want me to do?" Gary asked.

Gregg told him. He explained it all, going over the plan again from the beginning. When he finished he said, "I want to make sure you guys are serious. You're sure you want to do this?"

"This thing killed my girlfriend," Gary said, his features looking more animated now, possessed with a vitality and spark that hadn't been present earlier. "You fucking bet I'm in."

"I'm in, too," Ray said.

Gregg turned to Don. "Don?"

Don nodded. He looked scared, but also determined. He took a deep breath. "Yeah. I'm in. And I want to go in the house with Gary when it's time."

"You sure?"

"Yeah, I'm sure."

They clasped hands firmly. Brothers bound in a mission.

CHAPTER TWENTY-SIX

Gregg Weaver rang the doorbell to Ronnie Baker's former home at precisely five thirty P.M., a little more than seven hours after the man had sealed their pact.

He was about to ring the bell again when he heard footsteps approach the closed door, then pause. He looked at the peephole, and a moment later Diana Marshfield opened the door. Her expression was frank, her demeanor standoffish and defensive.

And she looked absolutely drop-dead gorgeous.

She was dressed in a pair of stone-washed blue jeans that clung to her shapely legs and thighs. The top three buttons of her tight white blouse were unbuttoned, and Gregg could see the generous swell of her breasts. Her hair was clean, her face impeccable. Despite the anger in her voice and body language, she still exuded an incredible air of sexuality.

"Now what? Got your search warrant?"

"Diana, I want to apologize," Gregg said.

She blinked in surprise. "What?"

"I'm sorry," Gregg continued, feeling the emotion pour

through him as he let himself go. "I don't know what I was thinking this morning. I was scared and angry, and I'm still scared and . . . I don't know how to explain this but . . . I just want to say I'm sorry for what happened this morning. I overreacted. I feel like shit."

"Well, you should," Diana said. There was a hint in her tone that she was letting down her guard, a sense of playfulness that bordered on seriousness.

"I am sorry," Gregg continued. He was embarrassed as he looked around, shivering on the porch. It was chilly outside, in the low forties. "I didn't mean for what happened this morning to happen. I wasn't thinking straight. Um . . ." He looked at her sheepishly. "Can I come in? Can we talk?"

Again there was that look on Diana's face of having been caught off guard. For a moment he thought she was going to reject his offer, that her face would twist into a grimace of hate and disgust and she would say no and slam the door in his face. Instead she did the opposite. She opened the door and stepped aside. "Sure, come on in."

Gregg let out a sigh of relief. "Thank you," he said, pausing on the threshold. He reached out for an awkward hug and Diana allowed it, hugging him back. He could tell everything that was happening, this whole encounter, was taking her completely by surprise. "Thank you," he said again. "I'm glad you're home. I really need someone to talk to."

"Then let's talk," Diana said and this time her voice was softer, had less of a threatening edge. She moved away from the door, and as Gregg stepped into the house, he closed it behind him, quickly making sure it was unlocked, and then headed toward the couch, where he sat down.

Gregg leaned forward on the sofa, put his head in his hands. "I've been going crazy thinking about what happened Thanksgiving Day," he said. "And between losing Elizabeth and Jerry and Laura, and Mary missing today I'm just going out of my mind! I can't take it anymore!"

"I know," Diana said. She sat on the sofa next to him, and although Gregg wasn't looking at her, he could tell from her tone that she was relaxing more. "They say bad luck comes in threes, and that's certainly true in our case."

"First Cindy, then you and I losing our mates and their parents, then Mary turning up missing," Gregg said. He shook his head. "It's like a fucking nightmare."

Diana was silent. Gregg sighed, leaned back on the sofa. "God, I could use a drink."

Diana stood up. "I've got beer."

"A beer would be great."

Diana brought back bottles of Coors Lite, and they sat on the sofa drinking and talking. Gregg did most of the talking. He rattled on about how lost he felt since losing Elizabeth, how Eric was coping, then how things got jolted back into pure terror again early this morning when Brenda had called to report Mary missing. Diana nodded, saying she had been surprised by the disappearance, too. Gregg apologized again for being so accusatory this morning. "It's okay," Diana said, and this time there was genuine friendliness in her voice. It was as if she were saying, *Don't worry about it, everything's cool.* "I would have freaked out, too."

"Did Social Services ever come back today?"

"No. Bet you wish they had. They wouldn't have found anything, anyway."

Gregg had been expecting this answer. Diana's influence was gaining strength; he'd felt it earlier today when the police were at the house. Her power over the officers had resulted in a hasty search. He found it appalling that social services didn't follow up. Maybe the officers that responded this morning never made the request.

"God, I'm sorry."

"It's okay," Diana said, her voice growing softer. "It's over now."

"I mean, I know you were trying to make what you had with Ronnie a family," Gregg said, taking a swig of beer. "If this shit hadn't happened to us, things might have turned out different. I know kids sometimes take a while to get used to each other and new situations, but—"

"Mary was adjusting very well," Diana said. She was sitting closer to Gregg now.

"I think so," Gregg said. He took another sip of beer and looked around the living room. "By the way, where are Rick and Lily?"

"They're down the street at a friend's," Diana said quickly.

Gregg nodded and turned to her. He could tell she'd come up with the lie on the spot but he kept his expression neutral. "How are they taking everything?"

"As well as they can, I guess." Diana had lost a lot of the angry spark she'd had this morning, and when he'd first knocked on the door thirty minutes ago. She seemed downright friendly, the type of woman he would normally have enjoyed talking to and spending time with. "I've been letting them do what they want lately, just to get their minds off what's been happening. The more they can get away, the better they can deal with it."

"Yeah." Gregg finished his beer and placed the empty bottle on the floor. He leaned forward, head bowed, his eyes shut. "I wish it were as easy for me."

The silence that followed was awkward and what came next was both genuine and planned. It was genuine because Gregg was tapping into his emotions, allowing himself to feel the pain of his loss, his fear of Mary being in mortal danger. He let the emotion run its course, and he surprised himself when he started crying.

"I'm sorry," he said, pausing briefly before burying his hands in his face and sobbing. He could feel Diana stiffen beside him, obviously embarrassed at another sudden turn of events. "I'm sorry," he said, trying to hold his emotions in but failing. "I can't help it I . . . I just miss them so much! And . . . and I'm so *lonely!*"

"I know," Diana said, and she gently laid a hand on his shoulder. "It's going to be okay."

Gregg nodded, his chest hitching. "Yeah."

Diana rubbed his back, her touch comforting, soothing.

He reached out and touched her leg. The gesture was intended as an acknowledgment of her support but it had the opposite effect. The hand rubbing his back in a friendly, nonsexual manner now traced down to his hand on her leg. He felt her hand on his, her fingers caressing his arm. He took a deep breath and looked at her. "I'm sorry about that," he said. "I've been getting carried away with myself lately."

Diana smiled and, while he didn't let it show, he saw the undercurrent of sexual desire in that smile. "Sometimes when things are just real fucked up we all need to escape for awhile. We need to let off steam. You coming here tonight is your way of letting off steam. We're hanging out, talking about things, having a few drinks. It's cathartic."

Gregg nodded. "You're right." Her hand stayed on his arm, rubbing it, and he made no move to push it away.

"Want another drink?"

"Yeah. I could really use another."

Diana got them both another beer. And they talked more, drinking, relaxing. Gregg let himself ease into the conversation, pretending he was merely hanging out with a friendly and extremely attractive woman, sharing a drink with her, getting comfy in her house. Diana relaxed more around him and her tone became jovial, a little flirting. Gregg kept the conversation on the past tragedies, telling Diana how stressed he'd been since everything had happened and how he just needed to get away from it all, even if for the evening. Diana nodded, understanding on her features. "I've got some pot," she said. "Maybe we can just kick back here tonight and get stoned."

"That would be great!"

Diana smiled. "You do look tense. Turn around." She motioned for him to turn his back to her, and he complied.

A moment later he felt strong fingers kneading the back of his neck, and he winced. "Ooh, you *are* tense," she said, stopping her ministrations. "You need a massage."

"You can say that again," Gregg said, rolling his shoulders.

Diana stood. "I've got some pot in the bedroom. Why don't we go kick back on the bed and get stoned, relax a little bit, and then I can give you a massage."

"Sounds good." Gregg followed Diana into the bedroom and sat on the edge of the king-size waterbed she had shared with Ronnie. The room was dark, the top spread on the bed red velvet. It looked comfortable. Diana struck a match and in its dim glow Gregg noticed several candelabras perched on the dresser. There were candles on the nightstand as well. He watched as she lit the candles, and soon the room was bathed in a red glow. Once the candles were lit, she opened a dresser drawer and held up a plastic baggie containing a stick of weed and a small wooden pipe.

She filled the bowl of the pipe carefully and got it lit. She drew the smoke in, held it, then passed the pipe to Gregg. It was the first time Gregg had smoked pot in over ten years and he coughed on his first drag, expelling smoke from his lungs. He coughed uncontrollably, doubled over. Diana took the pipe from him and took another hit as Gregg got his coughing under control. "Sorry," he said sheepishly. "I haven't smoked pot in years."

"That's okay," she said, expelling a thin stream of smoke. She held the pipe out to him. "More?"

"Yeah." He took the pipe from her and managed to not only draw the smoke into his lungs, he actually held it in for a bit, coughing only slightly as he released it. He handed the pipe back to her. "That's it for me. This'll probably send me off to la-la land."

Diana laughed and took another hit.

"Mind if I use the bathroom?"

"Go for it. Want another beer?"

"Sure."

When he returned from the bathroom, he saw Diana had brought back two more beers. She handed him one and they lounged on the bed, drinking and talking. The pot was getting him nice and mellow, and it was relaxing. He lay back, his head on the pillow, feeling high. The flames from the candles flickered, casting wavery shadows on the heavy drapes that lined the windows. The candles were scented—jasmine maybe. It was a nice smell. He set his bottle on a nightstand. "I feel better already."

"Turn over," Diana said, gently nudging his shoulder. "Lie down on your stomach. Take your shirt off first."

Gregg unbuttoned his shirt and pulled it off, followed by the T-shirt he wore under it, and lay on his stomach. Diana went into the bathroom and came back with a bottle of lotion. She straddled his midsection, squirted a dollop of lotion on her hands and began rubbing it into his back and upper shoulders. Gregg sighed, his eyes closed. It really did feel good to have her massage him. Her fingers were working wonders on his sore muscles. They kneaded and prodded the tension away. "That feels good," he said.

"Good," Diana said.

Gregg let Diana give him a complete rubdown. She spent ten minutes massaging the kinks out of his shoulders, his biceps and arms and down his lower back. Combined with the alcohol and pot, it sent him straight to sensory nirvana. When she reached the waistband of his jeans, she paused. "I can do your legs if you want me to."

"Sure," he said, his voice dreamy.

"You want to pull down your pants?"

"Oh." He turned over, sat up and grinned at her, awkwardly fumbling to unsnap his jeans. Diana was watching him, a smile on her face, and in the red-tinged darkness she looked sexy and alluring. The pot was really influencing him now, tapping into his senses, and as he leaned over to unzip his pants, she leaned closer to him. He could feel her heat, smell the freshness of her skin, and he managed to unsnap his jeans and push them halfway down his legs before he stopped, leaned forward and kissed her.

It just happened. He could feel the tension between

them building, could tell the past forty minutes had been leading up to this. He had recognized the signs and subtle plays and went for it. She seemed a little taken aback but quickly responded, meeting his inquisitive tongue. His hands drew her closer so their bodies melted together. He felt her firm breasts press against his chest as her arms encircled him. And then she was leaning into him, being the aggressor, and he let her ease him down on his back, their lips still locked in a deep kiss.

They lay on the bed together with Diana on top of him, kissing passionately, their tongues dancing, darting in and out of each other's mouths, exploring. Gregg ran his hands along Diana's back, cupped her jean-clad buttocks, then roamed back up her body, his thumbs brushing the sides of her full breasts. Diana's hands darted down to the elastic of his briefs, slipped underneath them. He felt her fingers tickle his pubic hair. His penis, which had become hard the moment they first kissed, was now throbbing. Diana seemed to sense this and stopped their kiss to push his jeans down past his knees and off to the floor. Gregg helped by slipping his briefs off and Diana removed her blouse, flinging it aside. Her white bra seemed to glow in the darkness, a sharp contrast to the blackness of the shadows and the flickering glow of the candles. She flung the bra away and Gregg reached out and cupped her breasts, his thumbs circling her areolas. She moaned and was on him again, kissing him.

Feeling her naked breasts against his chest made his need for physical companionship seem more real. For a brief moment he thought about Elizabeth, but then pushed her to the back of his mind and got back into the role.

He helped Diana slip out of her jeans.

He ran kisses down between her breasts, taking each erect nipple in his mouth. Diana moaned; Gregg let the lust that was building carry him through; his only desire, his only wish now was to wallow in Diana, to fuck her, to unleash his seed inside her.

He ran his tongue down her naked belly. When he got to her panties he pushed her down on her back and pulled them off and down her legs with his teeth.

When they came together again in the dark, meeting in the hushed passion of lovers, Gregg allowed himself a quick prayer that his son would be safe, that Mary would be rescued alive, and that Don, Ray and Gary would be able to carry out the rest of the plan.

Then it was down to business.

And Diana went down on him.

And he let her take him.

His last coherent thought before she eased him inside her was, *My God, it's the best sex I've ever had, it's the best ever, no wonder she ensnares them like that, no wonder, I could never—*

He gave in to his lust for her.

"What do you think?"

They had just made their fifth drive by the house since embarking on their part of the plan, and the darkened bedroom windows were the first thing Don Grant noticed. Ray pulled the car over to the curb and killed the lights and engine.

The neighborhood was still. The interior of the car was warmed by the heater, but Don felt a chill nonetheless. He glanced at Gary, who caught his gaze and held it. Gary rubbed his gloved hands together and shivered. This was it. The time had come for them to finally put their part of the plan into action. "It's been at least forty minutes," Gary said.

"I know," Don replied.

"You think she's doing it yet?" Ray asked, looking at the house.

"Oh yeah," Don said. He couldn't keep his eyes off the house. His heart raced, and he felt sick with dread at what he and Gary were going to walk into.

They had dropped Gregg off a little after five-thirty P.M. and headed back to the motel room to wait, which had been torturous. The plan had been to give Gregg sufficient enough time to play his part, to let Diana seduce him and suck him in so she would be occupied for the remainder of the night. There had been some brief debate about how long the other guys should wait before the second part of the plan was put into motion, and Ray had let his bravado show when he'd boasted, "Well, shit man, I know she ain't a real woman and all, but you should be able to get into her pants within thirty minutes, don't you think?"

Gregg had shook his head and Don had dismissed Ray's boast as youthful machismo. He had suggested they play it safe and start their return surveillance of the house at nine P.M. "She should be fully connected by then," he had said, glancing at Gregg as if to give him another chance to back out of it. Gregg had remained stoic, committed to going through with it, and agreed.

They were to wait until the lights in the house were off, and then forty-five minutes after that. Then they were to put the meat of the plan into action. Ray would wait in the car with the engine running while Gary and Don, one of them bearing an axe, would enter through the front door, hoping Gregg had been able to unlock it; if it wasn't, they would use the axe to smash in the door. Once inside, the clock would start ticking: Their first job was to find Mary by checking those spots that had been passed over in the quick search the police conducted that morning. "Start in the attic," Gregg had said that afternoon as they drew up the plans. "The attic in that house has a pull-down ladder and you get to it from the hallway that leads to the master bedroom."

Once Mary was rescued, one of them would carry her out to the car and the other would venture into Diana's bedroom with the axe. Gregg braced them for what they would see. "Think of one of those morphing images you see as a special effect in a movie. It might just look like a shapeless lump and it'll be merged with me. You might not be able to tell where I end and it begins. I'll be unconscious, and it'll be in its most vulnerable state while it feeds on me."

Don had agreed. "It should not only be vulnerable, it'll be drunk."

"Take the axe and just start chopping into that thing," Gregg had said. "That should start loosening its hold on me. I don't know what state I'll be in, but—"

"He might not be able to wake up," Don had cut in, looking Gary firmly in the eye. "Do whatever you can to wake him up. For God's sake, watch out when you swing that axe, too. That thing'll be feeding on him, but do what you can to get Gregg to come out of it."

Whoever dropped Mary off at the car was to then head back to the house and help rescue Gregg. "If it wakes up and comes after you, run," Gregg said. "If you can't save me, save yourselves and get Mary out of there. Just get the hell out."

They hadn't thought about what to do if the cops showed up before they could get away. They hadn't had time to talk about that. The only time the subject came up, Gregg had waved the question aside and said, "We'll wing it if it happens."

Don hoped they didn't have to wing it too much.

"Well?" Gary asked.

Don glanced at Gary, who was sitting in the passenger seat. He nodded. "Let's go," he said.

"Jesus fuck, let's get this over with," Ray said, shivering. He looked nervous and scared as Gary climbed out of the car.

Don got out and reached into the backseat for the axe. The two men glanced at each other, then at the house across the street.

The darkened house was still.

The neighborhood was silent.

It was just after ten-thirty P.M.

"Let's go," Don said.

They started across the street. Don's heart beat hard in his rib cage, and he felt his limbs shaking. Gary darted ahead of him and around the side of the house, moving stealthily as they made their way to the porch. Don reached out and gripped the doorknob with one gloved hand and turned it.

The door was unlocked, just as Gregg had planned it.

They stepped inside the dark living room.

Silence.

Illuminated somewhat by the streetlight outside, they were able to make out the living room. Gregg had drawn a crude map of the layout of the house back at the motel room, and they both immediately glanced toward the master bedroom. They crept farther inside, and Don saw the half-opened door to the master bedroom at the end of the short hallway. About twenty feet from the threshold of the master bedroom, positioned on the hallway ceiling, was the square outline of the attic door. Gary grabbed a chair from the dining room and placed it under the door, stood on it and hooked his finger around the lock, pulling it down. Don moved the chair away as the ladder unfolded. He stood guard, hefting the axe, as Gary quickly climbed up into the attic.

Don's nerves were twitching with fright, his blood icy as he focused on the half-opened bedroom door. He could see the flickering glow of candles emanating from within. It was hard to hear anything even in the stillness of the house, and for a moment he let his imagination get away with him at the thought of Diana Marshfield (Lisa) suddenly appearing behind him, her naked form standing before him, a smile on her perfect lips. He felt the skin along the back of his neck rise, and he almost risked a look behind him, almost bolted out the front door because he didn't know if he was going to be able to go through with this. But then he heard a scraping sound and it was so sudden, so loud in the silence of the house that he jumped and almost dropped the axe. His heart leaped into his throat, and he looked back down the hallway, almost certain the loud noise of Gary in the attic would wake her up and she would creep down the hall, leaving Gregg's lifeless body in the bedroom, where she'd been feeding. She would instantly ensnare him with her look and he'd be unable to run, unable to escape, and Gary would come down bearing Mary's body, unaware of the danger that was now right below him and—

He saw Gary's feet trudging carefully down the wooden steps. Then he saw the dangling, limp hands of a child. Don sprang forward to help as Gary emerged from the gloomy attic. He was carrying Mary in his arms, carefully making his way downstairs. Mary's body was limp, her skin pale, her eyes closed. Don didn't know whether she was dead or alive; she could have been either. She was dressed in white and pink pajamas that were streaked with dirt. Gary looked at Don and mouthed, "She's alive."

Don nodded and gripped the axe. The minute Gary reached the living room floor he headed toward the front door with Mary. Don turned toward the master bedroom, gripping the axe firmly.

Please, God, give me strength.

He hadn't prayed to God in years, since Lisa had been taken from him. He said a quick prayer now, took a deep breath, and forced himself to walk down the short hallway toward the master bedroom before he lost his nerve.

He nudged the door open and stepped into the bedroom. The shades were drawn across the windows, and if it weren't for the dozens of candles glowing from candelabras perched on the dresser and end tables the room would have been pitch dark. Despite the fact the light from the candles hadn't been seen from outside, they illuminated the room perfectly.

The bed's large oak headboard was set up against the far wall, and the first thing Don saw was Gregg lying on his back, motionless. His eyes were closed, and he was naked, his right arm flung over his head as if he had just fallen into bed. The sheets were thrown back, and attached to Gregg's left side and spilling out over the other end of the bed was a mass of seamless flesh.

The sight almost sent Don into a heart attack. He felt the skin along the back of his neck crawl. His stomach did a slow flip-flop as he stood in the bedroom, bearing the axe, gazing down at the monstrosity feeding on Gregg.

Is he alive? Is he dead? Does that thing know I'm here? Oh God, I think it's moving—

Don stepped forward, raised the axe over his shoulder and then brought it down with all his strength on the mass of flesh on the right side of the bed with a sickening, wet *plop!*

There was a tension in the air, as if something invisible exploded. It was very faint, but it cast a warm, damp feeling around the room. Don ignored it, knowing that if he paused for just an instant, he would give the thing a chance to slip into his mind. He pulled the axe out of the fleshy thing. It felt like he was pulling the axe out of thick Jell-O or slime. There was a moist sucking sound, and the sudden scent of rot and decay, but he barreled past that, raised the axe over his shoulder again and swung it down a second time, hard. The axe blade sank deeper into the shapeless mass, and this time the change in the air was immediate.

It was waking up.

Shit! Don pulled the axe out and brought it down again, harder. The blade sank into another spot, up near the top of the bed, where he hoped Diana's head would have lain. He glanced quickly at Gregg and saw no movement. The thing was still attached to him. He pulled the axe out of the thing with a wet sound that resembled pulling a booted foot out of mud, and quickly nudged Gregg's shoulder with his left hand. "Gregg!" he yelled. "Wake up!"

He could feel the tension building as the stink rose. The stench was overpowering, and now he swore he could make out faint movement from the thing on the bed, as if something was swimming beneath the surface of its skin. He nudged Gregg again with the axe handle, poking him hard in the ribs. "Gregg! Wake up, come on, come on, *wake up!*"

Gregg was still.

Another quick glance at the thing sent his heart trip hammering again. It was *definitely* moving now.

"Goddamn you, motherfucker!" Don raised the axe high over his head and brought it down with all his strength in the center of the thing.

The blade sank into the mass of flesh. Something warm, wet and stinking of a cesspit spattered Don's face.

And the shapeless mass of flesh on the bed, the same mass that was attached to Gregg like a big cancerous tumor, began to undulate and shift.

When Ray saw Gary dash across the street carrying Mary, he quickly got out and opened the door to the backseat. Gary slid her in quickly. "Put a blanket over her and keep that engine running," he said.

Gary raced back to the house, thinking if Don was using the axe he would immediately assist in bringing Gregg to consciousness. He thought he heard Don yelling, and when he breasted the entrance of the master bedroom he saw Don bring the axe down on the bed. Gary paused briefly, taking the scene in quickly, then moved to the edge of the king-sized bed where Gregg lay and shook him roughly. "Gregg!" he shouted. "We gotta get out of here!"

"Die, you motherfucker!" Don screamed, bringing the axe down again.

Gary grabbed Gregg's arm and pulled. The room was pungent with the intermingling scents of garbage, rot and jasmine. He pulled Gregg halfway off the bed, saw the thing was still attached to him, and shook Gregg's face. "Wake up!" he yelled into Gregg's face. He slapped Gregg's cheeks, as if he were trying to sober him up. "Wake up, fight it off man!"

"Die, die, die, motherfucker, die!" Don panted as he raised the axe and then swung it down again and again.

Gary caught a movement out of the corner of his eyes and looked up. The thing was waking up. "Shit," he muttered.

"No!" Don screamed.

Something shot out of the mass of flesh and grabbed Don's arm.

Gary watched, momentarily stunned, as Don struggled with the thing. It had a firm grip on Don's right arm. He still clutched the axe in his hands, and Gary immediately grabbed Don around the waist and pulled him back. "Let go!" he yelled.

"You fucking bitch!" Don screamed. Gary felt him struggling as he fought to tear himself away from the thing.

Gary reached for the axe, and Don released it into his grip, the tradeoff happening so quickly it was as if they were linked psychically, as if Don knew what Gary was thinking. The thing still had a firm grip on Don's forearm, and it was now beginning to build into a shape as it gathered itself up on the bed. Gary got a firm grip on the axe and swung it down hard into the growing mass.

The blade bit deep into the flesh, releasing a wave of putrid air and a splash of something wet that spattered him like warm raindrops. The blow caused it to relax its grip on Don, who stumbled back violently, crashing into the dresser and sending the candelabras to the floor.

The carpet caught on fire. A second candelabra that had fallen down beneath the window caught flame below the heavy velvet drapes.

Don immediately lunged forward and grabbed the axe from Gary. "We've got it! Get Gregg the hell out of here!"

Gary grabbed Gregg's arm, pulling him with all his strength. His body slid across the bed, and Gary saw the thing that had been seamed to Gregg's side began to pull away with a wet separation of flesh. Don brought the axe down on the thing again as the flames began to rise higher, spreading rapidly up the velvet curtains.

The room grew quickly hot and smoke-filled as the flames raced up the walls, burning the wallpaper. Once they reached the roof the house would be engulfed. "We've got to get out of here!" Gary yelled.

"Die!" Don screamed, swinging the axe down again.

Gary tugged on Gregg's arm again, and this time he felt something give way from the thing clutching him. He shook Gregg again. "Goddamn it, wake up!"

"You cocksucking bitch, *die!*" Don said, his voice raspy and sobbing as he swung the axe down on the thing again.

Gary gave another ferocious tug on Gregg's arm, as if he were pulling a drowning man from a raging river, and this time the thing let go completely and Gregg stumbled back, his naked form falling over Gary in a crumpled heap. Gary quickly scrambled to his feet, grasped Gregg under the armpits and hoisted him up. "Come on, man," he shouted. "Fight it!"

The room was growing hotter and the smell of smoke stronger, baking the stench of rotting flesh into a thick, impenetrable thing. Gary stood up, Gregg slumped against him, and he thought he could sense Gregg stir slightly. "Don!" he shouted.

The flames that had been fanning their way up the walls of the master bedroom, feeding on the carpet and the dresser, suddenly rushed up to the roof of the house. Don felt the heat move over the walls and roof, and he knew any minute now the entire bedroom was going to be engulfed in an inferno. He hoisted Gregg to his feet and shouted again: "Don!"

And then the shapeless mass of flesh suddenly took form. It gathered up from the bottom, like some shimmering CGI animation effect from a horror film, merging into a distinct shape. Female. Naked. Standing beside the bed, facing him.

Diana Marshfield.

The smoke was getting thicker and it was hard to breathe. Gregg was stirring to consciousness quickly, and he leaned against Gary, coughing. Gary shouted again one last time: "Don!"

If Don heard him, he gave no indication. He faced Diana and threw the axe down. Gary took a step toward the bedroom door, dragging Gregg with him, unable to tear his gaze away from Don and Diana. Don was sobbing, and as the flames picked up in their intensity, the heat stifling now, he thought he could make out Don's sobbing voice. "Lisa . . . Lisa . . ."

Diana Marshfield locked eyes with Gary, ignoring Don completely, and he knew then she had him marked. Gregg stirred suddenly, as if he had been given a jolt of electricity. He was suddenly more conscious, more aware, and Gary immediately sensed Diana still had a hold on him and was trying to use her newfound strength to get a hold on *him* as well. "No!" he shouted.

Gary could feel Diana tense, could see the intense hatred and lust for him in her eyes. He could tell she was about to pounce; was about to leap across the room at them, utilizing whatever supernatural powers she had to capture her prey, when suddenly Don screamed, "Lisa!" and leaped at her.

The force of Don's leap knocked Diana down, and it snapped Gary out of his temporary paralysis. He bolted out the bedroom door, dragging Gregg with him just as the flames mushroomed, engulfing the entire bedroom in a fiery inferno.

Together they ran through the house and burst out the front door, feeling the heat chase them out. Gary was still clutching Gregg, pushing him out as he ran. As the bedroom behind them was engulfed in flames, he heard the screams of anguish and pain coming from the bedroom. He wasn't even aware of the blisters breaking out on his skin from the intense heat of the flames.

The sound of the screams made him run faster and Gregg almost fell against the car when they reached it. Gary fumbled for the back door and shoved Gregg inside and slammed the door. He ran around to the passenger side and dove in. He barely got the door closed as Ray peeled away from the curb, away from the burning house, away from the nightmare.

In the backseat Gregg was talking to Mary, crying. "Mary! Mary, are you okay? Oh God, *Mary* . . ."

Gary leaned back in his seat, trying to catch his breath. His skin was bathed in sweat.

"What happened?" Ray asked as he drove through the neighborhood too fast. "Holy shit, man, you okay? Christ, I think you're *burned,* man!"

"Slow down!" Gary said, coughing.

Ray slowed, and Gary closed his eyes, trying to catch his breath.

In the backseat Gregg was shaking Mary. "Mary, Mary, Mary . . ."

"She's okay," Ray said. "I checked her. She's breathing, she's okay."

A soft cry came from Mary, as if to confirm this.

Gregg: "Mary!"

And as Mary struggled from a sound sleep, a sleep induced by the gradual sapping of her soul and life force, Gary leaned back and closed his eyes and tried to tell himself the second voice he had heard screaming in pain along with Don Grant's had been human.

EPILOGUE

It had been a warm day, slowly building up to the intense dry desert heat New Mexico was known for, but Gregg Weaver didn't mind. He welcomed it. He was tired of the hot, humid summers of Central Pennsylvania.

He was standing on the back deck of the house he had bought earlier this spring just outside Albuqurque, looking out over the backyard. Eric and Mary were in the garage, teetering around on bicycles and skateboards, and their laughing voices made him smile. It was nice to hear them laugh like that. It was great to hear them play, let down their guard and just be kids. He hadn't thought he'd ever be at a place where he could hear that again.

The sliding-glass door that led to the kitchen opened, and Gregg turned around. Brad Campbell came out, bearing two bottles of ice-cold Molson. "Here you go, bro."

"Thanks," Gregg said. He took a deep swig. Cold beer, warm desert heat. Paradise.

"You picked yourself out a nice place, man," Brad said, stepping to the edge of the porch and looking out over the patchy backyard. Gregg's yard ended at the edge of a ridge that overlooked the valley below, which displayed a breath-taking view of the city. If he turned to the north he had a view of the high desert and the mountains beyond, which was even more beautiful. "What made you decide to settle in New Mexico?"

"I don't know," Gregg said. A warm breeze ruffled his hair. "When I decided to sell the house in Lititz, I asked Eric where he wanted to go and he said somewhere far away from Pennsylvania. I didn't want to go back to Los Angeles. Too smoggy, too crowded. So we picked somewhere in between. Plus, I've always wanted to live in the desert, and Elizabeth always loved it."

"It's nice out here," Brad said. He leaned against the fence that straddled the deck, admiring the view of the valley. His hair, which had been cropped short for Elizabeth's memorial service, was now a shoulder-length mullet.

"Yeah, it is."

"How do the kids like it?"

"They love it."

Gregg had hoped the kids would adjust, and they had. In the two months following Mary's drastic rescue from her father's former house, Gregg didn't know what the future was going to hold. He had to take a leave of absence from his job just to deal with taking care of Mary and the surmounting legal and financial maze, and Brad had helped out with Elizabeth's literary estate. In fact, Elizabeth's literary estate was one of the reasons he had flown Brad out to Albuqurque. He had some serious business to discuss with him, stuff he didn't want to bring up over the phone.

"How's Gary doing?" Brad asked.

"He's doing well," Gregg said, taking a drink, his gaze sweeping over the view. "His burns are completely healed." In addition to a rash of second-degree burns, Gary Swanson had suffered a third-degree burn along his left arm. Likewise, Gregg had suffered a lot of second-degree burns all over his body.

Ray had been quick-thinking enough during the frantic drive to escape Diana's clutches to pull over about a mile away from the development and call the police. By then neighbors had already called 911, and in the ensuing quagmire that followed that evening, Gary and Ray had been questioned by Lancaster County detectives and the Pennsylvania State Police. Gregg had been questioned extensively upon his discharge from the hospital after being treated for his burns, as well as dehydration and smoke inhalation. The three of them had all stuck to the basic story they had come up with earlier that afternoon during their planning, and it went something like this:

Gregg had gathered the three of them together in an attempt to get information out of them in his search for Mary, and they had voiced their individual suspicions that Diana was responsible for Mary's abduction. They'd gone to the Baker house to talk to Diana in the hopes of convincing her to reveal where Mary was. Once at the Baker house, the four of them had argued long and hard through the night with Diana. She had become hysterical and gone crazy, throwing the lighted candles in her bedroom around and assaulting Gregg. Don had tried to subdue her, and that's when Gary and Ray had started looking for Mary, starting with the attic, where they found her. By then the bedroom was ablaze, Don was unconscious, and Gary went in to rescue Gregg while Ray rushed Mary to the car. Unfortunately, Gary had been unable to save Don and had run out of the house just before it was totally engulfed in flames.

The police had been skeptical. Gary, Ray and Gregg had kept to this basic story with poker faces. Part of their planning included placing an extra set of clothes in the car for Gregg, which he'd donned quickly after Ray called the police; he didn't want to have to explain that he'd been having sex with Diana in the event the police did become involved. Luckily they were able to skate by during questioning that first night. When the fire was put out and Don's body was found, Gregg's heart had bled for him. And when they failed to find a second body—in the beginning only badly burned scraps of flesh were found—law enforcement turned the heat up on them.

They kept to their story. They insisted Diana had been in the house and that they had fought her. Gary had pointed out that Mary had been found in the attic unconscious, and the little girl had supported the story by saying Diana had kidnapped her from the Wandrei home. Of course the police questioned her separately, and Gregg had been worried at first because of it. But Mary had been through a lot that past month, and she'd known if she told the police she was lured out of Brenda and Donald Wandrei's house by her father they wouldn't believe her, so she told them Diana had snuck in the house and kidnapped her.

This had helped somewhat. The investigating detectives had wanted to place the three men in custody, pending their investigation, but Gregg had called the family lawyer, who intervened. There was no evidence the three men had committed a crime. Unless the authorities could prove otherwise, there were no grounds to hold them. So they'd waited for nearly two weeks as the fire marshal and the police conducted their investigation and returned their verdict.

And the verdict was . . . all the evidence suggested the three men were telling the truth. The fire marshal declared the blaze had been caused by the flame from several candles, igniting the curtains and bedspread in the bedroom. Because the bedroom had been furnished in oak with heavy velvet curtains and bedspread, it had gone up quickly. The coroner determined Don had died from massive burns and smoke inhalation; other injuries Don might have suffered were inconclusive due to the condition of the body.

When the investigators emerged with the badly charred remains of the axe and asked them about it, they claimed ignorance. *Never saw that before in my life, Detective. Had no idea Diana had an axe in the bedroom.*

The axe handle was so badly burned it was impossible to get fingerprints off it.

While the physical evidence at the scene seemed to lend credence to their story, once the police learned of Don Grant's arrest warrant for murder in California, they began questioning Gregg more: How did they meet? How long had Don been in town? Did Gregg know Don was wanted for murder? Gregg tried to prepare himself for the scrutiny when they learned Don had perished in the fire, and he came up with a story that would have worked in one of Elizabeth's short stories or novels, yet stayed pretty close to the truth: Don had contacted him shortly after Thanksgiving, inquiring about Diana Marshfield. He hadn't revealed his past in California, and Gregg had no idea the man was wanted for murdering his wife, Lisa. Instead, Don convinced him Diana Marshfield was a con artist, that she had married him several years back under another name; just which one Gregg couldn't remember. Apparently Diana would change her name every few years, move to a different state and city under this new identity, change her appearance, strike up a relationship with a man, marry him, then swindle him out of his life savings and leave. Don had finally tracked her down to Reinholds, Pennsylvania, where she was living under a new name, Diana Marshfield, with a new sucker, Ronnie Baker. This story segued well with further testimony from Elizabeth's family and their feelings regarding Diana; they'd known there was something fishy about her from the beginning, but they just couldn't place their finger on it. Now the pieces were falling together.

It fell together with the lead detective of the case, too. He checked computer records for Diana Marshfield and found close to a dozen aliases she'd used. Gregg had been astonished the detective verified what Don had told him, that there had actually been some kind of record. With the co-operation of law enforcement agencies from other parts of the country, they were able to corroborate most of the story Gregg told them; the only thing that didn't add up one hundred percent were physical descriptions. In more than one case, the woman whom Diana was impersonating bore no physical resemblance to her. Sometimes the description was accurate, other times it was way off the mark, and sometimes the description was sketchy at best. Detective Carson didn't know what to make of it, only that his instinct was leading him to believe Diana Marshfield was the best con artist he had ever run across, and the only thing missing was her body.

That had been the only thing left unexplained: Diana Marshfield's disappearance as well as that of her children.

Along with Don Grant's body, investigators found charred remains that could not be identified. Lab tests indicated that what was found was flesh . . . but just what kind was inconclusive. Gregg said nothing during the few weeks of trying to identify these pitiful remains. The only thing he could think of was what Gary had told him, that when he and Don walked in, they had seen that shapeless mass of flesh attached to his unconscious form in the king-size bed, draining him. He didn't want to suggest that the scant remnants of flesh were the remains of Diana Marshfield because then they would try to verify that in the only way they knew: by trying to get DNA samples.

In the end, the charred flesh remained unidentified. It was one of the many things about the case that puzzled the lead detective since it couldn't positively be tied to Diana Marshfield or her kids.

Gregg had suggested numerous times that maybe Diana had run out of the house after Gary and they hadn't noticed her. Maybe she'd been in shock and had simply raced out of the neighborhood, somehow made it to the main highway and hitched a ride somewhere. She'd left her car, her belongings, at the house and while it was possible she had identification on her person, it didn't seem likely she would get far. An all points bulletin had been placed with the state police with her description, detailing what she was last seen wearing, but she was never found.

At least officially.

In early January, a 911 call in Cockeysville, Maryland, just outside Baltimore, sent firefighters and police officers to a strip mall off Route 83. There they came across two frightened young men, one of whom was visibly ill. They pointed at a charred section of the ground, and the cop who approached the scene first later stated he didn't know what he was looking at. There had obviously been a fire; the wall of the building bore burn stains shooting up at least ten feet, and the unrecognizable mass that lay charred and still smoking on the ground at the base of the building surely couldn't be human, but it was. The ill young man vomited on the shoes of one of the other officers who had responded to the scene.

According to the two men, they had driven to the rear of the mall to urinate—they'd both been drinking and had to pee really bad—and they'd just turned the corner at the mall when they saw the fire start. It had gone up like a torch and the torch had begun immediately moving frantically, running around, bumping into the walls, and that's when they realized it was a human being who had been set on fire. They'd raced over to the hapless victim and tried to douse the flames with jackets and a blanket from the car, but it had been no use. The flames had been too intense, so they'd fled around the corner to a phone booth at a McDonald's and dialed 911. By the time they got back to the victim, the fire had burned itself out.

It had taken the coroner a week to determine that the victim was female, and two weeks later a shaky, tentative identification was made. The victim was Diana Marshfield. She was identified by a piece of jewelry that had remained untouched by the flames. Gregg and Mary both identified it as having been similar to something Diana had worn often. The physical stature of the victim matched Diana's description, but the body was so badly burned that no further testing could be done.

And with that, it became an open-and-shut case for the investigators. Diana Marshfield had committed suicide by pouring gasoline over herself and lighting a match. An empty can of gasoline had been found at the scene, and the coroner found traces of it on the victim and splashed on the ground where she was found. Gregg found it hard to believe Diana Marshfield would have killed herself, even if she *had* escaped. The more he thought about it and read through the account, the more he was convinced the body wasn't Diana Marshfield's. Rather, the body was that of a homeless woman Diana had ensnared, probably while assuming the role of a man: She had led the woman around the back of the strip mall, had given her the jewelry, then doused gasoline over her and set her on fire. Gregg had even tracked down one of the men who had come across the dying woman and asked him if he'd seen anybody else in the area, if he thought it was possible somebody had set the victim on fire. The man had emphatically stated he had seen nobody fleeing the scene. Yes, there had been other people around at the strip mall, but he hadn't seen anybody fleeing.

Hell, the succubus could have been one of them. Under a new identity.

And under a new identity, it could always come back to Lancaster County. It knew Gregg was widowed. Knew he would soon become lonely.

Best of all, it knew Gregg already had a taste for it.

That was another reason why Gregg felt the need to move far away from Pennsylvania. He wanted to get as far away from it as possible.

Gregg and Brad drank their beers and watched the sun set over the desert hills of New Mexico. A moment later Eric and Mary ran into the backyard from the garage. "We going to Avila's for dinner tonight?" Eric asked eagerly.

Since moving to Albuqurque, Eric had become addicted to Mexican food.

"You bet," Gregg said, finishing his beer, ruffling his hair. "How 'bout you, Mary?"

"I want a burrito and *sopapias* for desert!"

Gregg and Brad laughed. "You got it," Gregg said.

They went back into the house, the men taking their empty beer bottles with them and closing the sliding-glass door. Then they went out to dinner at Avila's.

Later that night, upstairs in Gregg's office, they talked some more.

The kids were downstairs in the den, watching a movie on Cinemax. Gregg had turned on the air conditioner; it had been almost one hundred degrees today and the evening temperatures were only supposed to fall to the high seventies. The two men had retreated upstairs with cold beers to talk. Gregg had sorted through Elizabeth's computer files and papers, had made copies for Brad, and he pointed these copies out to him now. He'd also produced a list of publishing contacts Elizabeth had maintained and a database of all her published and unpublished work. There was still an unfinished novel she had been under contract to deliver, and Brad had volunteered to complete it several months ago. He'd arranged with Gregg and Elizabeth's editor to finish the book, and Elizabeth's publisher had graciously extended the deadline. Now Gregg handed Brad a Zip disk containing the unfinished novel and the notes that went with it, along with other material. "Alan wants this by September," he said.

"No problem," Brad said, taking the disk. "I can have it done by then."

"Great." Gregg took a swig of beer. "I really appreciate you helping me out with this."

"Hey man, no problem. Elizabeth was my friend, and I'm only too glad to do this for her."

They drank in silence for a while. Downstairs, the faint sounds of the movie *Shrek* could be heard.

Brad grinned. "Mary really likes that movie, doesn't she?"

"Oh yeah. She's seen it at least twenty million times."

"How's she doing after all this?"

"Pretty well, considering all she's gone through." Gregg looked at Brad, deciding now the time was right. Brad knew only the bare basics, what had made the newspapers and the personal stuff that had been normal on the surface; the selling of the Weaver home, Gregg getting custody of Mary after Cindy's family agreed it would be better for her to be with Gregg and Eric, relocating to New Mexico. Now he was going to get the whole tamale.

"Brad, there's another reason why I asked you to fly out here for a few days."

Brad nodded and took a swig of beer. There was a calm knowledge in his brown eyes. "I kind of suspected that."

"You did?"

Brad grinned. "Dude! I'm a writer. And not just *a* writer, I'm a writer of the same weird fucked-up shit your wife wrote. Which means she and I thought a lot alike. I could tell something was up when you called and asked if I could fly out to discuss the literary estate. Shit, we could have settled that over the phone and by e-mail and Federal Express."

"You're right." Now Gregg was smiling. "And I know you can keep a secret. I know I can trust you; anybody who was Elizabeth's friend is somebody I know I can trust."

"I appreciate hearing that, man."

Gregg took another swig of beer, set the bottle on a coaster, leaned forward, elbows on his knees. "I have something to tell you. I know you'll listen with an open mind because like you said, you're a writer, and writers like you and Elizabeth have open minds to this weird fucked-up shit." He smiled again, catching Brad's eye. "What I'm going to tell you is what *really* happened. What the police never found out and what the press never found out and never will. Okay?"

Brad nodded, the grin fading from his lightly bearded face. He could sense the seriousness of Gregg's tone.

"Want another beer?"

Brad nodded. "I think so."

Gregg went downstairs and brought up an ice bucket filled with the rest of the case of Coronas they were drinking.

Then he told Brad Campbell what *really* happened.

And Brad believed him.

It was two hours later and both men were far from being sloshed. The summer heat had something to do with that, Gregg supposed. The kids had already gone upstairs to bed and the two men had retreated to the back porch where Gregg finished the story in low tones.

"So you believe me?" It was the fifth time Gregg had asked this.

"I believe you, man." Brad's tone comforted Gregg's nerves. He could tell Brad believed every word.

"Will you do me another favor?"

Brad looked at him, cradling an empty Corona bottle. "I think I know what you're going to ask me, but go ahead."

"Elizabeth's last book contract was a two-book deal," Gregg said, speaking slowly. "The Zip disk I just gave you contains only the first book. I told Alan I didn't want to break the contract and would like to fulfill it with a novel Elizabeth already has, one she wrote a few years ago that she never sent for publication. He told me he'd take a look at it."

"I didn't know there was another novel," Brad said.

"There isn't." Gregg fixed Brad with a pensive gaze. "Not really. But what I just told you . . . well . . . what do you think?"

Brad paused, understanding dawning on his features. "You want me to novelize what you just told me?"

"Can you?"

"Well . . . yeah, sure . . ."

"I detect hesitation."

"No, I'm not hesitant at all—"

"I'll pay you," Gregg said quickly. "Half her advance up front and a percentage of the royalties."

"It's not the money I'm worried about."

"Then what is it?"

Brad shifted in his seat, looked out at the vast desert night. When he looked back at Gregg, there was a grin on his face. "How soon can I start?"

Gregg smiled.

An hour later.

"There's something else I haven't told anybody," Gregg said, lying back on the chaise lounge. Brad was reclining in the lounge next to him. They were down to the last bottles of Coronas and were pleasantly shit-faced now.

"What's that?"

"You have to promise not to tell anybody," Gregg said softly. He heard his voice cracking, and he took a deep breath to hold the sudden wave of emotion that threatened to spill out of him. He felt like crying, but he couldn't, not here in front of Brad. Brad would think he was completely shit-faced, that the alcohol was magnifying everything, ex-aggerating things.

"Your secret's safe with me," Brad assured him.

"I know what it's like to be an addict now," Gregg said. "I think Mary knows, too. We've actually talked about it a lit-tle. Away from Eric's presence, of course. And I haven't told her about my . . . problem yet. But I think she knows. She's a very smart little girl."

Brad frowned.

"We've been very supportive of each other," Gregg con-tinued. "In a way, we're like each other's AA sponsors. We talk to each other about our mutual problem every day. And we both . . . take pains to avoid thinking about it or getting into the habits that would make us fall off the wagon. It's hard, though. It's real hard, especially for Mary. I mean, she misses her father terribly. I know she does, but you saw her room."

"There's no pictures of her dad in her bedroom," Brad said. "Just her mom."

"Exactly."

"But Elizabeth's picture is all over the house," Brad said, looking at Gregg. "Her presence is all over the house. So what's—"

"It's not thinking about Elizabeth that worries me."

Brad opened his mouth to respond but didn't say anything. It was as if he didn't know what to say.

"I miss Elizabeth terribly," Gregg said, feeling his voice crack again. "And I try to think of all the good times we had, and I'm very comforted that she died trying to help Mary and fight this . . . this evil that came into our lives. I'm very proud of her for that." Gregg felt his voice cracking more, and he took more deep breaths to calm himself down. "I suppose I'll always miss her, you know? And . . . and I know life will go on. I'd like to think that I'll get stronger, that I'll heal. I'd like to think Elizabeth would have wanted me to move on with my life, to be happy. She would have wanted me to go on living, to take care of Eric and Mary, and I'm going to do that. I've promised her I'm going to do that, and I think everything in that area has gone okay so far. I mean, what I did to save Mary—"

"You played the best role of your life when you did that," Brad said.

Gregg nodded. He took a deep breath. "Fuck yeah, I did. And it took that to kick me in the ass again. I've made a promise to Elizabeth now that I'm never going to abandon my muse again. It saved Mary after all." He took another deep breath, wiped his eyes, looked at Brad. He managed a small smile. "I have an audition next month with a local theater company. My way of reconnecting with my muse, keeping my promise to Elizabeth that I'll always feed it and take care of it."

Brad nodded, his features conveying that he understood, but he remained silent.

"But . . . I get lonely sometimes." Gregg turned to Brad, and a tear rolled down his cheeks. "You know what I mean?"

Brad nodded. "Yeah. I know what you mean, bro."

"No. I don't think you *really* know what I mean."

Brad was silent again, a confused look on his face that suggested he didn't know how to respond.

"You ever done hard drugs?" Gregg asked.

The question seemed to take Brad aback a bit. "Well . . . yeah. I mean, I'm not proud of it. I was young and stupid and did a lot of things I probably shouldn't have done. Why?"

"I've never done hard drugs," Gregg resumed. "Just beer and pot, that was the extent of it. And I was never a heavy drinker anyway, and for the longest time I could never relate to the mindset of an alcoholic or drug addict. I used to think people like that were losers. You know, that they couldn't control their drinking, that they were dumb enough to do cocaine and get hooked and . . . well, I used to think they deserved it. Is that shitty or what?"

"I guess," Brad said. "I mean . . . in a way it is, but then sometimes I feel the same way, too."

"You ever done heroin?"

Brad bristled. "No."

"Neither have I. And from what I hear, it's pretty heavy stuff. It's supposed to be the best high in the world, and that after doing it once you want to experience that feeling over and over again, so you do more. I guess that's the way it works for people who get hooked on coke or speed or booze. Something in their chemistry connects with whatever substance they take and feeds those pleasure centers, makes them want to feel that high, that pleasure, again, so they do more. That's when it hooks you. That's when you become dependent on it."

Brad didn't say anything and Gregg could tell his friend—Elizabeth's friend, but his now—was looking worried. Gregg shook his head, sat up in the lounge. "Don't worry man, I'm not strung out on smack or anything. And I haven't become an alcoholic. This is the first time I've been fucked up like this in a long time."

Brad mustered a smile.

"But I do know what it's like to be an addict now. And Mary does too. And I'll tell you why." He swung his legs over the lounge and sat facing Brad, summoning the courage it was going to take to make this confession. He took a deep breath, willed the tears back, then took the plunge. "I've been lonely and . . . sometimes . . . when I'm by myself and I get . . . lonely . . . I . . . I masturbate and . . ."

Brad had that look on his face that seemed to say, *Dude, we all play with ourselves. It's human nature, no need to get all guilty about it. Hell, I beat my meat at least once a week on general principle, and my wife and I have a very nice, satisfying sex life, thank you very much.* But he didn't say anything; he listened calmly, waiting.

Gregg read the expression on Brad's face and shook his head. "It's not what you think. Sometimes . . . when I masturbate . . . I . . . I think about Diana Marshfield."

There. He'd said it. And then he buried his face in his hands, feeling the shame pour out of him. "And I can't help it! I just think about how it was when I was with her, and I take my dick out and beat off like a teenage kid jacking off to a *Playboy* centerfold. And I know it shouldn't make me feel guilty, but it does! It just *does!* And the more it makes me feel guilty, the more I think about Elizabeth and how I wish she were here with me and then I turn right back around and think about what it would be like to fuck Diana just one more time and then I start playing right into the fantasy and I jack off again and—"

And then Gregg Weaver sobbed.

Brad Campbell sat on the chaise lounge, not knowing how to respond. He sat there awkwardly as Gregg cried, patted his shoulder, lending support. Gregg cried, wiped his eyes. "I'm sorry. I didn't mean to bawl like that."

"It's okay, man," Brad said, rubbing Gregg's shoulder. "I think if I were in your shoes I would've cried too."

"I just wanted to tell you so you'd understand a little more." He looked up at Brad, wiping tears from his face. "For the book."

Brad nodded. "I understand. For the book."

"Is that some fucked-up shit, or what?"

"Yeah. It is."

"All I can do is be a source of support for Mary," Gregg continued. "Be her sponsor. And she's mine. We've both been through the same thing, and we both have the same . . . afflictions you might say. Hers is a little different, but it's the same nonetheless. We help each other."

"When's the last time you thought about Diana while jacking off?"

"Three weeks ago."

"How do you feel now?"

"You mean like, am I over feeling this way?"

Brad nodded.

Gregg shook his head. "No. I feel the itch every day."

"What about Mary? How's she?"

"As long as we don't mention her father, she's okay."

Brad was now sitting up, stone-cold sober. He was leaning forward, looking Gregg square in the eyes, having a nice man-to-man talk. "So what are you going to do? Are you afraid she'll—that *it*—will come back?"

"Yeah. But only if I give in to my urges. Mary feels the same way. That's why we avoid all mention of Ronnie. If she thinks about him, sees his picture, she starts to get openly weepy and she dreams about him. She wants him to come to her, to take her away. And . . . well, we've both talked about this and we both feel that the more she dreams about him like that, the more it will awaken . . . *it* . . . and it'll answer that call. It'll come to her and she won't be able to resist." His voice dropped a notch. "She understands something happened between me and Diana that night and that . . . that I have to avoid thinking about Diana in the same way she has to avoid thinking about her father."

"So what do you do?"

Gregg smiled. "I do what it says in the book—what the AA guys call the Alcoholic's Anonymous Handbook. I bought a copy two months ago, and I've been imparting Mary with some of its lessons."

"Really?" Brad nodded.

"Yeah. I know it's going to be hard, but I think we'll make it. Long as we have each other, we'll make it. We just have to take it one step at a time."

"One step at a time," Brad said, nodding. He looked up at Gregg. "Yeah, I can dig that."

Gregg smiled back at Brad and they stood up, collected the empty bottles, and went back into the house, closing the sliding-glass door behind them.

SURVIVOR

J. F. GONZALEZ

It was supposed to be a romantic weekend getaway. Lisa was looking forward to spending time alone with her husband—and telling him that they are going to have a baby. Instead, it becomes a nightmare when Lisa is kidnapped. But the kidnappers aren't asking for ransom. They want Lisa herself. They're going to make her a star—in a snuff film.

What they have in mind for Lisa is unspeakable. They plan to torture and murder her as graphically and brutally as possible, and to capture it all on film. If they have their way, Lisa's death will be truly horrifying…but even more horrifying is what Lisa will do to survive.…

SLITHER

EDWARD LEE

The trichinosis worm is one of nature's most revolting parasites. Luckily, these worms are rarely more than a few millimeters in length. But guess what? Now there's a subspecies that's thirty feet long…

When Nora and her research team arrived on the deserted tropical island, she was expecting a routine zoological expedition. But first they found the dead bodies. Now members of her own team are disappearing, and when they return, they've…changed. And is there any sane explanation for the lurid, perverse dreams she's been having? Indeed, there are other people on the island. But the real danger is something far worse.

DEATH'S DOMINION

SIMON CLARK

Modern scientists have proven Dr. Frankenstein right. They have discovered a way to raise the dead. Unlike Dr. Frankenstein's monster, these gentle creatures docilely serve their masters, but the living have begun to despise the dead among them. They are disgusted by their creations, and the government has set out to systematically destroy every last one of the "monsters." The monsters cannot fight back—it's not in their nature to defend themselves. That is, until one of the creatures retaliates against humanity with shocking brutality. In the war between the living and the dead, a new leader has arisen.

RAPTURE

THOMAS TESSIER

Jeff has always loved Georgianne, ever since they were kids—with a love so strong, so obsessive, it sometimes drives him to do crazy things. Scary things. Like stalking Georgianne and everyone she loves, including her caring husband and her innocent teenage daughter. Jeff doesn't think there's room in Georgianne's life for anyone but him, and if he has to, he's ready to kill all the others... until he's the only one left.

> "Ingenious. A nerve-paralyzing story."
> —*Publishers Weekly*